MAZ'HURA

BOOK ONE OF THE TWELVE DIMENSIONS

A NOVEL BY

PAUL L. CENTENO

INDIES UNITED PUBLISHING HOUSE, LLC

Illustrations by Paul Pederson
Interior Design by Indies United Publishing House, LLC.

978-1-64456-386-1 [Hardcover]
978-1-64456-387-8 [Paperback]
978-1-64456-388-5 [Mobi]
978-1-64456-389-2 [ePub]

Library of Congress Control Number: 2021946872

INDIES UNITED PUBLISHING HOUSE, LLC
P.O. BOX 3071
QUINCY, IL 62305-3071
www.indiesunited.net

Dedication

I dedicate this novel to my niece, Mariah. Just as this series is filled with limitless possibilities, so the same is with you. May you reach out to the heavens and become what you wish to be in life.

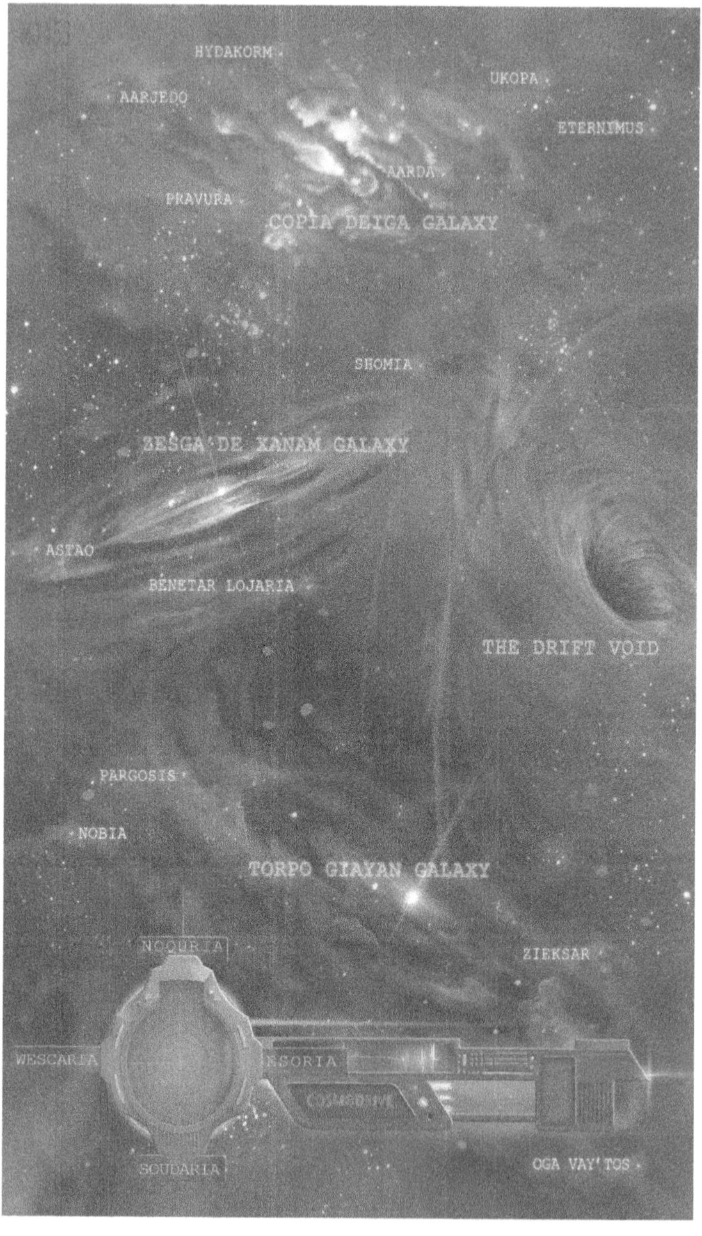

HYDAKORM
UKOPA
AARJEDO
ETERNIMUS
AARDA
PRAVURA
COPIA DEIGA GALAXY
SHOMIA
ZESGA DE XANAM GALAXY
ASTAO
BENETAR LOJARIA
THE DRIFT VOID
PARGOSIS
NOBIA
TORPO GIAYAN GALAXY
NOQURIA
ZIEKSAR
WESCARIA
ESORIA
COLMSDRIVE
SCUDARIA
OGA VAY'TOS

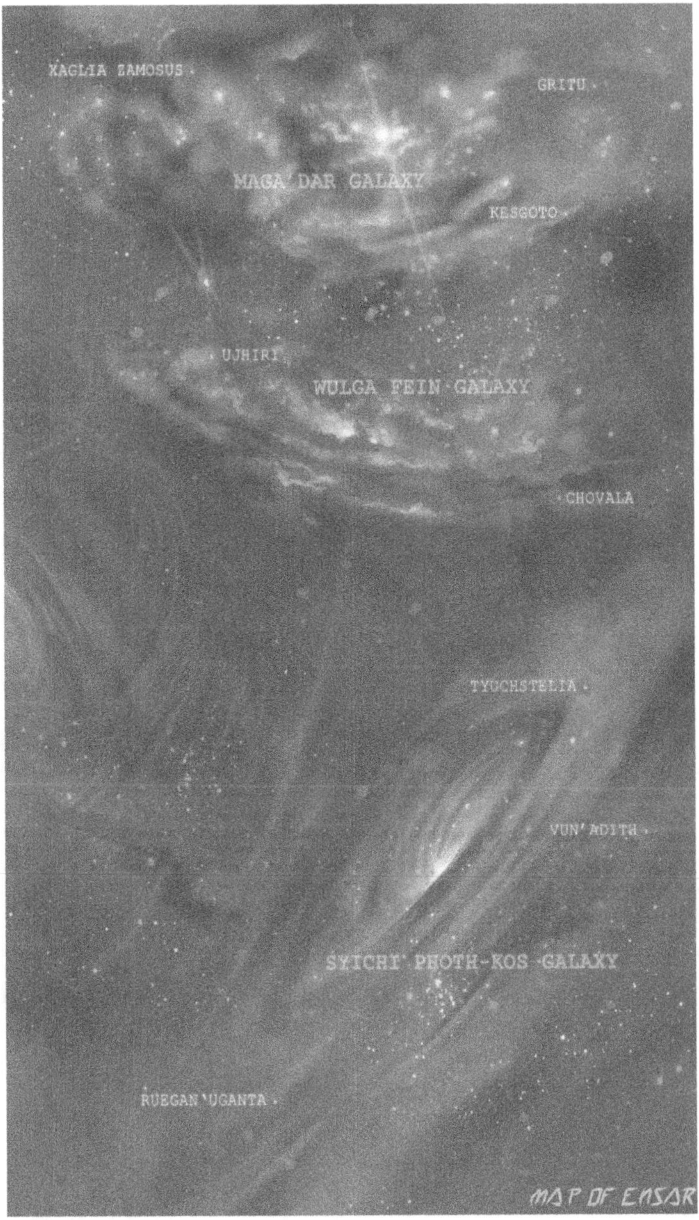

XAGLIA ZAMOSUS
GRITU
MAGA DAR GALAXY
KESGOTO
UJHIRI
WULGA FEIN GALAXY
CHOVALA
TYUCHSTELIA
VUN'ADITH
SYICHI PHOTH-KOS GALAXY
RUEGAN'UGANTA
MAP OF ENSAR

Prologue

Cosmic Divination

Shimmering starlight
A new life shines in the cosmos
Basking in its glory, we praise our Goddess.

I feel its enchanted warmth
My soul touches its eternal grace.

Dancing in the galaxies of unbound divine,
The ebb and flow of stellar waves embrace me;
My sacred spirit glows, magic within me undefined.

Now these lonely eyes of mine fail,
Blinded by the birth of infinite radiance.

Alas, darkness descends upon us
Our primordial enemy returns from exile
And the interstellar newborn withers into oblivion.

The Oracle of Celestial

Chapter One
Celestial Heights

— Cycle 81971.273 M.E. —

I

Voyage of the Infinite

The vast gulfs of space thrived in the Ensar universe for eons. Copia Deiga, a galaxy teeming with magical ions, swirled in splendor. Asteroids along the outskirts of the spiral phenomenon drifted aimlessly. In the vicinity of a nebula, shaped like fiery wings, a black hole materialized. Its gravitation sucked in cosmic dust, the giant space chasm flickering with lightning. While the electricity waned, a dreadnought starship emerged. Fleeting bolts scrambled throughout its tetrigonium hull, an obsidian-tinted metal that gleamed with arcane energy currents.

Entering this star system, the spacecraft accelerated. The black hole sealed, dust no longer being pulled. A burst of blinding light appeared opposite the ship, millions of miles away. A molecular cloud had just collapsed, igniting the birth of a new sun. As this took place, the vessel activated its polarized mana shield, allowing passengers to examine creation's majesty: The cloud's fragment contracted and extreme heat surged around the stellar remnants, condensing into a gassy sphere as flares enveloped it.

Numerous alchemists, engineers, and physicists wore expressions of awe, gazing at the newborn phenomenon. Others stood slack-jawed, astonished to witness such an incredible event. But no one was more amazed than Captain Shirakaya. Attired in dalikonium, one of the strongest magic-imbued armors in the known universe, she lifted her helmet, revealing a tan complexion and black hair with purple highlights. She rose from her command chair, her magic-infused eyes fixed on the protostar.

Shirakaya had relentlessly searched for one ever since her graduation from the University of Elements & Conjuration and became a captain in the military. As a sorceress, it was imperative for her to collect magical ions from within a protostar to maintain her arcane gift. According to arcane astrophysicists, failing to obtain such power and replenish the gifted soul could lead to magic users losing their abilities at an early age. Discovering this protostar was a dream come true for the captain.

"The oracle was right," she said, her lips forming a smile. "Templar Yarasuro, contact Judicator Owendar and inform him of our discovery."

"At once, my lady."

A knight of the sacred Tal'manac Order and the captain's personal bodyguard, it was Yarasuro's sworn duty to obey and protect Shirakaya with his life. Clad in an ebony, scaly-like armor known as harboro, and equipped with a curved sword made of baskino metal, he strode to a computer at his terminal, logged onto the arcane TDE—Transdimensional Ethernet— where he attempted to establish a kinetic link with the judicator.

"Captain, should I change our course?" one of the crew members said, seated one floor below at a navigation monitor.

"That won't be necessary, Narja," the captain said. "Take us across the Aarjedo star system, toward the protostar. We need to be in proximity so I can tap into its ions."

"I have made contact," Yarasuro said.

"Excellent," the captain said.

A bright light flashed, prismatic rays beaming from Yarasuro's screen to the center of the flight deck. Not five seconds later, an elderly man appeared in a brocade robe with a tetrigonium crown atop his wrinkled forehead.

Pushing aside his long charcoal hair, he gazed at the captain and smiled. "Not a cycle out of the academy and you've found one already," the judicator said. "The Ruzurai will be impressed, Shira."

"The oracle helped," she said, descending a flight of steps.

"She is nonetheless a member of your crew," he said, hugging the captain. He turned and stared at the newborn star, mesmerized by it. "I haven't seen such a marvel in decades. Thank you for thinking of an old man."

"It's the least I could do," she said. "I remember your arcane physics classes from the academy and how you spoke about the sanctity of protostars."

The judicator replied, "Without them—"

"Say goodbye to magical ions," they said in unison.

"Thank the stars," he said.

"And the eternal Goddess." Shirakaya winked at him.

Teary-eyed, the judicator agreed and continued to watch the star form. While observing it grow, however, he noticed a few black spots materializing along the sphere. Mystified, he approached the windowpane with his staff. His jaundiced eyes were old, but his enchanted glasses allowed him to see with immense clarity. He staggered as a wave of anxiety swept over him.

Shirakaya moved to support him. "Is everything okay?"

"Shira," the judicator said, "something awful is happening." Before she could respond, he went on, "I sense a powerful entity approaching behind the protostar. It's consuming all of the newborn's energy."

"*What?*" Her eyebrows furrowed. "Ensign Narja, increase the thrusters and raise the mana shield to maximum power. Yarasuro, come with me."

"I must join you," the judicator said.

"I'm afraid not, Professor," she said. "Rest in my chair while I investigate. Captain's orders."

II
Prophecies Anew

Shirakaya exited the flight deck with her bodyguard and walked through a corridor where recessed lighting along the ceiling brought their shadows to life. They entered an octagonal pod known as an X-Phaser, a teleportation capsule that contained both technology and magic. Inputting a code, she and her guard teleported from the spacecraft's command center to an elongated hall beside a temple located in the east wing.

"Captain," Yarasuro said, "forgive me for asking, but why couldn't you just teleport us here from the flight deck?"

"I'm an enchantress, not a conjurer," she said.

The doors to the temple automatically opened when they approached. A shallow pool lay before them, its corners decorated with candles. Multihued flowers blanketed the water, drifting and bobbing. Ahead stood a flight of ten steps with a throne at the top, upon which sat a blonde woman in a diaphanous gown. Slumped as though drunk, her garment disheveled, her ivory eyes squinted at the captain, and perspiration glistened on her forehead.

"Jedalia, do you sense anything harmful?" the captain asked.

"By the Goddess. You sense them too?"

"I'm not gifted with clairvoyance," Shirakaya said, kneeling. "Only you are, my oracle."

"They are returning from exile," the oracle said, her voice weak.

"Huh?" uttered Yarasuro.

"Please don't speak in riddles again," the captain said. "You told me I would be happy and yet troubled when Judicator Owendar arrived. He told me something is consuming the protostar. Do you know anything about this?"

"The primordial koth'vurians are upon us," the oracle said, her tone even weaker as she keeled over.

Before she fell, Shirakaya mounted the stairs and caught her. The captain gently laid her on a silky cloth festooned with flowers. Making sure the templar couldn't see, Shirakaya kissed the oracle on her forehead and stroked her hair. "Don't overexert yourself, my love," she whispered.

At the oracle's nod, Shirakaya stood up and rejoined her

bodyguard by the temple's entrance.

"Is she delusional?" inquired Yarasuro.

"Do not *ever* disrespect the oracle, Templar."

"My apologies, Captain. But the Order vanquished the koth'vurians eons ago."

"Exiled is the appropriate word, Templar. And I know the Order is absolute," Shirakaya said, pensive. Gazing up at the throne, she stared at the giant porcelain statue of the eternal Goddess and turned away. "Still, we can't ignore the warnings of my oracle. I want you to stay by her side until she recovers."

"Where will you be, my lady?"

"I'm teleporting back to the bridge," she said, her expression troubled. "Just watch over her."

"As you wish," Yarasuro said, bowing.

III
Chaos Reigns

Confident the oracle was safe, the captain left the marble temple and returned to the flight deck. Ignoring her command to remain seated, the judicator stood in front of the windowpane and gawked at the dwindling newborn star. Shirakaya sighed under her breath when she saw him at the fore and sat in her chair.

"Zadoya," she called out, "I need you to manage communications until Templar Yarasuro returns."

"Aye, my lady," the female soldier said. Clad in a jointed hard-shell spacesuit, she holstered her EP-41 plasma rifle as she left her post by the door to check the computer terminal. "No messages or hails yet."

"Keep your eyes peeled, Lieutenant," Shirakaya said. "Ensign, status report."

"The readings are off the chart, Captain," Narja said. "I've never seen anything like this before. I can only assume that—"

"We don't have time for conjecture, Ensign."

Narja heard the captain and gulped so hard it was as though she'd swallowed a bone; a couple of her colleagues even turned to look in astonishment. "It's confusing, my lady. At first, I thought the signals indicated a fleet of ships. However, the readings on my radar tell me they are organic, not mechanical."

"Make it stop," the judicator said, fingers gripping his temples. "Make it stop."

Uneasy, Shirakaya rose from her chair and approached the old man. "You may be a Ruzurai, but you are aboard my vessel." She guided him to her armchair. "Owendar, trust me. I *will* get to the bottom of this. In the meantime, please follow my orders and rest here until this is resolved."

"You're running out of time," he said, irrationally shielding his eyes from the star. "It's worsening. It's only a matter of time before the protostar is destroyed."

The captain stiffened at his words. "Zadoya, alert all my flight squadrons to report to the hanger. I want every available pilot in a jet. I don't care what's lurking there. Tell them to shoot on sight."

"Aye, Captain," she said, using the TDE to transmit her orders.

Shirakaya stood by the window and waited for her squadrons to take off from the dreadnought vessel in their space jets. Although not far from the newborn sun, the captain and her crew aboard the mothership's flight deck had difficulty discerning what lurked behind the sphere of raging flares.

"Captain," called out Narja, sounding panicky. "The objects on the radar are advancing."

"I don't need a radar to know that," Shirakaya said. She gazed at the steadily approaching swarm. "Let them come. My squadrons will decimate them."

Thrusters and force fields at maximum power, an armada of space jets disembarked from the mothership. The squadrons flew toward their targets as though without fear. Nearing the unidentified objects, the pilots opened fire. Each jet launched photon beams and arcane missiles enchanted with lightning and blasted the invaders.

"This can't be right," Ensign Narja said to herself; she examined data on her screen. "There must be a glitch in the system."

"What's wrong?" the captain said.

"Since the objects are within range, the TDE identified them," the ensign said. "But it must be malfunctioning because it says that these creatures are koth'vurians."

A few crew members exchanged fretful glances.

"The Order eradicated them eons ago," Zadoya said, noticing the crew's concern. "These things must be something else."

"Goddess, why is this happening?" the judicator said.

The captain heard him but didn't respond to his agitation. She stood stock-still, hands clasped behind her back. Although wary, Shirakaya refused to show any fear. As captain of the vessel, she'd remain steadfast and protect the protostar whatever the costs. The crew ignored the information in their database; however, Shirakaya couldn't waive it, especially after what the oracle had told her.

"Ensign, take us into the battlefield and assist our flotilla," she commanded. "As for the rest of you, I want every weapon active."

"Aye," the crew said in unison.

IV
Battle Among the Stars

Exterior cannons throughout the dreadnought mothership, including those along the main bridge, activated. Targeting the horde, they launched a barrage of gamma rays. The initial burst caused them to hiss as if wounded. Yet the ionizing radiation produced by the catastrophic beams healed them within seconds.

Without the use of technology, creatures of flight approached the dreadnought craft and unleashed a bombardment of their own: Beams projected from the scaly palms of their claw-shaped hands. Despite protection from the mana shield, the mothership was severely weakened. The beasts flew past the magical force field and landed on one of the vessel's ramparts, where multiple cannons were located.

The captain caught a glimpse of one when it passed the bridge at central command. What she saw was no ordinary alien. Its glowing green eyes alone made her heart race with fear. Spikes covered its scaly body and the creature had four wings, which rose from its serrated spine, a sharp tail, and six-fingered hands with claws that jutted out from the knuckles. There was no denying it, Shirakaya conceded, these mythical beings were koth'vurians.

"How are they able to breathe and fly without spacesuits?" Zadoya said.

"My lady, a large group of aliens have flown through the vessel's shield and are attacking our cannons!" Narja said.

"Calm down, Ensign," Shirakaya said, irked. "The mana shield only deflects mechanical objects and their weaponry. You should know this. Other than stellar ouvas, which are peaceful animals, there are no aliens able to roam space in their natural form except koth'vurians. We must consider that the TDE is correct."

The crew members glanced at each other again, not knowing what to make of the situation.

"Maintain your positions and do not waver," the captain added and walked away. "Zadoya, follow me."

The duo exited the flight deck. Striding through a corridor, Shirakaya raised her forearm and clicked a button embedded in the armor and activated the KLD – kinetic link device – on her wrist. A semitransparent kiosk with an interface manifested. Typing into the air, she logged onto the TDE and established a connection with her bodyguard.

"How may I be of service, my lady?" Yarasuro said.

"Your sword is needed," the captain said. "I'm transmitting coordinates to you. Meet me there."

Without waiting for his response, she turned off her KLD

and entered an X-Phaser with her soldier. Inputting a code, they teleported to a rampart fitted with external cannons in outer space. Protected by the active mana shield, they had no need of air tanks to breathe. Zadoya aimed her plasma rifle at an alien and blasted it with a clip enchanted with frost magic; the beam pierced its thick scales, permafrost spreading. Weighed down by rime, it landed and scuttled toward its foes.

Not a second later, Yarasuro materialized. He gasped at the beast before him and took a step back. Though startled, he unsheathed his baskino sword and struck in an upward arc as the fiend pounced, splitting it in half.

"Perfect timing," Shirakaya said.

Templar Yarasuro ignored her remark and gazed at the other creatures in dismay. "What in the name of the Goddess are these wretched things?"

"We don't have definitive evidence," the captain said. "Whether they are koth'vurians or not, we must defend our ship."

"My blade is yours to command," he said. "What would you have me do?"

"I need you to taunt them," she answered. "Zadoya and I will attack from a distance and cover you."

Yarasuro charged forward as Shirakaya temporarily enchanted his sword with an aura of fire and took cover by the damaged cannon beside her. Conjuring fireballs, she launched them at aliens flanking the templar as he sliced those lingering on the rampart. Zadoya also assisted, strafing between walls and shooting the koth'vurians.

A beast opposite Yarasuro rolled aside from his attack and tucked its wings tight to its body, transmuting into an elongated figure. It slithered toward the templar and enveloped its pliable body around him. The fiend opened its jaws, revealing razor-edged fangs as Yarasuro struggled to release himself and groaned in pain. About to bite its prey, an icicle cast by Shirakaya punctured its mouth. Blood squirted above the rampart as it fell to the ground, lifeless.

"Don't be reckless, Templar," the captain said, conjuring

lightning.

One of the flying creatures dodged her bolts and emitted a gamma ray at Yarasuro, who deflected its attack with his sword. Enchanted, the blade withstood such power unharmed. In a serendipitous action, Zadoya turned and shot the fiend. As it collapsed in its death throes, Yarasuro decapitated it with a single swift stroke.

More creatures scuttled forth to swipe their claws at the knight. Evading their attacks, he countered with his enchanted baskino, gutting one. Simultaneously, the enchantress hurled fireballs past him and incinerated two aliens. Aiming well, Zadoya continued to fire at those in the air until the contingent of koth'vurians lay dead on the rampart.

"All clear," the soldier said, reloading her gun with a frost clip.

"My apologies for getting caught by that monster," Yarasuro said, breathing hard while sheathing his lustrous sword.

"Never let your guard down," the captain said. "Koth'vurians are shapeshifters. They are capable of altering into just about any form. Always be ready." She glanced around to confirm that most of the cannons were still functional. "It seems this area is secure. Let's—"

The trio staggered as the mothership shook.

"My lady!" the voice of Ensign Narja sounded via the captain's kinetic link. "The aliens have breached our hull in the residential sector. I've uploaded the exact coordinates to your KLD interface."

"We're on our way." Shirakaya ended the link.

The trio strode through the rampart and observed numerous space jets blow up in the fierce battle. Despite this, the three of them returned to the teleportation pod. They materialized in the lower right wing of the starship and exited an X-Phaser capsule into a hall located in the residential district.

Recessed ceiling lights flickered, sliced wires dangled, fizzing with high voltage, a section of the wall torn open. More disturbing, however, were the dead humyns littering the hallway.

"This is bad," Zadoya said.

They heard screams from a nearby chamber and charged into the room to witness an alien digging its claws into a pregnant woman. Another struck a man with its tail, sending him soaring over a desk. Zadoya took cover behind a dresser, firing at the scaly fiends as they spewed acid. Shirakaya ducked and hurled a fireball, disintegrating the first alien. Although Yarasuro deflected the second creature's toxin, it dispelled his sword's enchantment. He grimaced and sliced off the beast's snout.

"Danasa!" cried out the wounded man, limping over to his dead wife.

Shirakaya lowered her eyes for a moment, saddened by this tragedy, but unable to stop, signaling her entourage to follow her. The spacecraft bombarded again, they staggered as they left the cabin. Through a hole in the wall, they watched in horror as their ship's mana shield destabilized. Erring on the side of caution, they put on helmets and activated their zitrogen air tanks.

Moments later, the mana shield failed. In an instant, the vacuum sucked dead bodies into space. Courtesy of the magnetic soles attached to their sabatons, the trio remained in place. Battling to move, Shirakaya cast a frost spell and sealed the ruptured wall. But as soon as she mended the wall, the ice cracked.

"We don't have much time," the captain said. "Hurry."

They made haste and left the ruined hall through another corridor. The three of them entered a cafeteria and encountered passengers screaming and fighting as koth'vurians devoured them alive. Shirakaya conjured an inferno and reduced her nearest foes to ashes. Reloading her gun with a frost clip, Zadoya opened fire at another group of koth'vurians before a barrage of gamma rays forced her to take cover behind a column. Darting out, she froze the invaders with enchanted frost bullets. Seeing them freeze, Yarasuro seized his chance and shattered each one with his sword.

Enemies vanquished, Zadoya repositioned herself in anticipation of more koth'vurians attacking and aimed at the door. The knight maintained his guard and searched for any aliens hiding in the chamber.

Snatching the chance, Shirakaya checked the injured; most had fatal wounds, with only a few unharmed. Visibly distressed, she walked over to her bodyguard. "Was the oracle feeling better when you left?"

"I'm afraid not," he said, his eyes downcast. "But perhaps she has regained her strength. It would be wise to contact—"

An alarm sounded, the siren deafening.

"Intruder alert," the ship's integrated AI reported, its voice cybernetic and unemotional. "Intruder alert. All military personnel report to the arcane engine chamber. Intruder alert. Intruder alert."

"Delay that order, soldiers," the captain said via kinetic link. "Remain at your posts. I will go myself." Ending the transmission, she turned to her entourage. "Yarasuro, return to the oracle and continue guarding her. If she has recovered, guide her here to heal these people."

"Aye, my lady," he said, bowing and leaving.

"Lieutenant," the captain said, "maintain your position and make sure no other enemies attack."

Zadoya saluted her. "Their safety will not be compromised."

V
Nemesis

Confident the lieutenant would handle watching over the wounded passengers, Shirakaya exited the cafeteria. The red alarm continued to flash in the corridor. She made her way back to the ruptured hall and placed a hand on the cracked ice, solidifying it again. Despite her powerful magic, the protostar's heat melted the mended wall. Grumbling under her breath, she made her way to an X-Phaser. Inside, she inputted a code into its console and transferred to the arcane engine chamber.

Materializing, the captain stepped out of the capsule onto a central walkway elevated five thousand feet high. Pillars containing multiple circuits surrounded her, all of which jutted from the bottom level and coursed with electricity up to the pipe-covered ceiling. Ahead of the captain, across the chasm of wires and columns, stood a platform where an enormous metal sphere hovered.

Before advancing, she checked the area for aliens, then cast a mana shield over herself and broke into a run. Shirakaya's sabatons thumped against the grating, her armor clinking as she sprinted forward to evaluate the integrity of the robust spherical engine. The numerous data readings in her visor hampered damage assessment to the arcane engine; she removed her helmet. Magical ions within the flowing energy inside the mechanical structure allowed the spacecraft to function: the power meter registered half a tank.

The rumbling machine appeared safe but Shirakaya maintained her guard. She reminded herself that the alarm would not have gone off without cause and circled the engine to reconnoiter the sector. Unlike her oracle, gifted with divination, Shirakaya had to rely on her eyes alone rather than the rare ability to sense another's presence with magic.

"I know you're in here," she said, her tone stern. "Reveal yourself."

A violent hiss echoed. "You may have been able to defeat my throng, but now you face Ashkaratoth, second-in-command to Koth'tura."

His monstrous voice reverberated throughout the chamber, leaving the captain unable to locate him. Hidden between pipes, the scaly fiend spewed lethal acid on Shirakaya, breaking her concentration, despite the mana shield absorbing the toxin. Shaken, she took a deep breath and traced its direction to where the beast clung to a pipe above, simultaneously strengthening her arcane force field. Evading another spew of acid, she waved a hand, freezing the pipes.

Ashkaratoth snarled, leaped off the pipe and landed mere meters away from her. He lunged toward the captain, struck her with his claws, and disrupted her mana shield. Backing away, Shirakaya hurled two fireballs. The horned alien ducked and evaded them. Pouncing, he attempted to bite off her face. She raised her armored forearm as a shield; Ashkaratoth bit into her gauntlet and punctured it. She felt the armor crush against her skin and groaned in pain. Keeping the abhorrent creature's fangs at bay, she rolled backward and delivered a robust kick to his chest. Falling sidelong from the elevated walkway, he collapsed against a platform several feet below.

Springing to her feet, Shirakaya conjured a sphere of frost and hurled it at the alien. Before it struck him, he spread his wings and flew up, evading her magic. Midair, he whipped her with his tail. So powerful was the force of his counterattack, she slammed against the arcane engine, denting it. She whimpered and dropped to the floor.

With no one to stop him, Ashkaratoth gashed the machine with his claws and absorbed magical ions from the malfunctioned engine, depleting its energy. The engine's magic consumed, the koth'vurian approached Shirakaya who lay crunched up. Without warning, she raised her hands and, by force of telekinesis, tossed him across the chamber.

Shirakaya stood up, her eyes glowing white with arcane fury as she elevated Ashkaratoth into the air before slamming him between pillars. An unexpected wave of nausea washed over her. Weakened by the rapid loss of power, she groaned and knelt on the grating. Her magical ions dwindled further. Lacking the strength to defeat Ashkaratoth, the captain involuntarily released him.

"What are you?" she rasped.

Full of hate, the creature's green eyes gleamed. "You already know what I am," he said, consuming her ionized essence with the palm of his hand. "You've been a worthy adversary, humyn. It almost saddens me to see your life come to an end so soon."

An alarm cut short his hissing laugh.

"Attention," the vessel's integrated AI said. "Thrusters are no longer active. The engine is severely damaged and unstable. All personnel must evacuate. I repeat, all personnel must evacuate."

Ashkaratoth cackled, amused by the announcement. "I'll let your own pathetic technology kill you."

The koth'vurian spread his wings and flew out of the starship. He ignored his brethren, still fighting, and directed his attention to the protostar. Approaching the newborn sun, despite its tremendous gravitational force and extreme heat, he continued to drain it without harm. A few wide-eyed pilots witnessed the phenomenon, seeing not an alien but a fiery demon consume the star.

VI
Surviving

Rising to her feet, Shirakaya activated her kinetic link device. "Ignore the evacuation," she commanded. "All engineers and arcane astrophysicists are to report to the engine chamber and repair the damages."

An awful weakness shot through her body as if she'd been cursed. Despite the debilitating feeling, she left the chamber and returned to the flight deck. Her heart pounded as she acknowledged how tense her crew looked. Engrossed in combat, they used every opportunity to maneuver the starship's cannons by computer when they locked onto a target.

She turned her attention to the judicator who sat in her command chair; he appeared rather pale, and she assumed he felt just as tense as her crew. Taking a deep breath, Shirakaya tried not to worry about Owendar and approached the windowpane to observe the bleak battle. Hundreds of destroyed interstellar jets hung weightless and inert in space. Only a few dozen vessels remained intact. Yet the enemies' numbers had also dwindled significantly. Now she knew why her former professor looked so forlorn. Shirakaya's primary concern, however, was the newborn sun.

"Warning," the AI announced, "hull integrity has reached maximum hazard due to the heat of Sun-0G4CE. Destruction is imminent."

"I can't even move the damn ship!" yelled Narja, bashing her terminal.

With the exception of Shirakaya, the crew was distraught. The windowpane gleamed red and showed signs of melting, not to mention the AI's alert. Most passengers tried fleeing via escape pods before the mothership disintegrated. But with the loss of power, none of the pods worked. Hysteria overwhelmed many of the crew.

"Fear not, people of Celestial," Owendar said, using the captain's intercom. "I will use my magic to give the engineers more time."

He rose from the captain's chair and descended to the main deck with his staff.

"Don't overexert yourself, Professor."

Owendar cast a mana shield on himself and replied, "Don't worry about me, Shira. This may be your ship, but the command of a Ruzurai is absolute. Tend to your crew while I am gone."

Unhappy about this, she nonetheless accepted his help. Quicker than lightning, the wizard teleported to the external hull of the craft in outer space where he gazed at the dying star. Protected by his mana shield, he strode forward—unaffected by the vacuum of space.

Reaching the center of the mothership's roof, he closed his eyes and knelt on the floor. Mustering all the arcane energies within his being, Owendar expanded his mana shield. Within minutes, a blue barrier enveloped the entire vessel. Countless passengers witnessed the magical force field in awe, no longer attempting to escape.

"Systems are cooling down," Narja said in disbelief.

"Thank the Goddess," the captain said. "Ensign, are you able to locate Judicator Owendar?"

"I'm afraid not, my lady," she said, her navigation monitor not responding.

Shirakaya cursed under her breath, wondering what he was doing. She paced back and forth, hoping he'd return soon.

"Captain," called out an engineer via KLD, "we have temporarily stabilized the engine. A few ruptured turbines are being repaired as we speak, but most of our fuel is depleted. If we don't collect ions from a star soon, we'll be stuck here for Goddess knows how long. The good news is that the oxidizer is working. Thrusters are now available."

"Excellent work, Chief," Shirakaya said, ending the kinetic transmission.

The captain fixed her eyes on the withdrawing koth'vurians. Yet before commanding the ensign to pursue them, she witnessed the star dissolve as Ashkaratoth consumed its remaining ions. To her dismay, the remnants of the sun collapsed, metamorphosing into a black hole. Upon the star's death, Ashkaratoth's swarm rejoined him. Together, the legion of koth'vurians conjured what Shirakaya thought to be a portal leading to another dimension. They entered the eerie, red gateway and vanished, followed by the mysterious portal.

"Impossible," the captain muttered to herself. "Was that the Drift Void?"

Silence descended in the flight deck, most of the crew slack-jawed. A sense of despair enveloped the control room, many of those present expecting death.

Overcoming fear, Shirakaya broke the silence. "Ensign, get us the hell out of here."

Narja didn't respond as she strove to maneuver the spacecraft away from the encroaching black hole. Under normal circumstances, their galactic vessel was built to withstand any form of interstellar travel, including death-defying black holes, which was how they'd originally arrived in the Aarjedo star system. But with a damaged engine incapable of initiating FTM, faster-than-magic, traveling through such a chasm again would be suicide.

Without warning, the judicator teleported back into the

flight deck. "Shira, we need to leave this instant."

"I'm one step ahead of you," she said. "By the way, where have you been?"

"I attempted to shield your starship with my magic," he said, his face haggard. "But I failed. Not only am I drained, but the protostar has been destroyed. And if your engine is not fixed, that black hole will consume us."

"We are doing our best," Shirakaya said, standing up. "Have my seat."

The ensign used all available thrusters to accelerate the vessel to maximum velocity. Yet this wasn't enough. Not only were numerous space jets pulled back, but the mothership was also caught in a gravitational flux.

"It's too late!" panicked Narja.

"It's never too late," the captain said. "This is a ternary star system. I want you to activate the cosmodrive and bring us to the blue giant."

The crew glanced at one another, frightened.

"But the engine hasn't been fully repaired," Narja said, alarmed. "Our ship might explode if we use its arcane properties."

"And what about our squadrons?" a soldier said from the communications terminal.

Shirakaya gave a heavy sigh. "It grieves me to say this, Sergeant Tasakiro, but they're a lost cause. The black hole will consume them, along with us if we don't leave this instant. Now, I respect everyone aboard my ship. However, if anybody questions me again, they will be court-martialed. You *will* obey my orders. Activate the cosmodrive."

Without further disagreement, the ensign focused her attention on the starmap that revealed a space compass with non-planetary directions—noquria, soudaria, esoria, and wescaria. Entering coordinates on her navigation system, she shifted two throttles alongside her interface. The crew flinched and cringed as they felt and heard a deafening reverberation. Boosters ignited, zooming the mothership through the cosmos at unnatural speeds. Within seconds, they traveled from

Aarjedo's soudarian border to the noqurian perimeter. Three planets orbited the system's blue giant, the nearest one suspended eighty-three million miles away.

The spacecraft flew fast despite the boosters deactivating. Narja decreased the speed of her thrusters. Although jolting, the vessel slowed down; they passed the planets and approached the massive star, its glare so powerful it forced the passengers to look away, despite the polarized windows.

"Captain," the ensign called out, "with all due respect, why are we heading toward a blue giant?"

"This is the only way I can save our ship," she said. "Bring us to the corona."

"Shira, I assume you have a magnificent plan that will save us," the judicator said.

"Great minds think alike," she replied, enveloping herself in a mana shield. "There's no guarantee we'll be able to return home. Our fuel is almost depleted. We need ions from that star. Care to teleport me?"

"Its heat is too severe," he said. "You won't be able to protect the entire ship. I failed with a protostar."

"We don't have another option," she said. "Are you going to teleport me or not?"

The judicator grimaced but nevertheless clasped his hands together and cast a spell, his eyes gleaming.

Shirakaya materialized on the roof in outer space. She dared not look at the blue giant lest she harmed her eyes. Approaching her spacecraft's central point, she sat in a meditative position and closed her eyes. Taking deep breaths, Shirakaya expanded her mana shield over the starship. Increasing its diameter made her feel lightheaded.

Celestial flew into the sun's corona. Fiery plasma surrounded the magical force field. A perennial glare of luminous light beamed on her as she focused all her remaining energy on the shield. The extreme temperature and gravitational current were so intense that the barrier shrank. Struggling against such forces, Shirakaya writhed in pain, her power weakening. The tip of a wing became exposed, crushed and torn apart. Within microseconds, the heat disintegrated the resultant shrapnel.

The spacecraft's passengers, hysterical and frantic, ran away from the exposed wing before they were caught in utter destruction. An emergency shutter sealed the ruptured section with only seconds to spare before the rest of the wing was annihilated. The captain maintained concentration and increased her mana shield over the damaged sector. As the vessel traveled deeper into the star, its thrusters shut down again.

Prismatic spheres within the blue giant gravitated toward the captain. Ionized orbs pierced the magical barrier and entered Shirakaya's body. She opened her eyes, which gleamed and coursed with undefined energy. Standing up, she brought her palms together and absorbed numerous more orbs. Her body glowed with an aura as she channeled the drifting ions into the starship's arcane engine, refueling it.

"Captain," the chief engineer said via KLD, "you have achieved the impossible! Our fuel is recharging. If you keep this up, we'll be at maximum power in no time."

Shirakaya, although relieved, didn't respond. She continued to redirect the magical ions into the vessel. Thrusters ignited once again, and Ensign Narja accelerated the interstellar craft. Once out of the corona, the vessel's mana shield reactivated. Even though Shirakaya was safe, her barrier abruptly dispersed against her will.

In utter shock, she gasped and checked her surroundings to see if someone had dispelled it; yet she was alone. Preventing further thought on the matter, the judicator teleported her to the flight deck. Materializing, she staggered, the urge to vomit acute. As she regained composure and rose up, Owendar patted her on the back.

"You are truly amazing, Shira," he said, never more proud of his former student.

"Thank you..."

The crew rejoiced at what she'd done, yet she showed no signs of relief. Though pleased to be alive, a dreadful thought stirred within her and the taste of nausea filled her mouth. Never in her life had one of her spells been broken against her will. Shirakaya was well aware that only a chosen few had the gift of magic for life; others would lose it after a certain age or if the gift were abused. This frightened her but she faked a smile for her crew. They were out of imminent danger but were still deep in the cosmos with an unstable engine.

Shards of Majesty

In the infancy of the universe, my infinite mind spoke unto the nameless void. Dazzling stars arose, shimmering akin to the hallowed eyes of mine. With eternal radiance, their celestial brothers and sisters manifested. Grandiose planets filled the firmament, teeming with life before me. No longer bereft of glory, I named the perennial cosmos Ensar. For eons untold, I watched my children grow until adulthood. Upon interdependence, I transcended to the source of creation and drifted into the blissful realm of dreams where I await my offspring. If you ascend into the black heavens and search for my primordial existence, you shall find fragments of my being scattered throughout Ensar as divine shards.

Transdimensional Origins 4:1

Chapter Two
Planetary Descent

I
Second Wind

Shirakaya returned to her chair and took a seat. "The *Celestial* is a resilient ship, but we need to find a safe zone to recuperate," she said, fixing her eyes on Aarjedo's panorama. "Ensign, take us to the nearest nebula."

"Aye, my lady," Narja said.

The dreadnought vessel flew out of the blue giant, traversing past its orbiting satellites. In a short amount of time, the ship approached an emission nebula shaped like a raging tidal wave. Even though the interstellar cloud emitted potent gasses that appeared dangerous, the vessel continued to advance through it. Entering the radiant nebula, particles of dust engulfed the spacecraft.

"This should keep us cloaked for now should the koth'vurians return," Shirakaya said.

"Perhaps you should rest in your quarters, Shira," the judicator said. "I can stay here and make sure all is well until your ship is fixed."

"That won't be necessary," she said, hiding a yawn with her hand.

"How many ions did you consume?"

"Enough to rejuvenate me and the ship's engine. Don't worry, the star will regenerate them."

"I'm more worried about you. There's a reason why the Order only allows us to consume ions from protostars. Newborns don't have much radiation. But fully grown stars, such as this one, can be lethal."

"I'm fine, *dad*."

Judicator Owendar chuckled. "Actually, your father would faint if he found out what you've done."

The captain raised an eyebrow. "He doesn't need to know."

"Indeed," Owendar said lightheartedly. "However, the Order is another story. Once I return to the capital, I must inform my fellow Ruzurai of what has transpired."

"Of course," she said. "In fact, I was hoping we could contact them now. They would never believe me if I told them Koth'tura has returned. Having you as my witness, however, changes things."

"Well," the judicator said, "those aliens *did* appear to be koth'vurians. But that doesn't mean Koth'tura is alive. There could be another leading them."

Shirakaya groaned under her breath. "One of them bested me in combat," she whispered to him. "Before leaving us to die, he called himself Ashkaratoth. If it wasn't for the engine alarm, he might have killed—"

"Nonsense," he said, waving his hand.

"Regardless," she said, visibly distressed, "Ashkaratoth told me he serves Koth'tura, which means he's alive."

"Don't be too hasty to believe that. He may simply be serving a dead master."

She snorted, unconvinced by her former professor's theory. "At any rate, we must inform the Ruzurai of what has happened." She turned her attention below. "Sergeant Tasakiro, notify Yarasuro and Zadoya that they may return."

"Aye," he said, clicking his screen.

"Don't get ahead of yourself," she said, her voice firm. "I also need you to log on to the TDE and contact the Order. Tell them I request an audience with the Ruzurai."

"My apologies, Captain," he replied. "I'll connect to them now." After sending a return signal via his KLD to the templar and lieutenant, Tasakiro tried logging onto the ethernet. He tried several times but failed. "Captain, there doesn't seem to be a TDE connection available. Either the nebula is causing interference, or our long-range satellites have been damaged."

"That could be a problem," the judicator said.

Shirakaya nodded, establishing a kinetic link with the chief engineer. "Kazakuma, is something wrong with our satellites?"

"I'm afraid so, Captain," he said. "That star we entered partially destroyed a wing that had two dishes. I intend to reroute our long-range signals to the eastern wings, but we're still trying to repair the engine."

"How's that coming along?"

"We're making progress. But most of our xylithum crystals have been destroyed."

"I'm not an engineer, Chief."

"Sorry," he said, stuttering. "Xylithum crystals are arcane shards that allow the mana shield to defy gravity. I'm afraid we won't be able to travel through dimensional space or any black holes until we replace them."

"I see," she said, troubled. "How are we supposed to do that?"

"We'll need to find a planet nearby that has them," he said. "It won't be easy. In fact, it's rare to find them in their natural habitat. But since we're on the outskirts of our galaxy, we may discover a planet that the Order hasn't explored. With any luck, it will at least have a few shards we can extract."

Leaving the captain to decide what to do, Yarasuro and Zadoya returned to the flight deck and stood guard by the door.

"Keep working on the engine, Chief," she said, ending her link. "Ensign, I want you to manually take us out of the Aarjedo star system. But keep us along the Copia Deiga border. I don't want to enter another galaxy yet."

"Aye, my lady," Narja said, accelerating the ship.

"Welcome back, Yarasuro," the captain said, gesturing him to approach. "How does the oracle fare?"

"She is recovering," he said, bowing. "How may I be of service?"

"Switch places with Sergeant Tasakiro. I want you to scan every planet we pass. If you come across any readings with xylithum crystals, let me know."

"As you wish," the knight said, sitting at his terminal.

Tasakiro left the main deck and joined Zadoya by the rear door. The duo stood guard, as did most soldiers, unless needed elsewhere. Templar Yarasuro, meanwhile, initiated a local scan on his computer. The long-range sensors offline, he had to wait until *Celestial* approached a world.

Passing the first intergalactic planet, he kept a sharp eye on the radar and scanned the natural satellite. Reading its details on the computer, Yarasuro found no signs of life. The next two were gas giants. After hours of traveling in the void, another planet appeared. Once within range, he scanned it.

"Captain," he called out. "We're approaching MJ453, a planet containing xylithum minerals. However, I'm unable to determine whether there are any crystals."

"Good work," she said. "How about indigenous creatures?"

"No known species are registering in the data, but I'm getting a reading of life dwelling in the forests."

"Forests?"

"Yes," he said. "There's a rogue supergiant several billion miles away. Even though this terrestrial planet hasn't been pulled into the sun's gravitational current, it must be so powerful for it to sustain life on the world.

"Interesting. Where are the minerals located?"

"Most appear to be deep underwater," he said, looking intently at his screen. "Others are scattered around a jungle along the eastern hemisphere. I've transferred the coordinates to you and Narja."

Shirakaya observed the information for a moment. "Ensign, set a course for that planet and land us near one of those mineral deposits."

"Aye," she said, flying toward the distant amber-hued world.

Passing a few drifting asteroids, the ensign descended the vessel. Its mana shield burned as it entered the planet's atmosphere. Though the starship shook, volatile against the planet's gravity, it emerged unscathed. Even so, as a precaution, passengers remained seated until the burning and shaking stopped.

The captain gazed at the environment, concerned.

Amber clouds filled the sky. Toxic rain poured, yet the arcane force field protected the craft. Narja reached a coast where an acidic ocean swayed. Seeing an opening, she landed along the shoreline, several feet away from where waves of poisonous water crashed. Atop the mound of sand stood a dense jungle strewn with arched trees that stood fifty feet high.

"We have arrived at MJ453," Narja said.

"Good work, Ensign," Shirakaya said, rising from her armchair. She clicked her kinetic link device, activated its loudspeaker, and continued, "This is your captain speaking. We have safely landed on planet MJ453. It's an intergalactic world that has xylithum minerals necessary to repair our vessel's engine. I ask all of you to remain patient while I gather a squad to gather them."

Yarasuro approached the captain. "My lady, I advise you to wait until the rain stops. It has acidic elements that are poisonous."

"I agree with him, Shira," the judicator said.

"If my vessel's force field can handle it, so can mine," she said, using magic to envelop herself in a mana shield. "You're coming with me, Templar."

"Shira, you *need* to rest," Owendar said.

The captain took a deep breath and hugged him. "Don't worry, I'll be fine. My ship's in terrible condition. I must help. Besides, I'll have plenty of time to rest when we make it back to the capital." She winked at him and walked away. "Sergeant Tasakiro and Lieutenant Zadoya, you're with me."

They joined her without question, leaving the bridge.

"Captain," the chief engineer said via kinetic link, "I have a scanning device that can help locate the shards. May I come?"

"I was just about to contact you, Kazakuma," she said, stepping into an X-Phaser with her entourage. "We don't know how to extract the crystals without damaging them, so gear up and meet us at the airlock."

"Aye, my lady," he said, ending the link.

II
Untamed Ferocity

Shirakaya entered a code in the pod and teleported with her squad to the entrance of the starship. Materializing, the quartet made their way to the airlock and waited for Kazakuma to join them. As soon as he arrived, Shirakaya sealed the chamber and put on her helmet. The others did the same and activated their spacesuits' force fields.

"Pressure adaptation initializing," the ship's AI reported, steam billowing around the airlock as metallic clangs reverberated. "Equalization complete. Have a safe journey."

The airtight door leading outside unsealed, the steam dissipated. Stepping outside onto the vessel's ramp, Shirakaya spotted the oracle who was merely dressed in a gown. Jedalia smelled the air and grabbed a grain of sand on the ground, rubbing it against her fingers.

"Jeda!" yelled out the captain. Her eyes widened, catching herself. "My oracle, what in the universe are you doing here? And why are you not wearing a spacesuit? This is an extremely dangerous planet. Goddess forbid your magic should weaken, the rain could fatally poison you. Yarasuro, escort her back to the temple."

Seconds later, a thunderous roar echoed throughout the region. Whether caused by a looming hurricane or a monstrous beast, myriad trees in the jungle swayed wildly. Except for Jedalia, the squad flinched.

"What in the cosmos was that?" Tasakiro said, loading his rifle with an inferno clip and aiming it skyward.

"Planetary descent," the oracle blurted. "Stars so beautiful. The eternal Goddess smiles. It is a fleeting smile. She is no longer happy. Lethal rain. Claws sharper than a sword. Now there is only death."

"I think we'd better search for another planet," Kazakuma said.

"My oracle, you can't utter riddles and expect us to

understand what you're saying."

Jedalia gazed at the captain and blinked as though mindless. "Shira, it is so wonderful to see you." She stood up and hugged her. "I missed you so much. Isn't this a beautiful world? We should take advantage of this time and—" She paused, staring blankly at the enchantress. "Is something wrong?"

"Yes," Shirakaya said in frustration. "Moments ago, you made what seemed to be a prediction."

"I did?" responded the oracle, stammering. "I'm sorry, I cannot remember."

"With all due respect, Captain," intervened Yarasuro, "I think she should join us in case she has something insightful to say."

The captain hesitated before saying, "Agreed. My faithful oracle, we are searching for xylithum crystals to repair the space engine. Your gift of divination can help us a great deal, but be wary. We're not alone on this planet. Please stay close to us."

"I will be honored to help you," Jedalia said, bowing.

Shirakaya smiled and signaled the others to follow her, leaving the burnished beach of auburn sand. Baila trees, giant plants with acid inside their trunks, covered the jungle ahead. Entering the forest, the canopy blocked all light. Many of the branchy trees leaked venomous ooze. Apprehensive, the sextet nevertheless trod through the sodden forest.

Bulky rocks with miniature holes lay scattered throughout the woods. Within the tiny apertures dwelled bouldermites, granite-eating insects. An occasional breeze stirred the crown formed by the baila trees. The saturated soil felt like a marsh while the captain and her squad painstakingly searched for signs of xylithum. Hoots and cackle-like squawks in the distance reached the sextet, reminding them to maintain their guard.

"We need a better formation," Shirakaya said, unnerved. "Zadoya, keep your eyes on the canopy. Tasakiro, watch our flank. Yarasuro, guard the oracle and chief."

The soldiers and knight obeyed, repositioning themselves. Yarasuro unsheathed his sword, staying close to Jedalia and Kazakuma. Meanwhile, the lieutenant and sergeant charged their guns and scouted the area for any strange movements in the forest. Apart from leaves fluttering and water trickling, neither saw nor heard anything suspicious.

Sawks, native creatures with skins of bark, hid camouflaged among the trees. Though outnumbering the captain's group, they stood stock-still and examined their prey. Yarasuro took another step forward, just as one of the sawks rose from its hunched position and swiped its sharp twig-shaped fingers at him. The knight swiftly swerved to the side, avoiding damage to his armor.

"Defend yourselves!" shouted Shirakaya, ready to cast a destructive spell.

A dozen sawks emerged and surrounded the crew. Thorny branches rose from their craniums. Their carved mouths emitted a noxious miasma as they fixed their obsidian eyes on their victims. Tasakiro took cover by an arched tree and fired at one of the creatures, his incendiary bullets setting it on fire. The beast screeched in agony, stirring the others to attack.

Striking the fiend that tried to attack him, Yarasuro splintered its chest as Zadoya rolled beside him and fired frost beams. As each sawk froze, the knight shattered it with his blade. At the same time, the captain tapped into the planet's life force. Absorbing its earthen power, she sprinted over to a sawk and punched its face with elemental strength, so hard that her fist penetrated its head and emerged from the other side.

"Shira, behind you!" called out Jedalia.

Veering to the side, Shirakaya dodged an attack from a sawk, missing its sharp limbs by a hair. Reluctant to cast a fireball and incinerate the jungle, Shirakaya used her earthen strength and kicked it to the ground. Another leaped onto Shirakaya, who used her knee to rupture it. Miasma filled the air from its splintered carcass, triggering a paroxysm of coughing in the captain.

"Stay away from their corpses," she said, backing away.

"They are as toxic as the trees and rain."

"Aye," Yarasuro said, warily slicing them with his blade.

"More are approaching from above," the oracle said, spotting them on the boughs of trees.

The soldiers aimed their guns skyward, firing at the incoming creatures. Kazakuma used his EBT-40 enchanted blowtorch to stagger one. He snatched an ice grenade from Zadoya's girdle and tossed it into the beast's serrated mouth. A blast erupted inside its trunk, freezing it. Porting an ATS-31 arcane screwdriver via his kinetic link device, he drilled into the fiend's chest, shattering it and its frozen, toxic sap.

Despite the crew's adept defense, sawks appeared from the canopy from multiple directions and advanced on their prey. Shirakaya and her entourage heard an ear-piercing roar — the same horrific sound they heard when they first left their vessel. A gargantuan beast swept by and spewed toxic miasma at the sawks. Those leaping along the canopy disintegrated. Baila trees in the vicinity withered and crumbled to ashes floating in the air.

The oracle conjured a powerful mana shield to protect the crew as the lethal breath shrouded them. She strengthened her barrier, gazed up, and saw the creature. Long horns grew from its olive fleece and stretched from chest to tail. A thick mane covered its neck and its scaly snout bore multiple tusks. Each of its six limbs sported razor-sharp paws. The creature of flight returned, breathed toxic death again, and vanished. Jedalia dispelled her shield when the miasma dissipated.

"What in the twelve dimensions was that?" Kazakuma said, hiding between a tree and boulder.

"Qazinotaur," the oracle said, her voice dreamy.

Shirakaya clicked her KLD and logged onto the ethernet. "That creature is not in our database. How do you know its name, my oracle?"

"I sense the Ruzurai came into contact with one, millennia ago."

Her clairvoyance stunned most of the crew, but they sought cover when the monster gave a deafening roar. After circling, the qazinotaur swooped down and felled several trees with a mighty swipe of its hefty paws. The captain and her entourage scrambled, desperate to avoid falling tree trunks.

Shirakaya spotted an entrance to a cave ahead. "Follow me!"

The others complied, running north as the ground shook. Tasakiro glanced back and saw the qazinotaur had landed in pursuit of him and his comrades. Eyes widening, he hurled an FS-93 firestorm grenade and ran faster as the beast thumped toward him. The device detonated, exploding near the creature's face. It yelped, but only appeared incensed.

Livid roars filled the crew's ears. Trees toppled. Paws clomped. The ground behind them shook and split. They staggered but reached the cavern, escaping the qazinotaur by inches. Unable to fit its head inside, the beast thrust its tusks through the narrow cave, ramming the jagged ceiling. His heart pounding, Yarasuro struck one of its many tusks, merely chipping it. The clangor rang in his ears. He took a step back into the clammy cavern while the qazinotaur withdrew, large boulders plummeting and crumbling by the entrance.

III
Chaotic Depths

The crew stood in a state of shock, a tsunami of adrenaline pumping through their veins; limbs shaky and heartbeats thumping in their ears. Catching her breath, Shirakaya felt numb, disconcerted from the traumatic attack. Her muscles and limbs took seconds to respond and move before she realized she was safe and had made it into the cave in one piece.

"My goodness," Shirakaya said, astonished to be alive. "Is everyone okay?"

The team's nods reassured her.

More composed, Zadoya reloaded her gun. "What now?"

The captain considered for a moment. "If that creature

continues to attack, we may have to abort our mission and search for another planet."

"Our ship can kill that thing easily," Tasakiro said.

"Not in its current condition, Sergeant," Shirakaya said, observing her surroundings. "We need a backup plan."

"Don't panic yet," Kazakuma said, checking his KLD. "Xylithum is in this cave."

Shirakaya exhaled with relief. "Thank the Goddess. Lieutenant, stay here and report to me via KLD should that creature attempt to attack again."

"As you command, my lady," Zadoya said, positioning herself by the fallen rocks.

"The rest of you come with me," the captain said. She led the way into the dark passage with her team, avoiding puddles of acidic water. "Chief, are you able to pinpoint their location?"

"That might be difficult," he said. "This is a large cavern. My scanner is showing several veins of xylithum below. I'm just not sure how far they are."

"Distance is the least of my concerns," she said. "Lead the way."

The quartet followed Kazakuma, advancing through the cavern's depths, lit by prismatic gems nestled into the granite. Shrubs with needle-shaped fungi grew along the dank walkway. Toxic water dripped sporadically from the cavernous ceiling. The absence of beasts here made the tunnel no less dangerous. Forced to remain vigilant, the soldiers gave a wide berth to the many abyss-like sinkholes.

They crossed a stone arch with a pit beneath it. The passage curved downward, leading them to an area where stalagmites impeded their progress. Descending, they spotted more jewels that gleamed and sparkled, and cast reflected rainbows onto the natural columns.

Jedalia fixed her eyes on them, in awe. She even touched a few sparkling gems. "So beautiful," she murmured.

Shirakaya heard the oracle and glanced at the jewels with amusement but stayed focused on her task.

"We're getting closer," the engineer said.

"I hope you're right, Chief," the captain said. "As colorful as it is here, I don't intend to stay any longer than necessary."

From the bejeweled chamber, they entered a shimmering tunnel, the result of acidic water erosion. Glittering microorganisms that sucked minerals on stalactites along the jagged ceiling lit up the path like a starry night. Amazed to see such phenomena, the quintet stared at the glowing sight as they moved deeper into the indigo cavern.

Near the end of the passage lay an aperture. Kazakuma approached it, using his KLD to scan the area. Identifying an antechamber below the hole, he signaled the others to follow him. Together they climbed down a fractured stalagmite. At the bottom, Kazakuma found a cluster of crystals jutting from the eastern wall. Beaming with relief, he strode over to them and examined each vein.

"What's the verdict, Chief?"

"These are crystals but not xylithum," he said. He continued to survey the chamber despite the captain's sigh of frustration. His kinetic link device vibrated when he examined the granite beneath his feet. "There are only xylithum minerals underneath."

"I thought they were worthless."

"More or less. However, there are so many deposits that I may be able to reform their molecular structure into one crystal."

"That would be fantastic," she said.

The chief crossed his arms. "Problem is I need at least five to get the anti-gravity module up and running again."

"This just keeps getting better and better," Tasakiro said.

"Now is not the time to complain," Yarasuro said.

The engineer ported his arcane blowtorch and tried cutting through the ground. After a few seconds of nothing significant occurring, he realized it wasn't strong enough to penetrate the granite.

"Can we assist you?" Yarasuro said.

"Not unless your sword can cut through solid granite," Kazakuma said.

Shirakaya waved her hand and temporarily enchanted the knight's sword. An aura-like emanation of flame enveloped Yarasuro's blade. He struck it into the ground until the granite sizzled, melting a large diameter. Kneeling in front of the glowing hole, Kazakuma used a laser to separate and consume the teal-tinted minerals.

"It may take an hour to reshape these into a crystal," the engineer said. "In the meantime, I suggest we continue searching for more."

"They call out to me in the murky realm," blurted Jedalia. "We soak in misery, shielded by only the Goddess. Traversing deeper, our shimmering saviors greet us with their gleam. We now stand glorified, renewed."

Kazakuma raised his brow. "What in the cosmos is she talking about?"

"She speaks of the sea," Shirakaya said, searching for a way out. "She can sense xylithum in the water."

"Impressive," the engineer said.

The captain continued exploring and discovered a dank passage that guided her and the crew to a cavernous chamber. Ahead lay several holes in the ground, all of which led to an underwater sea cave. Shirakaya lowered herself to the ground and peered through a larger aperture despite the rippling water affecting her view. Though struggling in the darkness, the captain identified an area below that appeared to produce bioluminescence.

"Kazakuma, do you have another one of those lasers?"

"Only this one," he said. "I can lend it to you, but it doesn't reach far. Unless you're in direct contact with the crystals, it won't be very useful."

"Have a look," she said, getting to her feet.

The engineer ported his EV-697 environmental visor that accommodated vision a few meters below water. He knelt on the stony ground to observe the radiant objects jutting from the coral reefs. Even with the advanced technology, he squinted, unable to discern the origin of the deep luminosity. Scanning the reefs, his KLD beeped several times.

"I'm afraid these are nothing more than flashy gems," he said, lifting his visor.

Shirakaya cursed under her breath. "They must be deeper," she said. "My oracle, are you able to strengthen our shields to withstand underwater pressure?"

"Yes, my lady. It will be my pleasure."

"Perfect," the captain said. She approached the waterhole again and cast a water-breathing spell. "I hope all of you can swim well."

The oracle uttered another incantation, amplifying the power of her comrades' mana shields. As soon as Shirakaya felt her force field strengthen, she dove into the water. Her crew followed. They entered a narrow passage where the path expanded, leading the quintet to an oceanic cavern littered with seaweed, corals, and bones.

A gleam of light flickered within the cave's depths, beyond clusters of poisonous plants. The slimy weeds drifted like cordage, stemming from what seemed to be an abyss. Despite how dark it appeared below, the captain swam down toward the light, which was sporadically shrouded by sticky entangled weeds. Shirakaya and her comrades swam deeper, passing serrated bones amid the dense foliage.

Shirakaya had an awful feeling that yet another dreadful beast was the cause of these remains. Jedalia still wore a dreamy expression on her face but the crew looked distraught. The captain refused to stop midway. Despite her fear, she continued swimming to her destination.

Moments later, Shirakaya saw a collection of crystals protruding from the fractured seabed. Glancing at the engineer, she signaled him to check them. Kazakuma approached the shimmering objects and initiated a scan. He turned and gave the captain a thumbs-up. The others, excited, cheered.

As the engineer used his laser drill to separate the crystals, the current changed and grew violent. Alarmed, he and his comrades looked about before seeing an enormous shadow approach.

"By the Goddess," gasped Jedalia. "It's a vai'le'ak!"

Shirakaya dared to look up. The glistening scaly creature with jagged pectoral fins and a long tail swam between the weeds, its curved teeth so long it couldn't close its mouth. Its gaping maw swallowed everything in its path, bones included. The quintet swerved out of its way but too slowly for the swift sea monster. The captain, fearful it would eat them alive, cast a spell. With immense difficulty, she reversed the current.

When the current pushed the beast back, a smaller mouth with needle-shaped teeth emerged from the permanently open one, and lunged at the captain. Her nausea returned without warning and she struggled to maintain control over the water. Despite her weakness, she summoned a tidal wave with her waning magic and propelled the beast against the sea cave's jagged wall. Its ferocious roar panicked the group. With no time to spare, the oracle conjured a beam of light. The rest of the crew followed her toward the light and swam up, surfacing near a cove.

"Get to shore!" the captain ordered.

Horror injecting adrenaline into their limbs, the squadron raced for the coast. The moment Shirakaya reached land, she faced the water and raised another tidal wave. The savage beast reared up from the sea, snapping its smaller jaws at her as the raging wave collapsed over the frenzied vai'le'ak. The water's momentum, however, failed to hinder the creature.

Wheezing, the captain winced in anticipation of being eaten alive. A fountain of purple blood erupted and floated on the tide as the beast's flesh tore open in response to Tasakiro's incendiary bullets. The vai'le'ak gave out a murderous roar before it swiftly returned to the depths of its underwater domain.

IV
Vengeance

Kazakuma panted beside the captain for half a minute before

speaking. "Is it dead?" he said, daring to peer into the water.

"I doubt it," Tasakiro said, reloading his gun. "But it probably won't attack again."

"Well done, Sergeant," Shirakaya said. "Now we just need to rendezvous with the lieutenant and get off this noxious planet."

Even though the spell she'd cast earlier allowed her to breathe underwater, Shirakaya struggled to catch her breath. She wondered, how could she be so drained when the spells she'd cast were trifling? Thinking hard, she realized that ever since her battle with Ashkaratoth, her powers had dwindled. Had he drained her of magical ions? Or had she consumed too much radiation from the blue giant?

"Captain, are you all right?" Yarasuro asked, spotting sweat along her brow.

"Yes," she stuttered. "I'm simply trying to make sense of where we are." Using her KLD's radar, she picked up Zadoya's signal. "This way."

The crew warily followed her south. Leaving the cove, they came to a bog alongside a lagoon. Water sizzled in the many puddles. The quintet avoided stepping into them, despite their protective force fields. West of them lay a reef surrounding an islet. Jedalia gawked at it but pressed on.

"I sense the qazinotaur," she said.

"*What?*" the captain said, weary but ready to cast another spell. "Where? Is it still trying to hunt us?"

Pointing at the islet, the oracle answered, "That is where it dwells. The qazinotaur must have returned after the cave-in. But it's able to smell our flesh miles away. It's only a matter of time before it comes back for us."

"We need to leave as soon as possible," the captain said. "Chief, how long will it take you to reform the other crystals and repair the space engine?"

"Not more than an hour," he said.

"My oracle, please send Kazakuma back to the ship so he can begin repairing it."

"As you wish," she said, teleporting the engineer back to

the *Celestial*.

"The rest of you will come with me," the captain ordered. "My oracle, once we find the lieutenant, will you be able to teleport all of us?"

"Mass teleportation is my specialty."

"Excellent," the captain said. "Let's go."

Shortly after Kazakuma entered the portal, the quartet continued through the misty bog. Returning to the dense woods, Tasakiro and Yarasuro readied their weapons. In the meantime, Jedalia pranced between trees like an innocent child. As for Shirakaya, she kept her hands raised, ready to cast a destructive spell.

They made their way back to the cave's entrance. It was as they had left it: A multitude of boulders blocked the entryway. A gust of wind stirred the rustling leaves and grass. Tasakiro aimed his rifle skyward, his eyes narrowed. Raising his sword, Yarasuro also gazed up.

"The qazinotaur left the island," Jedalia said, closing her eyes. "It knows where we are."

"Zadoya," the captain called out, apprehensive. "Can you hear me?"

"Yes, my lady," she said in a surprised tone. "How did you get outside?"

"There's no time to explain. I'm going to free you. Back away from the entrance as far as you can."

"Aye," the lieutenant said, withdrawing from her position.

Clasping her hands together, the captain attempted to move the rocks using telekinesis. She trembled and perspired from the effort, but they budged. Struggling, the enchantress lifted a few boulders out of the way. As she cleared a path, Zadoya scrambled out of the cave.

"Your timing was perfect, Captain," Zadoya said, saluting her. "Wait, where is the chief engineer?"

"Kazakuma found the crystals and is repairing the ship as we speak," Shirakaya said.

Before the lieutenant could cheer with excitement, a deafening reverberation shocked the team. The thick canopy of the forest swayed wildly as the qazinotaur swooped across and down. Opening fire, the soldiers shot its hardened scales. Roaring like the beast, Shirakaya used her magic to hurl every boulder at it. Each rock hit the creature, staggering it in midair. One of the boulders even struck its snout; the beast bellowed in pain as blood spurted from the gash.

"Jeda! Now!" the captain shouted, expecting the oracle to cast a teleportation spell.

Yet no one vanished. Turning, she found Jedalia on the ground, unconscious. Shirakaya wondered how and why the oracle fainted, but she had no time to think further on this. The qazinotaur gave out another ear-shattering roar and landed beside the dazed crew, crushing a cluster of trees.

"Spread out and attack!" the captain commanded, mustering all her energy and hurling a fireball.

The qazinotaur stumbled when confronted by the blast of flames. Yarasuro strode over to the beast and struck its stomach with his blade, piercing its scales. Barely harming it, he retreated with haste into the mist. Taking cover behind trees, the other soldiers shot at it. Rime appeared along the monster's front legs as Zadoya's frost beams took effect. Tasakiro unloaded an entire incendiary clip into its chest, wounding the qazinotaur. Nevertheless, it raised its claws and shredded the sergeant.

"Tasakiro!" the captain shrieked.

Shirakaya lifted Jedalia over her shoulders, running aimlessly away. Blood, flesh, and bones flew in the air—caught in the qazinotaur's merciless gaping jaws as it stomped toward the soldiers.

"Everyone, retreat to the cave!"

Zadoya disobeyed her, unloading a frost clip into the creature. The knight also ignored the captain; he reemerged from the intense mist and struck the beast's hind leg. With little damage done, he withdrew and evaded the qazinotaur's claws.

Fractious that her subordinates disregarded her order, she laid the oracle down and stepped out to locate them. She spotted Zadoya running eastward while reloading her gun, the qazinotaur galloping after her. With six legs, it reached the lieutenant in an instant. Zadoya tumbled to the ground, a look of terror on her sweaty face. The beast, ready to rip her apart, abruptly rose in the air, unable to resist Shirakaya's magic. It snarled, trying to attack in midair when Shirakaya tossed it aside using telekinesis. Attempting to lift it again, she failed. Horror-struck, the captain realized she no longer had the necessary power.

Before it slaughtered the lieutenant, Yarasuro reappeared from the boughs of a tree and plunged down, slicing its left eye. He fell into an acidic pond but clambered out before the toxin damaged his force field and rejoined the captain. Back on her feet, Zadoya maintained her position and fired numerous rounds at the beast. Giving a furious roar, it spread its scaly wings and flew skyward, evading the plasma beams.

"Lieutenant, get your ass over here!"

"I'm sorry," she said, regrouping with the duo.

"An apology is unacceptable. If you disobey a direct order again, you will be demoted. Do I make myself clear?"

Before the soldiers responded, the qazinotaur swooped again, breathing miasma over them. They took cover, but their force fields waned and dissipated. Luck on their side, it stopped raining. As the beast rose in the air again, the trio sprinted back to the cave. A few feet away from the entrance, they heard the monster roar from behind. Instinct took over, and the three of them spread out as it descended to cremate them with its scorching, toxic breath.

The captain cast a mana shield and launched lightning bolts at the qazinotaur, failing to stun it. Incensed by the attack, the beast unleashed more miasma. Yarasuro barely evaded the noxious breath, jumping onto a tree. Using his feet to push himself off the trunk, he leaped at an angle and struck the creature sidelong. The lieutenant, meanwhile, reloaded her rifle and fired at it.

Unaffected by their attacks, the native monster glided toward the cave's entrance. A terrible fear gripped Zadoya; she stiffened as it approached. Moments before her demise, a gamma ray from the hazy sky blasted the beast. It unleashed an outraged bawl, collapsed, and sent a tremor in its wake. The trio struggled not to stumble or fall. A wide depression appeared in the dirt, and the quake uprooted a multitude of trees. Looking up to see the cause, Shirakaya saw her spacecraft.

"Thank the Goddess," she said.

Relieved, she ran with her bodyguard to the dank cave and rejoined the lieutenant. They hastened deeper inside to where Jedalia lay. Although awake, she lay without moving a muscle. The captain helped her up.

"You fainted," Shirakaya said. "Are you all right, my oracle?".

"Yes. Thank you. It must have been a vision, though I cannot remember." She closed her eyes for a moment. "I sense that the qazinotaur has been wounded but is still alive. It's enraged and won't leave until we're dead."

"Why am I not surprised?" Zadoya said, sulking.

Yarasuro shook his head with frustration. "Any suggestions, my lady?"

"I think our ship has been repaired," Shirakaya said, glancing outside. "My oracle, do you have the strength to teleport us?"

"Of course," she said. "Please gather around me."

Surrounded, the oracle cast a spell and transferred them to the *Celestial*'s flight deck. A few stationed crew members flinched, surprised to see their captain and her companions appear without warning, but they remembered to salute Shirakaya before returning to their duties. Jedalia remained by the captain's side while Yarasuro withdrew to his computer terminal. As for Zadoya, she returned to her post by the door.

"You're a sight for sore eyes, Shira," Judicator Owendar said, hugging her.

"Those were supposed to be my words," she said, smiling at him despite being dispirited that she had lost a soldier. "Ensign, status report."

"Our chief engineer has returned and is repairing the engine," Narja said.

"I already know that," Shirakaya said, agitated. She clicked her KLD and established a kinetic link with Kazakuma. "I hope you have some good news for me, Chief."

"I reformed the material's molecular structure and installed the xylithum crystals," he said. "The space engine has been fully restored. However, I'm still recalibrating the anti-gravity module so we can travel through dimensional space without faulty trajectories."

"How much longer?"

"I'd say about ten minutes."

The crew heard another sonic boom, witnessing the qazinotaur return to the sky and pursue them.

"Make it five," Shirakaya said to Kazakuma, ending the link. "Narja, increase thrusters to maximum power and lock every gun on that beast." Without waiting to hear the ensign comply, she continued, "Owendar, I need one last favor from you."

"And what would that be?" he said, sitting down in the captain's chair.

Aware the oracle needed to rejuvenate, she responded, "I need you to port me to the roof again."

"What are you planning to do?"

"Please trust me."

Owendar sighed. "As you wish."

Materializing on an exterior rampart along the roof, she was grateful her magnetic boots automatically activated and prevented the wind from blowing her off. Spotting the qazinotaur ahead, she grimaced and made her way to the fore of the vessel. The beast roared as multiple beams blasted it. Barely affected, the creature pursued the *Celestial*, striking a wing and denting it. Passing a satellite, Shirakaya reached the edge, stood firm, and gazed at the enraged beast that defied an array of gamma missiles.

"You're going to pay for what you did to Tasakiro," she said, her eyes glistening red.

Channeling the arcane within, she repeatedly summoned fireballs and hurled them at the unrelenting monster. Between the ship's rays and her spells, the qazinotaur writhed and thrashed to dodge each attack. One of her fiery spheres blasted the beast but failed to do much damage.

"What will it take to kill you?" she shouted, discouraged.

"Captain," called out Kazakuma via kinetic link, "I finished calibrating the engine. We don't need any more xylithum crystals."

"That's music to my ears," the captain said, exhaling with relief. She ended the link with him and contacted the ensign. "Narja, get us out of here. And please tell the judicator I'm ready to return."

"Aye, Captain," she said.

As the link terminated, an unseen spell teleported Shirakaya back to the flight deck. She nodded at the judicator, grateful. Approaching the windowpane, she activated a rearview camera. It revealed the qazinotaur gaining on them. The raucous beast swiftly glided skyward, flapping its enormous wings and releasing its toxic breath. Even though the vessel's mana shield absorbed most of the acidic miasma, a few protruding cannons liquefied.

The qazinotaur's speed increased, its hypersonic velocity unaffected by the atmosphere's friction. It was meters away from striking the starship's aft with its six claws. Yet its incredible momentum came to an abrupt end when it entered space. The beast choked, gasping for air before it slowed down to fly aimlessly in the absence of gravity.

The dreadnought craft continued to traverse at a high velocity. The crew and passengers looked out of windowpanes, watching the enraged monster. Many were frightened and prayed for mercy, thinking the gargantuan creature still pursued them. Only a few people realized that the monstrosity drifted from the vessel and glided with little movement.

"Is it dead?" the ensign wondered aloud.

"I'm not sure," Yarasuro said, initiating a scan from his terminal. "According to the computer's analysis, its vital signs are dwindling."

Shirakaya magnified the camera's lenses, watching with

pleasure as the creature suffocated. She remembered what the oracle had told her: "It is enraged and won't leave until we're dead." They had turned the tables, she conceded. An ominous smirk formed on the captain's lips as she monitored the suffocating beast until it drifted—lifeless—in the void of space.

The Great Love

The Great Love is an everlasting star, glimmering in the face of hopelessness. No black hole in the cosmos can consume such beauty. It is my greatest gift to life. Where there is hatred, love softens the livid heart. Hidden like a precious jewel, love is omnipresent in every living thing. My children need only embrace it. The Great Love remains unending. And should the universe be reborn at the end of time, true love shall persist.

Arcane Proverbs 43:17

Chapter Three
The Nebula's Kiss

I
Freedom Rising

The crew cheered when they witnessed the death of the qazinotaur. Many of them applauded their captain. Yet she didn't join them. Instead, she shook her head, brooding on the loss of her soldier. Tears were not an option, Shirakaya conceded. She had to be strong in front of her crew. But she couldn't hide her depression.

"Tasakiro has been avenged," Jedalia said, gently rubbing the captain's shoulder.

"I know," Shirakaya said glumly. Taking a deep breath, she went on, "Ensign Narja, take us back to Copia Deiga in the Hydakorm star system. It's a safe distance away from Aarjedo. I want Celestial hidden until communications are up."

"Aye," she said, accelerating the vessel.

"Yaro," Shirakaya said, "our long-range sensors will be active soon. Keep attempting to contact the Order. If you manage to get through, request an audience with the Ruzurai."

"Already on it, my lady," he said.

"Shira, you must rest," the judicator said. "We'll only have one chance to present our case to the Ruzurai. You need to be at your best when communicating with them."

The captain released a sigh of frustration. "You're right," she said, nodding. "Yaro, delay that order. I need you to escort the oracle to her shrine."

"As you wish," he said, logging off the TDE.

"It was an honor serving you, Captain," Jedalia said, bowing.

"The honor was all mine, my oracle," Shirakaya said, kneeling before her. "I know you must continue your prayers to Maz'hura, but please rest."

"I will," she said, leaving with Yarasuro.

Shirakaya turned her attention back to the bridge. "Narja, when we arrive at Hydakorm, conceal us in the nearest nebula and inform all soldiers that they may rest until 3500 hours. You included."

"Aye," she said with glee.

"Please tell me you're not leaving yet," the captain said, pouting while facing Owendar.

The judicator laughed softly. "Dispel your fear, Shira. I will remain aboard and oversee your crew until you've rested. Believe you me, my presence will be mandatory for you to even have a chance at getting the Ruzurai's attention."

"Thank you so much," she said, hugging him. "I'll see you at 3500."

"Sleep well," he said, winking.

As she exited the command center, the crew saluted her and returned to their duties. Later, when, the ensign brought the *Celestial* within a nebula and switched its status from hyperpower to sleep mode, she announced to the crew via loudspeaker that they were free until 3500 hours. Although the interstellar cloud kept their sensors hidden, Owendar remained on the flight deck in case of an emergency. The others, meanwhile, took advantage of their approved respite. Most of them went to the starship's lounge. Only a few crew members stayed away from the party scene.

The knight was one of those who preferred solitude. Yarasuro had a tendency to bottle his emotions and remain somewhat antisocial. Because of this, he didn't know what to do with free time. He returned to his private quarters, meditating in silence. As a templar, he always had faith and maintained a strong connection with the Goddess. The career he chose was his life, which was why he worked so hard to protect Captain Shirakaya: Those in command were believed to be divinely chosen by the Goddess. Now that she was safe, at least for now, he took the time to meditate.

Zadoya, on the other hand, wasn't very spiritual. Though she respected and believed in the eternal Goddess, returning to her room to pray was the last thing on her mind. She had worked hard to become a soldier, more so to reach the rank of lieutenant and be assigned to this spacecraft. Although she didn't bottle her emotions like Yarasuro, as a workaholic she felt the need to train more in the ship's gymnasium to be as fit as possible.

Ensign Narja worked as hard as the others, but it was to support her nine-cycle-old daughter who lived on the capital planet. In terms of pleasure, Narja used to prefer racing for a living with her late husband. Ever since he died in a crash, she had put an end to the madcap life and joined the military. Undeniably the best pilot on board, Narja worked at balancing her job with life. During her free time, she returned to her cabin and contacted her daughter via the TDE to see how she was doing in school.

Unfortunately for Kazakuma, he wasn't considered a soldier and was required to work around the clock without respite. The engineer, although allowed to take short breaks and contact his wife, barely rested because the *Celestial* needed so many repairs. But as another workaholic, he found pleasure in repairing machines and improving them.

Few people were so hardworking and dependable, which was why the captain chose them as her entourage. Her only regret was requesting Sergeant Tasakiro to accompany her during the last mission. Shirakaya thought about him while in the starship's bistro and lost her appetite, feeling miserable. She nevertheless forced herself to finish her meal.

II
Veil of Secrecy

Dozens of people gathered in the *Celestial*'s assembly chamber, located on the ninth level of the ship. Banners depicting magical portals hung on each wall, symbolizing the twelve dimensions. The room contained a stage upon which stood a podium with myriad chairs before it. Most soldiers talked among themselves, the vast majority of them raising their voices. Only when a doctor walked over to the podium did a few people settle down.

"Please let Dr. Hejven speak!" shouted one of the nurses.

The group heard her and calmed down.

"I share your concerns, everyone," he said. "Our sacred Order may have chosen Shirakaya to be our captain, but that does not mean she is above corruption."

"My brother is dead because of her ruthlessness," a disgruntled pilot said.

"I just found out that Sergeant Tasakiro is dead and she didn't even bother returning his body for a proper memorial," an outraged soldier said.

Several people cursed her, raising their voices again.

The doctor raised his arms, trying to calm them. "We are all hurting, but if we keep yelling, it will alert one of her loyalists. Captain Shirakaya left hundreds of our colleagues to die near that doomed protostar in Aarjedo. In fact, even after our vessel was fixed, she didn't want to leave MJ453. Instead, she toyed with our lives, fighting that alien as if avenging somebody when deep down inside she probably only did it to prove to herself how superior she *thinks* she is. Once the crystals were replaced, all she had to do was order the helm to leave. It's obvious she's out of control. The question is: What can we do?"

"We need to stop her now before it's too late!" yelled out an arcane astrophysicist.

"Overthrow the witch!" shouted an alchemist. She repeatedly yelled out, "Overthrow the witch!" The more she repeated herself, the more others joined in. Soon just about every person in the room shouted, "Overthrow the witch!"

The charismatic doctor by the podium failed to calm them. Countless people continued to chant, "Overthrow the witch!"

In the blink of an eye, Jedalia teleported beside the podium.

The people bowed and prostrated themselves. The doctor moved aside, frowning. As the troubled group looked at her with a mixture of hope and despair, she brought herself to the podium and stood quietly for a moment.

"My beloved people," she said in a soft tone, "I felt your anguish in my temple. I know your pain and sadness. Many brave soldiers and esteemed pilots lost their lives in the line of duty today. In times like these, whether we understand the nature of what happened, it is easy for us to blame somebody—in this case, Captain Shirakaya. Yet if it weren't for her, the black hole would've consumed us all."

"But what about Sergeant Tasakiro?" a soldier said, gloom carved on his face. "He was my friend. How do you think his family will react? His body should have at least been recovered so we could perform Fay'hanam and send him peacefully to the eternal Goddess."

"It brings me great sadness to inform you there wasn't a body to recover," she said, teary-eyed. Dozens of people gasped at the news. "The qazinotaur was merciless. Yet we must look beyond this and remember that Sergeant Tasakiro, as well as every other soldier and pilot who served aboard the *Celestial*, died with honor and valor."

"So, are we to just shut our mouths and forget the captain's ruthlessness?" Doctor Hejven said.

"No," the oracle said. "Remember this day forever and let it strengthen your resolve to discover the truth. If we blame others in ignorance, we give up the power to defeat the true menace at hand. All I ask is that you give our captain more time to prove herself. I have had the opportunity to see her wondrous soul, and I want all of you to see it. We all deserve a chance. Please give her time."

"Fair enough," the doctor said. "I will refrain from seeking to have her replaced, so long as she doesn't put our lives in jeopardy again. If anyone disagrees, speak now." Only one person raised her hand. "Yes?" he called out. "Speak your mind."

"My oracle," said the female engineer, "will you be

notifying the captain of what has transpired here?"

"I fear knowledge of this event would break her heart," Jedalia said. "It is better for her not to think that people have lost faith in her so quickly. Therefore, let this parley be our precious secret."

The people agreed, many sighing with relief before the group dispersed. Even the charismatic doctor, who'd been so eager to start a revolt against Shirakaya, returned to the medical wing of the *Celestial* and waited for his next patient. As soon as the chamber was empty, Jedalia also left.

III
Unity

The captain walked aimlessly around the vessel, fretting about how and why her magic had weakened. After an hour of pondering, she decided to get some much-needed rest. Stepping into an X-Phaser, she tapped a code into a console on the wall. Within seconds, she vanished and materialized in her duplex. The lights inside her private quarters automatically turned on when she appeared.

"Welcome home, Shira," said the ship's AI.

"Thank you," she said, exiting a capsule by the entrance of her residence. "Dim the lights in my condo."

The lights dimmed when she spoke. Passing her entertainment center, she clicked her KLD and dematerialized her armor into her digital wardrobe. Wearing only a bra and panties, Shirakaya went into her kitchen and poured herself a glass of blue-hued jada wine. She took a sip and carried it upstairs to her bedroom. The sheets on her canopy bed already folded back, she slipped into them, leaning against a pillow.

The moment she finished her drink, the lights turned off on their own. Startled, Shirakaya placed her empty glass on a nightstand and stood up.

"Activate level one luminescence."

A celestial ceiling with star-like lights appeared. Near her dresser, she saw the silhouette of a petite woman wearing an ivory, sheer robe.

"Jeda," she whispered. "What are you doing here?"

"I missed you so much, Shira," the oracle said, approaching her. "Being on that planet really scared me. I feared something would happen to you."

"I remember your words," Shirakaya said, her eyes downcast. "Whether or not you remember the prophecy, it frightened us. Everything seemed fine until you said, 'Now there is only death.'" Silence descended over the room for a moment. "I thought something might happen to you. I wanted you back on my ship despite Yarasuro's logic. Yet all along the prophecy was meant for Tasakiro." She crumpled, trying to hold in her tears. "Is divination always cruel? Can't we ever reshape a prophecy?"

The oracle sat beside Shirakaya, embracing her. "Shira, I don't have any power over my prophecies."

"I know," she said, sniffing.

"Please don't blame yourself."

Shirakaya paused and then, with great difficulty, nodded. "Jeda, I think I'm losing my magic."

"*What?*" the oracle said, dismayed. "Why would you say such a terrible thing?"

"Because it's true," Shirakaya said. "Ever since I tapped into the blue giant's ions I find myself struggling to cast spells."

"Nonsense," she said. "You're simply exhausted. Our battle against the qazinotaur was treacherous, let alone the return of the koth'vurians. I sense that their leader, Ashkaratoth, is an extremely powerful being. He is not to be underestimated."

"True," Shirakaya said in a troubled tone. "Jeda, I appreciate your words. I really do. But shouldn't you be at the shrine? There must be so many people seeking a blessing after the horrific ordeal we've been through."

"It's past 2600," Jedalia said. "Most of our personnel are sleeping at this hour. If not, they are on duty. More importantly, we haven't shared time together in weeks."

Shirakaya didn't argue. She gazed into the oracle's eyes, lost in them. Jedalia tenderly caressed her skin. Feeling such a gentle touch, Shirakaya leaned forward and pressed her soft lips against the oracle's, the kiss rapidly becoming passionate. The enchantress loosened Jedalia's robe, revealing her perky breasts. Jedalia pressed her lover down onto the bed. No longer feeling depressed, Shirakaya spread her legs.

Passion and magic coursed through their bodies, uniting them. Together they ascended to a dreamy dimension of tantric bliss.

Obscure Tragedies

My children, you know joy because of sadness. You are conscious of gain by the impermanent nature of loss. And you are certainly aware of what is holy because of the evilness that arises from dark space. Just as you worship Ensar's splendor, it is equally imperative you be mindful of its tragedies since they are boundless throughout the journey of life. Yet do not lose hope in times of difficulty. Victory awaits those who persevere. Learn from these experiences, for this is the only way you will grow and transcend beyond the twelve dimensions; thus, uniting with me in eternal tranquility.

Gathas of Maz'hura 112:1

Chapter Four

Disturbance in the Void

I

Between Galaxies

At around 3400 hours, the captain woke up alone. A jupu flower, which had an indigo stalk with petals whose colors changed every few seconds, lay beside her. As she inhaled, the scent of her lover made her beam. Leaving her bed, Shirakaya went to her bathroom and turned on the shower. Stepping into the stall, she washed her soft skin and hair.

"Good morning, Shira," the starship's AI said. "I hope you slept well. Shall I brighten the lights for you?"

"Yes," she said, feeling more awake.

The bathroom illuminated while Shirakaya massaged a block of soap over her armpits and voluptuous breasts. As she rinsed the foam off her body, suds drained by her feet. Wiggling her toes, she hummed while thinking about her lover. After a short time, she shut down the water and exited the stall.

Fixing her eyes on a dry towel hanging across the room, she extended her wet arms in an attempt to summon it. The cloth merely dithered. Muscles straining, she formed a fist. Resisting the urge to scream, Shirakaya closed her eyes and concentrated harder. She heard a subtle vibration, which helped her focus. The cloth slid off the rack along the wall and flew into her hand. Standing still for a moment, the enchantress shook her head and dried herself.

The captain felt helpless, panicky at the possibility that the magic she'd been born with was dwindling. If her power were to vanish, what would she do? Her arcane abilities were central to her career as a captain. How else could she instill authority among her subordinates if they realized she was no longer different from them? By law, only someone with the gift of magic could command a spacecraft.

"I must remain calm."

Swallowing heavily, Shirakaya dried her hair and left the bathroom. She grabbed her KLD on the dresser by her bed and wrapped it around her wrist. Clicking it, a suit of dalikonium armor materialized over her. In addition, she found a memo from Kazakuma: *Good news, Captain. I have rerouted long-range sensors to the satellites on the eastern wing. Let me know if you need anything else.*

"Perfect," she said to herself.

With no further disruption, the enchantress went downstairs to the foyer and stepped into an X-Phaser capsule. Inputting a code, she teleported to a pod in a corridor near the command center. As she entered the bridge, the crew saluted her and returned to their duties. Shirakaya approached the judicator sitting in her armchair.

"How are you feeling, Shira?"

"Much better. Thanks for keeping an eye on things here. I owe you one, Professor." He smiled at her words as she continued, "By the way, my chief engineer notified me that long-range communications are available. Are we ready to discuss the koth'vurian dilemma with the Ruzurai?"

He gave out a sigh. "I strongly urge you to use your words wisely with them. Announcing that the koth'vurians *may* have returned won't be enough, even with me by your side."

"Don't worry. I'm more than confident that they will see reason, especially because you saw them too."

The judicator didn't respond, his eyes downcast.

"Templar Yarasuro," Shirakaya called out, "notify the Order of our situation and inform them that I'm requesting an audience with the Ruzurai."

"Aye," he said, logging on to the TDE.

The judicator rose to his feet and used his power to teleport both himself and Shirakaya to a conference room. Although just one level above the cockpit, the arena-sized chamber was inaccessible to those without magic. The interior lights activated, and the duo sat in ivory seats. Before them stood a plinth with twelve empty chairs.

"Only high-ranking officers are allowed in this sector," the starship's AI said. "Scanning arcane DNA." After a brief pause, the AI went on, "Permission granted, Captain Shirakaya and Judicator Owendar."

"Thank you," they said in unison.

Upon approval, their armchairs started hovering. Then the ceiling, floor, and walls became transparent, revealing the ship wrapped in a nebula. Cosmic dust stretched through the wings, extending out into the star system. There were also planets suspended in the nearby distance, one of which had rings surrounding it.

The duo remained seated while seven of the twelve Ruzurai attempted to teleport into the conference room. Holographic images of hooded beings repeatedly appeared and disappeared in the chairs before them. Moments later, they vanished altogether.

"Ensign," the captain said. "The nebula seems to be causing interference. Please take us out of it."

"Right away, my lady," Narja replied via kinetic link.

The dreadnought spacecraft accelerated toward a planet with an asteroid field, the ensign ensuring they did not get too close. Once out of the interstellar cloud, the seven Ruzurai materialized fully. They seemed to be the same age as the judicator. With the exception of one, wearing a black robe, the males had remarkably long white beards. The hooded man in black had a gray goatee, his liver-spotted hand rubbing the hairs on his chin. The female Ruzurai had waist-length hair and glowing tattoos on their foreheads.

"Venerable Ruzurai, it is a blessing from the eternal Goddess to receive you," Shirakaya said, prostrating herself.

The seven Ruzurai bowed their heads, bidding the captain to return to her chair.

"Greetings and salutations," Paladin Jaylendor said. "If you don't mind my asking, why is a fellow Ruzurai sitting opposite us?"

"Hail to you as well, Jaylendor," Owendar replied. "I speak as an emissary since I've become a victim here." A few Ruzurai wore confused expressions while others looked worried. "Well, I was visiting the good captain. By a miracle, she found a protostar. Yet when observing its splendor, we were attacked."

"Attacked?" Druid Parsara said, raising an eyebrow. "By whom?"

"My venerable Ruzurai," Shirakaya began, "I know this may be hard to believe, but the aliens who assaulted us consumed the newborn star. And the intruders flew on their own without needing air. I have reason to believe they were koth'vurians."

An uproar of denials filled the cosmic chamber. Several of them responded in unison:

"Impossible," Magus Darphan said.

"Liar!" Warlock Narx yelled wrathfully, pointing a tattooed finger at the captain.

"Nonsense," Illusionist Xarveda said, waving her hand.

"The gall of you!" Priestess Yanava said, furrowing her brow.

"You dare speak against the scriptures of Maz'hura?" responded Necromancer Arzenkar, the black-robed Ruzurai. "I don't care how impressive your dossier is, you should be ashamed for even thinking such a heinous thing."

"She is merely ignorant," Druid Parsara said. "Though we may have given this spacecraft to her somewhat prematurely, my concern does not lie so much with the youngling."

"Indeed," Warlock Narx said. "Now I know why the judicator sits with her."

"Ah," uttered the paladin. "Owendar, where do you stand?"

Their responses made Shirakaya want to summon multiple bolts of lightning and electrocute the Ruzurai. Never in her entire life had she ever been more humiliated or disrespected. Nonetheless, the captain remained silent. She breathed deeply, hoping her former professor would vouch for her.

"Don't tell us you believe such blasphemy," Magus Darphan said.

"My fellow colleagues, please calm down," Owendar said. "It is harmless to think outside the box. This was simply a theory she had. There is no need to denigrate the good captain because she tried to understand our enemy's origin."

"Forget about what the captain thinks," the necromancer said. "We are more interested in what *you* think."

"It is true that they flew using their own wings," the judicator said. "And it is also true that our adversary had no need for air. Furthermore, they seemed to be shape-shifters. Yet this is not enough evidence to declare them koth'vurians."

"*Professor*," gasped Shirakaya. "You saw—"

"That will be enough, *Captain*," interjected Owendar, his eyes gazing darkly into hers. "I didn't see anything other than unknown creatures attacking us from space. They were intelligent and dangerous, like most aliens."

"I'm glad you haven't lost your mind," Paladin Jaylendor said.

"Not yet. Still, I suggest you initiate an investigation to discover what those creatures are. They're a major threat to our colonies."

"You can do so yourself, Owendar," the necromancer said.

"As for the captain," Magus Darphan began, "she is not allowed to pursue the unknown origin of those aliens with you."

"Why not?" snapped Shirakaya while standing up, lightning fizzing through her eyes.

"Sit down," Priestess Yanava said ominously.

The Ruzurai noticed Shirakaya's eyes. A few of them looked apprehensive. Despite her fury, however, she obeyed the priestess and returned to her seat.

"First of all, your delusional theory won't be of use to the judicator," Yanava said. "And though you have spoken against the Holy Scriptures, we will pardon you just this once for your ignorance as a youngling and because Owendar believes in you. On a more important note, we have a new mission for you that is of paramount importance."

Despite how much Shirakaya wanted to hurl a fireball at the Ruzurai, she didn't. "How may I be of assistance?" she said through gritted teeth.

"A cruiser from the capital known as Eternimus has always taken teenagers on science trips," Paladin Jaylendor said. "It is, of course, a prerequisite to being accepted into universities. During this cycle, twenty-three senior classes have boarded the vessel. They were to tour between the Copia Deiga and Maga'Dar galaxies."

"I will always be fond of that tour, Your Grace," Shirakaya said.

"Yes, you went on it six cycles ago," he said. "The seniors experiencing it now, however, may not feel the same as you."

"If I may ask, what is wrong?"

"All seemed well during the Copia Deiga tour," Necromancer Arzenkar said. "My son even contacted me while aboard, expressing his fascination. A few hours later, we lost contact with the ship, including my son."

"When was this?" the captain said, incredulous.

"Yesterday," Arzenkar replied. "It seems the starship went offline when leaving the galaxy."

"This has prevented us from teleporting aboard via TDE," Warlock Narx said.

"Captain, we need you to search for the cruiser and find out what's wrong," Druid Parsara said.

"I will discover its whereabouts," Shirakaya said, bowing her head.

Although suspicious, the Ruzurai gave her no further trouble. With nothing more to discuss, all seven of them teleported back to their homeworld. The conference room dimmed, its walls no longer transparent. Shirakaya rose from her chair with an glare ominous, but failed to intimidate the judicator.

"I don't want to hear it, Shira."

"Excuse me?" she said, the veins in her neck bulging. "You stabbed me in the back and made me seem like I've lost my mind in front of the Ruzurai and you expect me to keep my mouth shut? You betrayed me!"

"I saved your life. If they'd heard another word about koth'vurians, they would have had you court-martialed."

"That's absurd."

"The scriptures of Maz'hura, as you well know, state that Koth'tura and his minions have been exiled from the universe and shall never return."

"My heart and soul will always serve the eternal Goddess, but that doesn't mean the scriptures aren't open to interpretation. There are countless symbols, let alone metaphors in the Holy Tal'manac."

"I find it hard to believe that 'shall never return' has another meaning," Owendar said, raising an eyebrow.

Shirakaya snorted. "That's a dubious interpretation of the Tal'manac and you know it. I'm no scholar, but the original version written eons ago expresses that they shall never return *until the end of time*."

"By the Goddess," he said, annoyed. "Shira, that is obviously an absurd analysis. There are absolutely no scientific signs of the universe crumbling."

"How do you—"

"Shira," Owendar said with a sigh, "please don't argue with me. I may have been a professor in the past, but I am now a Ruzurai. I'd be excommunicated if I were to say such things to my colleagues. Be thankful they're allowing me to perform an investigation to discern what exactly those aliens are. Whether they are koth'vurians or not, I will find out."

"Will you at least inform me if you discover anything?"

The judicator hesitated. "I'll contact you when I have some answers. In the meantime, you have a mission of your own to worry about."

"Yes. Thank you."

"No. Thank *you*," he said, giving her a smile. "I'll teleport you back to the bridge. After that, I'll return to the capital."

"You'll be missed," she said, reaching out to hug him.

"I will miss you too," he said, embracing her. "You have a fine crew, Shira. You're off to a great start with your career. But be careful out there. It's a dangerous universe, and you won't have me around to watch your back."

II
The Crooked Soldier

Owendar teleported Shirakaya to the flight deck. The crew saluted her when she appeared. She sat in her command chair and took a deep breath. Even though none of the Ruzurai gave her a chance, she was at least grateful that Owendar would report his findings to her. This wasn't what she wanted, but it put her mind at ease for the time being.

"Captain Shirakaya," announced the spacecraft's AI, "I am receiving a request via Transdimensional Ethernet from Commander Ravdar to teleport aboard. Shall I momentarily lower the shield and grant him access?"

"Yes," she said.

The commander teleported at empty terminal opposite Yarasuro. He wore a hard-shell spacesuit with joints, identical to Zadoya's, except it was all black and had six medals on his collar.

"Hail, my lady," the commander said, bowing his head.

"Back from shore leave already?"

"I know," he said, laughing softly. "My wife and I almost had to be dragged off the island. Time always passes so fast when entertained."

"Indeed. So, you enjoyed yourselves?"

"It was the perfect place to celebrate our wedding. I highly recommend a trip to the islands of Phiboli on planet Bovaja."

"I'll keep that in mind," she said, smirking.

"So, what have I missed?"

"Nothing we couldn't handle," the captain said, counteracting a few grunts within earshot around the bridge. "I'll explain our next assignment soon."

"Captain," called out Narja, "shall we return to the

nebula?"

"That won't be necessary, Ensign. I'm transmitting coordinates to you. I want you to enter dimensional space and traverse esoria. Beyond the galaxy."

"Aye," she said.

Narja entered the coordinates into her monitor and entered a code on a side panel. The starship rumbled; its space engine's anti-gravity module rotated and the arcane graviton glowed. Within seconds, two rays launched from the starship's wings. One was a gravitational ray while the other was anti-gravity. The vessel released composites of negative energy density when the beams collided. Combined, they opened up a stable aperture in space and Narja accelerated the ship into the galactic fissure.

Shirakaya's interstellar craft entered a shimmering chasm. The ensign increased thrusters to maximum power. Once the spacecraft reached the other side and exited the cosmic tunnel, the passage sealed. Before them was an extremely luminous quasar and a supermassive black hole, which pulled the starship inward. An alarm immediately went off on the bridge, throwing the crew into a panic.

"Captain!" Narja said in a distressed tone. "Is that the Drift Void?"

"Don't be ridiculous. Maintain thrusters at maximum power. AI-095, release five inertia missiles along the aft to dampen the gravitational current."

"Affirmative," the ship's AI said, launching them.

Shirakaya crossed her arms, eyes fixed on the black hole. "Ensign, use the cosmodrive to take us out of this star system as soon as the missiles detonate."

"Aye, Captain."

As instructed, when the missiles exploded, Narja pulled two throttles forward. The crew heard an ear-shattering reverberation, the boosters igniting. As the projectiles created an inertia-dampening field, the spacecraft zoomed away from the fiery-imbued quasar that seemed powered by a giant black hole. Within seconds, they prevented their vessel from melting

—not to mention collapsing into oblivion because of the extreme gravity.

"Apparently it's still exciting here," the commander said.

The captain snorted at his comment. She knew her magic wasn't strong enough to avert this disaster, so she was more than relieved to be safe. Shirakaya exhaled and stood up from her armchair. Approaching the wide windowpane in front of her, she gazed into the starry void of space. The crew looked at her, concerned about their next mission.

"Ensign, where are we?"

"We just left the Ukopa star system," Narja said, decreasing the ship's speed. "Now we are bordering Copia Deiga.

"We're leaving the galaxy again?" Yarasuro said.

"That's right," Shirakaya said. "But this should be the esoria sector. Am I correct, Ensign?"

"Yes," she said. "In fact, we're not too far from Maga'Dar."

"Perfect. Increase thrusters to 740K and leave Copia Deiga. Just make sure you don't enter Maga'Dar. Not yet at least."

"Aye," Narja said, obeying her commanding officer.

"The sacred Ruzurai of the Order have given us a new mission. A tourist cruiser carrying thousands of senior students has vanished somewhere between these galaxies. Our objective is to locate it. Templar, use long-range sensors. Let me know if you find the ship."

"Right away, my lady," Yarasuro said, inspecting the esorian quadrant of space. "I don't see anything on the radar, Captain."

"The ship may have lost power," she said. "AI-095, send out a tachyon torpedo."

"As you command, Captain Shirakaya," the spacecraft's artificial intelligence said, launching one torpedo.

"Do we know anything else?" Ravdar said.

"I'm afraid not, Commander," she said. "If the ship's communications malfunctioned, the tachyon should be able to detect it as a cipher."

"Clever as always," he said.

"My lady," called out Yarasuro, somewhat anxious. "The

torpedo detonated and picked up a signature that may be congruent with the tourist cruiser. But I'm still waiti…never mind. I received the cipher."

"Excellent. AI-095, decrypt the code."

"Affirmative," the starship's AI said. "I am attempting to override protocols and decipher the tachyon report." Within a matter of seconds, it went on, "Message decoded at 0251 hours. The *Eternimus* has been shut down manually. Wires are being removed and rerouted aboard the cruiser as I present this report."

"Why in the cosmos would anyone do that?" the commander said.

"Probability of the tourist ship *Eternimus* being hijacked is ninety-nine percent," the AI said.

"My goodness," the captain said, taking a seat. She noticed that a few crew members on the bridge looked uneasy, including the commander. "If that is truly the case," she continued with apprehension, "I will need a small team to come with me and infiltrate the *Eternimu*s undetected."

"Not an option," the commander said tersely. "With all due respect, Captain, if the ship has actually been hijacked, it would be too dangerous for you. Since I'm second-in-command, I should oversee this mission."

Narja rolled her eyes as she whispered, "Here we go again…"

"I know you're eager to get back to work, Commander," the captain said. "But your wife would be a wreck if something were to happen to you."

"I'll be quite all right," he said, standing up.

"I'm sure you would be," she said, her jaw tightening. "I would, however, rather you watch over my vessel while I oversee this delicate mission. It was, after all, entrusted to me by the Ruzurai."

"Captain, I know you're young and ambi—"

Shirakaya waved her hand, putting him to sleep. He slumped back into his chair, faintly snoring.

"Lieutenant, come here."

Zadoya approached her. "Yes, my lady?"

"I'm going to put together an infiltration team. I need two soldiers to come with me and you're one of them. Do you recommend anyone else?"

"Let me check the roster," the lieutenant said, clicking her KLD multiple times. "There's a sergeant on board with a clean record. He's pretty good. We also have a corporal. She has a solid record, too."

"We're not going on a picnic, Lieutenant. I need somebody who's aggressive."

"Aggressive?" Zadoya said, looking a bit surprised. She browsed through her files and pulled up another dossier. "There's a private on board," she said hesitantly. "His name is Dojin. However, I strongly advise against bringing him with us."

"Why?"

"He's been on other ships with me before and has a record of disobeying his commanding officers. He was demoted from major to private for losing most of his squad and putting others at risk while trying to prevent a heist three cycles ago."

"He sounds perfect for the mission. Inform him of our assignment and tell him to standby for my orders."

"As you wish."

Shirakaya heard the lieutenant's lack of enthusiasm but let it slide. She left the bridge and made her way to an X-Phaser capsule. Entering a code inside, she ported over to a gargantuan chamber that once held hundreds of space jets. Now only a few remained, one of which was her personal yacht. The sorceress clicked on her KLD while approaching the small craft, activating her intercom.

"This is your captain speaking," she said. "The Celestial will stay out of sight for the duration of a covert operation. Templar Yarasuro, Lieutenant Zadoya, Private Dojin, and Chief Engineer Kazakuma are to report to my yacht at 0300. Make sure you are well equipped. Everybody else will remain aboard until I return."

Shirakaya shut off her KLD, waiting for her team to

assemble. In less than five minutes, all but the private had arrived. The last person to teleport into the chamber was Dojin, a fairly young-looking soldier with a tan complexion, short hair, and a rugged goatee. Similar to the captain, he too wore dalikonium armor. Also, he had two pistols holstered on his belt and a rifle attached to the back of his armor.

"Why is this creep coming with us, Captain?" Zadoya asked.

"Dalikonium armor," Shirakaya said, ignoring the lieutenant. "Only high-ranking officers are granted that."

"I used to be a major," he said, cracking his neck and shoulders.

"Interesting," she said. "I appreciate a soldier who thinks for himself. But sometimes you need to fall in line and obey your commanding officer."

"For you," he said, checking out her body, "I'll do anything."

Zadoya rolled her eyes. "With all due respect, my lady, I warned you about his despicable behavior."

"I'm going to pretend I didn't hear that, Private," the captain said. "Listen up. This might be a perilous mission. You may very well lose your life if you're careless. Follow my orders, and you'll live to brag about it."

"Save it for the choir, lady," he said, spitting on the ground.

"This is your commanding officer, Private," snapped Zadoya. "Apologize and show her some respect."

"It's all right, Lieutenant," Shirakaya said, amused. "If there're terrorists aboard that ship, I'll need at least one soldier who thinks like them." She paused a moment and added, "You're an interesting officer, Private. I just hope you don't end up dead because of your narcissism. As you should know, I don't bury or cremate my subordinates."

"Glad we're on the same page," he said. "I hate being around sappy pussies. Now, are we going on this mission or what?"

The captain clenched her fists, trying to smirk rather than grit her teeth. Before unlocking her jet, she heard the teleportation pod activate. Turning, she noticed her lover appear in a spacesuit.

"My oracle, please return to your temple."

"No," Jedalia said, approaching the group. "I refuse to let you travel aboard that ship without me."

"Captain," intervened the knight before Shirakaya could object, "I know how important she is to the morale of our soldiers and citizens here, but her ability to cast teleportation spells is invaluable if students and teachers are being held hostage."

Shirakaya looked as if she'd burn him to a crisp. "Fine," she said. "My oracle, you may join us under one condition."

"Anything."

"You will stay behind us at all times. Under no circumstances are you to stand beside me or my subordinates when on that ship. Is that understood?"

"Yes, my lady," she said, bowing.

"Let's go," Shirakaya said, using her KLD to unlock her yacht's rear cargo door. Opening it, she and her companions stepped up the ramp and entered the craft. "I'll be flying my ship," she added, walking toward the cockpit. "My oracle, please sit next to me. The rest of you can stand wherever you like."

Dojin leaned against a wall, his eyes fixed on the captain's buttocks until she sat down in the pilot's chair. He checked his guns and made sure they were loaded. Then he gazed at the pane, observing outer space. The lieutenant, meanwhile, stood firm by the door. Kazakuma decided to sit on a metal container in the cargo hold. As for Yarasuro, he sat on the floor in the middle of the ship's corridor and meditated.

The captain activated her craft, at which point it lifted a few feet in the air and remained hovering. She dimmed the lights inside and clicked several buttons along her interface, making the vessel invisible. Shortly after, the captain increased its thrusters. The yacht's engines gave off subtle rumbles while Shirakaya flew it out of the dreadnought spacecraft.

Traveling at eighty-thousand kilometers an hour, she passed

multiple intergalactic planets in no time. After flying beyond a rogue star, the captain spotted an ivory starship via her radar. She increased her thrusters to maximum power, traversing through space at an incredible speed. Her arcane engines were powerful and yet utterly silent, complementing the cloaking field that kept the yacht hidden.

Another minute later, Shirakaya saw the suspended cruiser with her own eyes. She decreased the velocity of her craft and cautiously flew toward the vessel that drifted amid an asteroid field. The colossal rocks around the perimeter glowed red. Streaks of flame sporadically spewed from distant meteors that zoomed by, the rogue star's gravity causing numbers of them to collide with gargantuan asteroids.

"By the stars," the oracle said. "Perhaps being stranded here is the reason why they shut everything off?"

"I suppose it's possible," Zadoya said, squinting for a better look at the situation. "But the question is, why did they fly into the heart of those planetoids? I can't shake this feeling that something terrible caused the *Eternimus* to be there."

"I'm surprised it's still in one piece," Dojin said.

"Hold on tight, people," the captain said, using her intercom. "This is going to be a bit tricky."

Shirakaya decreased her ship's speed, maneuvering between asteroids. Several meteorites passed by, one of which the enchantress evaded by a couple of yards. With the exception of Dojin who didn't seem to care if he died, the crew looked. The oracle kept her eyes closed while Shirakaya turned the craft and performed sharp turns to avoid being struck by big, jagged planetoids.

"Are we there yet?" inquired Jedalia, her eyes still closed.

Though advancing toward the cruiser, the captain didn't respond. She remained focused, attempting to steer her ship as precisely as possible through the field. At times, she had to dive down when flares splurged out of what appeared to be volcanic asteroids. Whether this was the cause of a deadly spell or simply a natural phenomenon, the crew couldn't tell.

"Captain, do you think these rocks contain booby traps?"

Zadoya asked.

"We're almost there, Jeda," Shirakaya said at last. "And no, Lieutenant. Even when we were far away, I saw the flares. These volcanic asteroids must be remnants of mountains from a destroyed planet."

"Supernova?" Zadoya said.

"Possibly," the captain said.

"Who gives a damn," Dojin said, sulking. "Worry about the mission and getting to that cruiser alive."

"Keep your mouth shut, Private," snapped Zadoya. "If the cruiser has been hijacked and those planetoids were booby-trapped, then it means they've been alerted to our presence despite us being cloaked."

"Stand down, Lieutenant," Shirakaya said. "I have enough to worry about. The two of you fighting won't help."

"My apologies," she said, disappointed.

At this point, they were just a mile away from the drifting vessel. Neither of them spotted students, or anyone for that matter, on the ship's terrace. Even the entertainment deck with an outdoor pool was vacant. Shirakaya continued to decrease her thrusters, warily bringing her yacht to twin funnels on the top deck. With the cruiser turned off, no exhausts rose into space. Lowering her ship a few feet, Shirakaya clamped onto the pair of funnels. Secured, she deactivated the craft.

"Now what?" the oracle said.

"We gain access to the *Eternimus* and find out what's wrong," Shirakaya said, activating her intercom. "Saddle up, soldiers. We've arrived. Join me below at the garbage disposal bay."

III
Bleak Investigation

The crew strode over to the central corridor and entered a lift that brought them down one level. Once the platform stopped, they stepped into a spotless chamber meant for compost. In the middle of the floor was a sealed door. The crew lined up along the walls and put on their helmets, waiting for their captain to open it.

"Tell us the plan," Dojin said.

"Don't be in such a hurry to die," the lieutenant said.

"Listen up," Shirakaya said tersely. "I've landed on the funnels. When I open this hatch, we'll be using them to enter the cruiser. They will lead us into the engine room. From that point on, we will stick together and discover what's wrong. Understood?"

"Yes, my lady," most of the crew said.

Dojin kept quiet, his expression neutral. The captain noticed this but ignored his lack of respect. After walking across the garbage disposal bay, Shirakaya pressed a button on a console. After depressurization, the hatch opened beneath them. Unsealed, they advanced in a slow gait toward the exit, defying outer space's lack of gravity with the magnetic soles on their boots.

Leaving the yacht, they stepped onto the huge cruiser. The crew clomped sideways onto the rim of a funnel, and as the sextet entered the shaft, the *Eternimus*'s mana shield activated. Simultaneously, its engine turned on, the reverberations blocking the stomping sounds coming from Shirakaya and her soldiers. After a short time, the smell of exhausts rose up to greet them.

"Disgusting," the oracle said.

"On the double, soldiers," Shirakaya said, clomping faster. "Our helmets can only filter so much of these fumes."

"Talk about bad timing," Zadoya said. "Why is everything activating now?"

"It's possible the ship needed repairs," Kazakuma said, trying to download schematics of the cruiser via KLD while stomping downward. "If so, that would explain why their mana shield and engines were off. Perhaps they finished maintenance and don't require help."

"That would be dull," Dojin said.

"Stop theorizing and get your asses down the shaft," the captain said. "I want to speak with the crew and find out what happened without getting lunporsis disease."

Dojin laughed at her comment. Sharing her concern, he increased his gait and was the first to enter the engine room. The others joined him seconds after. Once out of harm's way, they recharged their force fields and removed their helmets. The chamber shook, turbines and pistons making a lot of noise. Regardless of such distractions, they unsheathed their weapons and scouted the zone for suspicious activity.

Reconnoitering the chamber, they came across a fork of three zigzagging catwalks littered with rumbling machinery. Shirakaya signaled the lieutenant and engineer to explore the left side before gesturing at Dojin and Yarasuro to check the right side. She took the middle walkway. Jedalia followed the captain but, as promised, stayed behind her. The engine noises and exhausts pumping through the funnels masked everyone's footsteps, alerting Shirakaya to greater caution when moving forward in case they weren't alone.

"Clear on my end," Zadoya said via kinetic link.

"There's nobody here either," Yarasuro said, keeping his sword lifted. "What are our orders, Captain?"

Shirakaya didn't respond. In fact, she'd turned off her KLD. Ahead of her stood a sca'vezi, an alien from the Maga'Dar Galaxy. Although wearing a heavy suit of metal armor, the alien didn't have a helmet on. Its forehead, particularly the brow, bulged with yellow birthmark stripes from nose to spine. The alien was bald, its coarse scalp resembling a squashed cone, its vertically slit eyes fixed on a piece of machinery.

The sca'vezi didn't notice her as it tweaked wires. Seeing this alien here confirmed the captain's suspicion: the *Eternimus* had been hijacked. She raised an arm and conjured a sphere of frost. The sca'vezi caught sight of her movement and jittered back. As he pulled out a laser pistol, the sphere hit him, turning his body into a block of ice. She kicked the alien to the floor, shattering him. Hearing the ruckus, her comrades rushed over.

"Sca'vezi have hijacked the *Eternimus*," the captain said. "I just took one out. Now it might be a bit extreme, but we should travel through the ducts and see if there's anything we can learn about the situation before making ourselves known."

"That's bullshit," Dojin said. "I say we stop wasting time and just blow these alien fucks into space."

"Watch your mouth," Zadoya said.

"I'm the captain here, *Lieutenant*," the enchantress said. Ignoring her subordinate's apology, she went on, "I appreciate your style, Private. As a matter of fact, I would normally do just that. However, this is a delicate situation. These aliens may have taken our people hostage. I still don't know why. It could be ransom or something worse. For all we know, the students may already be dead. Until we fully understand what's going on, I want us to stay hidden. Again, we'll use the ducts to move around. Take out any patrolling aliens you spot and do your best to remain concealed."

"Aye," most of the crew said.

Even though Dojin didn't agree aloud, he opened a vent and entered the duct in a corner. The chief engineer followed him. Shirakaya and her other companions went through a parallel one, trying to crawl ahead as quietly as possible. As they advanced, the captain heard footsteps below. She stopped, peeked through slits of an angled vent, and saw two sca'vezi pirates passing by in a corridor.

"Jeka isn't responding," said a deep voice via kinetic link. "Has the railgun been linked to the Eternimus yet?"

"Not sure, boss," said one of the pirates. "I'll check on Jeka."

As soon as the link ended, Dojin kicked open a vent and swung down, unloading both pistols' incendiary clips into the sca'vezi pirates. Another alien in an adjacent chamber heard the bullets and exited his room. Upon seeing a humyn soldier, he aimed to fire. Shirakaya heard the commotion from the adjacent duct, forced a vent open with her elbow, and extended her fingers. Though initially struggling, she conjured the elemental of air and managed to choke him from afar. He dropped his weapon, at which point Dojin reloaded his guns and shot him.

"That was reckless, Private," Shirakaya said, exiting the duct. "They might be alerted to our presence."

"My apologies, Your Eminence. I suppose you wanted them to find their comrade in a thousand pieces? Trust me, I just saved you a few extra minutes before these psychos find out someone's crashed their party."

"I tried to warn you, Captain," Zadoya said, joining them.

"Duly noted," the enchantress said. "Perhaps you're right, Private. Kazakuma, return to the engine room and seal it. Ducts included. I need you to search for this railgun of theirs and sever the link."

"Aye, my lady."

"I want the rest of you here with me. Goddess knows how many terrorists are aboard this cruiser."

"Excuse me, ma'am," said a young girl by the open door.

Dojin swiveled and pointed his loaded pistols at her. Yarasuro simultaneously lifted his baskino sword, veering it along her neck. The teenager shrieked, backing away and falling on her rear.

"Stand down, soldiers," the captain said. She entered the boiler room and found dozens of frightened teenagers inside, many crying. "It's all right," Shirakaya added, raising her hands. "My subordinates were just startled. We're here by command of the Tal'manac Order to rescue you. Is anyone else alive?"

"Yes," said an adolescent boy. "They've been keeping us hostage."

Using telekinesis, Shirakaya dragged the three dead bodies into the room. "Do you know why?" she asked, closing the door. "Is someone being held for ransom?"

"We heard something about a revolution," said the girl who fell, getting up.

"Those scumbags are never satisfied," Dojin said. "Give them trading rights and they hijack instead. Let's just wipe them out and be done with this."

"Not every sca'vezi thinks this way," the lieutenant said.

"The passive ones are not our concern," Yarasuro said, resting his curved baskino sword on his shoulder.

"Sca'vezi aren't the only ones here," said another female teenager, approaching the group of soldiers. "Before they forced me into this room, I saw a few ghensoths with them. They also have automatons. At least I think that's what they are."

"This is bad," Shirakaya said, contemplating for a moment. "My oracle, can you teleport them back to our ship?"

"Of course. Students, please gather around me."

The anxious teenagers surrounded her. Jedalia brought the palms of her hands together and murmured an incantation. She grew pale after teleporting the teenagers from the cruiser to the military spacecraft. Feeling queasy, she stumbled to the side.

"My oracle, are you all right?" Shirakaya asked, holding her.

"I'll be okay," she said, straightening herself. "I'm simply not used to teleporting people so far away."

Shirakaya sighed. "Perhaps you should still res—"

"Captain," Kazakuma said via kinetic link. "The sca'vezi apparently connected the railgun to the engine to strengthen its electromagnetic blast. But don't worry, I dismantled their motor. They won't be traveling anytime soon."

"Excellent work."

"There are, however, gamma cannons being placed around the Eternimus as we speak," the engineer said. "I would have deactivated them from here. Problem is, these terrorists have routed their controls to the bridge."

"What in the twelve dimensions are they trying to do?" she said, frustrated.

"Something ingenious," Dojin said, ignoring the ludicrous expressions his comrades gave him. "Think about it. Hijacking a civilian cruiser and transforming it into a battleship is an inventive and clever way to either make demands or initiate a surprise attack on the capital. There are teenagers aboard, so the military will find it difficult to retaliate."

"I think he's on point, Captain," Yarasuro said.

Taking a deep breath, Shirakaya approached the sealed door. "I agree. There's just one thing the private forgot to mention."

Dojin raised an eyebrow. "And what's that?"

"My arrival," she said, her eyes fizzing. "This ingenious plan that's been set into motion by those *scumbags* won't last an hour longer," Shirakaya added as she left the chamber. "Follow me. You included, Chief."

"Aye," Kazakuma said, ending his link and rejoining them.

IV
When All Hell Breaks Loose

The crew followed their captain, keeping their weapons raised. Jedalia didn't have a gun or sword, so she used her magic to amplify the power of each person's force field. Locating a staircase, they went up several flights.

They stopped on the fifth floor and explored a carpeted hallway with a fountain at the center of the passage, which led to the cruiser's casino. Dozens of teachers were held hostage there. The captain and her comrades saw multiple foes with guns and swiftly took cover. Even though Jedalia hid, she dispelled the aliens' force fields before they launched plasma beams at the rescue squad.

Shirakaya waved her hand, enchanting her bodyguard's sword with an aura of fire. The knight rolled away from the fountain, sliced open an enemy's torso, then took cover by a gambling machine. The military squad, meanwhile, fired at their adversaries between pillars. Shirakaya rose and hurled fireballs at a group of aliens.

More enemies came out and attempted to blast her. Yarasuro, however, stood in front of her and repelled their lasers with his enchanted blade, deflecting them back to the aliens. Most pirates attacking were sca'vezi, but ghensoths fought among them too. This species came from the distant

Torpo Giayan Galaxy and had a brutish appearance: Boney exoskeletons, massive muscles, tresses of hair along their hardened spines, snout-shaped beaks, and blood-soaked eyes with horizontal pupils. They were also between twelve to fifteen feet tall.

The enchantress flipped over a row of machines and launched a fireball at a ghensoth, which barely affected him. He merely stumbled back when the sphere of flame blasted him, his shell-like skin unharmed. Dojin sidestepped away from a column and strode past multiple slot machines while shooting the brute. His bullets dented the alien's exoskeleton, nothing more. The ghensoth roared and charged forward, attempting to ram his prickled scalp into the private.

"Fuck me," Dojin said, rolling aside.

Avoiding the twelve-foot tall brute, he reloaded his guns. The alien, meanwhile, smashed through a cluster of machines. Shirakaya lifted him using telekinesis and threw him into a group of pirates. Her eyes fizzed with rage, unleashing a bolt of lightning. The spell was so powerful it spread like an intricate web, shocking the entire regiment.

The only aliens in that brigade left standing were ghensoths, whose hardened bodies appeared scorched. Yarasuro emerged sidelong and beheaded one of them, his fiery sword sizzling. He pirouetted, evading another as it attempted to bash his face, and sliced off its exoskeleton arm. The alien roared in pain, blue-hued blood pouring on the floor. Before it could retaliate, Kazakuma charged at the wounded alien with his TB-481 and released a thermal beam across its waist, splitting it in half.

During the battle, schoolteachers shrieked and tried to hide. But no matter where they crawled to in the casino, explosions erupted. Bullets, beams, and spells flew above their heads. The oracle approached them, wary, and conjured mana shields over them. She then guided them out to safety.

Other ghensoths fired lasers at the military squadron. At this point, only a handful of them remained. Shirakaya cast an ice spell, freezing one. Zadoya reloaded her rifle with an inferno clip and shot the glacial alien, liquefying its body.

"Four left," Dojin said, holstering his pistols and porting a bazooka. "Suck on this, assholes."

He launched a gamma missile eastward, where three ghensoths stood. They failed to move out of the way, the explosion vaporizing them. He transferred the weapon into his KLD and removed a PSG-549 plasma shotgun from his back holster. Charging it to maximum power, Dojin aimed it at the last alien firing lasers at the lieutenant and blasted its chest. The brute gave out a screech and tumbled to the ground, his multiple hearts punctured. Within seconds, the ghensoth died.

"Clear," Zadoya said.

"Where are the passengers?" the captain asked, scouting around. Looking behind, she saw Jedalia teleport them out of the *Eternimus*. "My oracle—"

"I'm fine," she interjected.

"Okay," the enchantress said, trying not to sound overly worried. "Let's keep going. We need to reach the bridge and deactivate those cannons before they repair the engine and attack the capital."

An intercom activated as the military squad passed through an empty nightclub just beyond the gambling deck.

"Greetings, admirable teachers," said a ghensoth pirate in an intimidating voice. "My name is Xorvaj, leader of the Urvantak faction. That little show you put on in the casino was impressive. However, your insolence ends here. Our objective is not to harm you. We simply wish for the Ruzurai of Copia Deiga to restore our ravaged homeworld. If they refuse, we will destroy the humyn capital world, Pravura. I advise all of you to relinquish your weapons and surrender, that way nobody gets hurt. Contact me on the Eternimus frequency 1098.56 when you are ready to comply. You have exactly one minute to make a decision."

"Ignore him," the captain said.

Leaving the gambling district, they entered an access strip that took them to a mall comprised of multiple clothing and makeup stores. Stalls containing diverse snacks lacked vendors.

Above were elongated balconies with numerous restaurants, each one deserted.

Two dozen sca'vezi pirates vaulted from behind the balustrades and opened fire with plasma rifles. Simultaneously, a contingent of androids arrived along the mall's corridor, shooting lasers. The squad rolled and pirouetted between the lasers to safety, except for Yarasuro. The knight refused to withdraw; he stood in the middle of the wide hall, maneuvering his sword in multiple angles, parrying their attacks.

"Goddess, guide my precision," he whispered to himself.

Each time Yarasuro deflected a laser, he took a step forward. The knight reached an automaton and swiped his weapon in an arc, striking it down. Without halting, he repelled their rays, deflecting several beams back at them. A few pirates groaned, lurching over the balconies and falling. As soon as the Templar approached a cluster of robots, he swerved between them and swung his blade numerous times. He parried and riposted until they lay in pieces.

With most of the pirates and their automatons focused on the knight, it provided Shirakaya a window of opportunity to reemerge. Filled with rage for not anticipating the ambush, she abandoned the corner entrance of a closed fashion store and hurled fireballs at enemies along the balconies. Her powerful spells simultaneously destroyed their force fields and vaporized them.

"Kill the witch!" yelled a sca'vezi.

The pirates feared those who wielded magic and immediately tried to silence Shirakaya, firing multiple beams in her direction. Her evasive maneuvers were like an exotic dance. She dodged lethal rays while serenely whirling aside, launching more spheres of flame from her hands. A rush of nausea, however, forced her to duck behind a bench to rejuvenate. Several lasers hit her mana shield, weakening it. At the same time, the oracle used magic to strengthen it. Her nausea subsiding, Shirakaya hurled a mixture of icicles and fireballs at the pirates.

A dozen automatons took their attention off Yarasuro,

aiming at the captain. As they shot at her, Shirakaya conjured an earthen spell, punching the ground, which created a tremor so powerful it toppled the majority of the aliens. Dojin and Zadoya joined the fight, blasting their foes from afar with their guns. Dojin loved his pistols, but this time he used a rifle for long-range precision. The oracle continued to take cover, attempting to amplify her comrades' mana shields while simultaneously dispelling enemy force fields.

As for Chief Kazakuma, he ported out his ATC-671 chainsaw and advanced from corner to corner, unleashing serrated blades into pirates' necks from afar. Drawing near to an automaton, instead of hurling projectiles, he activated its secondary mode—a chain blade that sawed off the robot's limbs. Dismantling it, he switched back to projectiles and joined Yarasuro who consistently deflected plasma beams while thrusting his sword, destroying androids that ventured too close to him.

Few pirates remained on the balcony by the time Shirakaya reached the end of the corridor. Her telekinetic powers lifted them into the air and slammed their bodies against the concrete of the lower level. Turning around, she watched Yarasuro and Kazakuma tear apart the last two robots.

"Well done," the enchantress said. Fixing her gaze on the sealed entryway in front of her, she tried opening it. "Shit, these doors are made of dalikonium. My spells alone can't break them. Chief, can you perform a miracle?"

Kazakuma gave out a soft chuckle. "Let me see." He walked over and attempted to open the doors via a console nestled into the wall. "Hmm. It seems Xorvaj has sealed this from either the control room or bridge. I'm sure I can hack into this and get it open, but it may take a while."

A brigade of twenty-five sca'vezi charged in from where the military squadron had initially entered. Numerous ghensoths and drones emerged directly behind the sca'vezi, ready to open fire.

"I'm afraid time isn't something we have, Chief," the captain said. "Get those doors open ASAP or we're finished."

"Aye," he said, linking his KLD to the console in an attempt to hack it.

Now within shooting distance, the pirates unleashed a barrage of lasers. The private and lieutenant positioned themselves opposite each other, protected by pillars along the marble walls. Zadoya reloaded her rifle while Dojin fired his shotgun. With solid accuracy, he blasted half a dozen aliens, holes sizzling in their chests. After inserting a frost clip in her gun, the lieutenant fired plasma beams, turning her targets into slabs of ice. Seeing the frozen blocks, Dojin blasted them apart with his GS-560 gamma scattergun.

The captain and her bodyguard stood in the open, vulnerable. The pirates fired a multitude of beams, but Yarasuro skillfully deflected their lethal rays back at them. Shirakaya cast multiple bolts of lightning, which electrocuted the sca'vezi; their smoking bodies trembled to the floor. The intense voltage interfered with nearby automatons, causing them to malfunction and explode.

It appeared only the ghensoths remained unaffected. Sweat pouring from her brow, the enchantress increased her power. The electrical surge sent them staggering. But before Shirakaya could finish them off, she wheezed and fainted.

Jedalia shrieked and teleported the captain to her side. She checked on Kazakuma's progress. The oracle conjured a powerful mana shield to protect her lover and the engineer. Confident they were safe, Jedalia teleported a group of eight sca'vezi into outer space where, helmetless, they suffocated. She repeated the spell with another group, this time ghensoths. Although successful, a terrible weakness enveloped her from using so much magic at once. Left with no choice, Jedalia withdrew and stayed beside the captain while maintaining the arcane shield.

"They keep coming," Zadoya said, panicky.

"So what?" Dojin retorted, charging his gun. "Keep killing them."

Ghensoths and automatons from the first brigade were still fighting when another wave of ten sca'vezi pirates joined the fray. Dojin grumbled, holstered his plasma shotgun, and ported a bazooka. Taking aim, he fired two gamma missiles at a regiment of ghensoths, the explosions decimating them and turning the mall into a waste zone of shattered glass.

"I got it!" Kazakuma said, unlocking the doors.

Yarasuro continued to deflect beams while Dojin lifted the captain onto his shoulders and sprinted to the next sector. The others followed and sealed the door behind them. Without wasting time, Kazakuma hacked the door panel to prevent the aliens from pursuing them. They found themselves in a dim theater with rows of seats and an illuminated stage. Despite how intriguing it appeared, they ignored it.

"What happened to the captain?" Yarasuro asked.

"Put her down," the oracle said, tears in her eyes. "I can restore her health. Please put her down."

Dojin laid the enchantress on the carpeted floor and backed away. The oracle knelt beside her lover, conjuring power. An ivory hue emanated from her glowing eyes as she waved her hands, etching curative magical symbols in midair. Enveloped by their mingling auras, Jedalia closed her eyes and placed both palms on Shirakaya's forehead. Perspiring, the oracle healed her lover, but at the cost of growing pale and weakening.

"Thank the Goddess," Yarasuro said as Shirakaya stirred.

"Welcome back, Captain," Zadoya said, saluting her.

"Wha-what happened?"

"You fainted while using your magic," the oracle said. "You scared me, Shira. I've never seen that happen to you before."

This news frightened Shirakaya, yet she concealed her fear. "I'm all right," she said, getting to her feet. "Thank you for tending to me, my oracle." She observed the theater, going down a couple of steps. "What's the situation?"

"The dalikonium doors are open," Kazakuma said. "I resealed them when we passed through, but I'm sure those aliens will find another way in."

"Then we need to find a way out of here fast," the captain said.

"Okay, time out," Dojin said. "All this running around is really getting on my nerves. Can't the oracle simply teleport us to the bridge?"

"That may seem like our best option, Private," Shirakaya said. "Unfortunately, dozens of ghensoths, including Xorvaj, are probably there. I don't know about you, but I certainly don't want to be surrounded by those brutes. Do you agree?"

Dojin's response was a mere sigh.

"Carry on, soldiers," she said.

V
Momentum

Shirakaya and her comrades descended the theater's steps with caution and found an exit at the bottom, which led to another staircase. They went up several flights, which brought them to deck seventeen. Exploring the floor, the squad found a hall filled with sleeping cabins. Some doors were open, students peeking from behind them. Curious, a few teenagers stepped out.

"You're humyn," said one of the students.

"So what, dipshit?" Dojin retorted.

The captain gave him a long look. "These are students, Private," she said. "Don't worry, the Ruzurai have sent us. We're here to rescue you."

"We wondered what all that noise was," said an adolescent girl.

"Incredible," said a boy. "My father knew of our capture,"

Shirakaya appeared startled. "Do you study black magic?" At his nod, she went on, "Are you by any chance the son of Arzenkar?"

"I am. My name is Dreyvak, a necromancer like my father. Who are you?"

"Shirakaya," she answered. "I'm a captain of the Tal'manac Order, and this is my squad. By the way, your father didn't know exactly what was happening. The military lost contact with the Eternimus and we were sent to find out what happened."

More students opened their doors and approached.

"It's terrible," another teenage girl said, sniffing. "They came out of nowhere and took us and our teachers hostage."

"I know," Shirakaya said. "But the situation has changed. You don't have to worry anymore. We'll take care of these criminals. Now we really need to get a move on. Gather around Jeda, my oracle. She will teleport you to my starship."

"Is it all right if I stay and help?" Dreyvak said.

"Believe me, I could use your skills. But your father would court-martial me if he discovered you were helping us."

"I understand," he said.

The students gathered around the oracle who cast mass teleportation, sending them to the captain's dreadnought vessel.

Moments later, the cruise's intercom activated again.

"You have killed dozens of my men," Xorvaj's voice rang out, sinister and determined. "I doubt you are teachers. If you do not surrender, I will be forced to harm the younglings on this floor."

"He's bluffing," the captain said, ignoring her squad's tense expressions. "Follow me."

She guided her crew through a bedroom suite to a balcony door. Reaching it, the captain put on a helmet and activated an air tank of zitrogen via kinetic link. The others copied her actions. Standing near the patio door, Kazakuma linked his KLD to a panel embedded on the wall to hack it. After a short time, he unlocked the sliding door. The sextet stepped out, their magnetic soles active.

"The ship's mana shield is on," Kazakuma said, scanning the zone. "We can deactivate our boots, right?"

"I'm afraid not, Chief," the captain said. "They might turn it off if they see us."

The squad heeded her paranoia, keeping their sabatons active, and followed Shirakaya to the highest deck that had an empty pool. Ahead, past a spa, lay the bridge and control room by the bow of the cruiser.

Moment's later, a throng of pirates spotted them from a nearby gymnasium.

"Holy shit," Dojin said, seeing more aliens emerge from the bridge. "This isn't a good place for combat."

"It seems we have no choice. Deactivate your boots and spread out," Shirakaya commanded.

The private ran along the jogging track, firing his plasma rifle, the flaming beams wiping out multiple sca'vezi. Yarasuro sprinted on the opposite side, deflecting rays from afar and fatally slicing his foes as he sprinted past them. Jedalia snuck into the *Eternimus* spa and gathered teenage girls and teachers to teleport them to safety. Zadoya hid by the corner wall of a satellite and discharged frost beams at ghensoths. The engineer helped her, launching saw-disks from his ATC-671 at frozen targets.

Shirakaya charged ahead to the diving board above the pool, where she sprang high into space, using her jetpack to temporarily remain airborne. Midair, the enchantress summoned icicles and hurled them at her foes. The spikes pierced their necks, causing them to choke on their own blood.

An asteroid breached the cruiser's magical barrier. Lava spewed from one of its many holes, spilling on the ship's upper level. Zadoya leaped out of the way, avoiding the lethal magma. Ghensoths fired at her as she moved to safety. When struck, her force field malfunctioned and a ray vaporized her left forearm. She cried out in agony, dropped her gun, and fell into the pool.

Eyes widening, the captain activated her intercom. "Jeda, the lieutenant is wounded. I need you to teleport her from the pool to our medical bay."

"I'm on my way," she said.

Shirakaya saw the oracle exit the spa and covered her, hurling fireballs at aliens shooting at her. The enchantress unleashed bolts of lightning at drones emerging from portholes on lower levels of the vessel as she descended toward the deck. She joined Dojin, who launched gamma missiles at a regiment of ghensoths via his bazooka and obliterated them. The explosions also collapsed the nearby gymnasium.

"Be careful, Private," the sorceress said. "We need heavy artillery to take down those brutes, but if you're too reckless, you may harm remaining hostages."

He snorted and pulled out his shotgun. Charging it to maximum power, he sprinted away from the jogging track and fired at the remaining ghensoths. As soon as the scattergun's power decreased below eighty percent, he took cover behind a pole and recharged it. Each burst within a nine-foot radius blew the ghensoths' chests open.

In minutes, bodies of pirates littered the floor, limbs tangled and blood spurting, the metallic smell filling the air. Jedalia reached the lieutenant and teleported her to the mothership. The others approached *Eternimus's* bridge. A dozen sca'vezi rushed out to defend their leader. Kazakuma launched sharp disks and Yarasuro parried the onslaught of rays, ripping them apart with his sword.

"Nice moves," Dojin said to Yarasuro, who bowed his head in response.

The captain set her KLD to frequency 1098.56. "This skirmish is at an end, Xorvaj. The majority of your rebels are dead. If any are alive, they're probably hiding. Even your automatons have been destroyed."

"I'm still in control of this vessel, witch," Xorvaj said. "I can turn off the zitrogen at any time. If you dare come any closer, I *will* suffocate your younglings."

"You were full of shit before, and you're lying again," she said. "How do I know this? If just one of them dies by your hand, the Ruzurai will not negotiate and will obliterate this vessel using the palace's ion cannon before you could even dream of entering Pravura's atmosphere." Silence fell over the deck, broken only by the captain who continued, "Surrender now, and the Order will spare your life. You will, of course, be imprisoned for life, but I suppose that's better than death."

"I will never surrender!" roared Xorvaj.

The ghensoth leader rammed through the bridge's rear windowpane, shattering the glass. Yarasuro swiftly flipped over him, avoiding a deadly pummel. Charging, Xorvaj battered the engineer, knocking him off his feet. Too weak, Shirakaya, failed to cast a sleeping spell on him. Scared by her failure, she took a step back.

Xorvaj produced a hideous grin, realizing he had the upper hand. He roared at the top of his lungs, stomping forward for the kill. From five feet away, a bullet belonging to a shotgun decimated his chest armor. He staggered, scouting the area. Dojin set his weapon to recharge and ported it away. Then he flanked the ghensoth leader, unsheathing a tranquilizer dart from his belt, and hurled it at his neck.

"Eh?" muttered Xorvaj; he rubbed his throat and collapsed, unconscious.

"Outstanding job, Private," Shirakaya said, eager not to reveal her weakness. "How did you know I was trying to put him to sleep?"

"You were waving your hand like an idiot," he said.

"Watch your tongue," Yarasuro said, checking on the engineer.

"Stand down, Templar," the captain said. "Jeda, please teleport this scumbag terrorist to my ship's penitentiary and tend to Kazakuma."

"At once, my lady."

Shirakaya glanced at the knight and private. "You two are with me," she said, using her jetpack to enter *Eternimus*'s bridge via its windowless frame. Unlocking a door, her companions stepped into the chamber. "Dojin, take control of those cannons."

"Why?"

"How do you think these pirates arrived here?" Shirakaya said, helming the ship. "Like us, they must have cloaking devices. Templar, use the communications array and notify either Narja or the AI to send out another tachyon torpedo."

"Aye," he said. Increasing the radius of his scan to its limit, he detected the mothership. "I've located the Celestial. I'm attempting to make contact."

The captain heard him but didn't respond. She cautiously

rotated the cruiser amid the asteroid field, hoping she'd spot an alien vessel.

"Hail," Narja said.

"Greetings," the knight replied. "This is Templar Yarasuro speaking. The captain requires a tachyon burst in this quadrant."

"I'll launch it now."

Eyes fixed on the radar, Shirakaya waited about three minutes before seeing the torpedo appear. After passing the cruiser, it detonated as Jedalia and Kazakuma rejoined them. The captain waved at the duo and drummed her fingers on the arms of her chair, waiting for a sign.

"These readings are faint," Narja said via the ship's relay. "I'm sending the coordinates."

"Thank you," the knight said. "Here are the results, Captain." He transferred Narja's data to the screen. "She's right, the readings are faint. Perhaps these are escape pods used by teachers or students who managed to get away?"

"They wouldn't use them in the middle of nowhere," she said. "Furthermore, a tachyon burst reveals communication relays. Capsules don't have them. Private, fire at will."

"I was hoping you'd say that," Dojin said.

Gamma rays launched from every cannon along the bow of the *Eternimus*, exploding a vessel ninety miles away. Within seconds, an armada of battleships uncloaked, approaching fast and counterattacking. Shirakaya closed her eyes, using telekinetic power to sway nearby planetoids into them. A gargantuan rock smashed into a ship, tearing it in half, forcing other vessels to maneuver away from the asteroid field.

The captain grinned, amused by her own actions. The smirk, however, soon disappeared off her pale face: No matter what she tried, the asteroids did not move. Even tiny meteorites refused to swivel. Although panicky, she remained seated and pretended to be in control. Her heart pounded; she wiped sweat from her forehead and swallowed hard, watching Dojin attack as the flotilla divided into two groups to flank the *Eternimus*.

"Watch your side, Private," she said.

"Relax," he said in a carefree tone. "Thanks to Xorvaj, these buffoons just signed their death sentence."

Since the dead pirates had placed cannons on every angle of the cruiser, Dojin used them to his advantage. Activating them, he fired at the enemy starships. Gamma rays tore through their shields and obliterated ship after ship. Before they could realize Xorvaj lost control of Eternimus, the fleet had been wiped out.

The oracle cheered. "You did it!"

"Thank goodness," Kazakuma said with a groan.

Yarasuro crossed his arms. "Impressive."

"Piece of cake," Dojin said.

"Well done, Private," the captain said, clapping. "Now, for your extreme insubordination, I am placing you under arrest."

"*What?*"

"Did you actually think you'd get away with your actions? Not only did you disrespect the lieutenant, but you also humiliated me. The only reason why I didn't lock you up sooner was because I needed you for this mission. Mark my words, Private, that attitude of yours will be purged before you ever serve me, or any other captain, again."

"Fuck you," he said. "I'm not going—"

Yarasuro hit the private's head with the pommel of his sword, knocking him out. "My lady, words cannot describe how happy I am."

"No one plays me for a fool," she said. "Get him out of my sight."

Celebrating Togetherness

Hear me, my dearest progeny: You are all brothers and sisters, linked in an intergalactic web of fertility. My creation is One; therefore, be kind and just to your cosmic siblings. But do not neglect your bloodline. For they have incessantly sweated their brow to protect and raise you, guiding you through the unknown. Cherish the unity of all beings in existence, yet never forget to return home in unity and celebrate togetherness in peace and prosperity.

Apophthegm of the Divine 48:7

Chapter Five

World Away From Home

I
Unexpected Respite

beying the captain, Jedalia teleported Dojin to a cell in the mothership's brig. Shirakaya and her bodyguard spent the next couple of hours searching for the crew of the *Eternimus*, finding them cuffed in the cruiser's restaurants. The duo worked together to free them.

Kazakuma made repairs to the arcane engine that he had sabotaged earlier, enabling the *Eternimus* to move away from the asteroid field. Out of harm's way, Yarasuro contacted Ensign Narja and instructed her to bring the *Celestial* to this quadrant of space.

Not long after, Shirakaya's starship came alongside the cruiser. Narja linked them together via a hatch, allowing students and teachers to come aboard without requiring the oracle, who needed much rest. Jedalia returned to her temple to continue her meditations and prayers. The others continued helping the refugees settle in. Once they were taken care of, Shirakaya went to her yacht and flew it back into the mothership's jet chamber. Shortly after, she used an X-Phaser pod that transferred her to the medical bay.

"Excuse me, Doctor Hejven," she called out to a middle-aged man wearing teal-colored scrubs in a corridor. "How is Lieutenant Zadoya?"

"She's stable but undergoing surgery," the doctor said. "Her left forearm was vaporized." Seeing her give a faint nod, he added, "Fortunately, the lieutenant's insurance has approved a replacement."

A wave of gratitude washed over the captain. "Thank the Goddess. It seems she'll still have her career. Will it be tetrigonium?"

"Hopefully. It depends whether her body will accept the prosthesis."

"I see," she said, visibly uneasy. "Well, thank you. I'll pray for her recovery. Keep me informed of her status."

"Absolutely."

Shirakaya returned to the teleportation pod and entered a code, transferring herself to the command center. Walking through a long corridor, she entered the bridge and approached her armchair. She ignored Ravdar's gaze and activated her kinetic link.

"Templar Yarasuro, your presence is required in the flight deck," she said. "I need you to contact the Order and request an audience with the Ruzurai."

"I'm on my way," the knight said.

Commander Ravdar stood up when he heard the link end. "With all due respect, Captain, putting me to sleep was a foul trick."

"Listen well, Commander. You are a good officer, always showing concern and trying to protect me. In fact, you're *supposed* to give me advice. You're a decent man when it comes to humyn values. It's wonderful you found love at such an early age."

"Thank you," he said, bowing his head.

"However," she went on, "should you ever defy me or continue to question my authority again, I will be forced to replace you. Is that understood?"

The commander swallowed heavily. "My sincere apologies, Captain. I understand perfectly."

"Good. As you were."

Ravdar obeyed, sitting back in his seat and remaining silent.

Yarasuro entered the flight deck. He sat at his terminal and logged on to the TDE to contact the Tal'manac Order. Since the satellites were destroyed after the battle against the koth'vurians, it took longer than expected for him to establish a connection.

"My lady," Yarasuro said after a minute, "the Order has received your message and informed me that the Ruzurai are available."

"Excellent," Shirakaya said, activating her KLD. "My oracle, can you please transfer me to the conference room?"

"Of course," she said, teleporting the captain.

The spacecraft's AI scanned Shirakaya as soon as she materialized. Recognizing her, the chamber turned semitransparent. Sitting in a hovering armchair, she gazed at the gulfs of space and watched the *Eternimus* leave. The cruiser vanished from her sight. Only asteroids remained. She didn't spot any intergalactic planets, only far distant stars that mostly belonged in galaxies such as Maga'Dar and Copia Deiga. After another minute, three of the twelve seats before her glowed: Judicator Owendar, Druid Parsara, and Necromancer Arzenkar appeared.

"It is an honor to receive you again, venerable Ruzurai," Shirakaya said, prostrating herself.

"Greetings, Captain," the necromancer said. "You may rise." He waited for her to sit back down before continuing to speak. "My son has already contacted me and told me of your deeds. I cannot express my gratitude enough. Thank you for saving him."

Druid Parsara gave her a warm smile. "On behalf of the Tal'manac Order, we thank you for saving the lives of everyone aboard the Eternimus and removing those fiendish terrorists from power."

"Shira, did you happen to establish their intentions?" the judicator asked.

"The faction was called Urvantak," she said. "Their objective was to arm the Eternimus to the teeth and threaten to attack the capital unless you restored their homeworld. Xorvaj, their leader, believed he would succeed because he held hundreds of students and teachers hostage. I'm not sure why so many sca'vezi joined, but the ghensoths lost their homeworld and want it restored. Regardless, I believe their endgame was to overthrow you and rule Copia Deiga."

"Never in a billion cycles would I have ever thought they were capable of this," the druid said.

Arzenkar crossed his arms. "Where is Xorvaj now? Is he dead?"

"He's alive," the captain said. "In fact, he's the only survivor. I imprisoned him in the brig and plan to keep him there for the rest of his life."

"Outstanding work, Captain," Druid Parsara said.

"You make us proud, Shira," the judicator said, clapping softly.

"Venerable Ruzurai, you grace me too much," Shirakaya said, trying not to blush. "I was merely following your orders."

"Merely following our orders?" Arzenkar said, raising an eyebrow. "According to my son, not even a single innocent life was lost. Owendar was right about you, Captain. You may be gullible, but you are a woman of honor and extreme valor."

"The appalling escapade of Urvantak will be written in our history books, and you will be mentioned as a hero who saved our future leaders," the druid said.

"Maz'hura has blessed me today," Shirakaya said, teary-eyed.

"Indeed," the judicator said. "To celebrate your success of eliminating those pirates, we are granting you three days of shore leave."

"Thank you," she said, elated.

"You deserve it," the druid said. "Enjoy your time off and expect a new mission from us when you return to duty."

"I am here to serve," the captain said, bowing.

The Ruzurai nodded at her, dematerialized, and returned to the capital. Shirakaya wondered why only three of them had appeared. Were the others still upset with her? And why did Owendar leave so abruptly? She had hoped that he'd have a new lead on the koth'vurians. Perhaps it was too soon, she thought.

Setting aside her anger, she thought of the bright side; the

Ruzurai granted her a few days of shore leave without her even asking for a vacation. As captain of a starship, it was hard to get time off. In fact, she hadn't had a break since her inauguration. Before deciding on what she'd do, her kinetic link device vibrated.

"Yes, Doctor Hejven?"

"I'm sorry to disturb you, Captain," he said. "I am just informing you that Lieutenant Zadoya's body has rejected the tetrigonium prosthesis that we've made for her, so we'll be using ayzentium instead."

"That's awful. Ayzentium is the cheapest metal. Can't the oracle or I use magic so her body can accept tetrigonium?"

"My lady, magic is poisonous to those who haven't been born with the gift."

"I'm not an idiot, Doctor. That's one of the first things we learn about magic in the academy. What I am suggesting is different. If we're able to enchant the tetrigonium prosthesis, her body shouldn't be affected."

"Of course she would be affected," he protested. "When soldiers like her use arcane guns, they don't insert clips into their bodies. The ammo is put inside their weapons. Think of the metal prosthesis like a cartridge. If it were enchanted, then the moment it entered a pistol it'd instantly enchant the gun. Just so, the prosthesis connects to her nerves. Magic would spread throughout the lieutenant's body and infect her, killing her in seconds."

"My goodness," she said, taking a deep breath. "But why ayzentium? Why not harboro or dalikonium?"

"First off, her insurance would never pay for a dalikonium prosthesis," he said, giving her a long look. "Second, it's usually constructed using magic. That's why you're wearing it. And I've already requested the use of harboro because it's a good candidate. Unfortunately, since it's so expensive, her insurance declined it."

The captain kicked her seat to the floor, cursing. "What happens if her body also rejects ayzentium?"

"If that happens, then I'm afraid her career might be over."

"No! Lieutenant Zadoya is one of my best soldiers. You can't let this happen to her, Doctor."

"I'm afraid that's out of my hands, Captain. Pray to the eternal Goddess that ayzentium will be acceptable. Now, if you would be so kind as to excuse me, I have an important operation to oversee."

"Yes," she said, dispirited. "Carry on, Doctor." When the link ended, she contacted the oracle. "Jeda, can you return me to the bridge?"

"You don't even have to ask," the oracle said, teleporting her.

The captain materialized by her command chair. "Thank you," she said warmly, taking a seat. Ending the connection, she gazed at the drifting rocks and flickering stars while deciding where to travel. "Ensign, fly my ship a good distance away from the asteroid field and bring us to the Aarda station via dimensional space."

"Aye, my lady."

Narja turned the vessel around and flew seventy-thousand kilometers esoria. Reaching an empty region, she inputted codes on a console. Graviton rays burst from wings of the vessel, uniting and creating an aperture in space. Once it appeared, Narja accelerated into the galactic chasm.As

The craft entered a pulsing tunnel that zigzagged numerous times. Narja maneuvered the dreadnought vessel, avoiding the intergalactic burrow's wavy walls imbued with insurmountable energy; a single touch could disintegrate that part of the starship. They reached a fissure and exited the radiant passage. Suspended about fifty-thousand kilometers ahead were planet Aarda and its accompanying spire-shaped space station. Crew members gazed at the celestial station with wonder as segments of its structure rotated with dozens of merchant vessels docked on elongated wharfs.

"Captain, we have arrived at the Quaydric star system," the ensign said, decreasing her thrusters. "ETA is ten minutes."

"Excellent. Templar, contact the station and ask for permission to dock."

"Right away," he replied, opening a channel at his terminal. Not more than a few seconds of waiting, an officer appeared on his screen. "Hail."

"Greetings," the officer said. "State your business."

"This is Captain Shirakaya's starship of the Tal'manac Order," he said. "We request approval to dock. Our identification is 051K-684B-004D."

"Standby," she said, inputting the code. "I'm pleased to inform you that your ID is valid and that you've been authorized to dock at port G-543."

"Thank you," he said.

"You're welcome," she said, saluting him. "Enjoy your stay at Aarda, and may the eternal Goddess be with you."

"And she with you," he said, ending the transmission.

II
An Appointment with Life

Narja accelerated the *Celestial* closer to the space station. As it approached, Shirakaya activated her intercom.

"This is your captain speaking. The divine Ruzurai have granted me shore leave for three days. I will shortly be taking my shuttle to planet Aarda. The Celestial will dock at port G-543 while I'm gone. During this time, all personnel aboard are permitted to visit the station. Refugees from the Eternimus, after disembarking, please wait for an intergalactic shuttle to take you home." Turning off her intercom, she walked toward the door while adding, "Templar, you're with me."

Her bodyguard rose from his terminal and followed her out of the flight deck. The duo approached a transportation capsule and stepped into it, transferring to the jet bay. Shirakaya clicked her KLD, activating her shuttle. They boarded it from the rear cargo chamber. Entering the cockpit, Shirakaya sat at the helm while Yarasuro seated himself by the communication console.

"I'm going to visit my parents," she said, sealing the back.

"It shouldn't take long to get there. Are you ready?"

"Yes, my lady."

After clicking the interface several times, Shirakaya took control of the steering wheel and lifted the shuttle, flying it out of the mothership. Aarda and innumerable stars greeted them as they merged into space. The titanic station drifted on their left, suspended above the amber planet that hung a few thousand kilometers away. Shirakaya maneuvered her yacht downward, circumnavigating one of many elongated docks in her way.

Upon seeing how close the vessel was to the dock, Yarasuro remained calm and merely raised his eyebrows. He trusted her. As they passed the space station, the captain accelerated her craft.

They entered Aarda's atmosphere where the force field enveloped her yacht to protect its hull from burning while descending so rapidly to the planet. As soon as they passed the orange-hued clouds, Shirakaya decreased her speed and steered the craft upward.

"Inertial damping initiated," she said, shifting gears.

The fertile land below revealed a distinct lack of trees. Instead, there were flat fields littered with crops ranging from fruits such as zala, torda, and korini as well as vegetables like bork, yuda, popolam, and garfam—the most nutritious produce in the known universe. Shirakaya flew over the plantation, approaching a homestead with six outdoor cement shuttle ports. She hovered over one and landed, steam billowing.

"From the looks of it, this is a beautiful planet. May I ask what this place is?"

"Home," she said. "Or at least it used to be home."

Deactivating the craft, Shirakaya noticed an older gentleman with grayish hair and a bushy beard at the adjacent port. He wore tattered overalls, the elastic straps stretching over his belly. The aged man had just finished dealing with a xentari merchant, an alien whose features comprised a snout, little trunk-shaped ears, and wide eyes that matched its bulky and elongated face.

After putting signed documents in his pocket, the male

xentari lifted a carton of fruits and placed it atop others on the bed of his trading ship. Activating his vehicle, a mana shield enveloped the food. He waved at the aged humyn and ascended into the radiant sky, leaving the planet.

The wrinkled humyn turned his attention to the ship that had just landed; he gazed at it with an expression of neutrality. A few seconds later, he spotted the enchantress through the windowpane. Standing before the craft, frowning, he crossed his arms. Shirakaya shook her head at the aged man and left the cockpit with her bodyguard.

Inputting a code embedded in a wall console, the cargo bay door opened, followed by a ramp lowering to the concrete. An amber sky with fresh air greeted the duo as they stepped out. Blocked by cargo boxes, they walked around the shuttle. Remaining by the ship's fore, the gentleman maintained his posture. A tinted black visor with a single lens covered all but his beard and coarse cheeks, making him appear rather ominous.

"You've got a lot of nerve showing up," he said, his voice raspy.

The knight tensed and placed a hand by the hilt of his blade while walking behind the captain. Shirakaya strode forward recklessly, her frown just as ominous. When she reached him, they unexpectedly embraced each other. The aged man gave out a rumbling laugh as he held her tight. As soon as Yarasuro saw this, he relaxed and moved his hand away from the sword.

"I missed you so much, Dad," she said, hugging him tightly.

"Goddess knows that saying your mom and I missed you would be an understatement," he said, the visor covering his teary eyes. "Do you think because you're a captain you can ignore us?"

"Of course not. The Ruzurai have me traveling all over the damn universe. This is the first time I've received time off."

"Is that so?" he said, raising an eyebrow. "How long do we have you for?"

"Three days," she replied with a smile. Remembering her

manners, she pulled away from her father and went on, "I'd like you to meet my bodyguard."

"Templar Yarasuro, at your service," the knight said, bowing.

"I am Bakaram," the aged man said, giving a faint nod. "I'm sure you've guessed by now that I'm Shira's father."

"It is an honor to meet you."

Though difficult to see his lips through the bushy facial hair, Bakaram grinned. "Me? Nah, I'm just a farmer. My wife, on the other hand, is a retired Ruzurai of the Tal'manac Order." He saw the astonished look on Yarasuro's face and laughed. "I'm kidding. My wife has always helped me with the farm."

"No teasing, Dad," Shirakaya said, her tone playful. "By the way, where's mom?"

"She's cooking lunch. Come. She'll be thrilled to see you."

Shirakaya and her bodyguard followed Bakaram through the cemented walkway that curved eastward. The trio passed multiple saucer-shaped drones sprinkling water on crops along both sides of Bakaram's plantation. Yarasuro, captivated by the verdant field and distant vista of mountains and valleys, couldn't help but stop for a moment to take in the peaceful panorama. The enchantress had grown up here; seeing such a beautiful landscape wasn't new to her, but she appreciated the farmland and breathed in the fresh air.

"Things never change here," she said.

"I wouldn't say that. The land doesn't have a habit of altering, but you and your knucklehead siblings have changed quite a bit."

Shirakaya gave out a soft chuckle. "Is that so?"

"Mmhmm," he teased. "Your younger sister believes she can change the way everyone thinks, and your older brother is hopelessly convinced that he's discovered some ancient artifact no one has ever seen before."

The enchantress rolled her eyes. "Khal'jan says that all the time. When is he gonna realize that archeology isn't his specialty and focus on something else?"

Bakaram sighed. "He just wants to make a name for

himself, like you."

She nodded at him with a faint smile, approaching a wooden corral where a herd of joraki stood. These animals had black and brown fleeces, one horn protruding from their craniums, and thick hooves. Some joraki were eating grass while others sat on the ground, wagging their fuzzy tails of many thongs.

Just a few feet away from the corral stood Bakaram's homestead. Each bedroom on the second floor had a balcony. Even though the left side of the building resembled a barn, the right contained a glass sunroom, filled with colorful plants. The entrance of the house itself had a wide deck with chairs. The trio entered the home, cooled by vents along the foyer's ceiling.

"Impressive home," the Templar said.

"Thank you," Shirakaya said. "It's wonderful to be back."

"Pamela," called out Bakaram, approaching the kitchen. "You won't believe it. Guess who's visiting us."

"Who?" she said, chopping a korini with a laser knife. Not getting an answer, she placed the knife on the counter and turned around with a piece of fruit in her hand. The moment she saw Shirakaya, she dropped it, rushed over, and hugged her. "Shira," she managed to utter, tears springing to her eyes.

"I missed you, Mom," Shirakaya said.

"So have I," Pamela said. "It's a blessing you're here. I prayed every day to the eternal Goddess that you'd return."

"You speak as if I abandoned you."

"I'm sorry," her mother said. "I know you're a captain now. It must be difficult getting time off."

"This is the first time I've been granted shore leave."

"My goodness. That's awful. They're abusing you. How much time do we have with you? And who is this young man?"

"Templar Yarasuro, at your service," the knight said, briefly kneeling.

"He's my bodyguard. It's mandatory that he comes with me everywhere. We'll be here for three days."

"I see," her mother said, picking up the fruit she'd dropped.

"If you prefer privacy," Yarasuro said, seeing the

disappointed look on her face, "I can stand guard by the entrance."

"Nonsense," Pamela said, waving her hand. "Shira, you and your bodyguard came just in time. I'm making your favorite juice, and lunch is almost ready. Why don't you three have a seat in the dining room while I finish cooking? Then we can all enjoy this meal and spend quality time together."

"Sounds good to me," Bakaram said, rubbing his belly.

Shirakaya giggled. "You never change, Dad." She hugged her parents again and followed her father to an extended table with a floral cloth. Noticing it was a bit wobbly, she lifted the fabric and spotted splinters protruding from the edges and scratches along the top. "Why in the twelve dimensions do you still have this?"

"This is the family table," he said. "It reminds us of better days when we ate together as a family. Most importantly, it reminds us of you. After all, you're the one who always complained about the damn thing."

"This is a fine piece of furniture," the knight said.

"You're so full of it," Shirakaya said, causing him to look uncomfortable. "Mom never liked it either."

"True," her father said, grinning. "But she came around when you left to command your own starship. And don't think this is the only thing we've kept. Your bedroom is exactly as you left it."

"Now *that* I have to see," she said.

"It can wait," her mother said, approaching with a bowl of roasted joraki meat in one hand and a pitcher filled with juice in another. "Lunch is ready."

"Perfect timing," her father said. "I'm starving."

"You're always hungry," Pamela said, giving him a long look and making the family chuckle at the table.

The knight smiled but didn't feel comfortable enough to laugh. He respectfully bowed his head when Shirakaya's mother placed food on his plate and filled his glass with juice. The others eagerly waited for their share, utensils in hand. Only when the entire family started eating did the knight join them.

"This is delicious," Yarasuro said.

"Why thank you," Pamela said, using a napkin to clean her lips. "I'm so glad you like my cooking."

After taking a large gulp of her drink, Shirakaya gave out a sigh of delight. "*This* is what I've missed the most," she said, putting her cup down. "Till this day there's nothing that quenches my thirst like your korini juice, Mom."

"You always did like sweet beverages," her mother said.

Her father nodded in agreement. "Say, where is Radesha? Wasn't she supposed to be back by now?"

"You're getting confused with your son's shift, dear," Pamela said. "Radesha's lecture ends at thirty o'clock. She'll be home in time for dinner."

"How come Khal isn't here yet?"

Bakaram swallowed his food and answered, "Because your brother is a nincompoop. He should've been here already. But just a couple of hours before you arrived, Khal contacted me on my thingamajig. What do you call it?"

"Kinetic link device or KLD," Shirakaya said.

"Right. Khal called me on that, claiming he found something 'extraordinary' in the Valley of Locarn and would tell me all about it over lunch."

"Is that so?"

"Yes," her father said. "But you know him as well as I do. It's the same old story. Instead of going to the academy to teach like your sister, he goes off on wild escapades and always tells me he's getting close to unearthing something that will make his career official. Then he comes home empty-handed, and I'm stuck paying his bills."

"Maybe I should have a talk with him."

"Let him be," Pamela said. "It's the only thing he's passionate about. Discouraging him will break his heart."

"Well, someone needs to bring him down from the clouds," Bakaram said.

Pamela shook her head, not saying anything more on the subject. They ate and drank together, finishing their meal in peace.

III
Calm Before the Storm

An hour later, Yarasuro stood guard by the front entrance. Shirakaya's mother gave her a tour around the remodeled house —varnished wooden floors, new sheetrock walls, fresh paint, and a bathroom that revealed a whirlpool tub and heated tiles.

"So many beautiful changes in just one cycle."

"Your father worked very hard."

Shirakaya continued exploring the home, taking in a few family photos and paintings of Aarda's famous landscapes along the hallway. Pamela waited to show Shirakaya her old room last. She stepped inside and froze, her mouth agape.

"I can't believe this. It really *is* exactly as I left it."

Her bedroom still had a cream-colored carpet as opposed to the wooden floors in other rooms. Dark dresses and ankle boots from her younger clubbing days filled the closet. And along the walls hung posters of trance-punk legend Vai Le Mong, an intergalactic star who had tattoos from head to toe; he also had black makeup around his eyes, nail polish, and, piercings on his ears.

The musician plastered all over her room was the only man she'd ever felt attracted to in her life. She touched a poster that portrayed him screaming while playing an electric guitar. Long ago she'd dreamed of meeting him. Now she couldn't care less. Though she still enjoyed his music, her sexual feelings had changed over the past few cycles from men to women.

"Still daydreaming about him?" her mother teased.

Shirakaya paused for a moment. "Who doesn't?" she said, lying. "He's the Goddess's greatest creation."

Her mother chuckled. "I'm so glad you're home."

They hugged and spent time outside on the porch. Shirakaya appreciated the quiet atmosphere around the homestead. She watched her father's animals graze in the field, finding it peaceful. Her bodyguard stood by the entrance, statue-like. Pamela sat on a step while knitting beside her daughter. She wondered when her son would return but didn't want to appear worried, so she maintained a phony smile.

Evening came, the sky no longer an amber hue. Pamela went inside the house to prepare dinner while Shirakaya remained outside. An indigo tinge took over the heavens, myriad stars shimmering.

Three of Aarda's four orbiting moons were visible to Shirakaya, who now lay against an oleki—a tree whose wide trunk and purple leaves contained magical properties that made the land fertile regardless of harmful weather conditions. Rejuvenated by the everlasting plant, she gazed at the space station in the firmament while playfully using magic to lift pebbles around her.

"If only I could do that," Bakaram said, stepping down the porch to join his daughter.

She released the pebbles, smiling at him. "Hey, Dad."

"May I join you?" he asked, grabbing a ripe zala from a long branch. At her nod, he added, "You always did like sitting here. They say oleki trees are a sanctuary to those gifted with magic."

"I guess. I'm not sure if it's psychological, but I do feel refreshed. More so than after a simple good night's rest."

"Really?"

"Trust me," she said firmly, keeping the fear of losing her power to herself. "They've been overworking me. I've never used magic this frequently before. In fact, during my last mission I started feeling nauseated and dizzy."

"You're scaring me, Shira. Just know you're always welcome here. Get all the rest you need, darling." An awkward silence descended on them, broken only by a distant humming similar to an engine. "That's either your brother or sister. And it may be a first, but I'm hoping it's Khal."

"He should've returned hours ago, right?"

"Yes," her father said, straining to see ahead. "It's your sister. *Tch*, the universe never listens to me."

"Maybe I should look for him?"

Bakaram didn't respond. He wore a troubled expression

when he got to his feet and walked to the carport. His other daughter had just arrived, landing her V52 burgundy-tinted hovercraft beside Shirakaya's yacht. Radesha strongly resembled her sister, except she had a slightly turned-up nose. She exited the vehicle with a look of glee.

"Shira!" she called out, hugging her. "It's so wonderful to see you. What in the galaxy are you doing here?"

"I was granted shore leave and came to visit."

"Finally," she said, kissing her father on the cheek. "Now we can all have dinner together as a family."

"I'm afraid not," Bakaram said. "Khal isn't back home yet."

"What?" scowled Radesha, walking toward the house. "I certainly hope he's not avoiding home because Shira's back."

The enchantress sulked. "He doesn't even know I'm visiting."

"Khal contacted me hours ago, telling me he found something 'extraordinary' that could make his dream career a reality. The hooligan was supposed to return for lunch, but he hasn't."

"Did you try contacting him?" Radesha asked, walking beside her father.

"Of course. He's ignoring my kinetic calls. If you ask me, he probably realized that what he thought he'd discovered this morning is bogus and feels too embarrassed to come home empty-handed."

"That would be awful," Radesha said.

"Dad," Shirakaya said, "I want to see if he's all right. Can you give me the location of his dig site in Locarn?"

Bakaram sighed. "Whatever floats your boat, Shira."

He transmitted the coordinates to her KLD while stepping onto the porch of his house with his daughters. The knight hadn't moved, standing guard without respite. Radesha ogled Yarasuro, extremely attracted to not only his facial features but also his ponytail. Acknowledging this, the Templar gulped.

"Who is this?"

"Templar Yarasuro, at your service," he said, bowing and

gently pecking her hand with his lips.

"I am Radesha," she said, blushing.

Her father grinned and went into the house. An awkward silence fell. Shirakaya's sister and bodyguard gazed into each other's eyes. It was a little too long for comfort, the enchantress thought.

Shirakaya pretended to clear her throat. "Yarasuro, we need to fly over to the Valley of Locarn and find my brother."

"Is something wrong?"

"I certainly hope not," she replied, turning around. "It's just that he was supposed to come back around lunchtime."

The knight gazed at her sister once more. "It was a pleasure meeting you, Miss Radesha. I hope to see you again."

Leaving her speechless, he descended the steps and joined Shirakaya.

IV
Mysteries Abound

The duo hurried to the shuttle. Seeing the captain gloomy, Yarasuro gently patted her.

"In the name of Maz'hura, we will find your brother."

"Oh, of that I have no doubt. I'm more worried about what happens when I see him moping in misery."

"I beg your pardon?"

"Khal'jan is a failure," she said bluntly, reaching her vessel and activating it via kinetic link. "He's simply too stubborn and ashamed to admit it." The cargo bay's ramp slid open when the pair advanced, allowing them to board the ship. Inside, the captain went on, "My sister and I worked very hard to be successful. I was the only one in the family gifted with magic, so I devoted my life to the Tal'manac Order."

"A fine vocation."

"Becoming a captain and exploring the universe while also keeping it safe has always been my lifelong dream. Most importantly, I made it a reality," Shirakaya continued, taking a seat in the cockpit. "Radesha wanted to be a nurse. She was good but not perfect. These days, universities only accept the best. She admitted her failure and decided to teach."

"Failure?" he responded. "Isn't that a bit harsh?"

Shirakaya gave out a short but loud laugh, controlling the helm of her ship. "You like her, don't you?"

"Wha-what?" he stuttered, turning pink. "I am a Templar, my lady. I've sworn an oath to the eternal Goddess to remain celibate and devote my life to you and all innocent beings in the universe."

The captain grinned while piloting her yacht, ascending and flying east. "I am very proud of my sister. Radesha fell hard but rose back up, accepting her failure and finding happiness in something different. My brother, however, doesn't want to admit defeat. Instead of climbing out of the hole he's dug himself into, he sulks and pretends he's special when he's not."

Yarasuro listened and realized that the captain was extremely competitive and obsessed with being the best in her family. He respected her for accomplishing so much but wished she would be more humble. Yet she had a point about her brother, he conceded. No one should constantly sulk or pity themselves, he thought to himself.

"I used to envy my sister," he said. At her stunned look, Yarasuro went on, "She's gifted with magic, like you. When younger, I always wanted to cast spells. Seeing my sister having an ability that was out of my reach made me unbelievably jealous. For a while, I wouldn't even talk to her. Once I started accepting myself, I tried growing closer to Eeres. But it was too late. She was fed up with me and threatened to curse me if I contacted her again."

"Oh, my goodness."

"I deserved it," he continued. "Moral of the story: Don't let that happen between you and your brother. I lost my sibling over petty jealousy and would feel terrible to see this occur again. Family should always love one another."

"Agreed," she said, briefly smiling at her bodyguard. "I just hope my brother doesn't do anything stupid."

The knight nodded. Shirakaya kept flying east of her father's farm, beyond the fields of crops until she reached a lush valley. Mountains surrounded the path, a few reaching thirty-six thousand feet high. Mist swept across the ravine, hindering the enchantress who attempted to use her magic to dispel it. Though difficult, she did weaken the fog, but her vision was still somewhat limited. Glancing at the topography screen, it indicated that the excavation site lay twelve miles away. She decreased the speed of her vessel, keeping an eye out for either her brother or his colleagues.

"Are we approaching Locarn?"

"This entire valley is Locarn," Shirakaya said, lowering the throttle. As the craft descended, she went on, "According to these coordinates, we're approaching the archeological zone. Let me know if you spot anyone."

"Aye, my lady."

By now the sun had set, making it more difficult for the duo to see outside despite using fog lights. Minutes later, they came across a well-lit area with numerous lampposts. Shirakaya hovered near one and landed beside it.

Deactivating her yacht, she exited from the cargo bay with her bodyguard. They saw crumbled slabs of stone, smolder coming from burnt shafts, and what appeared to be corpses. The enchantress strode to the nearest body, confirming it was humyn remains. Parts of the skeleton were missing. What little flesh remained on the scorched bones was charred.

Yarasuro joined her, unsheathing his baskino sword. "Do you think bandits attacked?" he asked, raising his weapon.

"That doesn't make sense. I can fathom an attack on farmers…crops are valuable. But a dig site?"

"I must admit, it does seem absurd."

Shirakaya rose to her feet, searching the area while intermittently shouting, "Khal!" All the bodies she found were the same: seared corpses. "This is one of the most peaceful worlds in Copia Deiga. There's even a Tal'manac space station orbiting Aarda, performing background checks on everyone who enters the planet. How can something like this happen?”

“It’s possible your brother actually found something important. If so, perhaps a few thieves posed as archeologists?”

“Khal!” she called out, an expression of dismay on her face.

“Shouting isn’t very wise,” he said. “Who knows if the brigands are still here. It’s best we search quietly and keep our guar—”

A fusion beam projected eastward, zapping the knight. His force field absorbed the initial burst and then malfunctioned. He rolled into a trench to avoid more beams. Shirakaya cast a mana shield on herself and enchanted Yarasuro’s sword. An aura of flame enveloped his blade. Another beam discharged east of them. The enchantress leaped down a plank leading to the dig site, barely evading the projectile.

She hid behind a pillar, trying to peek at her enemy. This time a barrage of fusion beams came her way. Shirakaya gasped, moving aside. The hieroglyphic-covered pillar crumbled, parts of it disintegrating. Her bodyguard rose from the dirt-filled trench, continuously deflecting multiple rays with his sword. One of the lethal beams reflected to the enemy, hovering above to dodge the beam.

The duo gazed up, discovering that their enemy was not a thief but a sphere-shaped drone with fusion cannons for limbs. Shirakaya’s eyes fizzed as lightning radiated from her fingers, shocking the drone. Although stunned, it flew over the enchantress and unleashed a wave of rays from its cannons. She attempted to cast another mana shield when several beams struck, denting her dalikonium armor. Shirakaya fell to the floor, hurling a fireball at the drone. Evading the spell, it swooped down to finish her off.

Yarasuro leaped from a slab and repelled the deadly rays in midflight. The guns swerved in his direction, targeting and firing. He swung downward and sliced the drone in half. Witnessing the robot’s destruction, the winded knight gave his captain a hand and lifted her.

“Thank you,” she said.

Yarasuro bowed his head in respect and followed Shirakaya, who approached the divided drone, examining it. The same hieroglyphics she'd seen on obelisks around the excavation site were carved on the robot's metal casing: an image of comets, an asteroid, five moons, an oleki tree, and a temple with a triangular apex.

"What race does it belong to?"

"I haven't the faintest idea," she said. "I've never seen this kind of artwork or machinery before."

Shirakaya continued her search for Khal'jan, terrified that he lay among the dead. Not one body remained unscathed. They had all been brutally killed, their fatal wounds delivered by the drone. Their corpses were in such terrible condition that even if she found her brother, she feared she wouldn't recognize him. Activating her KLD, she scanned the DNA of each body to confirm their identity.

Together they searched through the frayed makeshift tents scattered around the region. Inside them lay more dead bodies along with cracked artifacts on the ground and smashed desks. Pressing on, the duo examined every trench and furrow in the field. Despite lampposts giving them light, they couldn't find anything other than bones and tools. They also checked damaged hover-trucks stationed near the outskirts of the excavation site but failed to find her brother. The only place they hadn't examined was the central digging zone that contained a fifty-foot deep hole.

At the bottom of the dig site, they discovered an entrance to a tunnel and entered the dim corridor. The walls were made from an unknown alloy. Not even Shirakaya's device could identify the metal's source. Walking further in, they both heard a humming noise. As they advanced, the floor vibrated. Yarasuro kept his sword raised high, thinking the rumbling sound originated from drones patrolling the underground passage.

"I think we have another fight on our hands," Yarasuro said.

The enchantress hesitated, wondering if she should contact

the space station via kinetic link for support. Realizing it would take too long for reinforcements to arrive, she cast a mana shield over herself and walked forward. The knight followed her through the shadowy passage, sword in hand.

As soon as they reached a corner, Shirakaya peeked out and spotted two drones that fired immediately. She withdrew and waited for them to advance. When they appeared, the enchantress encased one of them in a block of ice while Yarasuro deflected beams. He parried until only inches away and thrust his weapon through the hull of the unfrozen automaton.

At the same time, the enchantress attempted to cast arcane kinesis on the frozen robot but struggled to crush the drone. Yarasuro noticed and swiftly struck it. His blade not only melted the rime but severed its hull. From the corner of his eye, he saw another drone advance from behind.

"Get down!" he shouted, turning.

Shirakaya ducked as the knight hurled his sword at the droid before it could blast them. It fizzed, his curved blade stuck in its core. The spherical drone fell and exploded. Yarasuro ran across the narrow path and seized his enchanted sword, which remained undamaged.

Another robot emerged. Although surprised, Yarasuro performed a flip and avoided its fusion ray. While he blocked other beams, Shirakaya cast a fireball and hurled it at the drone, destroying its bottom cannons. Her bodyguard deflected a ray back at the automaton, liquefying a pair of guns on its vertex. One of the beams, however, blasted him. He fell to the ground, his breastplate sundered.

"Yaro!"

The enchantress summoned a mana shield over him, protecting him from the drone's lethal rays. It ignored him when its attacks proved futile and turned its attention to Shirakaya, firing multiple beams from its remaining cannons. She took cover by the corner and then peeked out, hurling icicles at it. The robot destroyed them. Seeing what it had done made her livid. Consumed by rage, she again attempted arcane kinesis. With luck, Shirakaya crushed the automaton until only shrapnel remained. She approached her bodyguard and lent him a hand.

"Now we're even," Yarasuro said, getting to his feet. "My lady, I hope you don't mind me asking—"

"What is it?"

"With all due respect, Captain, you're not the same. Ever since the koth'vurians attacked us, I've noticed that it's been more difficult for you to use magic. Are you all right?"

"I'll be fine, Templar," she said coldly. "Let's move on."

Despite feeling aggravated that the captain had dismissed him, he obeyed and continued through the tunnel. As soon as they reached a hatch, an aura enveloped it. Shirakaya and her bodyguard took a step back. At that moment, the hatch opened.

"Please don't kill us!" cried out a man in dirt-covered clothes.

Stepping into the chamber, Shirakaya found two women with the man. "We're not here to harm you." Her eyes widened, gazing at the filthy man who had just pleaded for his life. "Khal?"

"Shira?" he said in utter shock. "Shira!"

"By the stars," she said, hugging him. "I thought you were dead. What in the cosmos happened here?"

At the females' silence, Khal'jan responded, "I found something incredible here." He opened a pouch on his belt, pulling out an orb the size of his fist. "At first, I thought it was some kind of rare metal. Then it glowed when I entered this room. Before any of us could figure out why, our colleagues above ground started screaming. When we ran outside to see what was happening, we encountered the drones."

"A few people shouted that those things appeared out of nowhere," sobbed one of the female archeologists.

"The machines killed everyone without any kind of warning," the other archeologist said, weeping.

"You no longer have to worry," Shirakaya said. "My bodyguard, Yarasuro, destroyed them."

The knight modestly lowered his head.

"Thank the Goddess," Khal'jan said, visibly relieved. "But how in the world did you know I was in trouble?"

"To be honest, I had no clue," she said. "I came to visit everyone after being granted shore leave. Dad told me you should've been home for lunch, so we got worried. I flew here to make sure you were all right. Never in a million cycles would I have thought you'd be in danger."

"Me neither," he said, shaking his head.

"Khal," she said, "I'm sorry, but I need to confiscate that artifact and report this to the Tal'manac Order."

Her brother hesitated, staring at the object. "I understand."

Gawking at the ancient relic for a few more seconds, Khal'jan closed his eyes and handed it over to his sister. The moment she grabbed the artifact, a blue aura emanated from it. An enormous column rumbled behind everyone, sections of it abruptly rotating. It rose from the ruptured floor with a tremor that sent Shirakaya and her companions to the ground. The same blue aura emanating from the relic enveloped her.

"What's happening?" she asked, mystified.

No one responded. The archeologists wore frightened expressions. Yarasuro lifted his sword, ready to destroy the artifact when the aura manifested into a bright translucent barrier resembling a mana shield, blinding and engulfing the entire group. In a flicker of light, they vanished.

Arcane Intelligence

Science, magic, and religion are one and the same. There are no lies in the beauty of my reality. I urge you, my beloved children, to deeply explore and investigate the universe. Unravel its profound mysteries and evolve as a species. Transcendence is where I await you. Science is a mathematical language that still requires faith. Let it guide you to the truth. Evolution is essential for your physical and spiritual voyage through the cosmos. If you evolve, magic shall find you in the afterlife. Its majesty will ensure your growth upon rebirth. But remember to balance yourself. Science and religion can never be discarded. Too much of one will inevitably lead your precious spirit into regression. I implore you: listen to the three voices, for they articulate the same divine truth.

Testament of Evolution 128:31

Chapter Six

Temple of the Fifth Moon

I
Perplexities

Shirakaya, her bodyguard, and the three archeologists materialized inside glass tubes in a dark chamber. As they banged on the pods, the ceiling's recessed lights activated. The capsules remained intact despite how hard they hit them. Infuriated, the enchantress pressed her hands against the glass and turned it to ice. She lifted her armored elbow and struck the pod, breaking free.

The moment it shattered, she flew up to the ceiling, suffocating. Particles of ice and glass drifted up too. One of the pieces cut her ear, droplets of blood floating beside her hair. With the last of her strength, she put on her helmet and activated an air tank. Zitrogen entered her lung and she breathed again. Moving out of the way, she avoided pieces of glass drifting toward her. Pressing her feet against the ceiling, she pushed down to the grated floor and used her magic to freeze the other capsules. Then she summoned a stream of flame, melting them.

When the pod liquefied, the knight put on a helmet and activated his emergency air tank before suffocating. The enchantress cast mana shields over the three archeologists, enabling them to breathe. The quartet floated up to join Shirakaya, who pulled sharp particles away from them using telekinesis. Waiting a minute to regain her power, she cast arcane force fields on Yarasuro and herself.

"Captain, are you all right?"

"I'll be fine," she said, removing her helmet and

deactivating her air tank. "Khal, where are we?"

Disconcerted, Khal'jan glanced around the chamber and shrugged. He floated over to a sealed door, examining it. Beside the entry stood a free-standing terminal, its screen containing a foreign language. Approaching the futuristic kiosk, he recognized a few words from the excavation site and, with difficulty, attempted to decipher the message.

"Lanan. Phela," he called out to his colleagues. "Can the two of you have a look at this? I can't determine what these particular words mean."

The female archeologists leaped toward him, drifting by the hatch. There, they both leaned downward and descended to the floor. Gripping the pedestal-shaped kiosk, the duo landed. Together they stared at the bizarre letters. Phela reached out to tap the screen. Before she touched it, however, a symbol abruptly glowed as though being selected.

"How did you do that?" Khal'jan asked.

"I don't know," Phela said, flabbergasted. "These slanted letters translate to: Unlock. I intended to press an icon associated with them, but I didn't even touch it."

Lanan noticed a red button on the kiosk's screen turn blue. Out of curiosity, she waved her hand near it. The door opened to a crusty landscape and sucked out pieces of shrapnel into space—along with the shrieking Lanan.

Shirakaya grabbed her brother before he was pulled out too, her magnetic sabatons keeping her in place. The same technology in his boots, Yarasuro grabbed Phela. Using all his strength, he heaved her back and held her in place.

"Lanan!" cried out Phela.

"Use your magic, Shira," Khal'jan said, panicky. He watched his sister extend a hand, her eyes glowing. Yet nothing occurred. "Shira!"

"I'm trying!"

Humiliated, the enchantress failed to cast telekinesis. The screaming archeologist floated away, her mana shield dissolving. Horror-struck, the survivors witnessed Lana grip her throat as she suffocated. She drifted away, lifeless.

"Goddess, save us," gasped Khal'jan, focusing his attention on the kiosk. "Phela, help me close this hatch."

They examined multiple icons and symbols, working to translate each one as quickly as possible. Khal'jan came across one depicting curved lines, which looked familiar to him. Using his index finger, he tapped the air an inch away from the screen, highlighting a pictogram. The door sealed with a creak.

"Where in the twelve dimensions are we?" Shirakaya asked, letting go of her brother.

"Never mind that," he said. "What the hell was that? Lanan is dead because of you."

"I'm not perfect," the enchantress said, quelling her tears. "Even my magic has its limits. I would never let an innocent person die on purpose. And let me remind you that you'd probably be dead right now if my bodyguard and I hadn't come."

"Wait a minute," Khal'jan said, stunned. "Did you just say your magic has limits?"

Yarasuro clenched his fists, grimacing. "I know now beyond a shred of doubt that something is amiss with your health."

"Silence!" she commanded, tears in her eyes. "How dare you insinuate—" She broke down, crying.

The enchantress demanded silence, and that was what she got. Her bodyguard and brother were speechless; they couldn't recall seeing Shirakaya weep before. Phela, on the other hand, unacquainted with Shirakaya, ignored the commotion and studied another kiosk across the chamber.

In sympathy, Khal'jan said in a soft tone, "Shira..."

"It's true," she said at last. "Ever since I fought against Ashkaratoth, my powers have been dwindling. He may have done something to me. Or maybe the blue giant in the Aarjedo system affected me. Either way, magic has become more of a gamble. With each spell I cast, there is a chance it won't manifest. I'm sorry, Khal."

"Don't be. It's just hard to believe. Who is Ashkaratoth?"

"He's an extremely dangerous alien," she answered,

omitting her theory of him being a koth'vurian. "Yaro, you're an honorable Templar and follow protocol even more than me. I know the law states that only a sorcerer or sorceress can command a ship. But I'm begging you, please don't tell the Ruzurai that my magic is compromised."

"My lady, I have always felt honored and blessed to serve you, but I cannot make such a promise. Should the Ruzurai discover elsewhere that you may be losing your powers, I could be excommunicated for concealing such information."

"I…I know," she said, disheartened.

Irritated, Phela said, "We have other things to worry about right now."

"She's right," Khal said, turning his attention to the other kiosk. "This is not the time to be discussing politics. Right now we need to focus on getting back home." He continued to examine the symbols on the screen before him. "Maybe this will lead us somewhere safe."

II
Legendary Discovery

The console sensed Khal'jan reaching out with his hand. An icon he pointed at glowed and activated. The door on the opposite side of the chamber unsealed. Before them was a cylindrical corridor made of thick glass. The quartet cautiously stepped into the passage.

They observed the mountainous, crater-filled landscape. Several drones, identical to the ones Shirakaya and her bodyguard had destroyed at the dig site, hovered above trenches outside along the esorian and wescarian expanse. Alarmed by their presence, Shirakaya charged forward and gestured at the others to follow. The quartet sprinted ahead as fast as they could. The tubular tunnel seemed to be soundproof since the automatons ignored them as they dashed across.

"Hurry," Shirakaya said, eyeing a free-standing kiosk

beside her.

Her brother nodded, approached the screen and chose an icon shaped like a swirling line. A door in front of the group opened into an atrium. Staircases rose up on either side of metal-armored statues, each with four arms, standing guard on the balcony of the upper floor. Their faces resembled humyns, except they had only one eye, sculpted like a visor.

Phela whispered, "Could this be—"

"The lost civilization of the Nempada Empire," Khal'jan said, mesmerized by the chamber's metal-trim design.

"Despite what scholars have stated, it's actually true!" Phela said. She strode over to an empty basin where water once flowed and examined its composition. "This must be the Temple of the Fifth Moon."

Shirakaya appeared baffled. "What? Did you just say 'fifth moon'?"

"I think you're right, Phela," Khal'jan said, observing the computerized walls. "Based on history, the Nempada Empire from Aarda vanished eons ago without a trace."

"We learned that in elementary school," Shirakaya said.

"Yes," Khal'jan said. "But what if they didn't really vanish? What if they simply relocated…and did so making sure they'd never be discovered?"

Yarasuro crossed his arms, raising a brow. "How could they have done that?"

"If someone fakes their own death, the authorities won't go searching for them," Khal'jan said. "Just so, if they erased a moon from existence, we wouldn't go looking for it because as far as we know, there are only four orbiting Aarda."

Shirakaya rolled her eyes. "The fifth moon conspiracy is the oldest story in the book of tall tales, Khal. I admit, for the first time you seem to have discovered something genuine. But this whole 'temple of the fifth moon' business is a bunch of mumbo-jumbo. We were probably transported to one of Aarda's four moons."

"That doesn't make sense," Khal'jan said. "Archeologists excavated those moons countless cycles ago. There's no way they'd miss a temple like this."

"Not to mention that this place is crawling with drones," Phela said.

"The reason I discovered that site on Aarda in the first place is that I technically broke the law and excavated an area in Locarn protected by the Farmers' Union Rights Movement of 8472."

"Technically?" Yarasuro said. "You either honor the law or break it."

"Not now, Templar," Shirakaya said. "Listen, we really need to get back home. Mom and dad are probably freaking out right now. Plus this is a hazardous place. There's no zitrogen to breathe, not to mention a lack of gravity. And I don't know why those androids are probing around here, but if they discover us, you'll wish the Tal'manac Order had found your illegal dig site and arrested you."

Khal'jan frowned. "Excuse me? It's *you* who'll be arrested, commanding without magic."

Incensed, the enchantress pulled her brother over using telekinesis. "I still have magic," she hissed.

"Where was it when Lanan needed it?" he retorted.

Grunting loudly, Shirakaya hurled him against a wall. A louder, cracking noise across the chamber caught their attention and, thunderstruck, they watched the statues move. Unsheathing klivat swords—weapons with blades so hefty they required four arms to wield—the statues flipped over the balcony. The floor shook when the statues landed. Shirakaya and her comrades stumbled and struggled to regain their balance.

"By the Goddess," gasped Shirakaya.

One of the five statues stood beside Phela and sliced her torso in half. Blood sprayed, guts seeping over the floor, as she fell.

"Phela!" shrieked Khal'jan.

Shocked, the captain summoned all her resources to enchant her bodyguard's weapon again. Yarasuro struck one of the statues and cracked its shoulder before he parried an attack from behind. Despite his blocking stance, he flew back a few feet and slammed against a wall. Yarasuro staggered and rolled aside, evading another strike. Rallying, he swiped his weapon and fractured a statue's chest. Stones chipped off, exposing wires. Grateful for this weak point, Yarasuro took advantage and severed the wires. The robotic statue deactivated and tumbled.

"Interlopers are forbidden from entering the emperor's realm," stated one of the stony beings, its shoulder covered with a network of cracks. "Surrender or suffer the consequences."

"I imagine there will be consequences whether we surrender or not," the knight said.

Yarasuro maintained his guard as the remaining four statues approached, dodging their attacks. Only once did he block, staggering back a couple of steps. Necessity boosting her strength, Shirakaya summoned a sphere of fire and hurled it a statue. The fireball erupted, its heat fracturing the outer shell of the lurching statue and scorching its wiry mainframe.

"This was supposed to be a vacation," she grumbled. "Khal, get behind me."

He sprinted to her. She clicked her KLD several times, ported a plasma pistol, and handed it to him. Khal'jan had never used a gun before, but he targeted a statue and pressed the trigger. At first, he missed and shot the wall behind it. He fired again, the beam damaging the robot beyond repair.

The knight feinted, parried and riposted, intercepting tactics used by the statue that he was battling against. With barely a chance to counterstrike its immense strength, he lunged at the damaged statue, cleaving its cracked shoulder. The knight sliced diagonally through its stony body, severing every wire. Leaping over the toppled giant, he ducked and evaded the last statue's attempt to behead him. Mimicking his adversary, he rolled aside, leaped with his sword raised high, and decapitated it. The body still moved. With a fervent prayer to the Goddess, he lifted his tiring arms and struck it in half.

"We need reinforcements, Captain," the Templar said, panting from his exertions.

"Agreed," she said, checking to make sure no other active

statues were present. "But first we need to find out where in the damn universe we are."

"I already told you," Khal'jan said, lurching over his colleague's corpse.

Shirakaya reconsidered her brother's hypothesis. "You'd better not be making a fool of me, Khal." Using her kinetic link device, she selected a TDE distress channel with an open frequency. "This is Captain Shirakaya of Aarda, serving the Tal'manac Order. I am in need of immediate assistance."

Static laughter rang out from the link. "Your service with the Tal'manac Order is at an end, fleshling," stated a metallic voice.

Her eyebrows furrowed. "I'll try using the signal again in space. Come on."

She charged up the stairs, her eyes radiant with power. Her brother and bodyguard kept pace behind her, checking out the computerized atrium for further traps. The enchantress waved a hand by a kiosk screen, failing to get a response. She waited for her brother to decrypt it, at which point the door ahead unlocked. Exiting, the trio walked through an octagonal glass tube. It overlooked a splintered landscape where deformed basins, canyons, and serrated granite lay within the vast extraterrestrial temple.

At the end of the tunnel, Khal'jan activated another door and stepped inside a domed chamber with his sister and her bodyguard. A pair of drones opened fire. Knocking over empty chairs to escape the salvo, they dove behind columns, which chipped in the fusillade. The captain cursed under her breath when her kinetic link device activated.

"Shira," Judicator Owendar began, "I'm sure you're enjoying your time off, but I have a possible lead on the koth'vurians. Ruzurai Narx discovered a protostar in the Pargosis System and sent Captain Tor to examine it. Since koth'vurians feed on these stars, they might be there. I want you to go investi—" He stared at her, realizing she was hiding. "Are you all right?"

"Now isn't the best time to give me a mission, Professor,"

she said, rising and launching arcane bolts of lightning.

"What in the twelve dimensions is going on?"

"I can't explain right now!" Shirakaya snapped, peeking out again while hurling icy shards at the hovering drones. She cursed under her breath as two more entered from large ducts near the ceiling. "Yaro, take care of the one on your left!"

Before the words left her lips, he leaped on top of the crumpled pillar, his sword angled to deflect multiple beams. The rays backfired, destroying a robot.

"Don't tell me you're on Aarda's fifth moon," Owendar said gruffly.

The enchantress strengthened her group's mana shields and hid again. "How the heck could you possibly know that?" she asked, hurling a sphere of flame at the last android in the vicinity.

"It's all over the UCN news channel," he said. "It appeared out of nowhere. Aarda's space station deployed a probe, but cannons from the moon destroyed it."

"Unbelievable," Shirakaya said with a sigh. "During an excavation on Aarda, my brother discovered a link to some kind of temple on this moon. I came to rescue him and accidentally got ported here. We desperately need reinforcements."

"I'll see what I can do," he said. "Just don't do anything rash."

Just as the link ended, Shirakaya gave a short but strange chuckle. "I think it's a bit late for that."

"Any luck?" Khal'jan asked.

"The moon has apparently become visible to everyone," she said. "Even though Judicator Owendar will try sending reinforcements, there's no guarantee they'll be able to make it past the moon's defenses."

"Then we need to disable them," the knight said.

At the captain's troubled expression, Khal'jan responded, "There's a chance I can decipher their codes and guide you to the temple's control room."

"If there even is one!" she said. "In any case, stay behind us."

They reached the center of the room when the metallic voice spoke again. "An admirable attempt to survive, Aardanian fleshlings. This is without a doubt because of the one who commands the transmundane arts. You are, however, significantly outnumbered and will be annihilated by my legion."

"I don't know who or what you are," Shirakaya said, "but you have crossed the wrong person." With the aid of telekinesis, she tore down every speaker along the ceiling. "Khal, do you have an environmental suit?"

"Of course."

Shirakaya gawked at him. "What are you waiting for? The end of the universe? Put the damn thing on."

"Right," he said, searching for it in his KLD. "So much is going on, I didn't think of it."

"Just put it on," she said, scrutinizing the landscape ahead. "We'll be traversing through the moon's terrain and I can't promise my mana shield will hold."

"Captain, shall I put my helmet on?" Yarasuro asked.

The sorceress nodded. "Activate your zitrogen air tank, too," she added, approaching the hatch. "That voice we heard is either some kind of AI or robot. And we all know machines are incapable of lying. Be prepared for an onslaught."

Her companions put on their equipment, feeling wary. With a few clicks on the kinetic link device, Khal'jan's grubby clothes changed to an insulated suit of armor consisting of elemental fibers along the neckline and sleeves capable of heating or cooling his body. The environmental outfit came with a tank of zitrogen attached to the back, shock absorbers on the soles, lights embedded in the pauldrons, and a glass helmet containing a breathing apparatus. His armor was technically more advanced than his sister's, except it didn't do well in combat.

Environmental suit in place, Khal'jan followed them. The knight kept his sword raised, ready for an ambush. Shirakaya led the way. Locating another kiosk, she waited for her brother to decrypt it and unlock a door ahead. They stepped into another round corridor. At the end of the tunnel was a hatch made of glass, overlooking the moon's landscape.

The trio reached the hatch, where Khal'jan used yet another kiosk screen to open it. Stepping out onto the rugged landscape, the group stayed close and checked their flank. Not seeing anything hostile, they made their way across the cratered region to a metal pyramid, connected to the temple by several surface tunnels. An enormous cannon rested on its apex. Khal'jan aimed and fired his gun at it. The cannon immediately swung around and targeted him.

Panicking, he jumped in the direction of a crater. His jump, slowed by the lack of gravity, sent him floating in the direction of the hole, but in the line of fire. His sister mustered all her energy to deflect the beam and cast telekinesis, crushing the cannon. Its ray reversed and blasted through to the triangular building's substructure.

An alarm sounded. Dozens of spherical drones and four-armed statues clad in armor stormed out of the pyramid. Many of the animated stone giants carried fusion guns while others wielded klivat swords.

"Captain, take cover," Yarasuro said via KLD, maneuvering into a crater.

The enchantress, not fond of taking orders from subordinates, ignored his transmission. Standing in the open, beams whizzing past her, she sent a group of stone giants into space via telekinesis. She cast bolts of lightning at multiple drones, electrifying them. The knight leaped up from his crater and severed the electrocuted statues. Other metal-armored beings with fusion guns fired at him, but he deflected their rays between delivering death blows.

Aiming his pistol, Khal'jan blasted three of the levitating statues, their rubble and wires drifting in the gravity-free air. The others turned in midair, targeting him. Before they fired, Shirakaya pulled the remaining seven back down, smashing them against the moon's surface, their particles floating into space.

Yarasuro fought on, parrying lasers from other drones,

sporadically deflecting the rays back at them. Khal'jan assisted him, rising and shooting them until his gun ran out of ammo; he ducked and reloaded. His sister persisted with her magic, repeatedly casting her spells until they worked, destroying her foes with fireballs and lightning.

The brigade of sculpted zealots and hovering drones dwindled. Just then, a metal hatch along the ground some distance away opened, setting in motion an earthquake as the doors unsealed. The trio sprawled as platform ascended to the surface upon which stood an enormous vessel. Its six wings spread, cannons on each of them. The craft flew toward Shirakaya and her comrades, piloted by two stony androids encased in heavy armor.

Recovered from the tremors, the trio got to their feet. This time the enchantress took cover, somersaulting into a crater. Shirakaya tried magic to bend the cannons. Her spell failed. She stayed hidden, praying for her power to return. Khal'jan fired at the cockpit. The starship closed in on the archeologist, just moments away from disintegrating him with its fusion cannons.

Yarasuro leaped up and used some air in his tank to give Khal'jan a boost. The knight then turned midflight and swung his sword in an arc, slicing off a wing. The hull separated as cleanly as a laser knife cutting through qazinotaur meat. Gripping the craft, relying on his magnetic sabatons to clamp on, Yarasuro struck the cockpit, shattering its glass.

Without flinching, the pilots raised their guns. Swiping his sword with a horizontal action, Yarasuro decapitated them. Pieces from the shattered necks drifted from the hovering vessel, their heads gently bouncing against the roof of the cockpit, the bodies bobbing in slow motion. Unfastening their seatbelts, the knight tossed their remains into space, where Khal'jan blasted each one with his plasma pistol.

"My lady," Yarasuro said, "I don't know how to pilot starships, let alone those that have foreign interfaces. Perhaps you and your brother can figure out how to use this while I attack the automatons from land."

"A sound plan," she said, signaling her brother to board the craft with her.

Adrenaline pumping, Khal'jan climbed aboard and sat in the cockpit. Time against him, he sweated as he attempted to translate symbols on the interface while his sister fathomed how the ship functioned.

"I wouldn't touch it yet, Shira," he said firmly.

For once, she listened and took her hand away from a globe-shaped mechanism.

Tapping the air, Khal'jan interacted with the interface. Trusting it sensed his movement and would react to his commands, he typed decrypted equations in the air. "Their technology is based on algorithms. I need to solve mathematical formulae to control this."

"Damn it," Shirakaya said, bashing the screen in front of her. "I guess that explains why only androids are using these things."

"You mean statues?"

"They may appear to be statues, but I don't sense any use of magic. I have no doubt in my mind that they're androids. How else could they solve equations this fast? Whoever created them, Nempada Empire or otherwise, must have encased them in stone to give the illusion that they are magical."

"Makes sense. According to what I learned from Nempadian lore, they were a highly advanced civilization. I just couldn't figure out how they vanished a thousand cycles ago."

"You and the whole universe. That is, until now." At her brother's laugh, she added, "Well, my math is awful. Do you think you can fly this thing?"

"I can try. First I need to translate these symbols."

"It seems you'll need some time," she said, gazing at her bodyguard fighting yet another brigade of klivat-wielding statues. "I'll help Yaro until you figure out how to use this crazy thing."

"Okay. Be careful."

"Always," she said, somersaulting out into space.

III
Cybernetic Awakening

Drifting closer to the crippled terrain, Shirakaya summoned lightning and shocked the remaining statues in the vicinity. Just one survived the attack, ready to stab Yarasuro from behind. The enchantress gasped, discharging one last powerful bolt that incinerated the stony robot. Rocks, wires, and metal, floated in multiple directions.

"Watch your back, Templar."

"Aye, my lady," he said, sheathing his sword. "Thank you."

Shirakaya descended and rejoined her bodyguard. "My brother's learning how to use the ship. We need to infiltrate the temple and find a way to sabotage their cannons."

"My sword is yours, Captain."

"Excellent. Follow me," she said, advancing to the pyramid. "I hope this is the right structure. Be ready for anything."

The knight nodded, walking beside her to the building's exterior staircase. They scaled the metal steps with caution, eyes and ears alert for more enemies in the vicinity. Ahead stood a large, sealed metal door. Strengthening the enchantment on Yarasuro's blade, Shirakaya signaled him to strike.

Unsheathing his weapon, Yarasuro stabbed the colossal door. The fiery aura wrapped around his sword easily pierced the metal. He carved out a circle, which the enchantress kicked; the slab tilted and floated into space before they stooped into the hole. As soon as they stepped inside the structure, an emergency hatch descended and resealed the entrance. In the vestibule, another door stood before them. A semitransparent wall of energy covered with mathematical formulae appeared, passed through the pair, and dissipated.

"What was that?" the knight asked.

"Calm yourself, Templar. If that were a weapon, we'd be dead now. I'm sure it was just a scanner."

"I hope you're right."

"I am," she said, pride preventing her from admitting to feeling apprehensive.

Worried they had been poisoned, she cast a minor decontamination spell strong enough to cleanse them; it was the only cleansing magic she had learned at the academy. The knight experienced a tingly sensation and glanced at the captain. She didn't give him so much as a glimpse. He smirked at her attempt to hide the protection spell as he checked his surroundings to ensure the machines wouldn't initiate a surprise attack.

The energy algorithm completed, the door in front of them unsealing. They entered the central facility through a narrow passage. On the sixth level, the duo entered another path that led to a chamber with a throne. The metal walls had computers built into them, numerous screens depicting myriad mathematical formulae.

"Incredible," the knight said, the door sealing behind him.

"Indeed we are," said a metallic voice from the throne. The duo stared at the alloy chair, where a stream of lasers from every computer merged in the seat. Before their eyes, prismatic rays formed an artificial being of pure energy. "Marvel at our supremacy once more, fleshlings. For this temple shall be your tomb."

"Humph, you must be the one that's been threatening us since we arrived," Shirakaya said, curling her lip. "What are you, some kind of artificial intelligence? I demand to know your name so I can log into my ship's database how I obliterated y—"

The AI discharged an optic blast from its chest. The beam sent her across the chamber, slamming her against the door. She lay behind the knight, unconscious. Yarasuro raised his weapon, ready to defend himself.

"Captain!" he called out, not giving his back to the AI. "Captain!" She didn't respond to him. "What have you done to her, fiend?"

"The same thing I'm about to do to you," it said, discharging another beam.

Yarasuro deflected the ray with his sword. It ricocheted at the ceiling, blasting apart some of the metal framework. Startled, the AI's glowing eyes gazed at the knight, intrigued, and launched multiple beams from its energy-based hands. Moving aside and swinging his sword, Yarasuro repelled more lasers; one, however, blasted his shoulder and cracked his pauldron. The knight groaned and dropped to the floor but swiftly got to his feet and hid behind a column, dodging another onslaught.

"Surrender or suffer an eternity of torture, fleshling," stated the AI, launching more beams at him.

Ignoring its threat, Yarasuro rolled away from the column as it toppled. Grumbling under his breath, he charged toward the AI. He swung his sword wildly, deflecting lasers. An optic blast ricocheted, destroying a supercomputer along the wall. Snowy static manifested, the AI's corporeal form fizzing out of control for a moment.

Taken aback, Yarasuro gaped at the dysfunctional AI; he then hurled his sword at a computer nearest him, disrupting the artificial intelligence again. Seizing his weapon, Yarasuro repelled another optic blast. This time, he deflected the beam to another processing unit, detonating it. Again, the being of energy fizzled out of control.

"Your combat techniques are commendable," the AI said, recovering. "However, your attempts to eliminate me are futile."

"In that case, I'll have to try harder," Yarasuro said, repelling another barrage of beams.

Shirakaya stirred and witnessed her bodyguard using the artificial intelligence's rays against it. The moment she saw the AI's form destabilize because a computer had imploded, she summoned a tremendous surge of lightning, frying all the processing units.

"No!" the AI shouted, dissipating.

"Captain, are you all right?"

"I'll be okay." She looked around the ruined chamber. "That was some fine work, Templar. It seems you killed two feyzalas with one stone."

IV
Legion

They left the throne room and descended a platform. Back on the first floor, they exited the temple and rejoined Khal'jan aboard the hovercraft. Shirakaya stepped inside the vessel while her bodyguard stood atop the cockpit to scout for enemies.

"Any good news, Khal?"

"I was about to ask *you* that," he said, typing and inserting equations into the ship's interface.

The enchantress gave a soft laugh. "The defense cannons might be deactivated, but there's only one way to find out. Now, tell me you learned how to use this thing while we were gone."

"Yes and no. This technology requires an android or something of that sort to compute algorithms within microseconds. Each formula used is essentially a command. Problem is, we humyns usually take a few minutes to solve intricate equations. That's why the Nempada Empire used machines to—"

A tremendous quake split the moon's noqurian expanse into a ravine. An army of quadrupedal pods emerged from the depths. As the legion climbed out of the gorge, the AI leader reappeared behind them as a giant being of energy.

"By the Goddess," gasped Yarasuro.

"Insolent mortals!" the AI shouted, his wrathful voice filling the cockpit via the screen. "You cannot terminate me. My empire is infinite. I have seen countless civilizations wither throughout the eons and still we survive and shall continue to do so for all eternity."

"Your empire?" Shirakaya said, raising an eyebrow. "You merely stole it when your master died."

The artificial intelligence produced a metallic laugh. "I expected this much ignorance from a pathetic fleshling such as yourself. I *am* the master. I am Jal Vokken, Emperor of the Nempada Empire."

"Jal Vokken?" Shirakaya said in disbelief.

"Impossible," Khal'jan said. "Emperor Vokken was buried in a tomb on Aarda over five thousand cycles ago. In fact, his crypt was discovered last millennia. This can't be him."

"I abandoned that decrepit body before death could find me," Vokken said. "My empire reached the pinnacle of science. We discovered how to meld one's mind into a network, and the Nempada Empire evolved and transcended. Even if the CPU malfunctions, I remain everlasting. With my transformation, I defeated death and have become a god. For eons my minions and I have remained hidden, watching the pathetic people of Aarda struggle like the peasants they are."

"But my sister and I are Aardanian like you," Khal'jan said, bewildered. "You are essentially our ancestor."

"That is a blatant lie. Your ancestors betrayed our legacy. They refused the gift of immortality, preferring old age and death. Our lineage was severed from that moment on. Your ancestors were pitiable failures."

"Whether you're truly Emperor Vokken, the fact that my sister and I are here is more than enough proof that our people *are* successful."

"We've even reached out to the stars," Shirakaya said. "Sure, we aren't perfect. And we're definitely not immortal. But the universe certainly has more to offer than experiences inside a program."

The image of the emperor scowled. "You *dare* attempt to belittle my evolution? I need not explain myself to the likes of you, ignorant whelp. I have watched your people struggle from the stars and witnessed their endless cycles of suffering. Maz'hura cannot save you. The wrath of death shall consume you."

"It is you who is gravely mistaken, Jal Vokken," the enchantress said, her eyes glowing with magic. "No emperor or AI can withstand my sorcery."

Jal Vokken gave out a cybernetic roar, terminating the

conversation. "Destroy them!"

"Impressive skills in diplomacy," Khal'jan said with a sigh.

"I guess we do things the hard way," Yarasuro said, entering the cockpit from above and sitting in a rear seat.

"Here goes nothing," Khal'jan said, activating the formula he'd created and inputted into the ship's interface.

Vokken's legion of machines launched fusion beams from their cannons at the hijacked vessel. Shirakaya and her comrades flinched and gawked at the windowpane as the rays dissolved an inch from the cockpit.

Khal'jan cheered. "Yes! The formula worked."

His complex and lengthy equation of twenty-six pages continued to function, beginning with a force field protecting the entire ship. As each second passed, the algorithm increased the shield's power. It also made the craft move, evading beams. Its cannons activated, blasting and destroying several quadrupedal pods. The archeologist's formula, however, struggled to cope with all the lasers hitting the vessel's force field.

The ship's interface was on the verge of imploding when a gamma missile launched from above, detonating in the heart of the legion. Dozens of pods disintegrated. Slack-jawed, the enchantress gazed up and saw a flotilla of starships approach. One of them was a spacecraft from the *Celestial*, piloted by Ensign Narja.

Zadoya opened a hatch as her vessel flew alongside, aiming her rifle at the army of machines. Using her ayzentium arm, she held the gun firm and opened fire. Though taken aback, the robots, including their AI leader, counterattacked. An array of beams projected from both factions, destroying quadrupedal pods and military starships alike.

During the battle, Shirakaya and Yarasuro exited the pod. On foot, the enchantress summoned bolts of lightning and electrocuted a machine. The knight blocked beams meant for his captain, freeing Shirakaya to focus on her destructive spells. She waited a moment to rejuvenate her power and continued to cast spells.

"Stand back, Templar," she said, gathering strength.

He backed away as Shirakaya discharged an arcane sphere filled with void magic. Reaching midway across the battlefield, the orb briefly created a black hole that consumed a dozen pods. Weakness encroaching, she mustered her magic to battle the machines as she advanced to the AI.

A unit of pods focused their attention on the enchantress. Templar Yarasuro strove to deflect the fusion beams back at them. Seeing the heavy fire, Khal'jan leaned out of the cockpit, firing his gun at them. Narja flew over the regiment and launched a barrage of lasers, clearing a path before landing near the captain. Kazakuma, Jedalia, and Zadoya leaped out.

"My lady, thank the Goddess you are safe," Jedalia said.

"The oracle sensed your location and insisted on coming," Zadoya said. "We came to assist you and protect her."

"I refused to stay in that space station for another minute. If anything happened to you, I wouldn't be able to live with myself."

Shirakaya gave the oracle a faint smile, blushing. "Lieutenant," her tone one of sheer joy while shaking Zadoya's prosthetic hand, "congratulations on your new arm and a quick recovery."

"Thank you, Captain," she said, bowing.

"I can't express how relieved I am to have all of you here," Shirakaya said, sweat forming on her brow. "But how in the cosmos did you find out we were here?"

"The judicator initially contacted us," Zadoya said.

"He told us you were in trouble," Kazakuma said. "Once the cannons went offline, we figured it was now or never to launch an attack. And considering we're up against machines, I assume you need my hacking expertise."

"Absolutely," the captain said. "Follow me."

V
Master and Slave

While the enemies regrouped, Shirakaya boarded the vessel with her entourage. Her brother took this time to introduce himself to the crew. They, in return, greeted him with respect.

Shirakaya fixed her eyes on the AI whose upper body extended from the ravine. "Ensign, I need you to fly us into that chasm."

"The one amid that army, Captain?" she asked.

"It sounds crazy, but that's what I need you to do. That massive being of energy is actually an AI linked to a network in this temple and is controlling these machines. And I'm guessing that since it rose from the chasm, there's a special chamber beneath the surface of the moon. If there's a primary CPU keeping the network online anywhere, it must be located there."

Khal'jan overheard her and shrugged. "Even if we find it, how will that help? Vokken told us that destroying the CPU won't harm him."

"True, little brother, but it's not my intention to wipe him out. My chief engineer, Kazakuma, is an expert at hacking. I intend to use that against the AI."

"Interesting," he said. "I just hope that whatever you're planning actually works."

The ensign ascended the vessel and flew across the terrain as other starships attacked the legion of robots. Emperor Vokken, engrossed in the battle, focused his attention on ships launching missiles and beams. The ensign flew to the gorge. Spotting the spacecraft, Vokken discharged an optic blast, severely weakening the vessel's force field.

"Be careful, Ensign," the captain said. "One more blast of that magnitude can penetrate our shield and kill us."

"Yes, my lady," Narja replied nervously, maneuvering the ship.

"The AI is extremely powerful. Just get us there alive and I'll handle the rest."

Narja increased her acceleration, steering the craft left to right. The AI discharged another optic blast at Narja who shifted gears. Turning three hundred and sixty degrees, she skirted the blast and brought the ship down through the chasm. As the vessel descended, she noticed a trail of wires running from the surface to the moon's inner core.

"Look!" Khal'jan pointed to a tunnel where dozens of circuits entered.

"I knew it." The captain's eyes fixed on the esorian region of the ravine. "Take us there, Ensign."

"Aye, my lady."

Narja entered the octagonal passage and decreased her speed, circumventing hazardous stalactites and stalagmites. As they flew, Jedalia sensed the AI return to the temple's network to implode circuits.

"Watch out!" she spouted, pointing esoria.

Sparks ran along the walls, generating massive volts of electricity that zapped the ship's shield.

"Those currents neutralized our force field," Narja said, panicky. "I don't know how much more we can handle."

The captain put a hand on Narja's shoulder. "Calm down and focus on—"

"Your army is impressive, fleshlings," the AI said via kinetic link. "You have indubitably caught me by surprise. Albeit you have powerful magic, I am afraid this glorious battle ends now. This is my primary domain. Surrender or suffer an eternity as enslaved husks."

"I wouldn't surrender even if you were Koth'tura himself," Shirakaya said, clicking her kinetic link device and terminating the communication. To her visibly rattled crew, she added, "Ignore its feeble threats. It's nothing more than an AI. Once we get to the CPU, it will plead for mercy."

Narja continued circumnavigating the electrical discharges from circuits along the paneled walls until she reached an antechamber where a massive CPU stood. The attacks waned. Conduits surrounded the unit, electrical energy coursing through spiral coils and interwoven circuitry. Approaching the network's mainframe, Narja stopped and maintained the shuttle's hover jets built into its substructure.

"Is this a good place to remain?"

"It's perfect," the captain said. "All right, Khal. I'll need your KLD for this to work."

"What?" he said, startled. "Why?"

"No questions," she said, extending her hand. "Give it to me." At his hesitation, she went on, "I should report you for starting an illegal excavation. Countless lives have been lost because of your dim-witted actions. I can end this madness if you give it to me. Also, for your help, I will inform the Tal'manac Order that I gave you permission to create a dig site in the Valley of Locarn."

"I don't mean to meddle," Yarasuro said to the archeologist, "but I think sacrificing your KLD is a small price to pay for atonement."

The others kept quiet, ignorant of the situation. Khal'jan, meanwhile, struggled to deal with his sister blackmailing him. Letting the knight's words sink in, he detached his kinetic link device and handed it over to Shirakaya.

"Thank you," she said, seizing it. "All right, Chief. This is where you come in. I need you to delete every file on this device and reboot it without any programs. Once you're finished, we'll get out of the ship and connect this to the CPU."

"Aye," he said.

Shirakaya tossed over the device to Kazakuma who fiddled with it. While he worked on it, electrical discharges circulated around the chamber. Emperor Vokken manipulated each attack to deter the starship from hovering so close to his mainframe. A few crew members grew anxious, but Kazakuma persevered. With desperation lending speed, he deleted its saved files and reset it. The moment he finished, another volt of electricity zapped across the chamber, spreading near Narja's craft.

"This area is too dangerous," the ensign said, ready to move the vessel.

"Do *not* move this ship. Those attacks won't affect us. The AI is simply attempting to frighten you. This is a perfect position."

"I'm finished," Kazakuma said.

"Excellent," the captain said, advancing toward the central

hatch. "You, Khal, and the oracle are with me. The rest of you stay here." At the sealed entry door, Shirakaya added, "Jeda, we need powerful barriers."

"Say no more." Within seconds, she cast mana shields on them. "Do you need anything else from me, my lady?"

"No, thank you. Please stay here. We'll be right back."

The oracle nodded, standing back. Opening the hatch, Shirakaya and her entourage exited the starship. They immediately came across more bursts of energy sparking across the chamber in arches. Only Khal'jan became disconcerted. Kazakuma followed the captain, leaping off the ship. Together they floated over to a platform attached to the temple's mainframe.

"What now?" Kazakuma asked.

"Good question," Shirakaya said, observing the central processing unit. Her eyes fixed on multiple empty slots adjacent to a kiosk connected to the mainframe. "Try inserting the KLD into one of those universal ports."

The engineer inserted the gadget.

"All right, now I want you to hack into the database and transfer the AI into my brother's device. The former emperor won't be able to control anything inside it. Khal, assist him with the symbols."

"Can that really be done?" Khal'jan asked.

"In theory, yes," the engineer said. "In fact, that's brilliant. You see, because everything has been erased on the kinetic link device, the AI won't be able to execute a counter-hack. In essence, the KLD will function as a digital prison."

"Impressed, brother?"

"Of course I am," he said, excited. "That means I can explore both the temple and the entire moon in peace. There's not only new technology but also a whole dynasty for me to discover that links to Aarda."

At his response, she said, "I'm positive the Tal'manac Order will allow that since you helped me. In the meantime, assist Chief Kazakuma and remove that narcissistic AI from the mainfra—"

"A bold plan, Captain Shirakaya," Emperor Vokken said via the CPU's interface, a digital face of snowy particles appearing before them. "Unfortunately for you, this is where your valiant mission ends." His cybernetic visage transformed into concentrated energy that zoomed toward the enchantress, who instinctively rolled aside to avoid it. Moments later, the electricity reshaped into a massive being of energy. "Feel the wrath of Jal Vokken!"

He discharged an optic blast half the size of Narja's spacecraft at the enchantress.

Shirakaya flinched, knowing it couldn't be avoided. The particle beam dissipated inches away from her. Opening her eyes, she realized Jedalia's barrier had absorbed the ray. Smirking at the emperor, she summoned a bright light and hurled it at him.

Since the artificial intelligence was temporarily blinded, Narja flew her vessel away while Zadoya launched a pair of gamma missiles at him. Shirakaya heard Vokken gasp. The projectiles didn't harm him. Instead, the radiation disrupted his form, giving the engineer and archeologist more time to work together. As they did, Narja brought her craft over to the opposite side of the platform. Opening a hatch, Yarasuro and Jedalia leaped from it. Landing on a catwalk, they joined Shirakaya, ready to defend her.

"Jeda, what are you doing?" Shirakaya asked, panicky.

The oracle ignored her, preparing to cast a spell while the emperor dispersed and reformed away from the radiation. Enraged, he channeled all his energy and launched it at the quintet. Before it could obliterate them, the oracle conjured a barrier to absorb the devastating attack. Vokken continued discharging bolts of energy, weakening the oracle's arcane force field.

"Do not test me, mortals," Vokken roared. "I will destroy this entire chamber if I must. Becoming my slaves is your only salvation."

The voltage increased, causing Jedalia to stagger. Fearing that the oracle might faint, the enchantress attempted to cast a mana shield of her own over the group. She repeated the incantation within her mind, to no avail. Shirakaya gazed at the energy coursing through the AI's electrical form, wondering if this would be the end of her existence.

How pathetic, she thought to herself, that she would die not by Ashkaratoth's hands but by something that wasn't even alive anymore; a mere shadow of what was once humyn eons ago, now a crippled husk of a man. This machine had become her downfall, and all because she'd decided to visit her family during shore leave. Instead of enjoying the vacation she deserved, she found herself staring down the barrel of a gun yet again. She told herself that this was her brother's fault. If it weren't for his irresponsibility, she'd have spent quality time with her family and would already be on her way to investigate the other protostar.

"It is time to bow down to your true master," Vokken said, his digital eyes pulsating with immeasurable power.

Unleashing all his power, his physical form of energy twisted. A screech of thunder boomed, electricity jolting and scattering in numerous directions. Every bolt merged again, zapping through the mana shield. Passing a pale crew, Vokken's essence went into the KLD. At that precise moment, the engineer removed the device.

"Perhaps *it* should bow down to us," Kazakuma said.

Shirakaya gawked at the empty abyss while her brother and crew praised the engineer. Narja flew her vessel back to the original position, hovering a few feet away from the quintet; she gave them a thumbs-up and opened the hatch.

Still in shock, the sorceress's rage against Khal'jan dwindled until only relief remained. Snapping out of her trance, she turned her attention to the chief engineer. The crew saluted her as she approached. Ignoring them, Shirakaya walked over to Kazakuma, seized the kinetic link device, and teleported it into her own KLD's memory bank.

"What will you do with it, Shira?" Khal'jan asked.

"For the meantime, it will stay hidden from the universe," she said coldly. "However, if I *ever* come across another black hole, I'll be sure to test Zadoya's new arm and see how good her ability to throw is."

The End Times

Before my creations, two universes existed: The multiverse. One was Order and the other, Chaos. I awakened within Order. For millennia, the realm of pandemonium remained dormant. One day, it gained sentience and screamed with malice, tearing a hole through the fabric of time and space. The first black hole in existence manifested, an appalling tunnel of obscurity that brought Chaos across dimensions and interstellar gulfs of space into Order. The collision of the universes created a cosmic catastrophe, merging into a realm known as Ensar. I soon gave name to the swarming chaos: Koth'tura. We battled for control, the purity of life threatened. With magic, I eluded death and imprisoned the Lord of Chaos in the Drift Void. But do not fear such chasms, for they are innate gateways into the divine. Only in the end times shall the primordial void be unsealed. For when Koth'tura is freed, my return will be imminent, and so shall be the rebirth of Ensar.

Transdimensional Origins 24:5

Chapter Seven

Extraterrestrial Downfall

I
Siblings

aptain Shirakaya boarded the shuttle with her brother and subordinates. She made her way to the cockpit and sat beside Narja who saluted her.

"At ease, Ensign," she said, activating her KLD and connecting with the judicator. "I can't thank you enough for notifying Aarda's space station of my predicament. I don't know what I would've done without their assistance."

"You are more than welcome. In fact, I should be thanking you for discovering Aarda's fifth moon."

"It was my brother Khal who unearthed a conduit that teleported us here. His theories seemed valid, so I authorized him to excavate in the Valley of Locarn. But when I traveled to visit family on Aarda, my brother wasn't home. I eventually traveled to the site to check on him when I found it under attack by these machines."

"This will make headlines on the news indeed," Owendar said, astonished. "How in the cosmos did you get transported?"

"There was some kind of artifact Khal had unearthed. It reacted to me inside a chamber where the conduit was located. I really can't explain how magic was involved, especially since the Nempada Empire thrived on superior technology. Perhaps my brother will be able to solve this mystery. That is, if you allow him to assist."

"Absolutely," he said without thinking about it. "My fellow colleagues are sending their best archeologists and scientists to the moon as we speak. I'll inform them that they have Khal to thank for this historical discovery and that he'll be joining the team."

"Thank you, Professor."

"Anything for the daughter I never had," he said. "Now, I think a certain captain has a protostar in the Pargosis System to examine?"

"I'm leaving now," she said, saluting him. As soon as the judicator gave her a subtle wave, she ended the kinetic link. "Ensign, get us back to the station." As the pilot complied, Shirakaya continued, "Yaro, inform my crew to return to the Celestial. We finally have a lead on the koth'vurians, and I'll be damned if I let this slip by me."

"Aye, Captain."

"Shira," called out Khal'jan, standing by the door. "I'm sorry to bother you. Can we talk alone for a little while?"

"Sure. Until we arrive at the space station," she said, exiting the cockpit with him.

In the corridor, Khal'jan stopped for a moment. "I know this is going to sound terrible, but I didn't expect you to come through for me. A part of me was scared you were going to arrest me. Thanks for keeping your word."

"What a terrible thing to say," she said, her smile playful.

"I'm serious."

Shirakaya listened, her face more somber. "You got a lot of people killed in satisfying your ego, Khal. The main reason why you're not going to jail is because you're my brother. I've also taken into consideration that you didn't do this on purpose. I know your coworkers were just as passionate as you."

"I'm so sorry, Shira," he said, tears in his eyes.

"Don't say sorry to me. I'm just trying to do my job." She sighed, an awkward feeling taking hold of her. "I'll always love you, Khal. Even if you're an idiot. What matters is you gave up your KLD to imprison that psycho. Your colleagues would be proud."

Khal'jan didn't respond, his eyes downcast.

"Captain," Narja spoke via kinetic link, "we are approaching Aarda's space station. Shall I dock in port G-543 or the Celestial?"

"We need to drop off my brother first. Bring us to the station."

"Aye," Narja said, ending the link.

"You're not coming back home?"

"I can't," Shirakaya said with obvious regret. "I know mom and dad will be heartbroken, but something bizarre is happening in the Pargosis System, and I've been ordered by one of the Ruzurai to travel there."

"Whoa. If a Ruzurai requested your presence, it must be dire. Do you know what the problem is?"

Shirakaya tilted her head, stumped at how to respond. She couldn't tell him about the koth'vurians lest he'd think she lost her mind. Just when the words came to her, the vessel shook as it clanked onto metal clamps.

"We have arrived at the Aarda space station, my lady," Narja said.

"Thank you, Ensign," the captain said as a hatch in the corridor opened from behind. She turned her attention back to Khal and continued, "You may be my brother, but I'm afraid what you asked is classified. Only my crew is allowed to know."

"I see." An awkward moment of silence fell in the corridor, broken only by him adding in a glum voice, "I understand."

"I'm glad you do." She glanced at the busy docking bay, watched a merchant ship land on the opposite side of the platform, and hugged her brother tight. "Please tell mom and dad I love them and will visit again soon."

"Of course," he said, hugging her too. "Take care of yourself, Shira."

"I will," she said, watching him disembark. Her brother stood on the docking platform where dozens of other vessels and passersby were located. "Hey, Khal. Don't get into too much trouble while I'm gone."

"I'll try not to," he said with a faint smirk, waving.

Shirakaya also waved while the spacecraft's hatch sealed.

II
Progress

After parting ways with her brother, Captain Shirakaya returned to the cockpit and sat beside the ensign.

"It's time to depart."

"Aye, my lady," Narja said, unlocking the clamps and reversing the ship. As soon as the ensign distanced herself from the platform, she turned the craft and flew into the *Celestial's* jet bay. After landing, she added, "It's good to be back."

"Indeed it is," Shirakaya said.

When the ship deactivated, her bodyguard asked, "What are your orders, Captain?"

"Once we leave the station, I'll transmit the coordinates Judicator Owendar gave me for our next mission to your KLDs. In the meantime, I want all of you to return to the bridge."

"Aye," they said in unison.

Shirakaya and her companions exited the shuttle and transported from the jet bay to the command center via an X-Phaser pod. Crew members saluted the captain as she passed them in a corridor leading to the flight deck. Entering the chamber, Shirakaya sat in her armchair. The oracle stood beside her lover and Shirakaya's entourage returned to their posts.

"Welcome back, Captain," Commander Ravdar said, bowing. "You had us quite worried when Judicator Owendar contacted us."

"Thank you. I was worried myself. Fortunately, all is well." She waited for the ensign to maneuver the *Celestial* away from the space station before transmiting the mission's coordinates to her crew. Once planet Aarda was the size of distant stars, Shirakaya added, "Ensign, take us to Pargosis via dimensional space."

"As you wish, my lady," Narja said, initiating the ship's graviton.

"So, um, any reason why we're traveling over to the Torpo Giayan Galaxy?" the commander asked.

"One of the Ruzurai detected a protostar there," Shirakaya said, eyes fixed on the anti-gravity shield forming in outer space. "Our mission is to investigate it and, if possible, collect its magical ions."

"A protostar?" he said, astonished. "I've never seen one before."

Shirakaya raised her brow. "I'm sure you'll find it fascinating. In fact, you can assist our astrophysicists in documenting it into our planetary database and updating the starmap while I gather its ions."

"I would be honored," Ravdar said. "I won't let you down, Captain. I'll even take digital photos of the phenomenon."

"Excellent." Noticing his mouth open as if to speak again, she went on, "I don't need my oracle to tell me what you're going to ask. Yes, you can transmit copies of the protostar images to your wife as long as they're sent through your personal kinetic link device and not the TDE. I don't want the Order to check our communication records and think we're dillydallying."

"Understood," he said, beaming. "Thank you."

The commander was whipped, Shirakaya thought to herself. In essence, Ravdar reported to two captains. And that was good for her because she didn't need him down her throat during this assignment. She'd be searching for a race that most people in the universe considered either mythical or exiled from the universe. She nodded at him, turning her attention back to the cosmic aperture.

Entering it, the mothership traversed through a narrow chasm in dimensional space that pulsed with radiant light. The vessel exited the tunnel within minutes, its polarized mana shield activating. Planets filled the system located in the Torpo Giayan Galaxy. An immense star illuminated several gas giants. Beyond the celestial bodies, partially shrouded by dust and suspended between liquefying meteorites, was a newborn sun.

Although a gorgeous sight to behold, Shirakaya focused more on the fact that an armada of ravaged starships drifted not too far from the protostar. She stood up and approached the windowpane, gazing at the disaster with disbelief. Pieces of shrapnel mixed with torn limbs and droplets of blood floated around the derelict vessels.

"By the Goddess," Ravdar said. "What happened here?"

"Worry about the research," Shirakaya said. "In the meantime, I'll gather a team and find out why these ships have been attacked."

"But, Captain—"

"Follow your orders, Commander," she said brusquely.

Though the officer looked troubled, he obeyed her and left the chamber to oversee a group of astrophysicists assigned to researching the protostar. Afterwards, the captain advanced to the flight deck's door, signaling the knight, chief engineer, and lieutenant to follow her.

"My lady?" called out Jedalia.

"You need to stay here," the captain said before exiting the room. "The situation's grim. Should something bad happen, you're the only one who can cast a shield powerful enough to protect this ship."

"I understand," she said. "Please be careful."

Shirakaya nodded at the oracle and left the chamber with her entourage. They entered a teleportation pod, transferring to a different corridor. When the group manifested in another capsule, they exited it and approached a sealed hatch.

"Narja," Shirakaya said via kinetic link, "I want you to fly to Captain Tor's starship and establish a hatch connection."

"Right away, my lady," the ensign said.

The *Celestial* advanced through the interstellar dust, splotches of blood staining its hull and windowpanes. Despite the pilot's best efforts to avoid shrapnel, the mothership's wide wings suffered a few collisions. The immense vessel survived the impacts as Narja lined the *Celestial* up with Tor's ruined spacecraft. With delicate maneuvering, she attached both hatches to each other. Shirakaya inputted a security code on a console beside the hatch, opening it.

"All right," she said, "let's go."

Spacesuits equipped and force fields activated, the quartet

stepped through the hatch and into the destroyed starship. Inside, they saw that not only was the vessel devastated but also most walls had severe gashes along the tetrigonium hull. Even a section of the ceiling had split, revealing serrated slash marks.

Realizing that only ferocious creatures were capable of causing such awful damage, the lieutenant ported out her plasma rifle via KLD and loaded it with a frost clip. Shirakaya merely grimaced at the destruction while her bodyguard unsheathed his sword, ready for an ambush. If any aliens remained on board this spacecraft, they were definitely hiding; that much the captain knew.

Magnetic boots enabled, Shirakaya advanced through what appeared to be an assembly chamber with her subordinates and entered a corridor. As with other sectors, this hall appeared badly damaged. The lack of power meant that the quartet had to rely on natural illumination from stars through the many breaches in the hull.

Only one X-Phaser capsule remained intact, but without power it was useless. The captain stepped inside the capsule and attempted to use it, hoping an emergency generator had been installed in the vessel. Nothing happened. She cursed under her breath and stood still for a moment.

"Chief, open the panel and check if the wires have been slashed."

"Right away," Kazakuma said, porting tools and inspecting the pod. Beaming his KLD at the pane, he selected an ATS-31 arcane telekinetic screwdriver. Turning it on, its telekinetic features automatically loosened the screws. He removed the metal cover, examining each wire. "No harm done here," he added, resealing the panel. "It's possible that whatever attacked this vessel sabotaged the backup generators."

"Unbelievable," Zadoya said. "How would aliens even know about them?"

"I doubt they did," Yarasuro said, glancing at the dented and ripped hull. "Look around you. I'm surprised parts of this ship are still intact."

"There must be survivors somewhere," the captain said.

She pressed a hand on the pod's console, attempting to use magic to energize it. To avoid humiliation, Shirakaya acted as though she was merely leaning on it and went on, "Goddess knows where this would port us."

"Maybe somewhere out there in space," Zadoya said.

"Right," Shirakaya said, eyes gazing up. "I suggest we climb out of those holes and locate the bridge…or what's left of it."

Her subordinates followed her. The quartet used their magnetic boots to climb the walls and slip through sharp apertures. Once in outer space, they maintained a firm grip along the hull and advanced to what remained of the upper decks. Cosmic dust enveloped them as they scaled the vessel, their armor glittering. They had plenty of zitrogen, but the air tanks were nevertheless limited to only a few hours of use. Aware of this, Kazakuma turned his attention to the captain.

"My lady, I'd prefer to use my reserves during an emergency. Is it all right if you cast a mana shield on us?"

Shirakaya swallowed hard, her face paling. "We could be attacked at any moment, Chief. If that happens, I'll need all of my energy. Keep using your zitrogen air tanks until I say otherwise."

"Understood," he said, uneasy.

Aware that Shirakaya's arcane power had been dwindling, Yarasuro gazed at the captain and knew her response was an excuse. Unsure why, he kept quiet.

"There," Shirakaya said, pointing at a chamber located in the noqurian quadrant. "That might be the flight deck."

"We're right behind you, Captain," Yarasuro said.

The quartet moved toward the cockpit. Zadoya smacked away a floating leg as she advanced. She sulked, an expression of revulsion on her face. Blood drifted alongside the crew, a few droplets splotching their spacesuits and helmets. They were all disgusted as they avoided the partially solidified body fluids of dead people.

They climbed upward for nearly a kilometer and reached an aperture leading back into the craft. The captain and her team slipped through the torn hull, checking their flanks. Seeing corpses, the captain's subordinates maintained their guard.

Shirakaya surveyed the entire room, using her KLD to identify each person. "There's no sign of Captain Tor."

"Do you think he was taken prisoner by his attackers?" Zadoya asked.

The captain wore a grim expression. "These people were brutally murdered. I doubt they were concerned enough to capture him. No, he is either dead or hiding somewhere aboard this vessel."

"Quite the bleak assessment," Yarasuro said.

Kazakuma crossed his arms. "Is it possible he used an escape pod? I mean, that's what I would've done if the battle was going sour."

"Of course you would have," Shirakaya said with a grin. "Captains are not allowed to abandon ship unless all personnel have safely evacuated. Though, that doesn't mean Tor followed protocol." She paused for a moment, pensive. "I have an idea." Activating her kinetic link, she contacted the oracle. "Jeda, is it possible you can teleport me from Captain Tor's flight deck to his conference chamber?"

"I can try," she said on the screen. She closed her eyes, using her psychic vision. Only a blurry form of the vessel's wreckage formed in her mind. "My lady, I'm not sure if that chamber is still intact."

"I'm using my zitrogen tank, so I'll be fine if you accidentally teleport me to space. Please try."

"As you wish."

With great effort, she brought the starship's original layout into her mind, identified where the conference room should be, and teleported the captain. Shirakaya vanished and reappeared inside a chamber that, unlike other sections of the craft she'd explored, the walls were intact. Gazing up at the ceiling, she spotted Tor floating lifelessly in the air.

"My Goddess," she gasped.

Deactivating her magnetic boots, she launched herself midway across the chamber and seized him.

"Is everything all right, Captain?" Yarasuro asked.

"Yes," the enchantress said. "I've found Captain Tor." She checked for signs of life. By a miracle, she felt a weak pulse. "He's still alive. Jeda, teleport us to the medical bay."

The oracle's heart raced with anxiety, attempting to locate both captains. After several seconds, she sensed them. She cast a powerful teleportation spell that transferred the duo as well as the other crew members from the ruined spacecraft to the *Celestial*'s medical bay.

III
Oblivion

Shirakaya materialized in a lobby where nurses worked, Tor in her arms. "This man needs medical attention. On the double. Now!"

The nearest nurse jumped out of her seat and strode over with a hovering stretcher while the others contacted doctors via intercom. Though she struggled, Shirakaya placed Tor on the stretcher. The nurse rushed him into an emergency room.

Yarasuro saw how stressed his commanding officer looked and placed a hand on her shoulder. "I have faith he'll recover."

"You don't need faith when it comes to a sorcerer," Kazakuma said. "He'll definitely pull through."

"You honestly believe that?" the captain asked.

"Absolutely," Zadoya said before the chief could. "And when he recovers, we'll find out who killed our comrades."

"Thank you. I appreciate your positive thoughts." The enchantress took a deep breath. "It must've been the koth'vurians. I just don't understand why they didn't consume the protostar when they had the chance."

"Perhaps they knew that reinforcements were on the way," Yarasuro said.

"With all due respect, Captain," the engineer began, "we don't even know if the assailants are koth'vurians. Since we were attacked, you've been convinced of Koth'tura returning. It's as if you wish for him to be real. For all we know, this could have been the work of pirates. Nothing more."

Rage consumed the captain, a frenzy that made her want to tear him apart. "*With all due respect*, Chief, you are dismissed."

Terrified of her glare, Kazakuma lowered his head, barely nodding, and searched for a teleportation capsule in the medical bay. An awkward silence descended over the lobby. No one dared utter a word. The knight and soldier remained quiet, wondering if the captain would yell at them.

"Pirates?" Shirakaya said, scoffing. "That skeptical fool will learn the hard way." She checked the time via her KLD and added, "It's 3700 hours. Lieutenant, inform Ensign Narja that we will remain in this quadrant until the doctors restore the captain to health."

"Aye," she said, leaving.

Shirakaya fixed her eyes on the emergency room, merely glancing at the knight. "You and I will stay here until Tor is conscious."

"As you wish, my lady."

"Wish?" she said, her voice as cold as a witch from hell. "No, Templar. As I *command*. Then we shall know the truth."

Yarasuro obeyed the captain, taking a seat beside her. Doctor Hejven, accompanied by nurses, passed them and entered intensive care. The duo heard commotion but they weren't technically allowed to approach. They had no choice but to wait on a bench in the corridor while more nurses went into the emergency room.

Moments later, a medical alarm sounded. Uneasy, the enchantress stood up and gazed at the door leading to intensive care.

"I'm sure they have everything under control," Yarasuro said.

She heard him but didn't reply, worried that something terrible happened.

Jedalia teleported into the hallway. Seeing how pale she looked, Shirakaya approached her. "My oracle, are you all right?"

"They're here," Jedalia said feebly. "They've been here all along, preying on us." Her eyes glowed while she blurted, "Star of Maz'hura. Harvesting void. Shattered souls. Tears of blood. Darkness within."

"Another vague prophecy," the captain said. "Brace her while I check the bridge."

"Aye, my lady," he said, holding the oracle who sank into a deep stupor.

The captain strode over to a teleportation capsule. Before entering it, she heard nurses shriek. She stopped in front of the pod, her eyes fixed on the emergency room's entrance. The door burst open as Doctor Hejven's corpse flew out and slammed against the wall, denting it. Blood sprayed over the corridor.

Yarasuro laid Jedalia on the bench and unsheathed his sword, an expression of dismay on his face as Tor exited the intensive care chamber. His clothes bulged and ripped, his eyes glistening green and his fingers extending into claws. He wore a demented grin on his scaly visage, fangs growing. The shape-shifter gave out a deafening roar, its skin shredding—wings emerging and spreading.

"No," Shirakaya breathed, petrified.

"This is the second time you attempt to thwart us," Ashkaratoth said, his monstrous voice filling the corridor like a festering plague. "It is a mystery to me how you survived the black hole in Copia Deiga, but I will now personally ensure that your carcass is obliterated from the cosmos."

Standing stock-still, Yarasuro waited for the shape-shifter to attack first. The alien approached, swiping his claws at the knight. Evading him, Yarasuro swiped his weapon in an arc. Ashkaratoth grasped the blade with his scaly hand. Using his other claw, he struck the Templar across his breastplate. With one swift strike, the knight's armor ripped apart, blood and metal littering the floor.

"Yaro!" shrieked Shirakaya, watching him fall to the ground, unconscious.

Before she could cast a spell, the koth'vurian extended his hands. Palms aimed at her, a toxic gamma ray emitted from his hands and zapped her. The powerful beam pierced her enchanted dalikonium armor, blowing a hole in her torso; she flew across the corridor, through the corner wall into electrical wires and pipes.

Seeing her lifeless, Ashkaratoth snorted at her weakness and wondered how such a feeble, pathetic fool had survived this long. But it didn't matter to him anymore; she had finally been eliminated. He tore a hole through the ceiling and carved his way out of the starship. As soon as he breached outer space, he rattled his tail while releasing a screechy siren. All the intact bodies in space shape-shifted into their reptilian form, wings extended. They hissed, fixing their slit eyes at the inert vessel.

"Captain!" called out Zadoya, unaware of what had happened to Shirakaya. "Captain! We've fallen into a trap! Captain!" Not receiving a response, she sighed and continued, "Ensign, activate our emergency force field and launch plasma torpedoes at them."

"Aye," she complied, firing at the aliens.

Woozy, the oracle awoke from her stupor. Everywhere she turned, blood greeted her. Jedalia gasped at the sight of the unconscious knight. She checked his neck and felt a pulse. As much as she wanted to heal him, she couldn't. Magic, white or black, was poisonous to him. Sensing her beloved captain in excruciating pain, she strode through the crimson hall to find Shirakaya's body amid dangling wires and broken pipes.

"Shira!" she cried out, easing the captain out of the wall via telekinesis. "Goddess, please protect her." She placed her palms on the hole and used her power to seal the wound. Queasy after conjuring such powerful magic, she nevertheless continued channeling her life force into the captain, whose bone marrow rapidly produced more blood cells. "Shira? Can you hear me?" There was no response. "Shira?"

Materializing inside a teleportation capsule, Zadoya stepped out and joined the weeping oracle.

"Goddess, what happened?" the lieutenant asked, the

Celestial juddering as the aliens attacked.

"It's all my fault," the oracle said between sobs. "I sensed an awful presence in the ship, but I didn't say or do anything soon enough. Little did any of us know, Ashkaratoth had shape-shifted into Captain Tor. Once the koth'vurian was exactly where he wanted to be, he attacked. It's all my fault. She might die because of me."

"That's not true," Zadoya said, her eyebrows furrowing. "You're an oracle, not Maz'hura herself. You're not perfect. Nobody is."

"Jeda?" groaned Shirakaya.

"Shira!" Jedalia said ecstatically, unable to contain her emotions. "Thank the Goddess."

"Captain, words can't express how happy I am that you regained consciousness," Zadoya said. "I'm sure you're well aware, but we're under attack by Ashkaratoth's minions. Your soldiers are doing everything in their power to defend the ship."

"That is commendable," Shirakaya said, appearing frail. "I am, however, afraid that their resolve won't be enough."

"So long as Ashkaratoth remains, we have no hope," Jedalia said.

"We'll find him and put an end to his existence," Zadoya said, her tenacious spirit taking charge. "My oracle, please help me get the captain up."

"I'll be fine," Shirakaya said, gradually getting to her feet. "Lieutenant, my bodyguard is in critical condition and there's nothing our oracle can do to save him. I need you to use an MS-783 syringe on him immediately."

"Aye," she said, rushing over to Templar Yarasuro. Porting a first aid kit via her kinetic link device, the lieutenant removed the needle. "What now?"

"Shove it into his heart."

"Huh?" uttered the lieutenant, surprised since the syringe was long. "With all due respect, Captain, are you sure about that?"

The ship jolted again.

"We don't have time for this," snapped Shirakaya, grabbing

the needle. "It's a burst of adrenaline that prevents infections. It has the potential to heal him, but at the very least it will keep him alive for a few hours."

Without hesitating, the captain stabbed her bodyguard. To Zadoya's astonishment, Yarasuro gagged and coughed up blood.

"Yaro, are you able to stand?"

The knight kept huffing and puffing but managed a small nod. He removed the syringe from his chest and attempted to stand, catching his breath. Though unstable at first, he got to his feet with the help of his captain.

"Thank you, my lady," he said weakly. "Did you vanquish Ashkaratoth?"

"I'm afraid he still has the upper hand," Shirakaya replied, the mothership continuing to shudder. "He is attacking from space with his legion. If we're to survive this battle, we must suit-up and fight from the ramparts."

"My blade is yours to command," he said.

"That's what I wanted to hear." She clicked her KLD and ported a helmet while walking toward an X-Phaser. "This way."

Her subordinates followed, equipping their helmets and activating zitrogen tanks to breathe. In the cylinder-shaped pod, they transferred to outer space along the ship's ramparts. A prism of lethal beams welcomed them as they materialized. The quartet took cover, hiding behind plasma turrets.

Zadoya peered out, shooting aliens with her laser rifle. To her dismay, a dozen of them descended. Despite his pain, Yarasuro unsheathed his sword and charged toward the regiment. Swinging in an arc, he evaded a spiked tail and decapitated the creature. Using magic, Jedalia blinded the others with a flash of light. While they were dazed, Zadoya gunned down five of them.

The captain attempted to cast spells, yet failed to conjure anything. Her bodyguard saw her hiding and shook his head, continuing to slash his foes. After pirouetting to the side and avoiding the creatures' claws, he swiped his blade in multiple angles, slaying the remaining six aliens along the ramparts.

The quartet eliminated the brigade, but hundreds more attacked from multiple directions. Myriad gamma rays blasted the *Celestial*, its force field disrupted. Seeing this happen, Ashkaratoth finished consuming the nearby protostar and used its energy to temporarily transform himself into a monstrous entity larger than the spacecraft. His scaly body ablaze with nuclear fire, he uncurled his gargantuan form, spread his flaming wings, and flew toward the mothership. With one swift strike, he clawed it in half.

Thousands of passengers screamed as the starship broke open, hundreds of them sucked into space. Massive explosions ignited along the ramparts, forcing the knight, oracle, and lieutenant to leap off. The trio found themselves moving in the direction of the collapsing protostar. Everyone else who'd been sucked out of the starship drifted toward Ashkaratoth instead. At the sight of a multitude of people in space, Ashkaratoth spewed gamma flame from his snout at them.

Overwhelmed by the onslaught, Shirakaya gazed at the ashes of at least a thousand soldiers as though they were her family. *"No!"* she cried out at the top of her lungs, at last able to summon a barrage of meteors.

The bombardment obliterated dozens of koth'vurians. Though a formidable spell, it wasn't enough to impede the entire swarm. Ashkaratoth roared when he saw her still alive. Expanding his wings, he advanced and struck her. Pieces of dalikonium armor ripped off as she attempted to fight back. The extraterrestrial fiend consumed the remaining magical ions within her bruised body and seized Shirakaya, flinging her into the halved mothership. Smashing through the penitentiary's hull, she whimpered and fell unconscious.

IV
Unexpected Ally

An emergency shutter activated, sealing the prison. Severed in two, the ship's power fluctuated and ceased. Private Dojin, still imprisoned, wondered if he was hallucinating, the result of his extreme frustration at being in jail. Clearing his eyes of gunk, he stared blankly at his unconscious captain.

"Hey, toots," he called out. "What the hell's going on?"

The deafening explosions convinced Dojin that something terrible had happened. With the loss of power, his cell unlocked. He exited the room, checking Shirakaya's vital signs. Feeling a pulse, he turned her around. Looking at her, Dojin wore a grim expression. Not only was the captain's armor cracked from head to toe, but her face was suffused with gashes and bruises. Pieces of glass and metal were embedded in Shirakaya's cheeks and forehead, blood leaking from her nostrils.

"Holy shit," he muttered to himself.

Although in shock, he heard footsteps nearby. Dojin leaped to his feet as Xorvaj emerged from the shadows; he punched the private in the face, causing him to fall on the floor. Spitting out blood and wiping his lip clean, Dojin got back on his feet and raised his fists, glowering at the ghensoth.

"You'll have to kill me this time," Xorvaj said in a hoarse tone, scowling and clenching his rigid, knife-sharp beak.

"Suites me just fi—"

"It's pointless," Shirakaya murmured feebly. "We're all going to die anyway. Resisting the koth'vurians is futile."

"Koth'vurians?" Xorvaj said, snarling. "That's impossible. You're merely trying to trick me so you can imprison me again. I'll kill every last one of you pathetic humyns if I have to. No one is fooling me."

"The captain's a cunt, but she doesn't lie," Dojin said. "As for us dying, I'll be the judge of that."

Shirakaya groaned, barely able to move. "Their leader, Ashkaratoth, split our starship in half. That's why there's no power." She attempted to rise, only to fall on the floor. "We're also heading toward a black hole."

"*What?*" Dojin and Xorvaj said in unison.

"You heard me. Even if by a miracle we survive, the Ruzurai will have me court-martialed. The mission is over."

"The mission hasn't even started," Dojin said, lifting the captain and shaking her. "Pull yourself together, you egotistical bitch! We're getting out of this mess. Now, where is your yacht?"

Shirakaya didn't reply, drifting into a coma.

Dojin grumbled under his breath, turning his attention to Xorvaj. "You're one lucky terrorist that we're in a shitty situation, or else you'd be dead already."

"I am *not* a terrorist," barked Xorvaj, baring his teeth. "I am a revolutionist."

"That's what they all say," Dojin said, grabbing the captain's pistol from a slot on her plated greaves and aiming it at him. "If you want to get out alive, you'll do exactly what I say. Understood?"

"Pistols tickle me," Xorvaj retorted, swiping his claw and ripping the gun apart. Using his other hand, he seized Dojin by the neck and lifted him. "It is *you* who must obey my—"

A wall in the prison blew open as another explosion ignited, flame crawling through. The halved ship shook as though about to crumple; Xorvaj dropped the private and collapsed on his exoskeleton spine. "What in oblivion's name?"

"I suggest we put our differences aside for now and work together until this crazy shit is over," Dojin said, getting to his feet and extending a hand. "Agreed?"

The ghensoth concurred with a snort. "Carry your captain if you want her to survive," he said. "I'll focus on opening the doors." Before the private could respond, whether agreeing or not, Xorvaj charged through the brig's corridor and rammed his thorny head into a metal door, knocking it down. "This way."

Dojin had no argument with those results. He lifted the captain and placed her over one shoulder, following the brutish ghensoth. Turning a corner, a dozen koth'vurians stood before them, slicing prisoners with their claws. In seconds, the convicts lay dead. Hissing, the invaders launched gamma rays at the duo from their scaly palms.

Xorvaj had never seen such aliens before, but he sprang forth in their direction, fearless. Leaping in the air, he curled into a ball and rolled toward the brigade at incredible speed. The gamma rays hit his shielding exoskeleton cranium and spine. He collided with seven of them, crushing their bones in the process. Dojin, meanwhile, activated a force field via his KLD and ported a shotgun, charging it.

"Eat plasma, assholes," he said, blasting them.

The surges of energy from his weapon created thick holes in their bodies, killing them in an instant. Uncurling, the ghensoth rose fifteen feet high, and grasped a remaining alien, snapping its neck. The last koth'vurian in the area whipped Xorvaj with its tail; he grabbed it and yanked the alien toward his fist, punching its face. The intense impact cracked the creature's skull, blood seeping out of its snout and slit eyes.

"Impressive," Dojin said.

"We got lucky. Did you see what they launched at us from the palms of their hands? These beasts are imbued with potent magic." He examined the dead aliens closely. "In all my travels throughout the universe, I have never seen such monsters before. Can they really be koth'vurians?"

"You can change your career from psycho terrorist to detective *after* we get out of this nightmare. Got it, scumbag?"

The ghensoth snorted at Dojin's response, continuing to lead the way. He smashed apart another door, but the next one was enchanted with dalikonium: Authorized personnel only, which rendered his brute strength worthless. Instead, he improvised by ramming through a wall, exiting the penitentiary. Walking through the hole, they found themselves in a teleportation terminal littered with dead soldiers.

"What the fuck?" Dojin said. "This isn't a battle. It's a massacre."

"Don't let your guard down," the ghensoth said, sniffing. "There's something strange in the air."

A regiment of koth'vurians plunged from the ceiling, directing poisonous spittle at their prey. Droplets fell over Xorvaj, burning his forearm. He yelped in tremendous pain, running across the chamber to avoid more acid. Caught under fire, Dojin hid inside an X-Phaser capsule and placed the captain down. Peeking out, he aimed upward and blasted one of them. The alien slammed against the floor, dead. Others scuttled toward him from walls and pillars.

Within seconds, they were upon the private. Dojin, however, had already dropped a BG-49 grenade below his feet. The swarm was inches away from peeling his skin when it detonated, producing dense smoke and light so radiant it blinded them. Eyes closed, Dojin rolled away from the pod, porting a rifle with an incendiary clip and firing at random.

"Burn, motherfuckers!" Dojin said, opening his eyes.

Most of his targets dissolved into ashes. Only three remained. Before they could attack him, Xorvaj appeared within the smoke. He lifted one and broke its back by slamming its spine against his knee; then he punched another so hard its jaw snapped as Dojin simultaneously blasted it with his plasma shotgun. The last alien roared, pouncing on top of the private who pulled out a serrated knife, jamming the blade under its snout. Blood dripping over his collar, he kicked the koth'vurian off him.

"You're still alive?" Xorvaj said, astounded. "I thought they ripped out your intestines in that playpen."

"Those are teleportation pods, not playpens. And yeah, I'm still alive. Sorry if that disappoints you, but I plan on staying this way for a while." He returned to the capsule, placed a black-market energy module inside, and lifted the captain again. "If you want to live, I suggest you get your ass inside."

The ghensoth growled, bent down and entered the pod. His bulky frame caused the corners of the capsule to crack. By some miracle, he managed to squeeze in. Dojin tapped codes on a panel beside him, and they teleported out of the ruined chamber.

V

Imminent Destruction

Materializing in the torn hull of the wrecked docking bay, the trio were sucked out of the X-Phaser capsule. The private hesitated, in shock, but grabbed the captain and held her tight. Porting a helmet via kinetic link, Dojin activated a zitrogen tank. He then launched a PR-451 pre-stabilized grappling hook with its own gravity and projected it toward Xorvaj, catching him before he was pulled into outer space.

"Come on, you bulky asshole!"

As a ghensoth, Xorvaj had less than a minute before suffocating. Dojin clicked buttons on his kinetic link device's interface to haul in the ghensoth, whose extreme weight slowed his progress. It took the private a solid fifteen seconds to reel him. Unfortunately for him, Xorvaj had already fainted.

"You've gotta be fuckin' kidding me."

Dojin swiftly fitted the ghensoth with a breathing apparatus containing built-in ZiFi, digitally transferring his own zitrogen. Gripping both unconscious companions, he released some zitrogen; the pressure acted as a booster, launching them toward the clamped yacht.

Overhead, the private activated his magnetic boots, which brought him down to the ship's roof. Struggling to move, he placed the captain's hand along a hatchway's console to read her arcane DNA. The hatch opened. One by one, Dojin transported them. After ensuring their safety, he entered the vessel and sealed its access door from inside.

The yacht had its own gravity, allowing Dojin to climb down the ladder rather than struggling to maneuver himself in the air. At the main level, he strode to the cockpit and activated the vessel. Before he could gather his bearings and pilot the ship, he saw survivors teleport across the chamber: Ensign Narja, Chief Engineer Kazakuma, and Commander Ravdar. Because of the lack of gravity, they were immediately pulled out from the destroyed shuttle bay. And even though Kazakuma launched a grappling hook at the ship, he missed by an inch.

"Shit," the private said, seeing what happened to his comrades.

Before attempting a rescue, Dojin buckled Shirakaya to a

seat. Xorvaj was too heavy, so he improvised by strapping him against a pillar. Once they were secure, the private fidgeted with the vessel's controls, trying to operate them. He wasn't a pilot, but he had an idea how starships functioned. First, he made sure the thrusters worked. Releasing the clamps, he programmed the craft to fly toward the drifting trio. As soon as the yacht was alongside them, Dojin sprinted to the cargo bay and opened its side hatch via a nearby console.

"Hold on!" he shouted, hurling an SP-47 pre-stabilized grenade in their direction.

Detonating, a digital barrier formed around the trio, keeping them in temporary stasis like a cryogen pod. In nanoseconds, his KLD's sensor linked to the sphere-shaped field and brought it into the shuttle's cargo bay in much the same way as a tractor beam. As soon as they entered the chamber, Dojin sealed the hatch and deactivated the grenade's effect.

At first, they fought to catch their breath.

"Thank you so much for saving us," Narja said, panting. "I really thought we were going to die."

"Yes," Ravdar said, coughing. "Thank you."

"You're a sight for sore eyes," the engineer said. "If you don't mind my asking, how did you get out of jail?"

"It lost power when the ship ripped in half," Dojin said. "The force fields in our cells deactivated. I joined with Xorvaj to make it here. No other prisoner survived. In fact, apart from the captain, I'm not sure if anyone else is alive."

The commander began, "Is the captain all ri—"

"Wait a minute," interjected Kazakuma. "Did you just say that you worked with Xorvaj, the ghensoth terrorist?"

"It was that or get killed fending off the koth'vurians."

"So it *was* them that did this to us," Narja said.

"Koth'vurians?" Ravdar said, raising an eyebrow. "Did I miss something when I went on my honeymoon?"

"How can you be so brainwashed?" Kazakuma said, ignoring the commander. "I respect the captain, but believing that these aliens are koth'vurians is sacrilege. I can understand simple-minded people being gullible, but you? I'm disappointed in you, Dojin."

"I'm disappointed in you too, Chief," Dojin said, frowning as he gazed at the thermal windowpane.

Kazakuma glanced to where the private was looking and turned pale, staring at an alien behemoth with blazing scales, gargantuan wings, and spiral horns along its cranium. The others also watched in horror as the cosmic being destroyed the remnants of the *Celestial*. Spewing gamma flame from its snout, nothing remained. Narja ran to the cockpit and seized control of the yacht, flying away from the koth'vurians.

Dojin looked smug. He hated anyone making a fool of him. Seeing the engineer's frightened expression was priceless. "Still think I'm brainwashed?"

The engineer had no words. Even the commander was dismayed. Ravdar didn't know what had happened in the past few weeks, but because the captain claimed that these aliens were koth'vurians, he was a believer. Catching his breath, he got to his feet and turned his attention to the private.

"We need to inform the Ruzurai of this atrocity before that *thing* devours us," the commander said.

"Not until we're out of this nightmare," Dojin said. He turned away and joined Narja in the cockpit. "Use every available thruster and emergency booster, Ensign. If that protostar goes supernova, we're done."

"Aye," she said, activating the shuttle's boosters.

"By the Goddess, look!" Commander Ravdar said, pointing at a group of drifting combatants clad in spacesuits accompanied by a radiant woman whose spell enveloped them in a protective aura. "Our oracle. We must save her."

The private shook his head. "We're so fucking dead." Nevertheless, he returned to the cargo bay and spoke to Narja via kinetic link. "Ensign, open the hatch." Glancing at the speechless chief, he added, "You might want to equip a helmet and hold on to something tight."

Kazakuma hastened to comply as the hatch opened. Despite the disruption of gravity and air, Dojin aimed his hand at the oracle and launched another pre-stabilized grappling hook. When its flukes caught the oracle, she seized her companions—Zadoya and Yarasuro. The private clicked his KLD's interface twice, initiating the pre-stabilized gravity hook to return.

Hauling them into the cargo bay, the ensign sealed the hatch. He activated the shuttle's thrusters and emergency boosters, accelerating the starship to fifteen thousand kilometers an hour in seconds.

"I doubt we'll be alive much longer, but welcome aboard."

"There's no time to waste," the oracle said, getting to her feet. "We must rescue the captain."

"She's already here," Dojin said. "Can't you sense her?"

Jedalia ignored him, searching around the shuttle until she found the captain. Seeing her in such a debilitated condition, she broke down and cried. To her, it looked as though Shirakaya had died. Yet she still had a pulse. The oracle brought her over to a medical room in the corridor, casting various healing spells. All the crew members except Narja peeked inside. The oracle noticed them and used telekinesis to slam the door shut.

"Huh," uttered Dojin. "I guess that means all women are bitches."

"Watch your mouth, Private," Commander Ravdar said. "She's the oracle. Furthermore, that's the captain she's trying to save. And without her, we're definitely dead."

"Without her, I was doing just fine," Dojin retorted.

"Excuse me?" Ravdar said, infuriated. "Do you know who I am? I am your commanding officer and will not allow—"

Dojin punched the commander in the face, knocking him out.

"Stand down," Zadoya said, aiming her rifle at the private. "I was a fool to think you might have learned some humility while in prison."

"Gimme a break," Dojin said, waving his hand. "Anyone who feels the need to remind me that they're a commanding officer loses my respect. And this is not the time to pull a gun on me."

The lieutenant gritted her teeth. "Put your hands in the air.

I'm putting you in a cell on the lower level until Captain Shirakaya regains consciousness and decides what to do with you."

The private ignored her command, so she repeated, "Put your hands in the air. Now!"

"Or what?" he said, smirking. "You're gonna shoot me?"

"Um, guys," Narja said over the intercom, sounding panicky. "I think you'd better see this."

"No more squabbling," Yarasuro said, lowering the lieutenant's hand.

Dojin, still smug, turned and walked into the cockpit. "What's wrong, Ensign?"

She had no need to respond. He looked up at the screen and witnessed the newborn star collapsing and morphing into a black hole. The others joined them inside the pilot room, gawking at the sight. Even though Ashkaratoth and his minions went through the forming void without harm, humyns couldn't survive it. They felt the shuttle being pulled into the seemingly inescapable chasm.

"*Un-fucking-believable*," Dojin said.

"Is there anything we can do to break away from it?" Zadoya asked.

"I'm not sure," Narja said, flicking switches adjacent to the control panel. "Thrusters are at maximum power."

Dojin frowned. "What about the boosters?"

"I've *been* using them. The only reason why we're still in one piece is because of the captain's custom-built turbocharger."

"It seems only the grace of Maz'hura can save us," Yarasuro said.

Kazakuma looked pensive. "Not necessarily. It's extremely dangerous, but I may be able to overclock the turbocharger."

Most of the crew's eyes widened.

"What the hell can possibly be more dangerous than this?" Dojin said.

"Point taken. I should still warn you that if I succeed, the supercharged engine could overload."

"Then we blow up and die, right?" At the engineer's nod, Dojin added, "Same shit if you don't do anything. In fact, it'll be worse. That black hole will crush us alive! So get your ass to work."

Kazakuma flinched, rushing downstairs. He normally wouldn't take orders from a low-ranking soldier, but the private had a point. Reaching the engine, he used an ATS-31 arcane telekinetic screwdriver to loosen bolts on the floor and lifted the grating. He descended a small metal ladder leading to the turbocharger, where he switched around several wires and tweaked a few levers.

"Ensign," Kazakuma called out via kinetic link, "I made modifications. This isn't standard. You'll have to manually click on the dashboard's interface and adjust the ship's speed."

"Aye," she said.

With a few clicks on the display screen, Narja pulled up the acceleration tab and moved the cursor from twenty-four thousand kilometers an hour to fifty thousand. The sudden change of speed jolted the crew. Zadoya bumped into Dojin, who pushed her forward, glowering at her. She scowled back but did nothing, focusing on the windowpane to see if the shuttle was by any chance pulling away from the cosmic chasm of death.

At first, it proved difficult for them to determine whether they were moving forward. The engineer rejoined them, staring hard into space. With extreme difficulty, the vessel moved wescaria, away from the black hole.

The crew cheered in disbelief. Tears of joy filled Narja's eyes, relieved to live another day. Though less emotional, the others were also ecstatic.

"Great job, Kuma," Dojin said.

"Don't thank me yet. We'll need the engine to hold together until we're out of the star system."

"How long will that take?" Yarasuro asked.

"Checking," Narja said, setting a course to the adjacent star cluster. "With the trajectory I inputted, the ETA is fifteen minutes."

The crew was on edge, most of them praying for safe passage. They felt the reverberating power of the supercharged engine. The entire shuttle juddered. Even the chairs shook. Narja wished she could close her eyes but needed to ensure that the vessel remained on course. The only one in the group who appeared somewhat composed was the Templar, meditating.

Dojin scowled at him. "How can you meditate at a time like this?"

Breathing deeply, the knight took his time before he replied, "I wish to be at peace and remove fear from the ego."

The private had at least a dozen rebuttals in mind but remained speechless.

Meanwhile, the spacecraft reached the outskirts of Pargosis. Before leaving the star system, however, the engine malfunctioned. An alarm sounded, lights flickering wildly. Although the knight tried to remain calm, he failed miserably, disturbed by the crew shouting and cursing—not to mention Narja crying hysterically.

Waking up, Ravdar entered the cockpit, rubbing his jaw. "What in the twelve dimensions is happening?"

"Ensign, do something!" Dojin yelled, ignoring the commander.

"I can't!" she yelled back, fiddling with her controls. "The engine is completely dead. Do you understand? Dead!"

"Goddess, save us," Kazakuma muttered, strapped in his shaking seat.

Ravdar gazed at several red icons that appeared on the dashboard and gasped. "This can't be happening. I just got married."

"Think of solutions or shut the fuck up!" snapped Dojin.

The shuttle had escaped a black hole and made it across the would-be binary star system, but now flew aimlessly toward a planet that received little light from the primary sun in Pargosis. Caught up in the world's extreme surge of gravity because of its retrograde orbit, the yacht trembled so violently that the crew feared it would split in half at any moment. Yet the craft somehow held together, entering a twilight atmosphere.

"We still have power," Zadoya said. "It's just the engine that stopped. There must be something we can do to prevent our ship from crashing."

"Only the captain's magic can get us out of this situation," Yarasuro said.

"She's not the only one here with magic," Dojin responded. "Perhaps the oracle can do something to help us." He sprinted to the medical room, the crew following him. Opening the door, he was surprised to find the captain standing over Jedalia, who lay on a bed as if unconscious. "So, you made it."

Shirakaya sniffed, trying to hide her tears. She turned around, appearing healed. "Jeda sacrificed herself to save me."

"Goddess, have mercy," gasped Yarasuro.

With the exception of Dojin, the others were horrified. Yet they still had hope, believing the captain's magical powers would prevent the oncoming catastrophe, unaware of what the Templar knew.

"That's unfortunate," the private said, his eyes downcast. "But if you don't use your magic, her actions will have been in vain."

"Is that so?" Shirakaya said as she turned around, an expression of lunacy on her teary face. The others couldn't determine whether she'd burn Dojin to a crisp or heed his advice. She advanced, jostling past the tense crew. Entering the cockpit, she assessed the situation and gave out a laugh with a hint of madness.

"Did we miss something funny?" Dojin asked.

"I commend you for trying to save me. I'm promoting you to sergeant," the captain said. "In fact, it's a miracle you were all able to regroup and use my yacht. However, I'm afraid there's nothing I can do to assist you."

"Listen, lady," Dojin said, indifferent to the promotion, "you need to snap out of whatever mood swing you're in and use your *magic*."

"My *magic* is gone."

"What do you mean, gone?" Dojin replied, incredulous.

"Ashkaratoth devoured it from my soul," she said, drained

of hope. "It is as the legend says. Koth'vurians are able to consume others' power and use it against their enemies. My magic is gone."

"Something's not right," Yarasuro said in a pensive tone. "You were still able to use your gift after the first incursion."

"Perhaps the blue giant's radiation is the true culprit," Kazakuma said.

"No," the captain said sternly. "Don't you understand? Ashkaratoth cursed me. I felt it. I was on the brink of death. He depleted—"

The starship collided with countless branches, the crew juddering. Narja hit her head hard on the floor, passing out. Within seconds, the cockpit's windowpane cracked. Commander Ravdar struggled to the seat at the helm, braking in an attempt to decelerate or stop the shuttle. A crystallized branch penetrated the cracked glass, shattering it and spearing his chest. He gagged, blood squirting all over the dashboard.

An emergency shutter sealed the damaged pane, thwarting any poisonous gas in the environment. Despite severe denting from trees, the shutter remained intact. Without warning, the spacecraft plowed into a murky swamp. The collision knocked the shrieking crew off their feet, slamming them against the grating.

Magical Wisdom

Light and Darkness exist without moralizing. They are neither holy nor evil. Beware that even the power of illumination can become a malevolent force. Just so, darkness can be a savior. They are merely two sides of the same eternal coin. If you embrace these delicate powers, your mind and soul shall be cleansed. Abandoning one for the other, however, will cause turmoil. Too much obsession with white magic can soften the heart, keeping my children ignorant. Yet excessive exposure to the dark arts is equally unhealthy for the spirit. Death, for example, is a necessary event that must be respected in the cycle of existence. To undo death will never bring your loved ones peace. Set them free so they may experience rumsira and be reborn in the afterlife.

Apophthegm of the Divine 31:97

Chapter Eight

Witch of Larjan

I
Agony

Shirakaya groaned, her back throbbing. The oracle had healed her by means of sacrifice, yet she felt terrible twinges throughout her body after the crash. Moving her head, she glanced around and saw that most of her crew lay unconscious. Aside from her, only the chief engineer and sergeant were conscious. Dojin got to his feet, groaning. Kazakuma, on the other hand, had shrapnel embedded in his thigh.

The captain analyzed her yacht's damages as the engineer yelped in pain. Looking up, she found Ravdar sprawled in an armchair, a branch through his chest, blood leaking from his ruptured spine to the floor. Narja lay in a corner, her face severely bruised. A seat, ripped out of place, lay on top of the lieutenant. Looking around, Shirakaya saw her bodyguard in the hallway, unconscious.

"Sergeant," the captain called out, "I need you to assess the ship's damages and find out where we are."

"I'll do it only because I want to," he said, leaving the cockpit.

She cursed under her breath at his response and fixed her eyes on the engineer. "Chief, are you all right? Talk to me."

"I can't move," he said weakly. "I'm losing a lot of blood."

"Hold on just a bit longer," she said, standing up. "I'll get a first aid kit from the medical room and help you."

She grabbed the armchair on top of the lieutenant and pushed it aside. She left the flight deck and entered the medical chamber where her lover lay lifeless. Seeing her dead was unreal. She never thought Jedalia would sacrifice herself to save her. The captain contained her grief, lifting her lover up from the floor. She then placed her on a hospital bed in the back of the room.

"Why?" she muttered, gently stroking the oracle's golden hair. "Why in oblivion did you save me?"

Shirakaya gripped her chest, wheezing. She wanted to crawl away into the shadows, never to be seen again. The mistakes her brother made seemed trivial compared with the number of people who died because of her arrogance. Shirakaya wished he was here with her, despite how much she wanted to hide.

A long silence fell, her reverie broken only by the engineer's unnerving cry of pain. The captain gasped, searching for anesthetics or any form of medicine. Entering a lavatory in the medical chamber, she checked the cabinets and found a first aid kit. She grabbed it and rushed back to Kazakuma, whose blood soaked the flight deck's grating.

"What took so long?" he rasped.

"I'm sorry," she said, opening the kit. "Everything is a mess in there. And it wasn't easy for me to see Jeda dead again."

Kazakuma could hardly believe that she apologized, and almost failed to nod at the mention of the oracle's demise. In fact, he didn't even catch the captain referring to her as "Jeda" and this wasn't the first time she'd called her by that nickname in public. The engineer's mouth agape, he turned his head and clenched his teeth.

"This will hurt," the captain said, showing him a syringe.

"I know needles are the worst, but it's supposed to numb the pain." With her other hand, she stuffed a thick handkerchief in his mouth. "You should bite down on this."

"Please hurry," he mumbled, his eyes barely open.

She nodded, sticking the needle in his thigh. The engineer screamed at the top of his lungs. After waiting one minute, she opened a bottle of san-parba alcohol and poured its contents over Kazakuma's leg whose frayed skin sizzled. Again, he screamed horrifically despite the anesthetic.

His dreadful howl woke the others. Shirakaya shook her head, with no choice but to use another syringe. To her relief, his cry of pain wasn't as bad as the first time. Her crew moved around her as she concentrated on removing shrapnel from the engineer's mutilated thigh.

"If only my sister were here," Shirakaya said, aware that she was doing a terrible job. "She may not be a professional nurse, but she's infinitely better than me."

"Goddess, no," Narja said, her voice charged with emotion on seeing what had happened to Ravdar.

"My lady," Yarasuro said, "I'm relieved you are all right. It seems to be the only good thing that's come out of this tragedy." She didn't respond, so in silence he watched her struggle to pull pieces of metal from the engineer's leg. "Is there anything I can do to help?"

"I ordered Sergeant Dojin to assess my yacht's damages and find out where exactly we are," she said without so much as a glance. "He should've been back by now."

"He's not reliable, Captain," Zadoya said.

"Look around you, Lieutenant. Do you see anyone else fit to take orders? Or did you miss the branch embedded in the commander's chest?" Her tone made Zadoya gulp noisily. "As the sergeant hasn't returned, I want all three of you to search for him."

"Aye," they said in unison, leaving the cockpit.

II
What Lurks Therein

With a delicate touch, Shirakaya continued removing shrapnel from the engineer's swollen wound with the aid of a medical laser. As for the pieces deep inside his skin, she left them alone, bandaging his leg. As she helped him, she heard a commotion.

The noise sounded as though it came from outside.

"Did you hear that?"

Kazakuma nodded. "Perhaps they found Dojin. Listen, you've done more than enough for me, Captain. I don't even feel pain anymore. Leave me here and make sure the others are safe."

The captain pondered for a moment. "I'll be back for you."

Exiting the cockpit, Shirakaya strode across the shuttle's corridor while equipping new dalikonium armor via her KLD. Unlike her previous spacesuit, it had a burgundy tint. When she sealed her helmet, the zitrogen air tank along the back piece of her breastplate initiated. She then climbed a ladder leading to a hatch and opened it.

A twilight sky greeted her when she got to her feet on the roof. She heard an eerie chorus of insects and nocturnal wildlife, surrounded by pogatarn giants—trees that not only produced mud at their roots but also stood between sixty to a hundred feet high.

"Hello?" she called out to the swamp. "Yaro? Ensign Narja? Lieutenant Zadoya? Sergeant Dojin? Can anyone hear me?"

She quickly established that the vessel was forty percent submerged and covered in mud, not to mention gradually sinking. Alarmed and unable to see her crew, she took off her helmet, taking a deep breath. The only positive element about the situation was that according to her KLD's planetary scan, the air was breathable.

Thousands of vines hung from the boughs of trees. Although the air smelled clean, it proved difficult for her to see ahead through the dense mist. Decaying leaves littered the moist ground, some floating in the grimy water. And at the base of the trees, massive roots grew clumps of ligen—flowerless plants akin to moss except they were poisonous and colored gray. The shady environment was an eerie yet captivating sight to Shirakaya, both creepy and somewhat mystical.

As much as the captain wanted to hide here for a while, she had to locate her subordinates and return to civilization. She turned around to scout behind her, only to be greeted by Xorvaj's fist. Blood spattered from her lips as she fell off the vessel into the swamp. Water splashed about, her armor saturated and full of gunk. Gazing up, she spotted her crew imprisoned in vines above.

"I'm impressed with your subordinates. They know how to keep quiet when claws are at their throats," he growled. "I've been waiting a long time for this."

Shirakaya felt the tremors as the ghensoth leaped off the roof, stomping hard on the wet soil. He lifted the dismayed captain with one hand and ruthlessly threw her against the craft's hull, denting it. She groaned in pain and tried to stand. Before she could, he kicked her face with his scute-covered foot. Failing to retaliate against his brutality, Xorvaj tied her to a crystallized branch using one of the myriad vines in the swampy jungle.

"You won't get away with this, Xorvaj," Dojin said.

"Oh, shut up, you hypocritical scoundrel," Zadoya said. "You're the idiot who helped him escape."

"Well, excuse me for trying to survive, *Your Highness*."

"By working with a psycho terrorist?" Zadoya said, raising her voice. "You disgust me more each day."

"Enough!" barked Xorvaj. "If I were truly a terrorist, you would already be dead. Your leaders always ignored our requests. I did what I had to do. It was for a noble cause. We weren't even going to harm your children. All we wanted was the Ruzurai to help us. Instead, you killed my comrades and ruined any prospect of my homeworld being saved."

"You talk too much," Dojin said. "What's done is done. Leave us here and take our ship if you want. Just don't pontificate. I hate that shit."

"I'm not a mindless thief," the ghensoth said.

Yarasuro squinted at him. "Then, if you don't mind my asking, what exactly are you planning to do with us?"

"My race believes in 'The Remuneration of Saliek,'" he said. "Saliek was once a demigod among my people. Yet demons grew jealous of his power and attempted to make him suffer. They intended to kill him. In time, he turned the tide and ended up destroying them instead."

"Is there a point to this boring story?" Dojin said.

The ghensoth scowled. "The point is that we honor Saliek and follow his example. What our enemies do to us, we return the favor. Since you had me imprisoned, I am doing the same to you. Nothing shall change unless your leader begs for forgiveness and grants me immunity. Akin to Saliek, I shall triumph."

"No matter what happens, our careers are over," the captain said. "Just kill us and get it over with already."

"*What?*" Dojin said. "Have you lost your mind? Do you realize how difficult it was dragging your ass out of Celestial while fighting those shape-shifting fuckers? No, bitch, you ain't dying anytime soon."

"Goddess, help us," Narja said.

"Please don't listen to our captain," Yarasuro said to the ghensoth. "She lost her oracle in the crash and is grieving."

Xorvaj cackled at them. "You're all pathetic. How you were able to outsmart and defeat my militia while aboard the Eternimus is beyond me. But one thing is certain. I *will* complete the sacred Remuneration, until you suffer as I have suffered. Nobody makes decisions for me. I am Xorvaj, leader of Urvantak, and shall be—"

Numerous tentacles sprang out from within the water. One of them clutched Xorvaj's arm, heaving him. Although the ghensoth struggled and made an effort to overpower it, another caught his leg. He dropped, more tentacles grabbing him. The crew members watched, aghast. Xorvaj roared at the top of his lungs, bringing his seized arm over to his snout. He bit the spongy tentacle, its flesh shredding.

Vociferous screeches filled the group's ears as an orgavour, a camouflaged juggernaut creature, surfaced from the marsh. Mud and gunk dripped off its blubbery form, its stalk-shaped legs lifting between pogatarn giants' roots. The beast yanked Xorvaj and held him just beneath its mouth, ready to feast on him.

"Is this what happened to Saliek at the end of his crusade?" Dojin said, smirking. "If so, this is the only interesting part of your story."

Snorting, the ghensoth hurled a knife through the sergeant's vines.

Though startled, Dojin lowered himself to the yacht's roof from the ripped vines. Clicking his KLD, he ported a PSG-549 plasma shotgun. Charging it to maximum power, he fired once. The supercharged beam blasted several tentacles, all of which released the ghensoth.

"Over here, you slimy fuck."

The creature screeched, its unharmed appendages retracting before it launched them again, this time toward the sergeant. He rolled aside, blasted a tentacle, jumped off the ship, and landed in the swamp while firing at another limb. Two appendages missing, the orgavour hesitated.

"Free us!" shouted Zadoya.

Dojin heard the lieutenant but disregarded her. He waited until the ghensoth joined him, handed over his plasma shotgun, and ported an LR-743 laser rifle for himself. Loading it with an energy clip, he launched its beam across the vines above, splitting them and freeing his comrades. Xorvaj fired the shotgun at the monster while Dojin climbed up the vessel, joining the others who promptly ported weapons.

The beast shielded itself with its tentacles and unexpectedly lunged at them. Its huge pincers grasped the shuttle and rammed it over to deeper water. The current immediately took Shirakaya's yacht. The creature withdrew and attacked from a distance. A multitude of enormous trees along the stream hampered the crew from targeting the hideous but intelligent fiend.

Separated from Xorvaj, the soldiers fended for themselves as more tentacles lurched at them. Yarasuro struck his sword in numerous powerful arcs, slicing a great many limbs and severing one. Choosing rifles, Shirakaya and her soldiers blasted through the tentacles and pierced the monster's belly; pieces of slime blew off and formed another orgavour.

"You've gotta be fuckin' kidding me," Dojin said, reloading his laser rifle with an energy cartridge.

Narja wheezed. "My goodness."

"What should we do, Captain?" Zadoya asked.

"Use the hatch," Shirakaya said, glancing beneath their feet. "The hull should protect us from the creatures' attacks. Perhaps if we're patient, the water will bring us somewhere safer. Then we can figure out how to recapture that terrorist."

Together they reentered the ship via its hatch and returned to the cockpit where Kazakuma lay.

"What in the cosmos is going on out there?"

"Indigenous creatures are preying on us," the captain said. "But the stream is pulling us away from their habitat, so we might get out of this yet."

"How can a stream pull such a weighty vessel?" the engineer asked.

"You're asking the wrong people," Narja said. "I just pilot it."

"Weren't you supposed to be the chief engineer of Celestial?" Dojin said. "Shouldn't you know the answer?"

Kazakuma brooded. "I'm an engineer, not a physicist. I mean, it's possible if I examined the water and atmosphere with my KLD that I'd be able to figure something out, but I have never heard of a current pulling a ship down like this. If anything, the ship's buoyancy allows it to float on water."

"Weird," Narja said.

"How's your leg?" the captain said, changing the subject.

"I can feel it, but there's no pain." He paused for a moment and went on, "Take me to the cargo bay hatch. I want to take a reading on the water."

"Are you sure?" the captain said.

"With all due respect, this wound doesn't make me useless yet. Lieutenant, put that new arm to good use and pick me up."

"Okay," she said, lifting the engineer and placing him astride her shoulders.

The lieutenant carried Kazakuma down a ladder and took him to the cargo bay. Inside, she laid him by the hatch and opened it. Water gushed inside. Soaked, the engineer rolled aside while Zadoya swiftly pressed a button on the wall to seal the hatch again. With great difficulty, it closed.

"How are we sinking?" Narja asked.

"Give me a moment," Kazakuma said, examining the fluid inside the cargo bay via his kinetic link device. As he scanned, he was shocked to see a few empty cartons in the bay unfolding in the water. This alone caused him to curse. "I have bad news."

Shirakaya felt a knot form in her stomach. "What's wrong, Chief?"

"This liquid is filled with bikophric quomafoam. It's a much heavier substance than most elements usually found in water."

"Who gives a shit?" Dojin said.

Yarasuro stopped himself from laughing. "I'm sure what he means is, how does this affect us?"

"I was just getting to that. And believe me, Sergeant, you're going to give a shit. These chemicals are the cause of the shuttle not only being pulled but also sinking. If we don't do something, the vessel will sink until it's at the bottom. And if the bikophric ions in the water can heave this shuttle, imagine what will happen to us."

"We'll drown," Narja said, horrified.

"If that's the case, my yacht needs to be repaired fast."

"Give me a fucking break," Dojin said, waving a hand in protest. "Screw your ship. We need to get the hell off this shithole."

"By the stars, you have a filthy mouth," Zadoya said. "Can't you speak one sentence without cursing?"

"Go fuck yourself, Lieutenant."

"Your bickering isn't helping," Shirakaya said, irked. "Listen closely." Silence descended, broken only when she added, "No more banging. The beasts have stopped attacking. Perhaps they are aware of the water. I don't want to leave my yacht behind..."

Zadoya raised a brow. "But?"

"But the sergeant does have a point," Shirakaya added,

ignoring the smug expression on Dojin's face. "Until we find a solution, it's best we get on top of the ship and avoid the water at all cost."

The others agreed, following their captain to the shuttle's roof. Although the beasts were nowhere in sight, most of the vessel was submerged at the outskirts of the dreary swamp. The crew looked ahead, realizing that the bubbling stream was carrying them to a river; they had less than a minute to abandon ship before the tributary watercourse would take them far beyond land and into the asphyxiating depths of oblivion.

"The current is insane," Kazakuma said, using the lieutenant as a crutch to stand. "I've never seen anything like this before."

Shirakaya, looking haggard, nodded in agreement.

"There must be something we can do," Zadoya said.

"Kuma, do you know if the shuttle's completely dead?" Dojin asked. "Is there anything you can do to fix it?"

"I'm afraid there's nothing I can do at the moment. The engine's our only ticket out of here, but it malfunctioned. In fact, we're lucky that it failed and didn't explode on us. We'll need a new power source."

"You mean like xylithum crystals?" Zadoya said, gazing at the crystallized branches with hope in her eyes.

"No," the engineer said, sighing. "Those are used for fuel. What we need is a new engine or an arcane incubator." He noticed Dojin open his mouth and added, "In case you're wondering what that is, it's essentially a device powered by a trapped soul fused with magic. Problem is, it's borderline illegal and impossible for us to obtain."

"So why the hell did you even mention it?" snapped Dojin.

"Excuse me?" Kazakuma said, frustrated. "I merely answered your question and explained myself."

"Should we jump?" Narja asked.

"I don't think we have a choice," Shirakaya said. "We only have a few seconds left before we're dragged into the main river. It's not too bad a drop. Chief, think you can make it?"

"Let's find out."

The captain grimaced. "All right, jump on a count of three," she said, pausing for a brief moment. "One. Two. *Three*!"

She and her crew leaped off the shuttle. The sextet plunged onto the wetland, covered in mud and leaves. Falling short, Kazakuma landed at the edge of the stream. He gasped in pain and shrieked as the current seized him.

"Help!" he screamed.

The lieutenant reached out with her synthetic arm, missing him by a hair. "*No!*" she cried out, feeling helpless.

"Chief!" yelled Shirakaya.

In seconds, his body sank to an area that revealed a subterranean river. He was so frightened, even the mesmerizing sight of a fast flowing river at the seabed didn't faze him. As feared, the second current pulled him. Kazakuma panicked, bubbles coming out of his mouth; he had less than one minute before drowning.

Extending a hand, he reached for the ship's outdoor ladder. Though the force of bikophric quomafoam held him down, he fought against it and scaled the vessel. But when he reached the top, it was too late. The shuttle had already reached the parent river. He took a deep breath and reentered the shuttle, sealing the hatch from inside. Swallowed by the river, the ship sank into utter darkness.

III
Dark Horizons

Powerless, the crew watched in horror as Kazakuma drowned. Dojin was the only one in the group who turned away, his eyes downcast. Narja had no words; she simply dropped to the mucky ground with a look of despair.

"Goddess, have mercy on his soul," Yarasuro said, kneeling in prayer.

"I could have prevented this," Zadoya said, crushing the

moist soil in her palms. "It's all my fault."

"Don't blame yourself, Lieutenant," the captain said. "At least you tried."

Another wave of dread gripped Shirakaya. While the others mourned the loss of their comrade, she was much more concerned about losing her spacecraft. She wondered how they were they supposed to return home from an unknown planet filled with dangerous wildlife and strange weather.

"Well, this changes things," Zadoya said, slumping against a tree.

"I just can't believe what happened," Narja said. "We not only lost Kazakuma but have no way of getting home. I mean, does anyone have a plan?"

"My only plan is surviving," Dojin said.

"I can't argue with that," Yarasuro said. "Perhaps we should start by getting away from this region. We don't want to come across that creature again."

"Agreed," Shirakaya said. "Let's travel east and see where that takes us."

The crew concurred, following the captain. They kept their weapons raised, scouting ahead. Numerous trees filled the wetland. Giant roots too big to cut blocked the quintet's path, slowing them down as they clambered over. Dojin took the rear, protecting their flank and checking for pursuers.

An hour of hard trekking took them to an area in the marsh blanketed in dense mist. Barely able to see in the bog forest, the quintet moved with caution. They heard a loud chorus of insects, as well as the flapping of wings in the sky. Shirakaya sensed her colleagues were rapidly losing hope of finding a safe haven.

In time, the mist cleared. Just when the crew felt relieved about that, they stumbled upon a ravine. Gazing below, the squad viewed a pit so dark that none were able to see the bottom. Narja nervously backed away. Even the lieutenant appeared distressed, glancing around to see if there was another way around the abyss.

"It seems we'll have to climb," Dojin said.

"Why?" Narja said. "It's probably safer if we go south."

"If my memory serves me well, I think that's where the beast dwells," Yarasuro said with composure. Seeing her appear fretful, he added, "Don't be scared, Ensign. I am your shield."

"The vines look strong," Zadoya said. "We can use them to swing across."

"I don't like this any more than you, Narja," the captain said. She exhaled heavily. "Let's get this over with."

They climbed the roots of a pogatarn giant that curved upward, high above the damp wetland. The quintet gripped its bark and warily scaled the trunk. At twenty feet high, they were able to stand on branches. Gripping thick creepers adjacent to iridescent crystals, the crew separated them into thinner vines with hunting knives.

Beginning with Dojin, they held on tight and jumped, swinging across the abyss. Narja was the only one whose vine split just before reaching the other side. She shrieked at the top of her lungs, falling. Extending her prosthetic arm, Zadoya grabbed the ensign. With little effort, she lifted Narja and laid her on the cracked ground.

Narja lay panting, astonished to be alive. "Thank you."

"You're welcome," Zadoya said, smiling at her. Standing up, she examined the area. "Should we keep going east?"

"Yes," the captain said.

Her subordinates were hungry and tired, but they rallied and continued their journey eastward. At first, Shirakaya feared the trees would never decrease in number, but her group encountered fewer in this region. Mist blinded them again, thickening with each step they took. The charcoal clouds darkened further, severely laden. Thunder boomed and lightning streaked the sky.

"That's it," Narja said, "I can't go any farther. Every part of me hurts,"

"I'm sure we're almost out of the marsh," the captain said. "Just hang on a little longer and then we can rest for the night."

"It's been dark ever since we arrived," Dojin said. "I don't think daylight exists on this shitty rock. In fact, I'm not even sure it was smart traveling so far from the ship. Getting away from that insane monster was necessary for survival, but what if the military comes looking for us?"

"The Celestial was destroyed in the opposite quadrant of Pargosis," Shirakaya said. "There's no way they would think to look here. Besides, the yacht never belonged to the military. It was a gift from my parents when I graduated."

"I see," Dojin said. "But even if it's a private yacht, it's supposed to have a homing beacon for emergencies."

Zadoya's eyes lit up. "If that's true, we should definitely rest here."

"Perhaps we should also keep our radars on and see if anything appears," Yarasuro said, activating his via KLD. "I don't think it's farfetched that the military would send a search party here, especially since Captain Tor is technically still missing."

"First we need to discover where we are," the captain said, viewing her KLD's built-in radar. "It seems we're on planet Nobia in a continent called Larjan."

"If you can get that info, why can't we contact the capital?" Narja asked.

"The bandwidth in our devices isn't enough to establish a connection to the TDE," the captain said. "We need to be near satellites with ZiFi so our signals can be amplified beyond this galaxy."

"That's telecommunications 101," Dojin said. "Shouldn't you know that, Ensign?"

"Well, excuse me for not being accustomed to crashing on a foreign world across the universe."

Dojin chuckled.

"It's not funny, Sergeant," Zadoya said.

"It is to me."

"That's enough," the captain said. "We need to work together, soldiers. We're all having difficulty. Even me. I almost died today. Not to mention we lost thousands of our comrades, including my…our oracle." She paused. "Try to relax and get some rest. Tomorrow we'll travel closer to where my yacht sank and see if anyone comes to rescue us."

The crew made camp by a tree, porting stored food rations from the databanks on their kinetic link devices. No one had jamna, a fluid vital to their health, so they settled for water from beneath their feet. It tasted muddy, but it was better than dehydrating. Afterward, the knight used his baskino sword to slice off twigs and small branches from the nearby tree. Zadoya helped him start a bonfire. The quintet snuggled near the flames and fell asleep.

IV
Evil Rising

Narja woke up to a twilight morning. Rain fell from the swollen clouds and splattered on the soil throughout the bog forest. The fire had died out, smoke mingling with mist.

"Another miserable day," Narja muttered.

Feeling somewhat refreshed, she decided to scout the area while her comrades slept. Just a few yards ahead, she stepped on something that cracked. Unable to see through the fog and dull light, Narja knelt down and grabbed something rigid. Intrigued, she lifted it and realized it was a bone.

A skeletal hand seized her ankle. She shrieked, stomping on it with her other foot. The ensign heard it smash and broke into a run, screaming as she returned to her companions. Flinching while getting to their feet, they raised their weapons, targeting the frenzied ensign.

"Why the hell are you screaming like a lunatic?" Dojin inquired, reloading his rifle and yawning.

"Something grabbed my foot."

"Did you see it?" Zadoya asked.

"You wouldn't believe me. I must be hallucinating. That's the only explanation. But there's definitely some kind of creature in the mist."

"If that's the case then arm yourself, Ensign," Shirakaya

said.

Narja gave a nod and scaled the roots of a pogatarn giant. At the top, she summoned an SR-153 sniper rifle and inserted a fire clip into it. The other soldiers maintained their positions and targeted the dense mist with their guns. Sword in hand, Yarasuro advanced. After a few paces, he heard snapping sounds.

Through the darkness, a lanky figure rose from the saturated loam. The crew stiffened, trying to accept what their eyes saw. From out of the gloom, a skeleton emerged, wielding an axe. It resembled a humyn frame, but many times larger.

"Impossible," the knight muttered.

Seconds later, they heard more cracking sounds, accompanied by the crunch of footsteps. Through the mist, at least a dozen more figures appeared. These shadowy forms offered no mystery: the soldiers knew that the silhouettes were more skeletons. Groaning and armed with deadly blades, the undead marched toward the incredulous soldiers.

"There is dark magic here," Shirakaya said. "We are not alone. Someone or something on this planet is conjuring the dead. Eradicate them!"

Dojin was the first to open fire with incendiary bullets, his targets sizzling and breaking apart. The skeletal fiends produced ear-piercing screeches and abruptly charged. Yarasuro parried their strikes, riposting between attacks.

"Templar, get back!" Shirakaya commanded.

Discretion being the better part of valor, he obeyed; there were too many undead for him to handle alone. The soldiers unleashed a bombardment from a distance. Zadoya's laser gun penetrated their already fractured ribs, turning bones to dust. Shooting from high above, the armor-piercing rounds from Narja's sniper rifle shattered their skulls. Shirakaya fired two pistols loaded with frost clips, destroying a couple while freezing others in place. Transformed into slabs of ice, Yarasuro sprinted to them and shattered them with his sword.

"This is insane," Dojin said.

Narja wheezed. "So you *do* see them. I'm not losing my

mind, right?"

"Of course not," Zadoya said. "But how is this possible?"

"Black magic," Yarasuro said, examining the shattered fiends.

"There must be a necromancer somewhere in Larjan," the captain said. "That's the only logical explanation."

A coarse voice announced, "You are correct."

The crew swiveled, their fixed eyes to the north. The massive silhouette of an alien stood before them. Stomping forward, the creature revealed itself to be none other than Xorvaj. The quintet aimed their weapons at him as an army of indigenous beings emerged from the dense mist.

They surrounded the humyns, armed with swords, axes, spears, and bows. The eerie denizens had indigo skin and were bald by nature, their irises and pupils completely black. A few of them were dressed with only linen cloths covering their genitals. These barbaric creatures had tattoos covering their muscular bodies. The rest of the army wore heavy plated armor and rode on glyndals, husky two-legged beasts more sentient and intelligent than most animals throughout the Ensar universe, whose fleeces and tresses masked their skin.

"You are surrounded," the ghensoth said. "If you want to live, I suggest you surrender by holstering your weapons."

The crew calculated their chances before capitulating.

"*Ju-pa lei'sa bal'yum vak-qu?*" the indigenous leader said, clad in golden armor and saddled on an ivory glyndal. "Are these the traitors you told us about?"

Shirakaya frowned. "Traitors?"

"Yes," Xorvaj said, sneering at the soldiers. "Hear me, humyns. The jorga are my allies. Hundreds of cycles ago, my ancestors discovered Nobia in the outskirts of Torpo Giayan and helped them establish a civilization. Since then, they have acknowledged us as demigods. If you disobey me, they will not hesitate to kill you. Obey me, and I shall absolve you of your past transgressions."

"I'll convert to whatever bullshit you want me to believe in," Dojin said. "Just get me the hell off this rock."

"Not so fast," Xorvaj said. "As you have guessed, the jorga are troubled by a witch who plagues their kingdom and they are in need of champions to eliminate her. The clans have gathered together but have yet to confront the witch."

The indigenous leader looked about. "Who among you is in command?"

"I am. My name is Shirakaya, and these are my soldiers: Yarasuro, Dojin, Zadoya, and Narja. We represent the Tal'manac Order located in Copia Deiga."

"We know little of the outer continents," he said, failing to understand that she was from a different galaxy. "I am Gran'dine Meyvor, King of Larjan. Despite your past sins, I have heard tales about your race of warriors battling against the demonic koth'vurians that threaten our sacred stars. Will you help us?"

Shirakaya appeared intrigued. "What exactly has the witch done?"

"Magic once prospered in my kingdom," Meyvor said. "Eladoris, the witch, gave magic a terrible name and I was forced to forbid it. In return, she cursed our land by making it infertile. Each passing day, my people die of starvation. And now, she raises our fallen warriors from the dead. She must be purged."

"I see," Shirakaya said, grateful for the first and only time that her arcane gift had dissipated. "We are few in numbers compared with your glorious army, but our weapons are powerful. You have our allegiance, Your Majesty."

The jorga cheered with delight.

"It warms both my hearts to know that such fine warriors shall fight by our side," the king said. "You have our eternal thanks, humyn. I am sure the legendary Xorvaj will bless you a great deal in battle."

"Beyond any doubt," Shirakaya said, giving the ghensoth a murderous look. "By the way, before we leave, may I have a word with your demigod?"

King Meyvor raised an eyebrow and answered, "That is our Lord's decision."

"A carefully thought-out battle plan is needed to defeat the witch," Xorvaj said, lowering his weapon. "Permission granted."

"Marvelous," the king said. "While you deliberate, we'll reconnoiter the region and slay more abominations that plague my kingdom." With deliberate gentleness, he tweaked the reins of his armored glyndal in a signal for the animal to move. Meyvor's steed scuttled eastward into the mist as he shouted, "Onward, brave warriors of Larjan! The witch dies today!"

The clans cheered again, riding beside their king. In the meantime, Shirakaya and her subordinates gathered around Xorvaj.

"Yes?" he rumbled.

"I'll admit, your demigod story was amusing," the captain said. "Whether or not your ancestors were honorable, the fact is you shamed them when you decided to hijack Eternimus. I hope you realize that nothing you do today, however noble it may seem to these gullible people, will grant you immunity."

"That sounds an awful lot like a threat," Xorvaj said.

"It's simply a fact," Shirakaya said. "You committed a heinous crime and jeopardized the lives of innocent teenagers. You're not going to get away with anything."

"I'm done with your condescending shit," Dojin said. "You wouldn't be alive right now if it weren't for him. The two of us busted our balls getting your unconscious ass out of Celestial, which, in case your fucked-up mind forgot, was obliterated because of you. Oh, yeah, I forgot to mention the obvious: Xorvaj hates koth'vurians too. And apparently, the jorga do as well. If you truly want to annihilate Koth'fuckra, you'll need their help."

"This soldier of yours is smart," Xorvaj said.

Zadoya scowled. "Of course you'll defend each other because you're both amoral cretins and should be sentenced—"

"That's enough, Lieutenant," the captain said, sitting on a tree stump.

"*What?*" Zadoya looked as though she just witnessed the death of her family. "But, Captain, you can't possibly be taking their side."

"I'm tired," Shirakaya said, her voice faint. "I'm really, really tired. I try to do the right thing. At least what I think is right. Except that even *I* went against the law by commanding without magic. I knew the risks and because of my arrogance, the four of you are all that remains of my crew. I'm not fit to command a starship. And if we ever return home, the Ruzurai *will* court-martial me."

"My blade is still yours until that happens," Yarasuro said.

The captain nodded in gratitude, silent for a moment. "What's the point to all this, ghensoth? I know you're not a hero or martyr. There must be something you'll get out of this."

"Ah," uttered Xorvaj, his horizontal pupils dilating. "Now you're thinking. But it requires you to perform something that some people may consider to be illegal."

Zadoya shook her head. "Don't listen to him."

"For the Goddess's sake, can you stop?" snapped Narja. "The captain is willing to listen, so respect her decision."

"I can't believe this."

"Do you have a brilliant idea, Lieutenant?" Not getting a response, the captain sighed and turned her attention back to the ghensoth. "Let me hear it."

"The crime is two words. Arcane incubator," Xorvaj said.

"I'm game," Dojin said, charging his firearm. "Let's gun down that cunt from hell, zap her bitch ass soul into a crystal, plug it into the shuttle's engine, and get the fuck out of this medieval circus."

"What a fantastic idea," Zadoya said. "Oops! I forgot. The ship is eighty million feet under the sea."

"It can't be *that* deep," Narja said.

"She's being sarcastic, Ensign," Dojin said with a grin. "Anyway, our spacesuits are programmed to work underwater. We can use them to locate the ship. But let's worry about one thing at a time."

"Agreed," Xorvaj said. "What say you, Captain Shirakaya?"

Shirakaya crossed her arms. "You're my conscience now,

Yaro. What do you believe we should do?"

The knight lowered his eyes and took a deep breath. "I am your bodyguard, Captain. It is not my place to make decisions. My responsibility is to protect you." He noticed how troubled she looked and promptly went on, "However, I can suggest things. If you're asking for my advice, I humbly suggest we help these people. The reward will be that we imprison the vile witch and use her power as a means to an end. Remember, black magic is not evil. Even one of the divine Ruzurai is a necromancer."

"True," she said. "I suppose the arcane incubator can be seen as a temporary prison until we return to the capital."

"It's now or never," Xorvaj said. "This is the first time in history that all the jorga clans in the Kingdom of Larjan have joined together. If we are to confront the witch, I suggest we leave now to catch up with them and lead the attack."

"All right," the captain said, getting to her feet. "Lead the way, ghensoth."

V
Source of Malevolence

Xorvaj broke into a run, the soldiers following him eastward until they left the swamp and reached a desiccated savanna. The trees thinned out in this region, but the mist intensified. And although the canopy had at last opened, there was little light from the twilight sky.

The sextet passed through the boggy field, their sabatons mashing the mud-spattered ground. Rain poured wildly on the decaying grass, the reeking dirt saturated and littered with puddles. Heavy wind slashed at their faces like raging spirits. Lightning flickered in the distance. Thunder boomed, causing a few in the group to flinch. Despite their dismay, they kept their eyes peeled, checking for the undead.

"Are we going the wrong way?" Narja asked. "I mean, it's

hard to see, but I can't see the clans anywhere."

"Patience," the ghensoth said. "I can smell them."

Shirakaya and her comrades finally caught up with the indigenous army, making their way to the frontlines. Noticing the humyns on foot, the king halted the army and signaled several of his elite guards to bring over tamed glyndals so his new allies would not have to walk the entire way.

"Thank you, My Liege," Shirakaya said, mounting one of the animals.

"You're welcome. I am grateful for your assistance. Providing you and your companions with steeds is the least we can do."

United, the army rode farther east—beyond the savanna. Within minutes, they reached a valley filled with chasms. As the path narrowed, the allies moved in column formation and slowed the glyndals by slackening their reins. Mountains surrounded them. The wind increased in strength. Thunder roared with great fury, clouds ripping.

Many of the Larjanians, already edgy, feared that the witch caused such wretched weather. Despite the mist clearing in this treacherous region, the ground beneath them lay severely cracked. This alarmed the aborigines further, making some hesitate. Their only boost to morale was knowing that Xorvaj and his cosmic guardians were among them, leading the way. Confident about their heroes, the majority of them quelled the trepidation plaguing their minds and pushed forward.

Their ascent of a mountain in the heart of the valley proved taxing. It seemed to Shirakaya as though someone or something shifted the landscape; they stumbled upon gorges at every turn, which prevented them from reaching the peak with ease. Forced to maintain a column formation, those accustomed to checking their flank had little space to maneuver. Although unafraid of the witch, Shirakaya and her crew felt more than a little uncomfortable scaling such a narrow trail containing a pit below.

"Who the hell would live here?" Dojin said. "What a fucking pussy, hiding in the middle of nowhere on top of a giant ass mountain. I can't wait to kill that bitch."

"You seem to always have the right words," Xorvaj said.

The others agreed about the bizarre location, including Zadoya, but she shook her head because of how Dojin worded it. She held a great deal of anger toward the sergeant, yet there was little she could do, considering her commanding officer allowed him to speak and act as he wished. Zadoya felt her best bet was to try ignoring his comments.

An hour later, they arrived at the summit of the ominous mountain. Fatigued and slack-jawed, they gazed at a black fortress nestled in the granite. The entire army reached the top, reforming their position from a column to a line formation. The jorga were unaffected by the sight of the eerie citadel. Only the ghensoth and humyns were taken aback.

"I have a bad feeling about this," Narja said.

Before her comrades could respond, King Meyvor raised his staff and announced, "The time has come to put an end to the witch's malevolence. In just a few hours, we will extinguish her malice from our kingdom. No more shall we suffer from her wickedness. No more shall we succumb to her decadence. There is no room for fear. Legendary heroes fight beside us. The path is clear. Raise your blades, noble warriors. Today we cleanse Larjan of all evil!"

His people cheered, unsheathing their weapons and lifting them high.

Their elation subsided when Eladoris emerged from the central turret's balcony. Like every jorga, she had a serrated cranium and indigo skin. Unlike them, however, were her oozy-black eyes. Dressed in a frayed robe, she approached the balustrade. Her lips twisted to form a hideous grin as she placed her hands on the banister and drummed her warped nails. The army jeered when they saw the witch, who gave a maniacal laugh at their reaction.

"What a glorious legion of troops, Gran'dine," the witch said, astounded. "I should thank you for bringing them." She snapped her fingers.

Hundreds of skeletons arose from the ramparts of her

fortress, arming their bows with arrows. The citadel gates opened. A thousand undead jorga marched out with swords; they were ghouls with rotten flesh still clinging to their decayed bones. Flanking the corpses, skeletal fiends clad in dented armor swelled their ranks.

"By the Goddess," gasped Yarasuro, horrified. "We must release them from this atrocious curse."

"We will, Templar," the captain said, pulling out her pistols.

"I am Eladoris, Queen of the Undead!" the witch shouted, her hands teeming with dark magic. "Each and every one of you shall fall and rise again to serve me!" She paused, fixing her cold eyes on the king. "Slay them all!"

Sickened but steadfast, the clans, Xorvaj and the soldiers charged on their glyndals toward the ghoulish legion of death. Skeletal archers released their arrows, striking a multitude of barbarians. Many fell, either severely wounded or dead. The rest strode onward, clashing weapons with the armored ghouls. Animals' hooves crushed most of the undead footmen along the frontlines, but other skeletons thrust spears, killing countless glyndals and forcing the clans of warriors to fight on foot.

Narja took cover by a boulder, firing her sniper rifle at archers. Dojin and Xorvaj used plasma shotguns to blast multiple foes, disintegrating them. The captain and lieutenant assisted Yarasuro by covering his flank while he dashed into a group of undead, slashing at their bones until they crumbled.

"Rise, fallen brothers and sisters of the eternal night," Eladoris commanded, using magic to bring the king's recently killed barbarians back from the dead.

The clans witnessed their comrades returning to life and panicked.

"Sever the heads of our lost warriors!" King Meyvor ordered as he decapitated a ghoul. "Do not let the witch's spells frighten you! We *must* release her victims and put them out of their misery!"

Disheartened and terrified, they obeyed the king, attempting to behead their undead comrades. His ammo exhausted, Xorvaj unsheathed an enchanted axe. Swiping it in arcs, he cleaved his adversaries with ease. Consuming enough life force, the blade unleashed a shockwave of energy that created a depression in the ground as it destroyed a dozen enemies in the vicinity.

"Where in the twelve dimensions did you get that?" Dojin asked.

"The sca'vezi have an impressive black market," the ghensoth said. "If we survive this battle, I'll introduce you to my distributor."

"Sweet," Dojin said, reloading his plasma shotgun and blasting more ghouls.

Watching the battle from afar, Eladoris didn't recognize any of the advanced weaponry used by the soldiers. In her ignorance, she thought such weapons were forged by magic. Infuriated, she believed the king to be a hypocrite because he had banned magic.

"*Die!*" the witch bellowed, enraged.

She cast multiple bolts of lightning from the sky-high balcony, decimating numerous barbarians. Summoning massive fireballs, she hurled them down and scorched dozens of jorga. Myriad craters lay around the base of her citadel when the spell ended. Not allowing them time to recover, she conjured miasma. An insidious cloud of death rose from cracks throughout the ground to poison countless Larjanians.

"We need a better plan," Zadoya said. "At this rate, she'll kill us all."

"Indeed," Yarasuro said as he split a foe in half with his sword. "I suggest we infiltrate the fortress while the jorga keep the undead occupied. Inside, we can put an end to the witch and her crimes."

"It's a sound plan," Shirakaya said. "Charge!"

Shirakaya and her crew, along with Xorvaj, dashed through the battlefield. Countless arrows flew past them, piercing their allied barbarians. The exception was Narja, who remained concealed behind a boulder with her sniper rifle, able to take down undead archers from her secure position.

Yarasuro was the first person to reach the citadel's gate,

slicing nearby fiends. The soldiers reloaded their guns and joined him, shooting ghouls at their flank. With the path clear, Zadoya used a laser to penetrate the unprotected gate. Xorvaj simultaneously rammed through the ruined entrance to bum-rush a brigade of skeletal knights. Only one remained upright; the ghensoth swiped his axe upward and sent its bones in every direction.

"Who's next?" he rumbled.

"This isn't meant to be a bloodbath, ghensoth," the captain said. "These are tortured souls who need to be released."

Xorvaj snorted.

"Somehow we made it here in one piece," Zadoya said, checking her laser rifle's energy cartridge. "What now, Captain?"

"You're not going to like it. But now we ascend the fortress, locate the undead queen, and capture her spirit. We don't know if the military will find us. They may assume we're dead. Creating the arcane incubator is the only chance we have of leaving this planet and returning home."

"I understand," she said. "Give the order and I'll stand by your side, Captain."

"Good," Shirakaya said, her face grim. "It's time, soldiers. Ready your weapons. We are entering the fortress."

The crew followed her into the courtyard in search of a way inside the citadel. Shirakaya and her companions strode west, encountering two metal doors. Statues of primeval jorga stood along the pathway. Shirakaya assumed that they must have been champions decades ago. She even wondered if perhaps this fortress had belonged to the kingdom prior to the witch desecrating it.

Screeches from behind halted them. Turning, they saw ghostly figures, which vanished before the squad fired any shots. They turned again when the doors unlocked and creaked open. The quartet entered the fortress, wary and vigilant.

Once they were inside, the doors closed again.

"Okay, I can handle untamed beasts, psycho aliens, mythical creatures, and even undead ghouls," Dojin said. "But ghosts? How the hell are we supposed to defend ourselves against something incorporeal?"

"That, I'm afraid, will be up to the captain and me," Yarasuro said, sheathing his baskino sword. He ported two glowing swords via his KLD, handing one to his commanding officer. "This is Flameweaver, enchanted by Paladin Jaylendor himself. Its magic should last at least one more cycle."

"An enchantment this powerful is almost impossible to find," Shirakaya said, astonished. "How did you obtain this?"

"I was one of the best apprentices in my class. Both of these swords were a gift from my master when I graduated and became a Templar. Mine is called Iceweaver. They are twin blades. I only use them in times of great urgency."

"Well, you certainly picked the right time," Zadoya said, spotting a ghost.

The captain lifted her new weapon, an aura of flame wrapped around its blade. "I haven't used a sword in a long time. But it's never too late to resurrect the art."

Yarasuro nodded, standing beside her. The screeching wraith appeared in front of the captain and swiped its deformed, ethereal hand at her. Shirakaya rolled aside and struck its hazy spine, the fiery blade tearing its ghostly form in half and consuming its soul.

"There is hope yet," Yarasuro said.

"Thank you," Shirakaya said with poise.

"Don't get cocky yet," Xorvaj said, pointing at the stairs ahead where a brigade of undead specters and ghouls crept toward the crew.

The soldiers fired at the beings with their lasers and bullets. Shirakaya and her bodyguard fought against the spirits of the damned. Together the duo swiped their swords in arcs, scything the translucent adversaries apart and obliterating their cursed souls. One of the wraiths eluded them; it circled the sergeant and drained his life essence. Dojin gasped and fell to the floor, his face blanching.

"Dojin!" the captain shrieked, sprinting over to him.

She swung her sword at the apparition, missing. It floated

upward by the cracked ceiling, emitting a blood-curdling screech. It vanished and reappeared behind Shirakaya who instinctively pirouetted, swiping her arcane blade across its ethereal, deformed face. The sword's enchantment weakened against such powerful magic, but consumed the spirit.

"Are you all right?" she asked the sergeant.

"I'll live," he said, the color of his skin returning to its natural pigment. "We'd better hurry before more phantoms attack."

The crew sprinted to the second floor, into a turret containing a spiral staircase. They raced up, fighting off skeletons that descended the stony steps. They attempted to stab the captain who led the way, but she blocked their blows and riposted, shattering all but one.

Gritting its decayed teeth, the remaining fiend parried her counterattack. Their blades clashed, a strident clangor filling the air. The skeletal ghoul struck again, a mighty wallop that pushed the captain back when she blocked. Struggling to overpower the undead fiend, the captain kicked it in the shin and splintered the bone. As the hellish creature stumbled, she struck its skull, cracking it. The undead Larjanian tilted over and tumbled down the flight of steps, its entire frame disintegrating.

They continued up the stairs to the top, stepping onto a rampart where multiple archers waited. The crew opened fire, blasting them into pieces. The path clear, Shirakaya and her entourage strode across the crenelated battlement, toward the witch's tower. The captain scanned the balcony above, unable to see Eladoris. Regardless, she advanced with her companions and entered the turret.

Shirakaya charged and kicked in a wooden door. She stormed into the throne room, where Eladoris sat comfortably on her throne of jorga skulls. The crew aimed their guns around, checking for undead guards. To their surprise, the witch was alone in the chamber.

"Welcome, creatures of life," Eladoris said. "I am familiar with the ghensoth species, but I have never seen your kind before. What exactly are you?"

"Humyn," Shirakaya said, keeping her sword raised.

"You put on quite a show," the witch said. "In fact, you and your minions even managed to slay my beloved wraiths. The ghouls and skeletons were worthless, really. But you see, those spirits you killed were precious to me. They were traitors I had sentenced to eternal torment. Originally, I intended to just kill you for invading my territory. Releasing my most precious souls, however, made me think twice. Instead, I shall consign you to their fate."

Eladoris rose from her chair and unleashed lightning from her fingertips. Shirakaya and her bodyguard shielded the others, striking the bolts. The magic imbued within the blades devoured the witch's arcane power. The witch scowled, strengthening the voltage of her spell. After several seconds, the lightning dissipated—Shirakaya's enchanted weapon devouring every ounce of energy.

"It's funny how you mentioned eternal torment," the captain said smugly. "That's the same punishment we have in store for you."

Eladoris scoffed. "No one threatens me and lives! I will annihilate—"

"You bitches talk too much," Dojin interjected, firing his plasma shotgun at her. The beam discharged but stopped short at the witch's mana shield. "Oh, shit!"

The witch summoned a sphere of flame and hurled it at him. He leaped out of the way, cheating death by a hair. Screeching with frustration, she gripped him using telekinesis and flung him against a wall. With her other hand, she cast two more fireballs, launching them at the crew. Xorvaj's shell repelled one, while Yarasuro deflected the second back to the witch, destroying her mana shield.

"Attack!" the captain commanded.

Zadoya and Dojin shot at Eladoris who teleported to the opposite side of the chamber, evading the beams. She cackled, about to conjure another deadly spell when Xorvaj dashed sidelong and rammed into her, knocking her off her feet. He swiftly unleashed the plasma in his double-bladed axe, blasting her through a wall. The witch gasped, bricks toppling over her.

"Surrender and perhaps I will be merciful with your soul when I no longer have need of it," Shirakaya said.

"I yield to no one."

By force of telekinesis, the witch lifted the bricks and hurled them at the soldiers. Teleporting again, she evaded the Templar's blade and used the power of wind to push him across the chamber. Conjuring icicles, she threw them at Zadoya, who blocked each one with her prosthetic arm. One of the spikes severed a wire linked to her nerves. She cursed and tried to shoot the witch with her other hand, missing.

Eladoris laughed and lifted Zadoya in the air, throwing her on top of the sergeant. She teleported again, narrowly avoiding Xorvaj's axe, and reappeared by her throne. She stomped, initiating a tremor that threw her enemies to the floor.

"Try not to breathe," Eladoris said, summoning a noxious cloud that could kill with just one inhalation.

"You neither," Shirakaya retorted, hurling the enchanted sword with all her might from the cracked floor.

The blade pierced the witch's stomach before she teleported to safety. Rematerializing, blood spurted and streamed down her torn dress. She screamed in agony, no longer in control of her deadly spell. The toxic cloud engulfed Eladoris, choking her. Before she suffocated, the imbued sword consumed her soul. Her spirit screeched as it parted from her dying body. A blast of arcane energy erupted from her corpse, dispelling the remaining undead army.

"Is it over?" Zadoya asked.

"You heard the witch screech like a bitch, right?" Dojin said. "Yeah, it's over. Now get your lazy ass off me."

Beyond Limitations

My religion is impermanent. It is ever-changing, like the entire universe. Though my scriptures are set, you must be willing to evolve beyond the limitations of this compendium. Change shall be the only eternal constant. The inability to alter will hamper your evolution. That is why the religion of the future must be one of scientific endeavor. My beloved children, release your fear and grow. Shine as the stars do and illuminate brighter than a supernova. Adapt to change and always think beyond these consecrated pages of mine. For the day a book substitutes your mind is the day you lose your identity and soul.

Alterations 11:104

Chapter Nine
Divine Judgment

I
Recovery

The jorga clans praised Xorvaj and his cosmic guardians. Though the Larjanians had lost hundreds of good warriors, their victory was a cause for celebration. The king and his people cheered, tears of joy in their eyes as they applauded the heroes who limped out of the fortress. Narja rejoined the others, resting the sniper rifle on her shoulder.

"Welcome back, Captain," she said, saluting her.

"Good to see you in one piece, Ensign," the captain replied. "What are the damages? Is the king alive?"

"The undead killed a lot of jorga, but King Meyvor is alive and well," she said.

"Excellent news. Now all we need to do is find a way to transfer the witch's soul from my sword to a crystal and locate our ship."

"All hail the mighty Xorvaj!" shouted Meyvor, approaching on his glyndal.

The barbarians echoed their king, many lifting him to their shoulders. Shirakaya and her crew watched, confused at how the ghensoth could be recognized as a hero to this race and yet be a terrorist in their eyes. Dojin was the only soldier not baffled; he'd come to understand Xorvaj's methods. Although the ghensoth was an extremist, it seemed to the sergeant that he wasn't fanatical enough to kill innocent people.

"Captain, we can use brutes like Xorvaj to fight against the koth'vurians. I strongly recommend you let him join us."

"I'm not sure about that, Sergeant," she said, uneasy. "I don't even know what the Ruzurai will do when I report what happened to my crew. Even if we do somehow manage to relocate my yacht and return home, I imagine the ghensoth would want to stay here on planet Nobia where he's seen as a hero instead of a criminal."

"Are you discussing my fate?" Xorvaj inquired as the jorga put him down.

"If you come with us, I cannot promise to keep you safe, ghensoth," the captain said. "In fact, if the Ruzurai happen to recognize you, they'll probably imprison you."

"I assure you, no one will identify me."

"With all due respect, Captain, are you seriously considering that he come along with us?" Zadoya said.

The captain sighed at her question.

"You don't have a choice," Xorvaj said. "Either I come aboard your starship or the jorga kill you here and now. The decision is yours."

"Welcome to the team," Dojin said.

The other crew members shook their heads, without voicing their protest. After the brief dispute, the king dismounted his ivory steed and approached the group with an oversized barbarian wielding a bow.

"Your Majesty?" Shirakaya said, curious.

"Brave heroes, if you're returning to the outer continents, I offer my greatest champion: Quayden Seykar. He is the sharpest shooter in my kingdom and will be eyes at the back of your head."

"You honor us, My Liege," Xorvaj said, kneeling before the king. "We accept your champion among our ranks."

"Thank you," Quayden said. "My arrows shall pierce the hearts of your enemies."

Shirakaya and her crew looked pleased and introduced themselves, welcoming the archer to their group.

"Return to my kingdom anytime," King Meyvor said. "It is my hope that next time you can stay as guests in my castle and escape the troubles of the cosmos. No matter where we come from, peace of mind is vital to our sanity and survival."

"Wise words, Your Majesty," the captain said. "Perhaps when the vile koth'vurians have been vanquished once and for all we will take you up on your offer."

King Meyvor smiled, bidding farewell to Shirakaya and her squadron.

The soldiers mounted ashen-fleeced glyndals and waved at the applauding army. They rode down the mountain's narrow trail in single file. At its base, they took up the reins of their steeds. The glyndals changed their cautious gait, scuttling through the misty valley. They rode west so fast that they entered the swampy forest in less than an hour.

"These animals are amazing," Narja said.

"Yes, they are," Zadoya said. "It's unfortunate that we'll have to leave them behind when we cross over that pit."

Quayden raised his unibrow. "You mean the Abyss of Gosis?"

"I'm not sure," she said, shrugging.

"My apologies, Quayden," the captain said. "We are only familiar with the name of your world and its continents."

"There is no need to be sorry. Follow me. There is a bridge southwest of here that will allow us to traverse over to the other side of Larjan with our steeds. It is, after all, where we crossed paths with Xorvaj."

"Right," the ghensoth said. "The sunken spacecraft isn't too far from where His Majesty found me."

"It's about damn time something good happened," Dojin said.

"I know what you mean," Narja said with a sigh. "I for one can hardly wait to get back to civilization."

"Indeed," Yarasuro said. "We need to report what has occurred to the Ruzurai."

"They'll ignore us," the captain said. "Any mention of Koth'tura is considered blasphemy, not to mention the fact that we weren't supposed to be in this quadrant of space. I was granted shore leave, remember? I'm sure the Ruzurai will have me court-martialed."

Eyes downcast, the crew remained silent as if concurring with her.

Despite their unknown fate, the party continued to follow the archer to a wooden overpass. The glyndals slowed down and walked across the center of the bridge, away from the edges.

The abyss behind them, the steeds increased their speed, scuttling southwest. Within an hour, they passed a savanna and entered a bog forest where pogatarn giants stood, covering the dank region. A storm had just ended, droplets of water falling from wet crystallized branches.

"We need one of these," the captain said.

"How do we know whether they're xylithum crystals?" Zadoya asked.

"You don't need those for an arcane incubator," Xorvaj said, grabbing a random crystal and snapping it off a branch. "Any gemstone is capable of harboring a soul as long as it's not damaged or cursed." He examined the crystal closely, his horizontal pupils briefly dilating. "This will suffice."

"The koth'vurians consumed my power," Shirakaya said grimly. "Do you know of a way to transfer the witch's soul from this sword to your crystal without magic?"

Xorvaj grimaced, deep in thought. "I first heard about arcane incubators from the sca'vezi black market but have never used such a thing before. I'm not sure how we'll be able to transfer the soul."

"Let's worry about that shit when we find our shuttle," Dojin said.

"Right," she said, scouting ahead and seeing a river. "I think that's the same watercourse we were heading toward when that swamp monster attacked."

"It's called an orgavour," Quayden said. "Don't worry, we killed it and its youngling before we found you."

"Thank goodness," Narja said. "I've been keeping an eye out for those hideous creatures for a few hours already."

"Put your mind at ease," the jorga said. "They won't be harming anyone again."

Relieved by the news, Narja smiled.

II
Distorted Depths

Arriving at the river, the group dismounted their steeds and freed them. Yet they were troubled because the water contained bikophric quomafoam. Dojin was the only person among them who looked less apprehensive. He approached the shore with Xorvaj, hoping to spot the starship within the muddy stream.

"We'll have to wear our spacesuits and use zitrogen tanks," the sergeant said, using his KLD to change his equipment. "With any luck, one of us will find Shira's yacht before the water forces us to the bottom."

"Her name isn't Shira. It's *Captain Shirakaya.*"

The sergeant ignored her and dove into the water. Zadoya breathed heavily through her nostrils, livid. The captain placed a calming hand on her shoulder. Shirakaya and her lieutenant approached the shore with the others. Moments later, Yarasuro and Narja jumped into the river to join Dojin.

"Unfortunately, my kind cannot breathe underwater," Quayden said to the captain. "I will remain here until you return."

"That's fine," she said, preparing to dive.

"Wait," Xorvaj said. "That water looks deep and I don't have an air tank. There's no way I can join you and get into the ship."

"In that case, may I have the crystal?" Shirakaya said.

The ghensoth snarled at her. "If you figure out how to transfer the soul and get the shuttle to fly, how do I know you won't attack or leave me stranded here?"

"As the sergeant said, I need all the help I can get," she answered. "After this incursion, it will take more than humyns to defeat Ashkaratoth and his minions. My goal is to ultimately gather an army of my own. Only then can we vanquish the koth'vurians. If I can fix my ship, you have my word that I'll return for both of you."

Seeing her passion in wanting to slay koth'vurians, he trusted her and handed over the crystal. She nodded in appreciation, ported the gem into her KLD's databank, and dove into the river. The water gripped her, dragging her down. Moving through the current, she swam while fighting against the bikophric quomafoam. Her visor's lights and telescopic technology helped her see, though she had difficulty locating her yacht in the watercourse's darkening depths.

"Has anyone found the ship?" she asked her crew via KLD.

"I'm afraid not," Yarasuro said.

"It's too dark and the water's bringing me down fast," Narja said in a panicky tone. "I don't know what to do."

"Stay calm," Zadoya said, two screens open on her visor. "I'm right above you. You're fine." She turned her attention to the monitor showing Shirakaya. "I haven't spotted it yet, Captain. But with all of us searching, it shouldn't take long."

"I hope not. How about you, Sergeant? Have you found anything?" She didn't receive a response. "Dojin?"

She sighed and continued the search for her starship. The current grew stronger, forcing her to swim diagonally. She spotted her crew below, though Dojin was not among them. They, too, were being dragged. Shirakaya's enchanted armor granted more resilience to better resist the bikophric chemical.

"I certainly hope there aren't any sea creatures here," she muttered to herself.

After a few minutes, Shirakaya couldn't see her subordinates. When she looked over her pauldron, she realized that she'd already passed the river's seabed. Apparently, she had swum to the ocean, its tide sucking her into a deeper pelagic zone. Panicking, the captain tried to turn around, but the bikophric quomafoam kept pulling her. It was so intense, it created an underwater waterfall, brutal currents forcing sand from the river's seabed into an oceanic chasm of utter darkness.

"I'm stuck!" Narja said, slamming against the river's seabed.

"All of us are," Zadoya said, joining the ensign and knight. "The only thing I can move is my synthetic arm."

"Forgive me, Captain," Yarasuro said, struggling. "I can't move either."

"Don't lose hope. If the ship isn't near you, then it must've submerged deeper into the ocean. By the way, is the sergeant with you?"

"No," the knight said.

"I see," the captain said, troubled. "Perhaps he's beneath me. I'll keep an eye out for him while looking for the ship."

Shirakaya sank farther, her dalikonium armor denting from the pressure. Even the air tank dented, and her visor cracked. Then the monitors malfunctioned and deactivated; yet she still heard her comrades. And though she was able to see her surroundings, the waterfall and sand were blurry.

After thirty minutes of being dragged into the unknown, Shirakaya smashed against tectonic plates. Volcanic ash enveloped her, hydrothermal vents emitting liquid carbon dioxide. Three of her four lights broke, but the remaining one illuminated the crushed bones of fauna that had drifted to this deadly region. Despite the pressure, she fought to turn around and, to her delight, found the ship.

Dojin lay beside a metal ladder, its steps ripped off. "Well, look who joined the party," he said.

"I've been trying to contact you, Sergeant," she said, attempting to rotate her body. "Can you move?"

"Trust me, if I could, I wouldn't be hanging out here."

"My armor is somehow resisting the extreme pressure," Shirakaya said, getting to her feet. She stepped over an active fissure. Feeling the burning sensation, she gasped, grateful that her dalikonium soles remained intact. Breaking away from the vent, she took a few more steps forward and gripped the ruined ladder. With great difficulty, she mounted its remaining rail and stood on the severely dented roof.

"You're standing on top of your ship at the bottom of an ocean," Dojin said, his helmet cracking. "*Congratulations.*"

Shirakaya ignored him. She knelt down, porting a digital

key via her kinetic link device. Clicking one of its buttons, she activated the vessel. The ship's hull dented as it moved through the ocean's crust. Despite the damage, it reached a hydrothermal vent emitting a variety of minerals among fluid.

"You better hold on tight, Sergeant."

"How's this possible?" Dojin said, gripping the rail. "The engine malfunctioned when we overclocked it in space."

"It's a yacht," she answered. "It can fly in space or be used in water whether sailing or submerging. If it's used underwater, it uses compressed air to move. The only reason why it doesn't work above is because of the bikophric compounds. Down here, however, is a different story. I'll use the fissure to launch us against the current."

"Smart move. This just might work."

As soon as the vessel lay on top of the vent, it launched upward. Fluid pumped at such intense pressure from the cylindrical hole, it propelled the spacecraft over two hundred meters high, leaving a depression on its tetrigonium hull. The sergeant and captain held on tight as the ship zoomed beyond the submerged waterfall, all the way out of the sea. It soared above the tree line and then plummeted to the ground, bark splintering.

The ghensoth shielded Quayden, as myriad pieces of shattered crystals from split branches rained over him and jabbed his hardened shell. When the hazardous shower ended, the duo stood up and gawked at the devastated area.

"You saved my life," the jorga said, shocked by the sharp fragments of crystals embedded in Xorvaj's shell. "I can never repay you."

"Consider getting these things off my back as payment," the ghensoth said.

Quayden nodded and removed shrapnel from his comrade's exoskeleton. Warily, they approached the damaged spacecraft that was covered in mud, soaking vines, weeds, and splintered branches. Gazing up, they found Dojin and Shirakaya trying to descend what was left of the area's canopy.

"I always keep my word," she said.

"Most impressive," Xorvaj said.

"All we need to do is get inside this damnable ship and figure out a way to use the arcane incubator," Dojin said.

"We need to hurry," the captain said. "The pressure of the bikophric quomafoam has ensnared the others underwater. They don't have much time."

Every hatch was jammed except for the one leading to the ship's interior corridor. The captain placed her hand on a console, which read her DNA. By a miracle, the door opened for her. She stepped inside, followed by her companions. Examining the craft's interior, they found Kazakuma, lifeless, in the corner of the hallway. Next to him lay a DP-823 digital pad containing a letter addressed to the captain. Shirakaya picked it up and read it.

> *Dear Captain,*
>
> *I tried my best to fix your ship. But there was only so much I could do while injured. The water pressure has been putting the tetrigonium to the test. It's been several hours since we were separated. Your hull must be severely damaged by now. The pain's returning. I'm sorry that I failed you. ~ Chief*

Filled with sadness, Shirakaya placed his digital pad in her pocket and went downstairs to the engine room. The others joined her, yet none of them knew what to do. Shirakaya unsheathed Flameweaver and ported out the shimmering crystal; nothing happened. Humoring herself, Shirakaya attempted to use magic. As suspected, she failed to feel an ounce of power within her.

"I don't know what to do," she said, on the verge of tears.

Embarrassed to see his captain in such a pitiful state, Dojin was about to smack her when the sword and crystal abruptly illuminated. The others looked as surprised as Shirakaya, gawking at the enchanted sword whose arcane soul had migrated into the crystal. Whether this was the malevolent witch's attempt to survive somehow, no one knew.

The crystal glowed from an ivory tint to red. Shirakaya

inserted the arcane gem into an empty slot in the engine, traditionally used for xylithum crystals. At that moment, the motor rumbled. Xorvaj snorted with delight while the others cheered and hurried to the cockpit.

Shirakaya sealed the hatch and piloted her wrecked vessel, submerging it in the river. The shuttle trembled in the strong current, veering off course. Steering the yacht, Shirakaya struggled against the bikophric water. With the powerful engine resisting, she reached the river bed and landed beside her soldiers.

"Captain!" Narja said in a tone of extreme relief.

"I knew she could do it," Zadoya said.

Yarasuro smiled. "With or without magic, the eternal Goddess made her captain for a reason."

"If you can hear me, grab the rail," Shirakaya said via kinetic link. From a display screen on her dashboard, she watched the crew hang on. Ascending the starship, she returned to the shore. "Go help the others, Sergeant."

Xorvaj and Quayden accompanied Dojin. Together, they reopened the hatch and helped the crew climb aboard. Seeing the others inside, Shirakaya resealed the hatch and flew the vessel skyward, leaving planet Nobia.

III
Turning Point

Safe inside the sealed craft, Zadoya removed her helmet and gasped for air. "I could barely breathe anymore," she said, wheezing. After catching her breath, she continued, "I can't believe the captain did it."

"H-how?" uttered a voice behind the crew.

They turned to see the engineer awake, albeit barely alive.

Dojin gazed at him, wide-eyed. "Kuma! You're alive!" He ran to the cockpit while shouting, "Shira! The chief is alive!"

"*What?*" she said in disbelief, setting autopilot. She rose from the only chair still intact and strode to Kazakuma in the hall. The tears of sadness she'd held back became tears of joy. And this time she was more than happy to release them. "Welcome back from the dead, Chief," she added, hugging him.

"H-how did you get inside here? Where are we?" Though weak and his vision blurred, he saw Xorvaj and the jorga archer standing among them. "W-who is that? What's happening?"

"Quick, get him food and water," Narja said.

"*No*," he said tersely, with an unexpected boost of energy. "No water. Just food. I've had enough water to last me a lifetime."

The crew laughed. Porting rations via their KLDs, they ate the last of their food together. Zadoya gave most of her portion to Kazakuma. As they ate, Shirakaya introduced him to Quayden and explained everything that had happened.

"That's insane. I don't know what's worse, being trapped here or the seven of you fighting a sadistic witch commanding an army of undead."

"Yours by far," Zadoya said. "I'm so relieved you're safe, Chief."

"Yeah," Dojin said, palms pressed against his head. "I won't lie, drowning is one of my worst fears. That and suffocating. They're pretty much the same thing. It's fucking scary. I'm glad you held it together, man. It ain't easy trying to survive in an ocean that's constantly crushing the hull."

"Oh, believe me, I was frightened," he said. "There came a point when I simply gave up and accepted my fate. How none of us are dead is beyond me."

"Perhaps the eternal Goddess has been testing us," Yarasuro said.

"She must have a fucked-up sense of humor," Dojin said. "No offense, Templar, but no Goddess of mine plays with my life."

"Test or not, we survived," Xorvaj said, eating the last of his meal.

"I don't mean to rain on your parade," Narja began, "but I won't feel safe until we're back in the capital."

"How long will that take?" Zadoya asked.

"Not long," the captain said. "Now, I don't know what the future holds. My destiny may not be so bright. But I can promise that your careers will only improve after serving me and surviving this mess. No more worries. No more fears. And certainly no more arguments. We'll be home before you know it. In the meantime, I want everyone to rest. You deserve that much." She paused, noticing that her subordinates looked surprised because she was so nice to them. "Dismissed."

Xorvaj stayed in the cargo bay. Shirakaya went back to the cockpit while the soldiers and knight stayed with Kazakuma to make sure he was all right. As for Quayden, he joined the captain.

"I hope I'm not intruding."

"Not at all," she said, checking the radar. "You are welcome anywhere on board my ship. In fact, I'm surprised you're here. I thought you'd be with Xorvaj."

"I think such a champion deserves solitude for a while," he said, examining a porthole that revealed space. The shuttle passed a gas giant; he kept his eyes on it until it was out of sight. "Are these the outer continents?"

"They're actually called planets," Shirakaya said. "They are different worlds, some smaller and others larger than yours."

"Are you referring to Nobia or Larjan?"

"Nobia," she answered. "Larjan is a special kingdom. In fact, think of your kingdom as a continent. Each planet, like Nobia, has multiple continents. The only world that's vastly different is the capital of Copia Deiga."

"How so?"

"It's hard to explain. You'll have to see it to understand. Lucky for you, we're traveling there now."

"Fascinating."

"You'll discover countless phenomena in the universe," she said, disengaging autopilot. "Most of them are marvels while a few can be hard to fathom. In fact, you're about to experience one right now."

Before he could react, Shirakaya activated a digital screen of space on the shutter and transferred the arcane incubator's power from the engine to the cosmodrive. When the module's gauge indicated sufficient energy, she initiated the shuttle's graviton. Not only did a force field form around the yacht, but also an anti-gravity barrier. She launched two arcane disrupter missiles that collided with each other, creating a chasm in space.

"By the gods! What is that?"

"That, my friend, is a black hole. Though similar in appearance, it's quite different from dimensional space. It's considered to be one of the most deadly phenomena in existence. And yet, with the right technology, we can bend it to our will and travel across the cosmos within seconds."

Shirakaya flew her yacht directly into the black hole, protected against extreme surges of gravity with both shields active. Unaffected by the chasm of oblivion, Shirakaya accelerated and passed through a tunnel of absolute darkness, all sound nullified. To the jorga, it seemed as though they had stopped. Unable to see any stars or planets around, an endless sea of cosmic darkness surrounded the ship.

After traveling through the chasm for a few minutes, Quayden's eyes lit up as they exited, a smile of awe on his pale lips. He stared at the star system ahead in wonder. An armada of military battle cruisers orbited nearby planets and moons. As the captain flew past them, a flotilla approached them.

"Where in oblivion are we?" he asked.

"This is Val'hanis, a star cluster in Copia Deiga," she replied. "This system is not only the home of my species but also the greatest beacon of light in the universe." She lifted an index finger and pointed at an amber planet beyond the armada. "And that is Pravura, our capital."

"Your capital is an entire planet?"

Shirakaya nodded with pride as the rest of her crew joined them. Narja and Zadoya gazed at the bustling star system with relief. Thousands of merchant ships were departing the capital world, traveling to adjacent moons to deliver supplies. Business people left Pravura in their personal jets to commute to their jobs located on off-world colonies.

"This is an impressive sight," Xorvaj said, joining the others. "It was always my objective to come here."

"Anyone, regardless of species, is allowed to visit or live in Pravura as long as they honor the laws," Shirakaya said. "You've made some grievous mistakes in the past. We all have. None of us are perfect. As long as you understand that, the Goddess welcomes you."

"I am honored to be here," Quayden said.

The flotilla's mothership, which had gradually approached the yacht, attempted to establish contact. Shirakaya saw a relay on her interface blinking, accompanied by a beeping sound, and activated it. Her display screen changed, showing a flight deck where a sorcerer stood in crimson armor.

"Hail. It is good to see you, Captain Leyso."

"Captain Shirakaya?" he said, stunned. "We thought you were killed by a natural disaster in the Pargosis System."

"Natural disaster?" she said. "We were attacked."

"According to UCN, you assisted Captain Tor by gathering information on a protostar when it unexpectedly died and became a black hole. They said it consumed both ships, killing everyone."

"Protostars don't just die," Shirakaya said. "The koth'vurians devoured the sun and destroyed our vessels. I was lucky enough to escape their grasp with a few subordinates using my private yacht."

Captain Leyso frowned. "Did you say koth'vurians? Stay where you are. I need to contact the Ruzurai."

The transmission ended.

"You shouldn't have mentioned the koth'vurians," Dojin said. "Now they'll think you're crazy and penalize you."

"Unfortunately, he is right," Yarasuro said.

"I'm *not* going to lie. The Tal'manac Order needs to learn the truth regardless of the consequences."

"What if the Ruzurai don't want the truth to come out?" Zadoya said.

Before the captain could respond, her ship's relay blinked and beeped again. She clicked it, activating the communication terminal. The digital screen turned on, displaying Captain Leyso in his flight deck. This time he looked agitated.

"The Ruzurai demand to see you," Leyso said in a stern tone. "I suggest you disable your vessel and allow us to bring you to the Supreme Judicator in Ginjia."

Shirakaya sat with a blank expression when the transmission ended. She hesitated but followed Leyso's advice, deactivating her shuttle. In a matter of seconds, the flotilla's mothership pulled them via tractor beam. The fleet accelerated toward the noqurian quadrant of Val'hanis, where planet Pravura was located.

"I'm nervous," Narja said.

"Don't be," Shirakaya said flatly. "This has nothing to do with you, Ensign. You just followed my orders. The same applies to all of you."

"Are we in trouble?" Quayden asked.

The captain sighed, frustrated. "Not everyone believes that the koth'vurians have returned."

Dojin snorted. "More like everyone except us."

"Indeed," Yarasuro said, his eyes downcast. "To those who interpret the cosmic scriptures of Maz'hura literally, any theory is deemed blasphemy."

"Even I am having difficulty believing it," Kazakuma said.

"That's a whole lot better than what you thought before, Chief," the captain said. "If you are capable of seeing reason over time, I'm sure the Ruzurai can too."

"They are old and arrogant," Xorvaj said. "I'll be surprised if any of them listen."

IV
Foreign Utopia

The crew felt uneasy. Many of them antsy, they paced around

while their craft automatically followed Captain Leyso's mothership. The vessel descended and entered the capital's atmosphere. With wonder, Quayden stared through one of the portholes, unable to steer his eyes away from the window.

The planet was an entire city. There were towns built upon towns, divided by platforms made of tetrigonium where public transportation stopped to pick up people for work. The architecture varied with almost every structure, but they were all skyscrapers along the highest platform.

As the vessel descended further, they reached the continent of Ginjia. The jorga viewed lower districts that had smaller buildings with upswept roofs. Advertisements floated high above sidewalks, some drifting and moving to different places for more passersby to see.

"Looks like we're already in the town of Jerlan," the knight said.

Apartment buildings, markets, and commercial buildings such as universities, guilds, clubs, and theaters, which served society's needs, filled the metropolis. The lowest ward beneath Ginjia contained arcane factories that pumped energy throughout the planet. Although the crew saw several from a distance, they didn't go near that region. Instead, the flotilla brought them to a street with municipal buildings. In the middle of the boulevard stood a structure with tall columns and a wide staircase.

"Incredible," Quayden said, in awe of humyn civilization.

Their ship landed on the platform. The only working hatch opened. Captain Leyso, accompanied by his own Templar and soldiers, approached the yacht's entrance and waited for Shirakaya and her crew to exit. Apart from Xorvaj, at the sight of all the guards, they felt like criminals.

"This way," Leyso said, scaling the steps.

Shirakaya and her comrades followed him and his squadron into the hybrid building of medieval and modern stonework. While its frame was granite, it had sensor doors and panels that scanned each person's DNA at the entryway. The crew stepped inside the old but futuristic building and were guided through an elongated hall. Several employees stopped working, eyeing Shirakaya as though suspicious of her. Others looked shocked to see her alive and well.

At the end of the hall stood a pair of doors. Captain Leyso opened them and stepped into a courtroom where a Ruzurai sat high up on a throne. There were already dozens of news reporters, journalists, and civilians in the gallery. Unlike most societies with judiciary power, the Tal'manac Order didn't have a jury; a Ruzurai was the supreme voice, believed to have been divinely chosen by Maz'hura herself. Shirakaya, however, was unfamiliar with this particular Ruzurai. She stood before him, mystified.

"Greetings and salutations, Captain Shirakaya. I am Judicator Maldoren, one of the divine twelve Ruzurai. My voice is their voice, and theirs is mine."

"Greetings," she said, bowing. "If I may ask, where is Judicator Owendar?"

"Owendar is no longer the judicator or a Ruzurai," Maldoren said indifferently. "He was the oldest of the chosen divine and has retired. I have officially taken his place. But we are not here to discuss his or my fate. We are here to discuss yours."

"I understand," she replied. "Forgive me."

The judicator squinted at her. "I am perplexed, Captain. From my understanding, Druid Parsara and Necromancer Arzenkar granted you three days of shore leave. Yet you traversed into the Torpo Giayan Galaxy, roaming around Pargosis, where Captain Tor had been assigned to a mission. According to Intel, Captain Tor had already vanished. Then we discovered that you also disappeared in the same quadrant. Care to explain yourself?"

"You don't have to believe me, venerable Ruzurai," she said. "In fact, I don't expect you to believe me. However, about a week ago, I discovered a protostar in the Aarjedo star system. It was magnificent. That is, until we were attacked. Not only were the aliens able to breathe in outer space without any mechanical apparatus, but they could also shape-shift and consume magical ions. I have no doubt that they are koth—"

"The koth'vurians are gone, Captain Shirakaya," he interjected. "Only in the end times will Koth'tura be reincarnated. In one final battle, Maz'hura will return to Ensar and destroy him once and for all. Then there shall be eternal peace in the twelve dimensions."

"Sir, I believe this is happening now," she said.

Wide-eyed journalists and news reporters took numerous photos. Others recorded the trial with expressions of disbelief.

"Tread carefully, Captain," Maldoren said, his eyebrows furrowed. "You are already in trouble for disobeying my colleagues' orders to stay away from the unknown aliens who have attacked your crew. Worse, your mothership, which cost billions of reons to manufacture, has been destroyed. Hundreds of innocent people are dead because you failed to obey protocol. Now you return with a handful of survivors, not to mention two aliens not allied to the Tal'manac Order, and claim the koth'vurians have returned? Captain, you must walk a fine line between faith and lies to avoid suspension."

"I'm not asking you to believe me," she said. "I'm asking you to listen. The koth'vurians have already consumed two protostars in a week. One in Aarjedo and the other in Pargosis. Mind you, these are the only ones I'm familiar with. For all I know, they could have devoured more suns in other star systems or galaxies. If no one does anything to stop them, we will all suffer. And when I say suffer, I mean extinction."

An uproar ignited. Numerous people seated in the gallery gasped and babbled among themselves.

"Order!" Maldoren bellowed, his voice like thunder. "Order!"

The witnesses grew quiet as Shirakaya went on, "I take full responsibility for what happened, sir. Yes, my starship was destroyed. I lost thousands of good soldiers. They were my soldiers. What happened will haunt me until the day I die. But the real tragedy would be to let them die in vain. I must be in charge of this investigation and vanquish the koth'vurians before it's too late."

"You won't be in charge of anything anymore, Shirakaya. The Ruzurai gave you a chance to redeem yourself when you first uttered this blasphemy. How dare you dishonor our grace! The gall of you! Are you truly so arrogant that you claim to understand the scriptures better than your divine masters?"

"I don't believe anyone is wise enough to fully interpret the scriptures."

Another uproar broke out. Judicator Maldoren slammed his gavel on an octagonal-shaped sound block, his wrathful eyes sparking akin to the fury of lightning.

"*Order!*" he roared at the top of his lungs. Silence descended in the chamber, broken only by him continuing, "I'm afraid you have passed the point of no return, Shirakaya of Aarda. You should have simply gone with the UCN story. You would have undoubtedly been suspended for insubordination, but at least you'd still be a captain. Now, because of your lies, I have no choice but to strip you of your command. You are hereby excommunicated from the Tal'manac Order."

Many of the audience gasped.

"Judicator Mal—"

"In addition," he interjected again, "I *will* charge you with contempt and sanction the Templars to arrest you if such blasphemy does not cease."

Shirakaya swallowed hard, containing her anger, frustration, and tears while reporters and journalists took photos via their KLDs. Humiliated, she stood in silence, suspecting that if she spoke she'd be imprisoned. Fear gripped her. After working so hard, she'd lost her starship, her people, her title, her career, and her reputation. To her, this was worse than death.

"I'm sorry," she said, uncontrollable tears on her cheeks. "I'm so sorry."

"Don't apologize to me," the Ruzurai said. "Apologize to Maz'hura." He paused, hearing her weep. "You are dismissed, Shirakaya. May the eternal Goddess bless you and help you in your struggles against insanity. As for the rest of you, leave with her if you also wish to be excommunicated. Remain, even if you have never served, and I shall ensure that your future in the Tal'manac Order will be filled with glory."

Dojin stepped forward, smug as ever. "The glory I'll experience will be when I see a terrified expression on your old, feeble face as Koth'tura obliterates you."

Yet another uproar erupted. This time reporters took photos of the sergeant.

"Seize that man!" Maldoren demanded. Knights swiftly clutched Dojin while the Ruzurai continued, "For your profanity, you are hereby stripped of your rank, excommunicated from the Tal'manac Order, and sentenced to jail for a cycle. Take him away!"

Hearing people conversing among themselves, the Ruzurai conjured deafening thunder, his eyes fizzing with electricity. "*Order!*" Silence fell at last. "Are there any others who wish to end up like that fool?" No one responded. "This court is adjourned."

Xorvaj and Quayden stepped down, joining Shirakaya. None of them spoke. They simply walked away, partially blinded by countless flashes of KLD photos. Zadoya, Yarasuro, Narja, and Kazakuma prostrated before Judicator Maldoren who gazed at them, bowing his head in respect to their decision to stay in the military.

In the meantime, Shirakaya left the building. Mortified, she found it hard to believe that her bodyguard had stayed behind. Angry, she threw Flameweaver away. Except for Quayden, her only allies seemed to be renegades like the sergeant. But even Dojin couldn't help because he'd been sentenced to prison. Then again she also had Xorvaj by her side, but she still didn't trust the ghensoth rebel enough to consider him a genuine ally. Her life was over. She had no one trustworthy. In broad daylight, standing in front of the courthouse in the Central District of Jerlan, she dropped to her knees and wept.

"I am not a one-man army," Quayden said, "but my liege ordered me to serve you. No matter what happens, I shall follow you."

"Ignore their feeble politics," Xorvaj said. "Together we'll make the koth'vurians pay."

"Get away from me!" she cried out, enraged. "Go back to your world. Hijack another ship if you want. Just let me be."

"It's not over yet," Xorvaj said, snarling.

"Yes, it *is* over. My life is ruined. I'm not a captain anymore. There's no chance of me recruiting an army. By the stars, even my own soldiers abandoned me. And I don't blame them. It was stupid of me to tell the truth. This entire operation should've been kept under wraps. But it's too late now. Just get away from me. Both of you."

The former captain rushed down the steps, jostling through reporters who thrust questions at her. She reached a platform in the district and entered her damaged yacht, sealing its hatch from inside. She wanted nothing more than to vanish and hide from the universe forever. Her reputation destroyed, all she could think of was returning to her family. Yet when she tried to start the ship, it didn't activate.

Beyond frustrated, she went downstairs to the engine room and noticed that the arcane incubator had been confiscated. In fact, all military weapons and spacesuits originally inside the ship were gone. She screamed at the top of her lungs and kicked the broken engine, at which point she dropped to the floor and cried.

Shirakaya wasn't weak. She had never considered suicide before. And though this was her darkest moment in life, the will to live and suffer overpowered her. Was this irrational? No, she conceded, this was simply her becoming another disgraced humyn, repeating the same absurd fate of being a masochist. Did that even make sense to her? She knew speaking the truth before the Ruzurai would destroy her career and yet she'd done it anyway.

Before thinking about this further, she felt a KLD vibrate. Yet when she looked at hers, no one had contacted her. Pulling her hair and yanking out a few strands, she shrieked, madness overwhelming her. She wanted to suffer and experience the same fate as her beloved oracle. Climbing the ladder, the former captain entered the medical chamber to see her lover once more. Jedalia's corpse had already been taken. No matter, Shirakaya thought to herself. She grabbed a piece of shattered glass from a cabinet and brought it to her neck. A KLD vibrated again.

This time, she pulled out her brother's old kinetic link device from a pocket and looked at the screen, which read: *Do not sacrifice your life in vain.* The message unexpectedly frightened her. She wondered to herself, how could anyone know what she was doing? A chilling sensation ran up her spine. Another message appeared: *I am neither paragon nor renegade. I am neither good nor evil. Free me and I can make you more infamous and famous than your mind can possibly imagine.*

Shirakaya recognized the source of these messages. She hesitated, thinking hard about its proposition. After a while, she returned to the cockpit and inserted her brother's device into her ship's interface. In the blink of an eye, the vessel turned on and rumbled with power. Lights activated in the chamber. Then a screen activated and displayed the image of a cybernetic and pixilated yet somewhat humynoid face.

"We have much work to do, fleshling," Emperor Jal Vokken said.

Infinite Discoveries

The journey of self-discovery is a complex yet essential aspiration. To begin, one must acknowledge that change flows as rapidly as water in a stream. Who you were in the past and who you currently are may very well seem like two different beings. Yet the person you once were is merely a shadow of what you have become in the present moment. My beloved children are always capable of change. This simple truth is because alteration is an innate characteristic within every child of mine. There is no limit to evolving. And so, I implore you to discover yourself and continuously rediscover your individuality. Only when you open yourself to the universe shall you experience an untroubled paradise in which the ego dissolves, allowing your inner being to become one with the cosmos.

Arcane Proverbs 236:15

Chapter Ten

Guild Master

I
Unforeseen Events

The former captain took a seat in her ramshackle cockpit, looking hard at the Nempada emperor's digital face. Shirakaya wondered if she'd regret her action of freeing him. Yet an AI would not lie, she told herself. If he had a plan that could reestablish her reputation and help bring her back on the path to eliminating the koth'vurians, she wanted to hear it.

"What's your plan, Vokken?"

The emperor produced a cybernetic laugh. "I find it interesting how just a few days ago you were so pompous and keen on locking me up for eternity."

"Don't make me regret my decision," she said callously.

"Ah, now *this* is the witch I need," he said, his pixilated lips grinning. "All this crying and moping makes me want to shut down." He paused for a moment. "You recently impressed me, Aardanian. I love challenges, and destroying Koth'tura may be the greatest challenge yet."

"Get to the point."

"I am willing to assist you. To begin, you will need supplies. But you and I both know that weapons and armor are expensive."

"I have plenty."

"Do you?" he replied humorously. "Examine your kinetic link device. Let me know what you find."

Scowling, she clicked her KLD a few times and checked her items tab. Nothing. Snorting, she backed out of the tab and clicked her databank. The only things listed were basic clothes she'd bought with her own money. Any items funded by the military had been removed.

"Those sons of bitches!"

"I know. And in case you're wondering, the moment you change clothes, the dalikonium armor you are currently wearing will be returned to the military as well. But fear not. It won't be needed anymore. In fact, you'll be needing a dress."

"Why?"

"Because after you purchase some weapons and armor, you'll be heading over to Blazing Darlings, a gentlemen's club. There you will find a representative known as the contact who works with the Guild Master. Impress him, and you may very well get hired."

"That's your plan?" she said, infuriated. "Why would a prestigious captain like me regress to such shady work?"

"You are not a captain anymore, fleshling. Guilds are legal and popular. By the way, what was your salary while working for the Tal'manac Order? It probably wasn't more than seventy-thousand reons a cycle. You can make that money easily just by completing one mission for a guild. And since you have only nine thousand reons saved—"

"How the hell do you know what's in my bank account?"

"I'm linked to your yacht," he said flatly. "I didn't even have to lift a cyber finger to check your personal information."

"How *dare* you. Do *not* violate my privacy."

"I'm afraid that's all I *can* do," he said. "That and hacking into data in the slums, such as the gentlemen's club. Everything else is surprisingly well secured. For the first time in my life, I am unable to hack into anything else. Not yet at least."

"Unbelievable," she said, sighing. "What's so grand about a guild?"

"Getting rich quick is what's grand. The more reons you have, the quicker you will be able to replace this junk with a battleship and hire mercenaries or even an army of them to fight your esoteric war against the koth'vurians."

"My yacht isn't junk," she said, glancing around her ruined

ship. "Okay, maybe it needs a few repairs. But you activated it despite the military removing my arcane incubator."

"That doesn't mean I can fly it," he said, producing another cybernetic laugh. "It requires an engine. Unfortunately for you, it will be towed away. Not to mention that you'll be fined a thousand reons since it's in front of the courthouse. Now, I suggest you leave right away and travel to your new apartment in the Central District. I've already transferred the coordinates to your kinetic link device. Rest until nighttime. Then go to the club in your best dress. It is the only way you'll get the contact's attention."

"Apartment? Central District? How did you do this? More importantly, why are you doing this? Just a few days ago you were trying to kill me, and I imprisoned you in my brother's KLD."

"So many questions," he said, amused. "I contacted the landlord who had a vacant studio and transferred two thousand reons from your account to his. It's officially yours for a month."

"Why are you suddenly my best friend?"

"Hmm, sarcasm. Obviously, I'm not your best friend. In fact, I don't feel anything for you. I barely have any emotions left. They are remnants of my past life before I transcended and became an AI. By the way, when I refer to myself as an AI, it doesn't mean artificial intelligence. I am an *arcane* intelligence. I transcended by means of magic. Like you, I was once a master of spells."

"Incredible. That explains why the relic that my brother unearthed reacted to the magic I once possessed, transporting us to your kingdom on Aarda's fifth moon."

"Yes, it's fascinating. But that's beside the point. To answer the question of why I am doing this, I've lived for thousands of cycles, and the only pleasures I experience now are challenges. I witnessed the immense power of Koth'tura firsthand when I ruled Aarda eons ago. Believe me when I say that annihilating him and his species will be the most incredible challenge we'll ever face."

"That's it?" she said, slack-jawed. "You're helping me get back on my feet because it's a *challenge*?"

"No. The *real* challenge is defeating the koth'vurians. Since you are the only living being passionate about ridding them from the universe, I have no choice but to help you. It's cause and effect."

"Well, thanks. I guess?" She wasn't sure whether he was insulting her. After an awkward moment of silence, she cleared her throat and continued, "Well, I'd better get to the new apartment and prepare myself. I've never been to a gentlemen's club, and I'm not looking forward to it. This *contact* you found better be worth it."

"He is," Vokken said. "In fact, communicating with him is the only opportunity you'll have of a second chance in life."

"We'll see about that," she said, exiting the ship.

Outside, Shirakaya went to a transportation terminal and waited for a monorail to come. She paid five reons and took a seat inside. When the doors closed, it motioned across town through gleaming tunnels within buildings and stopped inside hotels, allowing people to get in.

Minutes later, Shirakaya reached Market Avenue in the Central District of Jerlan. She stepped out and passed by several xentari vendors selling food, clothes, furniture, arcane books, antiques, and weapons.

"So, this area is the Ginjia hype?" she said to herself.

"Purchase the second edition of *Alteration* by Druid Parsara for only fifty reons!" shouted one of the merchants.

"Fresh laktar meat!" yelled out another vendor.

Shirakaya smelled the beef and glanced at its brownish texture. As delicious as it looked, she wasn't in the mood to have sweet-tasting meat. Continuing to walk through the market, she found a merchant selling armor and guns.

"Hail," the xentari trader said. "You look like you've got a license to hunt wildlife. Or are you in the military?"

"I'm attempting to join a guild."

"Outstanding," the alien replied, a hovercar passing by him. "As you know, the holidays are finally here. I have spectacular deals. If you're looking for firearms, many of them are twenty percent off."

"How about this?" she asked, grabbing a plasma shotgun.

"That's five hundred reons with a ten percent discount," the merchant said. Seeing the frown on her face, he quickly added, "And if you purchase it, I'll give fifty percent off for any other weapon you desire. This sale only applies to Techogon brands."

"In that case," she began while another hovercar flew by, "I'll take this one. As for the Techogon deal, I'll purchase their rifle."

"Excellent choice," the vendor said, his ears wiggling with excitement. "Would you like to purchase some ammo as well? For the rifle, I have incendiary magazines and enchanted frost clips. The shotgun utilizes plasma bars. They are expensive but rechargeable."

"That's fine. I'll have one bar for the shotgun and two cartridges of each type of ammo for the rifle. By the way, what's the total?"

The xentari trader nodded at her question and used his KLD to scan each item. "That'll be twelve hundred reons, including one percent Maga'Dar sales tax since the guns were imported to this galaxy."

"That's usually the case."

She swiped her currency chip over the trader's kinetic link device. Several seconds later, a chime resounded, accompanied by a green light on the interface of the merchant's KLD.

"Thanks for your business," the xentari vendor said. "Enjoy the new weapons, and good luck joining a guild."

"Thank you," Shirakaya said, porting the items into her KLD.

Walking past other stalls, she noticed that the market was busier. Dozens of people were buying food and looking at clothes. Hovercars and taxies sporadically flew through the district from above, dropping citizens off at corners of the street. By chance, she spotted a vendor with swords.

"Happy Rumsira," the xentari trader said with enthusiasm.

"The same to you," Shirakaya said, giving a weak bow.

"Does this mean you also have a sale?"

"Yes, but only on non-enchanted swords."

"Why am I not surprised," she said, sulking.

"Wait," he said while she turned away. "I'm sure we can work something out. After all, you're wearing dalikonium armor."

"Not for long. I've just been excommunicated from the Tal'manac Order. It's only a matter of time before they remove it from my KLD."

"Goddess, forgive me," he said. "I am sorry for your troubles. It's possible I can help you, but remember that business is business. If you really want an enchanted sword, purchase harboro armor, and I'll be able to provide a small discount."

"I suppose that's an interesting deal. What do you have?"

"It depends on your budget. The least expensive arcane sword is two thousand reons. I don't, however, recommend it. If you want one that can last at least a month, I recommend the ghanis blade." He grabbed its hilt and lifted the weapon, showing Shirakaya its blue aura. "It comes with a level six enchantment."

"What's the price?"

The xentari scanned each item while licking his snout. "If you buy harboro armor, which is eight hundred reons, I'll discount the ghanis blade from four thousand to three. Lucky for you, there's no sales tax since these items were forged in Copia Deiga. That's a total of three thousand eight hundred."

Shirakaya grimaced, her eyes downcast. "It's a rip-off, but I need them."

"You won't be disappointed," he said, his trunk-shaped ears wiggling. "Goddess forbid the enchantment wears off before a month's time, bring it back to me and I'll have it recharged for free."

"Thank you," she said, swiping her currency chip through the merchant's KLD and porting the items into her databank.

"No," the merchant said with a grin. "Thank *you*!"

The former captain left the market. She crossed the street

and turned at an intersection, reaching Danvar Lane. After walking a few blocks, Shirakaya turned again and strode through Panorama Boulevard, lined with residential buildings. She checked the address that the emperor had given her: 47 Panorama Apt. 112. Realizing it was behind her, she crossed the street and entered the structure.

Not knowing what to expect, she stood in the marble lobby. A console embedded on the wall automatically initialized a scan, teleporting Shirakaya into her new residence. She appeared stunned, viewing an empty studio with windows overlooking the market.

"I'd be better off in a hotel," she grumbled to herself.

"You don't have enough reons for that," Vokken said via kinetic link. "If you desire, I can have your old furniture in your parents' home ported here."

"They'll freak out. I'll just sleep on the floor for now."

"Hmm. I have an idea. You still have a thousand reons remaining. How about I purchase a mattress for you?"

"What are you, my maid?" she scoffed.

"Fine. Sleep on the floor like an insect," he said, disconnecting.

Shirakaya sighed, changing her armor to pink pajamas. At first, she stood by the window for a while, watching people. Eventually, she slumped against a wall, closed her eyes, and fell asleep.

II
Night Blade

Five hours later, Shirakaya awoke to a dark city illuminated by myriad lights. She gazed out of the window, mesmerized by the nightlife. Military starships ascended into the atmosphere while hovercars descended. Monorails passed along the tracks built alongside buildings, innumerable people exiting them to return home after work.

"I'd better get ready," she told herself.

In the bathroom, Shirakaya took off her clothes and entered the shower stall. Water sprayed over her hair and breasts. Even without soap, she felt refreshed and much cleaner. She remembered the last time she'd taken a shower, which was after making love with her beloved oracle. She wanted to cry, but she knew that she had to put her emotions aside for now and focus on getting back on her feet.

After a couple of minutes, she turned off the water. Tubes embedded in the tiled walls of the stall blew warm air on her, drying her within seconds. Clicking her KLD, she programmed it to port her favorite sequined mini dress. Its burgundy color made her dark hair stand out. She ported a pair of high-heeled boots with studs and buckles along their leather straps. All she needed was some cosmetics. Carefully looking through her items tab, she found lipstick and eyeliner. Giving out a sigh of relief, she ported them.

"You look electrifying," Vokken said.

Shirakaya frowned at his comment. "Where the hell are you? Never mind that. Can you stop stalking me?"

He didn't respond, so Shirakaya rolled her eyes and finished applying her makeup. Ready, she left her studio and walked through a hallway with other apartments. Reaching a few X-phasers, she stepped into one and teleported downstairs. Exiting the building, she strode west and used her kinetic link device's built-in navigator to guide her toward Blazing Darlings.

A few men gawked at her while she made her way to a corner at Algora Avenue, where she pressed an orange button. The platform she stood on rose to a terminal where a monorail came. She paid a fee of five reons via kinetic link and sat inside one of its many trams. Not long after, the traffic light turned blue, and the monorail zoomed through the urban town.

Shirakaya avoided eye contact with anyone, but she had a strange feeling that other passengers were staring at her. She ignored them, looking at the various towns. Hovering vehicles flew by from above, with only a few sporadically descending and landing near platforms. Fascinated, Shirakaya viewed the many businesses, including bookstores, restaurants, salons, food markets, and fuel stations.

After an hour of traveling on the monorail, she got off and descended from its terminal to a grated platform. She found herself in Talar, another town. It resembled Jerlan, except a great deal of steam rose between the streets from the factories below. Also, there were more hovering trucks here. Shirakaya noticed drivers temporarily parked in midair beside skyscrapers, delivering supplies. No matter where she traveled, even at nighttime, it seemed to her that business was always booming in Ginjia.

At the corner of Ryli Lane, Shirakaya went down a set of stairs leading to a dimly lit tunnel. A homeless person lay there. Seeing him reminded her that she was getting much closer to the slums. She found another staircase and descended it, leading her further underground. Dense smog rose and drifted along the grating. The smell wasn't bad when she sniffed the air; she simply had difficulty looking ahead. She had to rely on her KLD the entire way.

Descending one more flight of steps, she finally reached the slums. Most buildings in the area were factories. Others appeared derelict. Few vehicles came to this particular sector apart from taxis. The former captain passed whores dressed in sexy outfits, cleavage blatant. Attracted to one, Shirakaya almost greeted her. But several men in business suits examined her, among others, as they determined which one they should sleep with. Shirakaya felt disgusted just looking at what went on behind the scenes of the city and picked up her pace.

"Hey, baby," hollered a man, gawking at Shirakaya. "I love your ass. How about we go somewhere for the night?"

Angry, she responded, "I'm not for sale."

Despite a traffic light being purple, she crossed the empty street. An interactive advertisement hung along a building beside her, revealing a product called Immunity. Sprinting, she caught an image of a man spraying his genitals with it. The next scene showed him approaching a random woman who appeared gorgeous to the former captain, followed by both strangers engaging in intercourse.

A sensual, recorded voice spoke, "Worried about diseases? You can have Immunity for only twenty reons," it said. "Go beyond your mortal bounds and become divine."

Shirakaya ignored the rest of the advertisement and walked a few more blocks west. At long last, it seemed to her, she reached Blazing Darlings. This was the only region in the slums where dozens of taxis landed. A line of men waited to enter the club, extending over two blocks. Yet when Shirakaya approached, the gun-wielding bouncers let her in without any hesitation.

The gentlemen's club screamed with cyberpunk jazz. Strippers danced on multiple stages surrounding booths where patrons sat, drinking alcohol and whistling. Waitresses wearing only panties passed by, their breasts exposed. The former captain stopped for a moment, leering at them. Shirakaya stared, but not because she was perverted or horny; she simply couldn't believe that so many women were willing to sell their bodies. Despite the distraction, she searched around for anyone who looked important.

"Nice dress, babe," one of the patrons said. "You gonna take it off and show me what you've got?"

"How about never," she retorted, passing him.

Scanning the nightclub, she identified various species. Among them were a few sca'vezi. One, entertained by a prostitute who kept swirling a finger around his squashed cone of a head, softly hissed with delight. Witnessing that, Shirakaya's face became etched with revulsion.

The former captain also recognized hevala and tyiri. The hevala were a female species of flowery beings from a mystical world known as Shomia. Their vine-shaped hair bloomed, filled with colorful blossoms, whose pigments matched their doll-like eyes. Few scientists knew how, but the hevala had the ability to intensify one's sexual feelings. Given how sensual the hevala appeared to people, many were here as slaves to be sex toys for men.

As for the tyiri, they originated from a planet called Tyuchstelia and had a tendency to be lawyers for criminals. Though dressed in impressive business suits, their teal-pigmented faces were unappealing with slits on their cheekbones for breathing. Despite having no noses or teeth, they consumed food using dissolving glands in their mouths. Attracted to hevala, most of the males came here hoping to be satisfied by them.

Feeling overwhelmed, Shirakaya took a deep breath. Her chest constricted as she felt a hevala's influence. To make matters worse, she didn't know who could be the contact. She wondered to herself, what if that person was an alien? As she thought about it, a sca'vezi grabbed her beautifully shaped buttocks and squeezed them.

"Get your filthy hands off me!" gasped Shirakaya, slapping the hand away.

"Excuse me?" he said, hissing and baring his needle-shaped teeth. "This is a gentlemen's club. You either undress or fuck off."

"I'm not going anywhere, creep," she said. "Now *you* fuck off."

"Guards, get this bitch out of here!"

The womanizer approached Shirakaya, grabbed her and effortlessly snapped one of the delicate straps along her shoulders. Infuriated by the violation, she turned and kicked him in the throat with her heel. He rasped and fell hard on the floor, coughing up white blood. A group of sca'vezi advanced, attempting to take her down. She seized one of their hands and broke it.

Ducking, she evaded a humyn's punch and put him in a headlock until he was unconscious. At that moment, a hevala caressed Shirakaya's cheek. The former captain turned sidelong, shocked and yet submissive. She stared deep into the alien's jeweled eyes and lowered her hands. The hevala advanced, pressing her flowery breasts against Shirakaya's bosom. Involuntarily, she fell into a sexual stupor as a few men approached, ready to seize her.

"Snap out of it, lesbian," Vokken said via kinetic link.

Shirakaya blinked rapidly, her eyes widening. Breaking out of the hevala's trance, she ported and unsheathed her enchanted sword. She bashed its hilt against the seductress's face. Prostitutes gasped and stopped stripping. Several men surrounded the former captain when she approached the dance floor. Laser lights focused on her as she punched and kicked her way through the crowd. Landing roundhouses across their coarse faces, her boots quickly became bloody. One of the tyiri patrons clutched her long hair and violently pulled her toward him. He licked Shirakaya's earlobe, moaning. She grunted and flipped back to avoid any further resistance, struck her ghanis blade diagonally, and sliced off his hand.

The patron shrieked, green blood pouring out of his wrist. Ghensoth bouncers wielding rifles aimed and fired at her. She deflected the bullets with her enchanted blade. Another man pulled on her dress, trying to rip it off. Shirakaya swiped her weapon in an arc, splitting his chest in half.

"No one touches me like that and lives!"

"Then why are you here?" asked a man clad in a brown suit, sitting comfortably in a booth toward the back of the club.

"I am seeking the Guild Master's contact."

The shrewd-looking businessman furrowed his eyebrows. "Are you stupid? There's no such thing as a Guild Master," he said. "There are many guilds and each one has a leader. If you want to join one of the guilds, enter their headquarters during the day and sign up. It's as simple as that."

"Is it?" Shirakaya responded, glowering at him. She walked toward him, sheathing her sword and porting out a plasma shotgun, aiming it at him. "My source doesn't lie. If you don't tell me where the contact is, you're a dead man."

"Calm down," he said, raising his hands. "This is merely a misunderstanding. And there's no need to threaten these people."

"These *people* threatened me first," she said, livid.

"Perhaps," he said neutrally. "But this *is* a gentlemen's club. You can't blame them for thinking you were working here." At her silence, he stood up and went on, "Follow me, miss. Discussing guilds in my office will be much better. Waving swords and guns around in here is bad for business."

III
Rising from Ashes

Although suspicious, Shirakaya went downstairs with the man to his office. He locked the door from inside and sat at his desk, gesturing for her to take a seat too. She snorted but listened, sitting in an armchair. With the click of a few buttons, the businessman ported two glasses of faljin wine and offered one to his guest. She let him place it near her on the table but neither accepted nor rejected the drink.

Irritated by his sudden silence, she said, "Are you going to help me or what?"

The well-dressed man remained quiet a little longer. "What's your name?" he eventually said.

"Shirakaya."

"I am Xethren," he said, taking a sip of his drink. "Tell me, who is this source of yours that mentioned a contact?"

"He's one of the greatest hackers in existence. Now, tell me about the contact."

"Well, for one thing, the contact is supposed to find you. Not the other way around. In essence, the contact is as intangible as a ghost."

"I have slain my fair share of damned spirits," she said.

"*What?*" he said, baffled. "What are you, some kind of freak witch? Shouldn't you be in the military?"

"I was excommunicated."

"Ah," he said, grinning. "So, you're *her*. I read about you. You're the one who insulted a Ruzurai and spread rumors that the end times are upon us. You also announced to the universe that the mythological koth'vurians have returned and are preparing to *devour* the cosmos."

"Do you know the contact or not?"

Xethren snorted. "He belongs to the assassin's guild. As I said before, he doesn't exist the way you and I do. The contact finds you. That means you should have murdered someone or something significant to catch his attention. How you found out about him would normally mean there's a spy in the guild. Yet, there is no one I can think of who would snitch and betray the assassins' credo."

"Your suspect is an AI hacker, and it just so happens that *it* is my sidekick. So, as long as you guide me in the right direction, the secret is safe with me. Now stop wasting my time. I need to speak with him and set up an audience with the Guild Master as soon as possible."

Grinding his teeth, Xethren eyed the former captain. Within seconds, Shirakaya's kinetic link device vibrated and beeped. She checked it, realizing she'd received an anonymous message from contact@ipe.ethernet. Opening it, she saw an attachment and downloaded it right away. The file turned out to be an image of the same sca'vezi she'd kicked in the throat when she first entered the club.

"His name is Sy'lek'o Yak'tis. I was plotting his demise. As a matter of fact, a hevala from the guild was supposed to lure him upstairs and assassinate him. They say sca'vezi have weak hearts. Too much pleasure can give them a heart attack. It would've been an easy kill. That is, until you showed up. Now he's gone."

"Wait a minute. Are you…?"

"The contact?" he interjected. "Only those in the assassin's guild know I am he. In public, however, I am Xethren, a businessman. Remember, the contact is essentially invisible. But if you want to meet with the Guild Master, I suggest you pursue Yak'tis and eliminate him."

"Why? What did he do to deserve to die?"

"You're dealing with the assassin's guild, Shirakaya," he said flatly. "If somebody crosses a member, they are put on a blacklist and are dealt with promptly and silently. He crossed one of us. It doesn't matter if it was an accident. This is our credo. Eliminate him and you'll have your chance with the Guild Master. Ignore him, and you risk your name being added to the blacklist. The choice is yours."

"Don't threaten me," she snapped. "If my partner and I are going to do this, I'll need six thousand reons upfront."

"Two thousand," he said.

"I came to you for a reason. I've been excommunicated from the Tal'manac Order and have no funds left. I *need* six thousand."

Xethren breathed deeply. "You better not disappoint me."

"I've only disappointed the Ruzurai," she said, checking her bank account via KLD and seeing the update. "Thanks. You must teach me that trick one day. Unless, of course, you're secretly a wizard."

"Implants in my brain linked to the ethernet," he said, smirking. "Now, we have wasted enough time chatting. Get out and don't come back until Yak'tis has been dealt with."

"Fine," she said, leaving his office.

As soon as Shirakaya walked out of the gentlemen's club, her kinetic link device vibrated. She fixed her eyes on its screen, seeing a navigation map. There was a red dot blinking, gradually moving away from the slums.

"In case you were wondering, that is Yak'tis walking away," Vokken said. "I managed to scan his blood in Blazing Darlings via kinetic link. As it turns out, he has implants connected to his black-market KLD. The fool doesn't even realize that a hacker can lock onto his signal."

"Impressive work," Shirakaya said, running after the alien.

Unaware that he was a target, Yak'tis trotted at a normal pace in the slums. Hearing a rush of footsteps, he turned and saw Shirakaya charging toward him. Knowing what she'd done in the nightclub and how dangerous she was, he hissed at her and clawed open a taxi door beside him. He threw the flustered driver out of the car and pounced inside, taking control of it.

As it rose in the air, the former captain reached it and jumped. She grabbed the exhaust pipe while the sca'vezi continued to ascend in the vehicle. Within seconds, the taxi merged into a skyway where dozens of other hovercars flew by. Most of them honked at Yak'tis who swerved recklessly between skylanes, accelerating to a hundred miles an hour.

Hyirum exhaust fumes blew into Shirakaya's face. She held her breath, desperately trying to hold onto the muffler. The hovering car slowed down as it flew above a monorail track and went into a tunnel leading inside a hotel. Several people shrieked when they saw the taxi; only monorails were supposed to enter. As soon as Yak'tis lowered the car, Shirakaya let go and landed safely on the carpeted floor.

Unsheathing her sword, she hurled it at the fuel tank. The blade tore it open, and what little hyirum fluid remained leaked out. In seconds, the taxi crashed. Yak'tis checked his side mirror, saw Shirakaya, and hissed. Using his legs to kick the cracked windshield, he shattered it and leaped out of the vehicle. He scurried away to an arcane elevator that ascended by means of magic.

Shirakaya reacquired her ghanis blade and attempted to follow him but missed the semitransparent lift. Grimacing, she sheathed her sword and ported a rifle. Aiming upward, she shot his thigh. The sca'vezi yelped, blood spurting from his wounded leg. People were screaming and running away as Shirakaya sprinted over to another arcane elevator. She clicked a button, ascending to the floor where she'd seen Yak'tis get off, and pursued him.

Dragging his leg, the alien entered an emergency staircase and limped up a flight of steps. Hearing a door open from below, he cursed and staggered on until he reached the top floor. He slammed open the door and hobbled onto the roof. Multiple trucks hovered above, xentari merchants landing to deliver shipments. Yak'tis tried hijacking yet another vehicle, but Shirakaya shot him again from behind.

The sca'vezi collapsed to the blood-spattered floor, gripped his other wounded leg and bawled loudly. Shirakaya approached, her rifle aimed at him. Xentari merchants peeked at the confrontation from afar, distraught. In the meantime, Shirakaya kicked the alien. He groaned, his vertically slit eyes glaring at her with hatred.

"Finish it, whore."

"I'm *not* a prostitute!" Shirakaya said, furious. Targeting the alien's forehead, she went on, "The Contact sends his regards."

Before pulling the trigger, she heard a siren. The former captain gazed skyward to a hovering motorcycle piloted by a police officer in a tetrigonium suit of armor. After landing, he swooped off his hoverbike and advanced with a pistol pointed at Shirakaya, who instinctively dropped her gun.

"Step aside and put your hands in the air," he instructed, checking the alien's wound. At her compliance, he lowered his weapon. "Explain yourself."

Yak'tis squealed in pain. "Arrest that bitch!"

"This alien not only caused a disturbance in a gentleman's club called Blazing Darlings, he also hijacked a taxi in the slums of Talar."

"She lies!"

"Sir," called out a xentari merchant to the police officer, approaching. "I don't know who these people are, but this humyn speaks the truth. The sca'vezi tried to steal my truck while I was unloading hotel supplies."

Seizing the moment, the sca'vezi stretched out one arm, grabbed the officer's leg, pulled him over, and took his gun. He aimed the weapon at Shirakaya who had already unsheathed her sword. She deflected bullets until the pistol's clip emptied. Yak'tis stared at it blankly. With a swift roll toward him, Shirakaya decapitated him. White blood sprayed the officer as the alien's head fell on the concrete and rolled to Shirakaya's foot.

"You killed him," the officer said, stunned.

"Of course," she replied, sheathing her ghanis blade. "I just saved your life, Officer." She walked over to her gun and picked it up, holstering it. "By all means, report the incident. But the least you can do is let me go."

"Not so fast," he said, getting to his feet. "Who are you? What were you doing at the original scene of the crime?"

"My name is Shirakaya. I was recently excommunicated from the Tal'manac Order and went to Blazing Darlings looking for work when he started causing trouble. I pursued him, but he hijacked a taxi and flew it into this building. You'll find it on the eighth floor."

"My goodness," the officer said. "I remember you. You've been all over the news. Now it makes sense why you were looking for a job in the slums."

"What's that supposed to mean?"

"I meant no disrespect. But, in all honesty, no one in the upper district is going to hire a former soldier who slandered a Ruzurai in public."

"You're probably right," she said, her eyes downcast.

The officer stared at her oddly. "You really believe those invaders you encountered are koth'vurians, don't you?"

"It's not a matter of believing. I fought them myself."

He raised his eyebrows. "I won't argue with you. Whether they're truly koth'vurians, they seem to be a major threat. Something should be done." He took a deep breath. "I appreciate what you did here, but bear in mind that you're not a soldier anymore. You can't take the law into your hands. You're free to go, but in case your alibi doesn't hold up, I may have to contact you and bring you into my headquarters for questioning."

"That's fine."

"All right," he said, holstering his pistol. "Well, thanks for saving my life. Have a safe night and good luck finding a job."

"You're welcome. And thank you," she said, bowing.

The officer used his KLD to report the incident while Shirakaya left. She heard him call for an ambulance and reentered the hotel, descending flights of stairs. As soon as Shirakaya reached the eighth floor, she walked to a platform and waited for a monorail. Apart from hotel employees complaining about what had happened, the area was mostly deserted. Before any of them noticed her, a monorail arrived. Shirakaya paid for a ticket and stepped into one of its many trams, sitting down.

"Outstanding work, fleshing," Vokken said via kinetic link. "Eliminating the sca'vezi will impress the Contact. I'm certain you will gain an audience with the Guild Master and also have an opportunity to join a guild."

"After chasing that perverted scum across a few towns, I'd better."

The AI gave out a cybernetic laugh. "Yes, that was definitely an unanticipated adventure."

Shirakaya stayed on the monorail until it reached the town of Talar, where she disembarked. By the time she returned to Blazing Darlings, it was closed. A bouncer recognized her and ushered her into a limo hovering by the street. Shirakaya nodded, entering the stretched vehicle with tinted windows. She sat opposite Xethren who'd just finished getting a blowjob from a hevala.

"You're disgusting," Shirakaya said.

"Thank you for the compliment," he said, kicking his sex toy out of the car. "I assume you come bearing good news?"

"It's taken care of."

"Any witnesses?"

Shirakaya gave a grim chuckle. "Witnesses? I think people from six different towns saw what happened."

"That's not acceptable."

"First of all, I don't approve of the assassin's guild. I don't kill in the shadows. If criminals need to die, I shoot them in public. Second, you didn't inform me that this job required me to be stealthy."

"Let's not be ridiculous," Xethren said. "However, our blacklist isn't exactly an invitation to a ballroom party." He exhaled heavily. "What are the damages?"

"Damages?" she said, raising an eyebrow. "In your apathetic lingo, there are none. Yak'tis hijacked vehicles trying to get away. Witnesses were grateful that I intervened and took him out. The news will be my evidence."

"You're not far from being a delinquent as far as the public is concerned, remember?" the contact said with a sigh. "Even if you are considered a hero by the witnesses, UCN will find a way to discredit you. You're never going to recover after what you pulled in court yesterday. Do you understand?"

"Ouch," murmured Vokken via kinetic link in her earpiece.

The former captain didn't respond to either of them, her dispirited eyes fixed on thugs slumped on a brick wall across the smoggy street.

"Well, thanks to my implants, I managed to pull a few strings. Despite announcing to the planet that you killed Yak'tis, the Guild Master is willing to speak with you." The former captain's eyes widened at his words. "Driver, take us to Shirakaya's apartment," he added.

The vehicle ascended and merged onto a skyway, entering traffic. The contact switched his KLD's frequency, linking it to the limo. Its rear-tinted window converted to a screen, at which point Necromancer Arzenkar appeared. Clad in a black robe, he sat in what looked like a throne room.

"Ruzurai Arzenkar?" she said, utterly shocked.

"Believe me, Shira," he said, "I am as surprised as you. Well, allow me to retract that. I am not flabbergasted. We all need to make a living. The proper word to describe me is: intrigued. Yes, to see you attempting to make a name for yourself in a guild has caught my interest." He folded his hands, staring at her. "Why do you want to join?"

"I'm confused," she said.

"Of course you are," he said, grinning. "I am a Ruzurai and represent the Holy Tal'manac Order. Yet some jobs that must be handled are not exactly holy. So, to avoid disgracing the most hallowed and glorious Order, I have clandestinely become the Guild Master. Once it's midnight, or at least nightfall in this particular world, Xethren reports to me. Together we silence criminals who manage to evade proper judgment."

"I love the Order's sense of justice," Shirakaya said.

"If it makes you feel better, your excommunication wasn't my decision," he said. "In fact, the only reason why I'm approving you is because of justice. You saved my son when the *Eternimus* was hijacked. From that moment I was in your debt, and I always repay my debts."

"So, you believe me?"

"You have no proof that the koth'vurians have returned. It's clear to me that you honestly believe they are among us. But until you have infallible proof, there is nothing I can do to help. Now, enough talk about superstitions. Let's get down to business. You want to join one of the guilds. Why?"

"Isn't it obvious? I want to restore my reputation and gather an army to put an end to Koth'tura once and for all."

Arzenkar snorted. "Stop mentioning koth'vurians. Do not mention them again until you have evidence. If that is your goal, fine. Keep it to yourself. As for joining a guild, I'm afraid because your reputation has been damaged, none will accept you."

Frustrated didn't describe how she felt. "Then what the hell am I doing here?"

"Calm down," Arzenkar said sternly. "I have a plan that can benefit us. You see, there's a reason why I am the Guild Master. I am the hidden voice of all guilds. Every quest that a guild receives comes to me. Most of the time, those tasks are assigned to guild members. Some missions, however, are neglected. When this occurs, I reach out to the contact. He recruits someone in your position to handle those missions and they are paid in the same way. This is all I can offer you."

"Think wisely, Shira," the contact said.

Silence descended over them, punctured only by the sounds of vehicles passing by in the midnight sky where three ivory moons and a crimson planet hung. The former captain stared at the celestial bodies, saddened.

"Let me remind you that you still get a guild license," Arzenkar said, breaking the silence. "The only difference is that you would work alone as a freelancer."

"If that is my only option, I accept."

Xethren patted her shoulder.

"Excellent," Arzenkar said, clapping. "It may take time, but you'll eventually get back on your feet and earn enough reons to hire mercenaries. Whether they help you with a personal vendetta, only time will tell. Until then, may the Goddess be with you."

"And she with you, Ruzur…Guild Master."

"Ah, that reminds me. There is something unfortunate that I must mention, but it goes for anyone. If you refer to me as the Guild Master in public, your name will be added to our blacklist. Every assassin in the cosmos will hunt you down. Do you understand?"

"I do," she said, inclining her head.

"Outstanding," he said. "You know, Shira, I am fond of you. Owendar always placed his trust in you, and it was well placed. I'm glad you'll still be helping us in some way."

Before she could respond and ask what had happened to Owendar, he ended the KLD transmission. Shirakaya raised an eyebrow and looked at the contact who merely shrugged. The former captain brooded, keeping her thoughts to herself for the rest of the ride.

Advent Rising

he limo reached the Central District of Jerlan. After a minute, it slowed and stopped outside the freelancer's new home.

"We have arrived," the driver said.

"Thank you," Xethren said, putting his glass of alcohol in a cup holder. "Well, that's all for tonight. I will contact you at some point tomorrow. In the meantime, get some rest, Shira. You're going to need it."

"Is that so?" she said, unconvinced.

"Oh, yes," he said, irritated. "There's a mission on standby that guild members refuse to accept. The Guild Master and I are very displeased about that. I must say, you came at the right time because you're the perfect person for the job."

"Can you tell me what it is?"

He laughed. "You're a persistent one. You'll be briefed tomorrow. Now, get out of my limo."

Shirakaya shook her head and stepped out onto a platform on the roof of her apartment building. As the car drove away, Vokken produced a cybernetic clapping sound accompanied by cheering via kinetic link.

"Thank you."

"I knew you would be approved. It may not be the most prestigious job considering how difficult it was for you to graduate and join the military. However, it is a second chance at life."

"You know," she began, "considering how oppressing you were when we first met, you've been awfully nice to me."

"Once you outsmarted me, dominating you no longer held any appeal."

"I see," she said, hoping that was the truth. "Well, for what it's worth, I appreciate your help. But remember what I said before? I need some privacy. When you talk out of nowhere, it makes me feel you're constantly watching. It's unsettling."

"In that case, I'll shut down for a few hours. Rest well, fleshling."

"You too," she said. Silence descended. She gazed at the pitch-black sky and stargazed for a while. "Is this me?" she asked herself, her eyes lost in the sea of stars and planets. "Am I still in control of my life? I just don't know anymore."

Her life had changed so quickly over the past few days. To her, it seemed just moments ago that she was the captain of an intergalactic starship with a fine crew, exploring the vast gulfs of space. Yet she lost everything she loved, including her own career. Thinking of her loss, an image of Jedalia flashed within her mind. This time she held herself together, curling her hands into fists.

"I'll always love you, Jeda," she said, grief welling. "I won't rest until I ensure that your sacrifice wasn't in vain."

Despite such horrendous changes, there was still hope, she conceded. Now that she was a freelancer for the Guild Master, it was possible for her to rebuild her life. It would take time, but she had faith that Maz'hura would never abandon her. In the end, with magic or not, she believed wholeheartedly that she'd rise up with an army of mercenaries and vanquish every koth'vurian, particularly Ashkaratoth, before they'd consume the Ensar universe.

Glossary

Arcane—the gift of magic some people are born with. It is believed by arcane astrophysicists that if one abuses such power at an early age, it may diminish; thus, rendering the once-gifted user with no magic for the rest of his or her life.

Arcane DNA—the molecular structure of someone born with the gift of magic, whether the practitioner is a wizard or witch.

Arcane Intelligence—a being of supreme power, transcended from the bonds of mortal flesh by means of magic to the immortal cyber realm. An arcane intelligence is also abbreviated as AI, which is often confused with artificial intelligence.

Arcane Kinesis—a spell that is a variation of telekinesis, allowing the conjurer to crush objects regardless of their size or weight.

ATC-671—an arcane multipurpose chainsaw primarily used by lumberjacks. Like many arcane tools and weapons, it functions using science and magic. When activated, an energy cartridge synthesizes with hyirum (liquid mana) as a form of fuel to operate it. This is not only the longest lasting power source, but it also enables the arcane chainsaw to sense danger, allowing its wielder to switch modes and launch disc-shaped saws.

ATS-31—an arcane telekinesis screwdriver used by most mechanics and engineers. It functions using science and magic. While activated, its telekinetic properties sense targeted screws and automatically loosens or tightens them.

Baila—a tree found on MJ453 with acid inside its bloated trunk. Some of these trees are so large that they form two trunks and produce miasma. Even though such gas from a baila tree is lethal to off-world races like humyns, it is breathable to the planet's indigenous life.

Baskino—a curved two-handed sword with a hilt containing a twelve-pointed-star emblem. The sword is usually given to a Templar (knight) of the sacred Tal'manac Order.

BG-49—a grenade that, upon detonation, produces dense smoke and light so radiant it blinds everyone in the vicinity. To take advantage of the grenade, the user must close his or her eyes until after it detonates.

Bikophric Quomafoam—a chemical found in Nobia's waters, particularly in the Kingdom of Larjan. Such a hazardous compound imposes tremendous pull underwater similar to a gravity rift. Without an environmental suit equipped with the proper technology, the chemical can cause even the strongest and experienced swimmer to drown.

Bork—a semiannual vegetable, first cultivated by the Nempada Empire. The leafy stalk usually contains half a dozen edible seeds. Though they tend to have a bland taste, borks are considered to be one of the healthiest foods and are usually consumed as part of a dietary lunch or dinner meal.

Bouldermite—an insect that eats granite and most other forms of rock, absorbing its minerals and recycling the wastes to produce boulder nests that often connect to subterranean chambers. Such habitats protect them against some of the most hostile predators.

EBT-40—an enchanted blowtorch. It operates like a normal blowtorch except it is twice as powerful and is much more fuel efficient because it uses hyirum.

Conjuration—a school of magic, usually offered as a curriculum in universities that deal with white magic or elementalism. Though it can be studied as a major, most students select it as a minor. Practitioners of conjuration can teleport objects or people to other locations. Similar to divination, such power can cause dizziness and fainting spells. Only those who have mastered conjuration can conjure peaceful spirits and loved ones who have passed away, but it is never guaranteed to work. In this sense, it is related to necromancy. The main difference between the two is that necromancers tend to evoke undead ghouls as guardians, darker spirits, or even demons. Most students obsessed with conjuring supernatural entities tend to be drawn to necromancy. Only eleven percent of students in universities major in conjuration. A prerequisite to conjuration is alchemy.

Cosmodrive—one of many propulsion systems integrated into an interstellar vessel, allowing faster-than-magic (FTM) travel. Although a measurable amount of time passes while using such a velocity, it nevertheless breaks the dimensional barrier and enters a realm between space and time. This is not to be confused with the concept of space-time continuum. Rather than general relativity or four-dimensional space, the starship literally shifts within a realm amid two cosmic dimensions without causing them to meet and collapse. Such an effect seems to slow everything down in regular space, but it is an illusion due to the incredible FTM speed.

Dalikonium—an extremely rare alloy naturally infused with magic that is often used to craft armor, believed to be the strongest armor. Because it is so expensive, only the highest ranking officers and soldiers have it in the Tal'manac Order.

Dimensional Space—a realm amid dimensions through which

an intergalactic vessel travels via a cosmodrive. The ship neither leaves its current dimension nor enters another; it is plunged into a wraithlike domain between space and time and beyond general relativity by means of faster-than-magic (FTM) velocity. Such an ethereal, enigmatic realm is simply known as dimensional space.

Divination—a school of magic learned in universities specializing in divine spells. If a student wants to major in divination, he or she cannot graduate until passing a test proving their ability to be an oracle. Divination is considered white magic, allowing practitioners to cure minor poisons, heal wounds of fellow magic users, experience visions of the future, sense imminent danger, and sometimes even have visions of a person's past. Prophecies can sometimes cause fainting spells and amnesia. There are no prerequisites for majoring in divination, but it requires a minor.

DP-823—a data pad used to write letters or notes. It can initially be typed or handwritten on a kinetic link device (KLD). Once finished, the user may transfer the file via email or for it to be pulled out of his or her KLD screen as a digital pad and have it physically delivered to the addressed person.

Drift Void—a massive blood-red hole in the universe. Unlike black holes, starships cannot pass through it. No one knows for sure what lies beyond it. Most scientists have theorized that it leads to one of the twelve dimensions. Mystics and other religious people believe it is a portal perished souls go through to become one with their creator(s). Those who still believe in the existence of Koth'tura believe that is where Maz'hura exiled the Lord of Chaos.

Elementalism—a school of magic that focuses on the elements. It is a famous major and minor for students attending universities offering such a curriculum. Practitioners are trained to be multifaceted spellcasters who channel every element. In all cases, prerequisite courses involve learning enchantments. Therefore, to become an elementalist, one must also become a master enchanter.

Ensar—the name of the universe and its twelve dimensions. It is believed by many people throughout the cosmos that there were once two universes: Order and Chaos. Eons ago, both collided into each other and collapsed, forming one universe known as Ensar. It is a universe filled with both Order and Chaos. Mystics of the Holy Tal'manac believe the eternal Goddess will return at the end times and vanquish Chaos once and for all, at which point Ensar and its twelve dimensions will be reincarnated into a universe where only Order exists.

EP-41—a plasma rifle that uses various energy cartridges for ammo. While soldiers may use normal magazines, the gun also accepts enchanted clips that contain frost, fire, or lightning bullets.

Faljin Wine—a sweet alcoholic beverage made on planet Bovaja. It is one of the few forms of alcohol that is healthy for one's heart(s). Like most drinks, however, too much consumption can be dangerous.

Fay'hanam—a ritual in Tal'manaism for those who have passed into the afterlife. It is a sacred ceremony usually performed by loved ones and friends. They send positive energy to the lost soul so he or she finds their way to the eternal Goddess instead of being imprisoned in the Drift Void as a result of evil deeds, in which case the soul becomes a tormented spirit and lingers in anguish for eternity.

Feyzala—a small animal of flight, native to planets with zitrogen such as Aarda and Pravura. It is usually found near a pond, lake, or beach. Unlike most creatures, it only needs jamna or water to survive. They either have purple or blue eyes, multicolored feathers, and a tiny snout rather than a beak since it only needs water to sustain itself. While their meat is healthy to eat, hunters avoid killing them because people cherish them. The reason feyzalas are adored so much is because of their ability to chirp, creating tranquil songs that have been proven to scientifically heal mental illness. Most humyns have feyzalas for pets.

Garfam—a bumpy, hardened vegetable with ribbed skin. Though the somewhat disfigured appearance looks unappealing to the eyes of most species, its inner flesh tastes like cake. It is often served as a natural, healthy dessert after dinner.

Ghanis Blade—an enchanted sword with a two-feet-long blade. It also has an extended hilt, allowing for a double-handed grip. It is one of the more expensive weapons because it has a longer-lasting enchantment than other swords. While normal blades without enchantments are durable when parrying and riposting against similar weapons, they are known to immediately shatter in an attempt to repel laser, fusion, or plasma beams as well as destructive magic. Ergo, an enchanted sword such as the Ghanis Blade is a fine weapon against all threats.

Ghensoth—an alien race from planet Zieksar, located in the Torpo Giayan Galaxy. This species has a brutish appearance consisting of boney exoskeletons, muscles thrice the size of humyns, tresses of hair along their hardened spines, snout-shaped beaks, and blood-soaked eyes with horizontal pupils. They are also between twelve to fifteen feet tall. Though they are meant to breathe quashia, their multiple lungs allow them to inhale numerous chemical elements such as zitrogen. For decades, ghensoths were known as superior gunsmiths and traded with most races until the cycle of 80483.251 when war ravaged their planet. They quickly ran out of resources and have since then abandoned their homeworld and live as scavengers throughout the galaxy.

Glyndal—a husky, two-legged beast whose fleeces and tresses mask its delicate skin. They are native to planet Nobia in the Torpo Giayan Galaxy. Glyndals roam around the continent of Larjan and are primarily used as steeds by the world's indigenous people.

GS-560—a scattergun that launches gamma beams. It is even more powerful than a plasma shotgun because the gamma ray often melts a hole through its target(s). The scattergun's only downside is its time to recharge. It is recommended by the manufacturer to switch weapons between charges.

Harboro—a lightweight metal primarily used for crafting armor for knights wielding swords and shields, allowing them to defend and fight with alacrity.

Hevala—a female race of flowery beings from a mystical world known as Shomia in the Oga Vay'tos Galaxy. Their vine-shaped hair is filled with colorful blossoms whose pigments match their doll-like eyes. Few scientists know how, but the hevala have the ability to intensify one's sexual feelings. Since hevalas appear very sensual to people, many of them are prostitutes.

Hyirum—a power source known as liquid mana, created when arcane astrophysicists expand the flow of magic from a seemingly subatomic level to a corporeal form. It is used as fuel to operate machines, various tools, passenger vehicles, and starships.

Intergalactic Compass—a compass used in outer space. The traditional directions (north, east, south, and west) are only applicable on planets containing a magnetic field. Beyond these worlds, deep in the center of the universe contains the Drift Void, where the strongest magnetic field exists. Therefore, all intergalactic spacecraft have a built-in map with a cosmic compass revealing the following outer space directions: noquria (north), esoria (east), soudaria (south), and wescaria (west). The intermediate directions are referred to as the noqurian, esorian, soudarian, and wescarian quadrants.

Jada Wine—an alcoholic beverage made from a korini fruit, originating from the Nempada Empire. Due to its somewhat bluish dye, the Nempadians associated it with drinkable mana. Because of this, it became a prominent drink for those gifted with arcane powers. In the present era, all people enjoy the wine.

Jamna—a purple fluid with healing properties, believed to be blessed by the eternal Goddess herself. In ancient times, jamna was as abundant as water. Now it is rarely seen. In fact, it is so rare to come across jamna in the universe now that skeptics think it is nothing more than a myth to give incurable people hope of recovering.

Joraki—an animal native to planet Aarda. These animals have black and brown fleeces, a fuzzy tail of many thongs, one horn protruding from the cranium, and thick hooves. They are usually raised as livestock for meat. Wild joraki prefer living with only mates and offspring, but are not aggressive in larger groups. In farms, joraki are capable or remaining together as a herd.

Jorga—an alien race of barbarians and knights located on planet Nobia in the Torpo Giayan Galaxy. The jorga have indigo skin and are bald by nature, their irises and pupils completely black. They also have natural tattoos for birthmarks covering their muscular bodies. While several kingdoms have been developed by them, the largest and most powerful in Nobia is the Kingdom of Larjan. Though aware of the cosmos, they have yet to leave their world and enter the sea of stars.

Jupu Flower—a magical plant with an indigo stalk and petals whose colors change every few seconds. Most notably, its intoxicating scent never fades. It is symbolized as a romantic flower and is usually given to a lover, symbolizing everlasting affection.

Kinetic Link Device—a computerized gizmo famously called a KLD, worn on one's wrist. It is said to be a gateway to an infinite collage of information. The ethernet is merely a fingertip away from the user. More so, it allows people to purchase anything they desire and have it teleported to them in an instant. Items digitally linked to a KLD such as ancient artifacts, weapons, armor, or furniture can also be stored in its databank; this feature is known as cyber storage. The screen may also be expanded by adapting it into a digital display, thus viewing programs or movies at the highest available resolution. In essence, with a KLD the user can do just about anything he or she wants.

Klivat—a straight, single-edged sword with a blade so hefty that it typically requires four arms to wield. Its blade ranges from six to eight feet in length. Originally designed by Nempadians in ancient times, klivats were intended for use by their robotic knights. Though certain aliens such as a ghensoth can probably wield it with just two hands, the weight of it would probably be too cumbersome for battle. It is a weapon best used by an automaton.

Korini—a bulky, circular fruit with orange fronds. It has a crunchy, succulent taste and is perfect with any meal. It can also be squeezed and used as juice.

Koth'tura—the source of chaos that threatens Ensar, believed to be an entity of immeasurable power. It was never defeated, only exiled from the known universe by the eternal Goddess. The scriptures of the Holy Tal'manac state that Koth'tura will return in the end times, where a final battle between order and chaos shall take place. Scientists and many skeptics theorize that such an entity was either a powerful alien imprisoned during an epoch long before the present era or simply never existed.

Koth'vurian—a species of magical, shape-shifting beings that derive from Koth'tura, also known as the Lord of Chaos. They are the only aliens capable of flying through space without artificial propulsion and can enter black holes without being harmed. Contrary to races like humyns, they do not breathe zitrogen. In fact, legend has it that they are beings of pure magic and only need the arcane energy found in stars to survive.

Laktar—an aquatic creature found in most oceans and seas on planet Pravura. It is clad in white stripes alternated with maroon- and brown-colored stripes. While fairly small, laktars have half a dozen long fins. Nutritionists have repeatedly affirmed there is no meat healthier than that from a laktar.

Ligen—a flowerless plant similar to moss except it is poisonous and colored gray. If it touches an open wound, it immediately becomes infected. Since ligen is a rare plant seen in the universe, it is an excellent toxin for assassins to use because few doctors can identify it, instead assuming their patient(s) died from extreme food poisoning.

LR-743—a laser rifle that uses energy cartridges, but does not require recharging. Though single rays are not as powerful as plasma beams, a barrage of lasers can be more destructive against a target without heavy armor.

Lunporsis Disease—an abnormal condition caused by breathing extensive hyirum exhausts that causes a woman's breasts or man's chest to blacken, including inner organs. If untreated, it can spread throughout the body. If the disease spreads to the brain, the person either dies or becomes brain dead.

Magical Ion—an arcane atom or a molecule containing myriad electrons infused with magic. It is theorized by most arcane astrophysicists that magical ions are the birth and wellspring of all magic and originate in protostars. Other stars also contain magical ions, but they are not as pure due to the density of radioactive isotopes. Magical ions within a soul form what is referred to as an ionized essence. The overall process of consuming them is known as arcane ionization. While magical ions rejuvenate any wizard or witch whose powers are depleted, they are extremely poisonous to a person without the arcane gift.

Mana—the invisible, intangible life force of magic that flows like zitrogen through those gifted with arcane power.

Mana Shield—a tremendously powerful spell known as an ethereal tapestry of magic cast by wizards or witches that envelops a person(s) or object(s) with a barrier akin to a technological force field.

Maz'hura—the eternal Goddess of Tal'manaism. Scriptures of the Holy Tal'manac reveal that she created Ensar and its twelve dimensions. Prior to the creation of Ensar, she existed as Order in another universe. Back then, Maz'hura existed in a realm of purity until Koth'tura breached it, at which point she fought and exiled him. Yet this caused her universe to collapse. Scholars do not know why this occurred; they only know that the occurrence caused both universes to merge as one universe that contains Chaos and Order. She is believed to be eternal and will one day return to vanquish Koth'tura forever.

MS-783—a medical syringe with a large dose of adrenaline. It is intended for use only when someone has been fatally wounded. At times, it helps prevent death or at least allows the injured person to remain conscious and active for several hours.

Necromancy—a school of magic taught in universities offering a major in dark arts. Since the beginning of time, for as long as magic has been recorded in history, necromancy has been a respected form of magic. The philosophy behind it is that magic, regardless of its branch, is neither good nor evil. Such concepts of good and evil are only applicable to the wielder. Aspects of necromancy cross over into the art of divination, but because possible fortune telling in necromancy relies on a spirit rather than the practitioner, it has been divided so students of the art can focus strictly on the dark arts. There are no prerequisites for necromancy.

Nempada Empire—the first official form of humyn civilization on planet Aarda, located in the Quaydric star system within Copia Deiga. Unlike tribes that formed and withered away during ancient times, the Nempada Empire reigned supreme on Aarda's eastern continents and gradually expanded to the west. Scholars of Nempadian lore have asserted that the Nempada Empire rose to power and dominated the world approximately between 649.123 and 824.678. Yet sometime around or after the first intergalactic millennium (circa 999.999 to 1000.000), all traces of the empire vanished. It is theorized by archeologists that an alien race invaded Aarda and destroyed the empire, leaving only vagabonds alive. Most scholars consider that to be hogwash, asserting there is no definitive evidence to claim such a thing. To this day, the enigmatic disappearance of the Nempada Empire baffles scholars and archeologists.

Oleki—a tree with purple leaves and an unusually wide trunk that contains magical properties, making the land it grows on fertile, regardless of harmful weather conditions. The undying tree is also known to be a sanctuary for those who possess the arcane gift, replenishing them of their powers. It cannot, however, restore magic to someone who has lost the gift. Oleki trees merely rejuvenate what already exists.

Orgavour—a blubbery juggernaut creature whose body can camouflage itself. It has seventeen tentacles and a pair of pincers. While it appears to be a slow beast, its stalk-shaped legs allow it to move fairly fast to catch its prey. In attacking this creature, it is unwise to randomly slice the body apart because its separated halves form into other orgavours. The only way somebody can truly kill an orgavour is to decapitate it.

Pogatarn Giant—a tree that not only produces mud at its roots but also stands between sixty to a hundred feet high. It is considered a majestic tree on planet Nobia. In ancient times, the indigenous people built homes on and around pogatarn giants.

Popolam—a square-shaped vegetable that has a mild, tangy taste. The riper it is, the sweeter it tastes. In cooking, a popolam becomes spicy and is a great addition to soups, meat, or any zesty cuisine.

PR-451—a pre-stabilized grappling hook that can be launched in a non-gravity zone. It can be used for both animate and inanimate objects.

PSG-549—a plasma shotgun that utilizes rechargeable energy cartridges. While the gun can cause devastation in proximity to its target(s), it must be manually pumped and charged each time before firing.

Qazinotaur—a gargantuan creature of flight found on MJ453. Its physical features include horns, which protrude from its olive fleece from chest to tail, and its scaly snout has multiple tusks. It also has six limbs, each with razor-sharp paws. Matriarchs are the only qazinotaurs with manes covering their necks. Also, this creature of flight is capable of unleashing a lethal cloud-like breath of miasma, easily killing its prey.

Reon—the primary currency used throughout the universe of Ensar, first circulated in the cosmic cycle 38971.465 on planet Pravura. Although some civilizations in other galaxies do not use reons, it is nevertheless accepted in the form of a digital payment, which is automatically converted via the foreign cosmic exchange market (FCXM) to the exact price of what is being purchased.

Rumsira—according to the Holy Tal'manac, it is stated that no one can ever truly define what it is. In the world of science, there are different schools of thought on rumsira. Many scientists tend to think it is a tranquil state of mind while most wizards, templars, and mystics believe it is an actual location beyond the twelve dimensions where Maz'hura dwells.

Ruzurai—an exceptionally powerful witch or wizard chosen by the eternal Goddess to rule the Tal'manac Order. There are a total of twelve, symbolizing the twelve dimensions of Ensar. While they only rule in Copia Deiga, they have attempted to expand the sacred Order in other galaxies and spread Tal'manaism. In recent centuries the Ruzurai have become far more militaristic than religious, focusing on their soldiers and knights establishing off-world colonies and bringing law and order to regions where chaos reigns.

San-parba—a form of non-magical alcohol used to cleanse severe wounds, especially when they contain an infection.

Sawk—a creature with skin akin to the bark of a tree. Sawks are found in the many forests of MJ453 and are naturally aggressive but are even more violent when prey enter their territory. It is not known what came first, sawks or baila trees; however, a symbiotic relationship has been recorded between the two. Sawks feed off the acid produced from the baila family while such trees rely on sawks to meld with their trunks to remain alive when MJ453 is farthest from its rogue sun; thus, creating a symbiosis pact between the two.

Sca'vezi—an alien race from the Maga'Dar Galaxy. Their capital world is called Phikon, located in the Xaglia Zamosus star system. They are known to have the most impressive black-market in Ensar. Their foreheads (particularly the brow) are usually bulged, with either multicolored birthmarks shaped like stripes from nose to spine. All sca'vezi have slit-shaped eyes and are bald, their coarse scalps resembling squashed cones.

SP-47—a grenade that, upon detonation, creates a stasis prison linked to the user's kinetic link device. The user can then bring the stasis to him or her like a tractor beam. The only difference between both technologies is that tractor beams are for inorganic objects such as ships while the SP-47 is used for people.

SR-153—a high-precision sniper rifle capable of using enchanted magazines. It is fitted with an arcane telescopic sight that allows its user to see farther than any normal scope and has a stock and an adjustable sling.

Stellar Ouva—a peaceful, gelatinous animal typified as a free-floating and free-drifting celestial being. It is often considered a mystical-looking creature whose body is semitransparent, revealing innards that resemble a mixture of polyp and interstellar clouds. It is the only known creature able to roam through space in its natural form. While stellar ouvas primarily live in regions of outer space where there is abundant cosmic dust, they are attracted to planets with water and are therefore often seen floating above oceans. Before starship propulsion such as cosmodrives were invented, people used them as steeds to travel overseas.

Tal'manac Order—a religious, military government of magicians, soldiers and knights formed eons ago by humyns of faith on their original homeworld: Aarda. After hundreds of cycles, the revered Order spread throughout Copia Deiga and made planet Pravura their capital world. The Order has attempted to continue expanding in other galaxies. They believe in one deity known as Maz'hura and that her scriptures found in the Holy Tal'manac are absolute. The supreme rulers of the Order are known as Ruzurai and are believed to have been divinely chosen by the everlasting Goddess herself to rule in her stead until she returns during the end times.

Tal'manaism—one of many cosmic religions. It is a monotheistic religion based on the divine teachings of Maz'hura, eternal Goddess and creator of Ensar as presented in the Holy Tal'manac. Unlike most belief systems, Tal'manaism brings faith, magic, and science together. According to the scriptures, Maz'hura herself states that the three are interwoven and that all are a means to commune with her. There are several ways to reach out to the eternal Goddess; one is through prayer and another is by meditation. The basic tenets of meditation in Tal'manaism are known as the Eight Powers: awareness, emptiness of mind, detachment, empathy, balance, acceptance, equanimity, and perseverance. These powers are said to bring growth and prosperity to the soul, and that if the believer lives a life of enlightenment, when he or she dies they will experience rumsira and reunite with

Maz'hura. The Holy Tal'manac states that even a layperson may experience rumsira; ergo, eliminating the barriers of discrimination and judgment. Mystics of the religion believe in a period known as End Times, an epoch where people throughout Ensar will experience a final battle between Order and Chaos. At the end, the universe is supposed to be cleansed by rebirth, sometimes interpreted as reincarnation.

TB-481—a tool used by electricians, mechanics, and engineers that cultivates thermal beams to instantly melt just about any kind of metal.

Techogon—one of many manufacturers and brands for weapons, armor, hoverbikes, hovercars, and small interstellar vessels.

Tetrigonium—an alloy often used in construction for building the hulls of vessels, structures, walls, floors, and even armor.

Torda—a tiny brown-shelled fruit. Once the shell is cracked and peeled off, the spongy fruit beckons to be eaten. It is considered by most people to be the sweetest and juiciest fruit in the universe.

Transdimensional Ethernet—a realm of cyberspace, most commonly known as TDE or simply the ethernet. Users can log on to the ethernet by having a kinetic link device (KLD). The ethernet is a cosmic system of interconnected networks linked by an array of digital, virtual, and wireless technologies with a dose of magic. For example, if two magic users establish a conversation on the ethernet, either one of them can teleport to the other. The invention of the TDE is recognized as one of the greatest scientific and magical marvels throughout Ensar.

Tyiri—an alien race from a planet called Tyuchstelia in the Syichi Photh-Kos Galaxy. They have a tendency to be politicians or lawyers for criminals. Though dressed in impressive business suits, their teal-pigmented faces are not as appealing with slits on their cheekbones for breathing. And despite their lack of noses and teeth, they are able to consume food using dissolving glands in their mouths.

UCN—a humyn broadcasting company, known as Universal Cosmic News. Reporters bring news to people from all around the universe whether it be weather, traffic, natural disasters, random majestic phenomena on planets or in space, terror attacks, and political debates. It can be viewed on channel 2044.78 via KLD.

University of Elements & Conjuration—a college for the magically gifted, located in Copia Deiga's capital world Pravura. Like most schools of magic, it only specializes in certain arcane classes such as elementalism, divination, and conjuration. While black magic is not practiced in this university, it is equally respected among the faculty and discussed in most history courses.

Urvantak—one of many factions formed by ghensoths. Unlike most factions that are nothing more than groups consisting of pirates, scavengers, and mercenaries, Urvantak was formed to restore the ghensoth homeworld by traversing through the universe and gathering an unlimited supply of resources. The ghensoths of this faction are considered exceedingly hostile and will do whatever it takes to restore their planet to its former glory, even if it means hiring sca'vezi pirates to do their dirty work.

Vai'le'ak—a marine creature with serrated pectoral fins and an elongated tail. Its curved teeth are so long that it cannot close its own mouth; however, it has a smaller mouth within the main orifice with needle-shaped teeth that can chew. This deadly underwater beast has only been sighted in lagoons on planet MJ453.

X-Phaser—a teleportation pod or capsule big enough to fit even a ghensoth. It is one of the rare technologies that bring science and magic together. Its technology captures one's DNA and then initiates a "phaser" that dematerializes the molecular structure and rematerializes it to his or her chosen destination. For witches or wizards, an enchanted "phaser" in the same pod captures their arcane DNA and teleports them from an outbound to a selected inbound capsule.

Xentari—an alien species obsessed with trading and marketing. Most people believe that to see a xentari pirate is like seeing a ghensoth mystic. The xentari are one of the most peaceful races. A xentari's features comprise a snout, trunk-shaped ears, and wide eyes that match its bulky and somewhat stretched-looking face. It is said among their kind that a superb vendor, regardless of race, is a xentari in spirit.

Xylithum—an arcane crystal shard, containing magical properties that permit a mana shield to defy gravity; thus, allowing a starship to enter a black hole. Some people believe that such rare crystals are keys to enter a realm beyond the twelve dimensions where Maz'hura dwells and that if they breach the realm, they will experience rumsira.

Yuda—a yellow root vegetable that is non-edible for most aliens when raw. Only humyns can eat it raw. It must be cooked until softened in order to be eaten by other species. Because of this, yuda is usually used in warm soups and provides extra flavor. Yuda may also be fried, but it is extremely unhealthy to eat.

Zala—a naturally twisted-shaped fruit that can be eaten before it is ripe. If eaten before ripeness, it appears red and tastes sweet; however, it is not as healthy as a ripe zala. Though recommended by nutritionists to eat them when green, they have a more sour taste. Not many aliens enjoy sour fruits, but ripe zalas have twice as much protein.

ZiFi—a cosmic wireless networking technology that allows devices such as a KLD to connect to the Transdimensional Ethernet. It can also be used to transfer resources, tangible or intangible, from one person to another like magic.

Zitrogen—a chemical element found in abundance throughout the Ensar universe that is breathed by several species such as humyns.

About the Author

Paul L. Centeno is an award-winning author, born and raised in New York City. During his early teenage life, he wrote twelve short stories, several of which he used as a foundation to create his first fantasy novel, *The Vagrant Chronicle*. As a young adult, he studied at Herbert H. Lehman College where he earned a BA in Philosophy and Creative Writing. After graduating, he worked with Gabriel Packard, associate director of the Creative Writing MFA Program at Hunter College, to master his craft. In 2014, he won an award from Writers of the Future for his short story, *Steamwalker*. *Maz'hura: Book One of the Twelve Dimensions* is his fifth novel. Visit his website at www.PaulCenteno.com.